Something of Yourself

Amanda Sapp

ASAPP Publishing

For Russ & Sue
Best parents a girl could ask for

*"You only are free when you realize you belong no place—
you belong every place—no place at all."*
—MayaAngelou

"Careerism is death."
—Robert Penn Warren, as quoted by Ken Burns on
The Joe Rogan Experience; June 11, 2025

CHAPTER ONE

Summer 2008

Fluorescent lights buzzed above linoleum hallways. The only other sound in the government office came from the methodical *tick-tick-tick* of the analog wall clock. Each second, a judgment against the poor life choices that led Astoria Lyons to a dead-end job back in her hometown after college and the broken heart she carried with her.

Alone at the front desk of the local USFS Ranger Station, Astoria stared at the dot-com era relic of a hulking Compaq computer. Scanning the screen, she gave her resume and cover letter a final read before clicking "submit," launching both documents into the void. Another application to another newspaper job that may not even exist, for all she knew. Another dose of unrequited hope.

Was it too early for the ham sandwich she'd brought for lunch?

She'd graduated from college in the spring. According to MTV, it was supposed to be the most exciting time of her life—road trips with girlfriends (she had none), an engagement ring (the man she'd carried on with for two years, who also happened to be her professor, had ended their relationship and shattered her world instead), maybe a new job in a new city (she scoured online job boards daily, to no avail).

But here she was, back in her hometown, enduring the mind-numbing irrelevance of a desk job where her primary responsibility was to answer phones that never rang.

Her father, Ace, had secured this gig for her. A timber industry lifer, he'd called in a favor with the local forest ranger—an old-timer who'd been kind enough to take her on when her student loans came due, and her journalism dreams began to fade.

I'm grateful for the job, she told herself, taking a dry bite of sandwich as tears pricked her eyes.

Truth was, she resented the dead-end gig with its limitless downtime and ample opportunity to dwell on her shattered heart and bruised ego, consider her shortcomings, and rage against the professor for all the ways he'd done her wrong.

She was mentally cataloging her flaws and his betrayals when his name pinged into her inbox, causing her to swallow too soon, the mass of ham and soft bread lodging in her throat. Head between her knees, she wheezed and coughed, willing it up and out of her esophagus and finally hocking it into the bin. Eyes watering, throat on fire, she hacked once more, then clicked to open the email.

"Good morning, Astoria. I'm thrilled to introduce you to a long-time cohort of mine, Anna Mae Alcott. Anna Mae works for a digital marketing agency in Nashville. She's looking for someone with a knack for storytelling who understands digital. I told her you're the best I've seen. I'll let you take it from here.

My best —"

After sobbing in the ladies' room for twenty minutes, Astoria returned, wiped her eyes, and typed a reply-only to this woman, Anna Mae, hoping the lack of response would leave the professor wondering.

"Good afternoon, Anna Mae. I'd love to learn more."

***

She hadn't meant to fall in love with the professor. Not at first.

College was two years of pulling swing shifts at an all-night diner, serving her peers in a stained apron, hair smelling of grilled meat, face greasy like whipped cream.

By the spring of her sophomore year, Astoria decided she deserved to savor the freedom of her youth. She quit the diner, took out more student loans, and switched her major from English to Journalism, enrolling in an Emerging Media Studies course.

Rhododendrons blooming pink and red across campus, she walked into the lecture hall, selecting a seat toward the back. Situated with her pen poised over her notebook, she was taken by the young professor commanding the front of the room, hands on hips, chest out.

They locked eyes, and he smiled, his white teeth flashing against his golden tan. Her face flushed, but she held his gaze until another student approached the professor. He shifted his attention but glanced back at her once and smiled.

As the weather warmed and the days softened, many sought distractions beyond campus, but most of the students in the Emerging Media Studies course were female, and attendance remained strong. They filled the auditorium with energetic anticipation every Thursday afternoon at four o'clock.

In each lecture, the professor paraded about the room, telling stories about how the first job out of college was making music videos in Nashville, Tennessee. He painted the southern town as worldly, bustling, winner-take-all for anyone brave enough to take on the music industry, dropping famous country star names, sharing behind-the-scenes images of artists, and waxing on about the magic of creating content before the days of iPhones, MySpace, and Facebook.

Maybe it was the heady spring blossoming around her, but one afternoon, Astoria made her way to the front of the room after class. Her head felt hot; her vision was fuzzy. Voice cracking, she introduced herself. Locking eyes with her, the professor smiled as if to himself, then thanked her for saying hello.

"We're going to have a lot of fun," he said.

He left encouraging notes on her papers. As the weeks progressed, she selected a seat closer and closer to the front of the lecture hall, staring hard at the man lecturing in his button-down shirts, khaki shorts, and leather boat shoes. His tan hinted at family vacations on warm beaches, while his southern accent lulled her into a trance. There wasn't a thing she didn't like about him.

On a Thursday night at the end of the semester, while the rest of campus was out partying, Astoria was cramming for her last final in the recesses of the library when the professor left her a voicemail.

"You've exhibited a real mastery of what we've covered in class," he said. "I'd love to discuss these topics you address in your final paper. Swing by my office tomorrow. I'll be there after three."

She barely slept that night.

Floated through her exam the next morning.

The afternoon finally gave way to three o'clock. Astoria's heart raced as she walked down the hallway to the professor's office. She knocked, feeling like she might pass out on the pea-green carpet in that musty old building. The door opened; the professor stood smiling behind it.

"Astoria Lyons. I'm so glad you came by." He gestured for her to enter. They sat facing one another across his desk. They held eye contact; Astoria struggled to focus on what he was saying.

A purple and orange sunset held the world in a psychedelic haze as she floated across the quad an hour later. Could life be so beautiful? Maybe it was all in her head.

Fall semester of her junior year, she landed the editor role at her university's paper. A fire ignited inside her when she learned the professor would oversee the newspaper's staff. He saw her flush every time he entered the room, and she knew he saw her, so she started looking straight at him, holding his gaze and letting him see her glow.

She didn't care what the other students on the newspaper staff might say. Whenever the professor laughed at her sarcastic wit in an editorial meeting, her peers rolled their eyes, but she indulged in the rush, beaming back at him while everyone else in the room dissolved into the background.

Despite her love-drunk obsession, or perhaps inspired by it, Astoria thrived in her new role. From leading editorial brainstorms to translating the print version of the school's paper into an online edition, she'd never felt so alive. She wanted to pursue a career in journalism after graduation. In the meantime, the harder she applied herself, the more time she garnered working alongside the professor. It wasn't long before the tension became unbearable.

***

A rainstorm slapped against the windows. They were working late to get the weekly edition to print. Two lowball glasses of bourbon waited on the desk. Alcohol was prohibited on campus, but the professor kept a bottle in his desk drawer for nights like these.

That's what he'd told Astoria, grinning as he dislodged the cork stopper—*thunk!*

Hunkered at a large desk littered with marked-up preprint spreads, she re-read her editorial letter. The professor leaned over her, his left hand resting on the back of her chair, his right hand dangerously close to hers on the table. The bourbon and the smell of his cologne—something of black licorice and soft leather—made Astoria throb.

He analyzed her headline longer than necessary. Heat radiated from his body, and she sat there holding her breath, staring at their hands next to each other on the desk, wondering how he'd react if she shifted her wrist half an inch, finally making contact. Electricity ran down her neck and arms and spine and between her legs. What would happen should their currents meet? Intoxicated as she was—more figuratively than literally—she wondered if the instantaneous voltage might be more than she could handle.

After finishing the bourbon, but not the paper, he offered her a ride home. Sitting in his Audi with the engine running, their bodies and breath, and that dizzying cologne steaming up the windows, they focused on the windshield in silence. His fancy car warmed right up. Astoria couldn't take it any longer. It was dumb, she decided, to keep pretending.

"You know I want more than a ride home," she said. Rain streaked down the windshield. He gripped the steering wheel with both hands and swallowed hard. Without looking at her, he slipped the car into gear.

***

Sitting on the toilet in the professor's bathroom after they finished that first time, Astoria smiled at the mottled specks of blood on the toilet paper. Marks of achievement, like his red pen on her papers, they left her feeling like she finally mattered.

She hadn't told him she was a virgin. At twenty, the label had become a burdensome reminder of the loneliness of growing up a dreamer in a small town. She wanted to be done with all that, like a semester of boring math classes.

She assumed the professor would move along, perhaps out of shame or fear of losing his job or to pursue his next target.

But he surprised her, driving them to his place whenever they stayed late at the paper—nights turned into weekends, which turned into weeks. They drank his bourbon on Friday nights. He told her stories about the South while they listened to Taj Mahal CDs. Saturday mornings, he made Bloody Marys to soothe their hangovers while she burned the scrambled eggs in his white-tiled kitchen. Sundays, he brought her coffee, croissants, and print newspapers, which they read in bed until noon.

She became a fixture in his apartment, and it became their playground—a place of exploration and indulgence where she danced across the hardwood floors in her socks and his button-downs, smiling seductively, shimmying, beckoning him to consume her again. Afterward, he made them cocktails while she studied his well-appointed bookcases, running her fingers across the spines.

After almost two years of this thrill-turned-habit-turned-addiction, she allowed herself to see their arrangement as her perfect scenario. Sure, worry pricked at her mind whenever the professor spent holiday breaks at his family's vacation home in Florida, never remotely hinting at an invitation for her to join. But she ignored the trolling concern, just as she downplayed the professor's disinterest in meeting her father, even though her hometown was less than two hours away.

Silently, she accepted that their outer worlds needed to remain separate until she graduated. They had to protect the professor's reputation. She understood. In the meantime, the professor was helping her bridge her working-class upbringing with a future she hadn't been able to envision on her own.

She began imagining their future together, daydreaming of cocktail parties in his apartment with its leather furniture, tall windows, and exposed brick. In her fantasies, she played the hostess, offering refills while cohorts from the college congregated in tight circles, laughing and drinking themselves out of their academic pretenses, enchanted by the dynamic professor and his charming muse.

She conjured a plan: they would live together after she graduated. He'd pursue tenure at the university. She would get a job at the local daily, then a regional role with the Associated Press. Eventually, they would go on Sunday drives to see her father. The professor would love the pastoral scenery and quaint working-class community—a welcome escape from the stuffy confines of his university. They would travel. She would become worldly while maintaining proximity to her humble beginnings.

Yes, she told herself, she really could have it all.

She allowed this vision to blossom and bloom until one afternoon, a few weeks before graduation. An icy spring rain slapped at the windows. With his back to her, the professor uncorked a bottle of wine.

"So, Astoria," he said casually. "Where will you be moving after you finish your last exam?"

The question was a dagger. A dark tunnel closed in around her vision as she processed his words. Hot tears streamed down her cheeks. The world was collapsing around her.

He faced her, a glass of wine in each hand.

"Come on, Astoria." He held forth a glass like a peace offering for an argument he'd already won. "You'll never amount to anything if you stay here. You have to go make something of yourself."

The most painful part of all: she believed he was right.

CHAPTER TWO

Hot damn, the south can burn. It was well into September. Morning, no less, but Astoria was sweating, rings of perspiration soaking the underarms of her wool suit jacket, her legs steaming inside the slacks. She'd bought the out-of-season getup from the clearance rack at JC Penney's, wanting to look professional for her first day on the job.

The HR email titled "Your First Day at Dixon-Richards" told her to arrive at the agency around nine, but she pulled in at eight-thirty, hoping to appear eager and ready to contribute.

After parking her rusting Toyota Corolla at the edge of a sprawling office park, she checked her makeup in the rearview mirror; concealer pooled at the corners of her eyes, and her foundation was threatening to melt down her face. She needed to get out of the heat.

She stalked across the concrete lot toward a line of buildings, teetering on her faux leather heels, the air hanging like a wet blanket around her. Amidst a row of luxury cars, she paused and squinted up at the towers. Columns of one-way glass stared back apathetically. Throughout the complex, Hispanic men bent at the waist as they silently tended to pristine landscaping. Behind her, the Nashville skyline glimmered on the horizon. Overhead, a plane drew a white line in the sky.

Maybe it was the oppressive heat or the three-thousand-mile drive across the country (which had all but drained her bank account); of course, her broken heart had all but depleted her reserves—whatever the culmination of forces, she felt lightheaded, as if she were hovering outside her body, her soul trying to escape. Flexing her toes against the narrow boxes of her shoes, she walked on.

Cold air blasted her in the face when she heaved open the thick glass door.

Behind the reception desk, a young woman was unpacking tiny Tupperware containers from an oversized Louis Vuitton tote. The bag's logo reminded Astoria of the sorority girls from college—the ones who dressed like Britney Spears and carried designer bags embellished with names Astoria couldn't pronounce, let alone afford.

"Can I help you?" the receptionist asked without looking up.

"I'm Astoria Lyons. It's my first day," she said, smiling brightly.

"Oh?" Still avoiding eye contact, the receptionist dropped her tote to the ground and leaned over her keyboard, clicking her mouse around on its foam pad, firing up the computer. The office hummed. Fluorescent lights buzzed. Machines beeped.

Astoria wanted to turn and run, but she thought about her bank account and how she'd spent all her money hauling across the country and moving into a new apartment with a new roommate in this new city. She thought about the professor and how he'd told her to get out in the world and make something of herself, and here she was, proving she could.

"Anna Mae Alcott is expecting me," she said, lowering her voice. She'd read somewhere that women needed to speak low and slow if they wanted to be taken seriously. "I'm the new social media person."

The receptionist jutted her chin towards a set of Eames chairs and lifted the desk phone to her ear. "Have a seat."

Astoria obliged, sitting into her damp suit, which the air conditioning was turning cold against her skin. She hoisted one leg and then the other, yanking her pants at the knee to let her thighs breathe, then wiped strands of hair off her sticky face while stealing glances at the young woman across the room. They were around the same age, except the admin had perfect posture, punctuated by a flawless bun slicked high atop her head, her white neoprene tank top exposing a tight physique. Astoria decided the young women's *leave me alone* vibe was absurd for someone in such a public-facing role.

Finally, Anna Mae Alcott floated into the lobby, the sleeves of her caftan dress billowing around her. Anna Mae exuded a warm, soulful vibe. She spoke with a syrupy drawl, wore her salt-and-pepper hair in a messy pile, and smelled like eucalyptus. "You made it," she said.

Astoria smiled, relieved to see a familiar face. She had met Anna Mae two weeks prior during a whirlwind trip when she'd taken a red-eye from Seattle to Nashville for her interview, met a potential roommate she'd found online, spent the night in the airport to save on a hotel, and caught a flight home the next morning.

Still jet-lagged, Astoria stood, smoothing her jacket, hoping to present as the perfect employee. Anna Mae enveloped her in a firm hug; her cheek felt cool against Astoria's.

"I didn't know if you'd actually come," said Anna Mae, releasing Astoria from their embrace.

"Here I am." Astoria shrugged, intending to sound enthused, but her voice pitched high, making the statement sound like a question. Again, she thought of the professor. She wondered if he'd warned Anna Mae that she might not show—that she didn't have the nerve to shed her small-town upbringing and move across the country to pursue a professional career.

Anna Mae had hired the professor straight out of Belmont University a decade before he traded his career in music production for one in academia. Together, they'd produced music videos for artists like Garth Brooks and George Strait. The professor bragged about these experiences as thinly veiled lessons to his students. He repeated them as embellished stories when he was drinking. Astoria would remind the professor she'd heard the story the first time he told it in lecture, but he'd shush her and carry on. Now, Astoria wondered how much the professor had told Anna Mae about her.

"You're gonna be great," said Anna Mae. She wrapped an arm around Astoria's shoulders and ushered her past reception, the caftan floating behind them as they went. "Let's get you some coffee, then find your desk."

They walked down a hallway lined with conference rooms. Astoria had interviewed in one of them, but now, she couldn't remember which one, as they all looked the same.

They stepped into a sprawling, dimly lit workspace. "And here we have the floor," said Anna Mae, motioning toward pods of desks clustered throughout the room. "Aside from our conference rooms and executive offices, this is where everyone works. It's open seating, so it fosters collaboration."

"Sure," Astoria said. Her stomach tightened, and she clenched her toes again as she registered the sea of industrial carpet and office furnishings, people sitting at their desks, some looking drug-induced, their eyelids fluttering amidst the manufactured placidity of the Corporate America scene.

"The Account Team sits here." Anna Mae indicated a bank of desks in the center of the room, where several blonde women hammered away at their laptops. These women also sat with perfect posture, their faces flawless in the artificial glow of their screens. They wore uniforms of V-neck dresses and sparkly bib necklaces. Long soft ringlets, set to perfection, hung from each head. In unison, they glanced up. Thick black eyelashes blinked open and closed, their expressions otherwise blank.

Astoria waved, smiling hopefully, although her heart sank as she realized she'd waited on girls like this in college at the diner. They'd come into the restaurant at three o'clock in the morning, puke in their handbags, and pass out in their boyfriends' laps. By Monday, they'd be prancing about campus, surrounded by friends or sorority sisters, ready to repeat the cycle. Sure, they made fools of themselves, but something in her envied their inconsequential sloppiness. She wondered if the professor was now pursuing one of these types—a pedigreed, party-going young woman from a background more closely aligned with his own.

From the back of the blonde horde, a curvy girl with cherubic cheeks, heavy coal eyeliner, and a back-combed ponytail waved wildly toward Astoria and Anna Mae. The squad of pristine young women rolled their eyes at their friendlier cohort, then returned to pecking at their laptops.

"That's Evie," said Anna Mae. "At least we can count on her to bring up the welcome wagon. Shall we?" Anna Mae led Astoria deeper into the open workspace, stopping at a wall where colorful printouts of website designs hung floor to ceiling.

"Everybody gets to be creative here," she said. "We hold reviews where everyone from Creative Directors to Account Supervisors to Strategists ensures the work is as smart as possible before it goes to clients.

"There's the Creative Team now." Anna Mae pointed down the wall to where five men huddled beneath a halo of recessed lighting. These men appeared to procure their apparel from the same source, much like the Account Girls, except the Creatives wore skinny jeans, pearl-snap plaid shirts, clean leather boots.

Astoria was silently questioning the group's propensity for creative expression when a sharp voice cut through the mundane hum. She turned, coming face-to-face with a toy soldier of a man. He was short but stout, his salt-and-pepper hair coiffed high and tight. Crisp pleats lined his dress shirt and khakis. He stuck his jaw out like a sword.

"Who do we have here?" His question sounded more accusation than inquiry. Across the floor, the Account Girls straightened in their chairs, increasing the cadence of their keystrokes.

"Henry Hunter," Anna Mae said brightly, "you remember Astoria Lyons?"

Astoria offered a handshake, but her discount jacket was one size too small, so she could only extend her arm from the elbow. Henry Hunter lowered his eyes toward the gesture, then scanned Astoria from head to toe.

"Why are you here?" he asked.

Astoria flinched, withdrawing.

"Henry," said Anna Mae, an edge in her voice now. "This is the social media manager we've hired. You met her when she interviewed here a few weeks ago."

"Social media, eh?"

"Astoria recently graduated from college. She's joined us all the way from Washington."

The man brightened. "D.C.?" Now, he offered a handshake, which Astoria returned. His palm felt cool; his grip was soft.

"Washington State," said Astoria.

"Oh." Henry Hunter furrowed his brow. "Seattle is a great city. World-class food scene."

"I'm from a small town in Washington. Not Seattle."

Henry Hunter put his hands on his hips and lifted his chin even higher, eyeing the young woman in the cheap blue suit, hair plastered to her scalp. In the background, the Account Girls still projected an air of busy, busy, busy as they hammered away at their keyboards.

"And you moved to Nashville?" he asked.

"It seems like a great city."

"But you're fresh out of college. Why not go to an A-market like Seattle or Los Angeles?"

Astoria wobbled on her heels.

"Don't scare her off." Anna Mae swatted at Henry Hunter, but he didn't flinch, eyes remaining fixed on Astoria.

"No. I'm interested," he said. "You're just starting. Why not head straight for the big leagues?"

Wild responses raced through her mind: *Because I was fucking my professor, and he hooked me up with a job at your agency so he could feel better about all those things I let him do to me. Because I'm broke and couldn't land another job, and what difference does it make? I'm here now.*

"I applied for a job with *The Seattle Times* once but never heard back," she said, forcing a smile.

"I see." Henry Hunter turned robotically toward Anna Mae. "Carry on then." He strolled toward the Creative Team, jostling one man on the shoulder as he passed, commenting on something that elicited laughter from the group as if they all shared an inside joke.

Astoria burned with embarrassment, reinforcing her fear that she didn't belong. She glanced at the Account Girls, who remained propped at their desks, exuding effortless perfection. *The suit was too much*, she decided. Henry Hunter knew she was a fraud.

Gently guiding her by the shoulders, Anna Mae steered Astoria away from the Account Girls, the Creative Team, and Henry Hunter. "Don't mind him. He likes to give newbies a run for their money to see if they can keep up. Let's get you that coffee, then I'll show you where my office is in case you need a place to escape."

The agency's open-concept workspace was a standard corporate cattle chute, but inside Anna Mae's office, the air was softer, humidified. A paper lantern glowed against baby blue walls, and a jungle of potted plants stretched in all directions as if trying to escape the building. A trumpet waxed longingly from a CD player.

"I like to play jazz music for my plants," said Anna Mae, turning down the volume before sinking into her desk chair. "This place can be intense, so I created a little Zen studio. Come in here anytime you want."

Astoria examined a watercolor hanging on the wall. The painting captured large birds ascending mid-flight, their black and blue wings threatening to propel them off the canvas.

"You like my birds?"

"I do."

"Man-O-War Birds by Walter Anderson. He was a Mississippi artist, or at least we claim him."

"Do you collect art?" Astoria turned from the painting and studied her new boss for a moment, then moved to sit in one of mid-century leather and wood chairs facing Ann Mae's desk.

"I did before my 401k dissolved." Anna Mae gave a little chuckle. "But yes, I support the arts. Musicians. Painters. Potters. I would've spent my career promoting artists, but economics pushes us to places beyond our control."

"I think I told you in my interview how I wanted to be a journalist?" Astoria sank back into the chair and ran her fingertips around the broad wooden edge of the seat. "But then I realized I need to make money."

"Smart. Make money now. Follow your passions later. Besides, there's plenty of writing for you to do here." Anna Mae clapped her hands like they were breaking from a huddle. "Now. Do you know how a marketing agency like this is structured?"

Astoria shook her head *no*.

Anna Mae slid a piece of paper across the desk. "Let's look at this org chart."

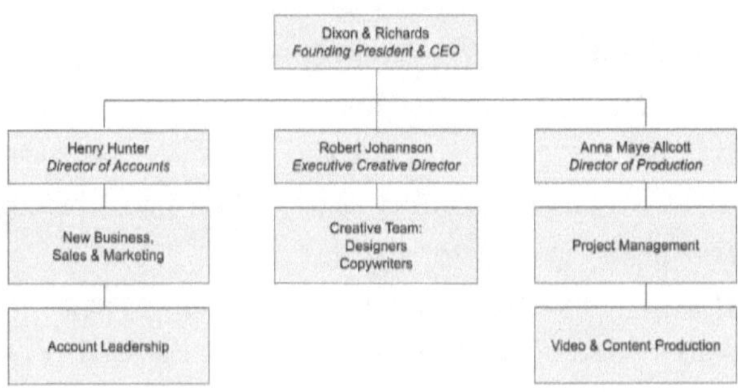

"They've completely misspelled my name on here, but don't mind that. I manage the production team and the project managers. We don't have a box for social media yet, but they say it's the future, so here you are to help us define what that looks like."

Astoria nodded, excited at how important her role sounded.

"Because you'll be producing content, I think it makes sense for you to report to me and the production team, but my partners have other opinions. Some believe social media should belong to Accounts. Others say it should be part of the CreativeTeam."

"Isn't it all the same company?" Astoria asked. "Why do we belong to different teams if we're all working for the same clients?"

Anna Mae smiled softly. "That's a good question and the right one, I suppose, but politics are always at play—nothing for you to worry about. A man named Robert Johannson manages the CreativeTeam; he's the man with the white mohawk. Everyone calls him Hanz—he says it's his part of his brand.

"Then we have Henry Hunter. He manages the AccountTeam and new business."

"The man we just met out on the floor?" Astoria asked, wrinkling her nose.

"He's from the east coast. You can't let him get to you." Anna Mae waved a dismissive hand, gold bracelets clinking down her wrist. "You'll want to build relationships with the Account Girls. They're the gatekeepers around here, and they pull a lot of weight, so tread lightly."

"I managed a team of sorority sisters when I was the editor at my college newspaper," Astoria said.

"That experience might serve you well." Anna Mae paused like she was about to offer additional advice, then decided otherwise. "And at the top of the heap, we have Dixon and Richards, the gentlemen who started this place. You'll see them around. They're retired, but they like to come in and critique our work on a whim. Drives the Creative Team crazy, but it's best to stay agreeable when they're in the room."

"I see."

"Keep that flowchart and study it. I need to run to a meeting, but you can get settled in."

Astoria slid the paper beneath the top sheets of her notepad and stood to leave.

"Speaking of the Account Girls, they're supposed to take you to lunch," said Anna Mae.

Astoria's stomach clenched, but she nodded agreeably.

"There is a new Account girl named Evie." Anna Mae pushed her chair back from her desk but remained seated, crossing her arms and holding a hand to her chin. "Her father and I go way back from our days at the University of Mississippi in Oxford, and I helped her get connected here. She's a character. We onboarded her last week, so ask her for help if you need anything. Seems she'll gladly lend a hand if it means getting out of work."

CHAPTER THREE

Astoria wasn't much of a planner. Before conjuring those daydreams of life with the professor, she'd never envisioned a future for herself beyond her hometown. But before flying to Nashville for her interview, she scratched out her best guess at what a budget might look like living off the entry-level salary Anna Mae mentioned in their email exchange.

She scoured Craigslist for an apartment to rent, dreaming as she scrolled, imagining what a fresh start might look like. But for a town built on the backs of working-class ballads, she was surprised to discover she couldn't afford a place on her own, so she searched "roommates wanted" listings instead.

One post read: *I'm Avis, an aspiring tattoo artist in my late 20s. Optimism. Love. Light. Email for pics and my contact info.* The accompanying images revealed nothing about the house or its amenities. Instead, two photos offered close-up views of a buxom woman with red-dyed hair wearing black lipstick. A horseshoe tattoo hung down from her collarbone. The words, *Giddy Up,* arced across her chest in a galloping font. The woman was sticking her tongue out in both pictures, winking at the camera while her breasts protested the restraints of a thin camisole.

In another post, a recently divorced man named Beau said he was looking for a roommate, preferably female, who was an excellent housekeeper and *open to considering a room-*

mates-with-benefits situation. Beau did not include a picture of himself, although he shared one image showcasing the façade of a grand antebellum home on a lake. Astoria wondered if Beau truly owned the home.

Yet another listing offered *an open room for any time you need to go on those trips to la-la land; $200 a week.* At least the accompanying picture showed an empty room with a single mattress on a wooden floor, so you knew what you were getting.

Astoria was questioning whether she wanted to move to such a seedy place when she stumbled onto a standout post: *Seeking FUN-LOVING but RESPONSIBLE and DRUG-FREE FEMALE ROOMMATE to co-rent a cute condominium in Hillsboro Village.*

Astoria was drug-free and believed herself responsible, but the term *fun-loving* made her think of how the girls she'd worked with at the newspaper might describe themselves in a room-mate-wanted post. They'd probably write in all caps, too. But she figured living with a sorority girl was preferable to renting a room in a halfway house, so she responded to the *ALL-CAPS* post.

The author's name was Elizabeth. They exchanged emails, agreeing to meet when Astoria was in town for her interview.

***

Hailing from Southern Illinois, Elizabeth carried herself with the prim confidence of an only child whose mother promised that the world owed her everything, and a corn-farming father who delivered on that promise, at least monetarily. Her online profile stated she received her BBA in Music Business from Belmont University and worked in sales for a major label in Music City, USA.

They met for drinks at Jackson's, an open-air bar in the bustling Hillsboro Village neighborhood.

Elizabeth wore bedazzled jeans, Lucchese cowgirl boots, and a tan corduroy jacket over a red T-shirt with "It's Five O'Clock Somewhere" in white cursive across the front. Astoria was still sporting her wilted suit. Before the drinks even arrived, Elizabeth launched into the briefing she'd prepared for the roommate screening session.

"I'm a very goal-oriented person. I always knew I wanted to work in the music industry. Belmont is where you go if you want to *be* someone in the music industry, so I went to Belmont and graduated with a job last spring. My next goal is to make VP with a label. It's so male-dominated, but women are the future of country music, and you're practically a shoo-in if you come up through Belmont. My father felt guilty about abandoning my mother and me when I was six, so I told him he could make it up to me by paying for private school. What did you study?"

Astoria's heart started racing when Elizabeth mentioned Belmont—the professor's alma mater—and she began obsessing about him all over again, tuning out Elizabeth's monologue. "I'm not sure," Astoria said, distracted.

"What do you mean?" Elizabeth asked. "Did you *not* go to college?"

"Oh—of course, I went to college. I have the student loans to prove it." Astoria laughed at her own joke.

Elizabeth blinked like an owl.

"Sorry, I meant to say I got a degree in journalism and tried to pursue a career as a reporter, but there aren't many jobs right now." She thumbed the edge of the beer bottle's foil label.

"So, why are you interviewing for a marketing job?" Elizabeth asked.

After the day she'd had, Astoria found Elizabeth's onslaught of questions exhausting, compounded by the effort required to frame herself as the ideal roommate. Still, she forged on, forcing a smile and pushing her tone to sound upbeat. "It's a great opportunity and a chance to live in a new city, you know?"

"I guess that makes sense. Everyone *loves* Nashville. They're calling it Nashvegas because there is so much happening here. It's like, *the* place to move right now."

Astoria frowned at the term *Nashvegas*, but Elizabeth continued.

"Everyone is moving here because there are, like, *jobs*, and it's not *that* expensive."

Astoria thought about all the unaffordable rental properties she'd scoured online.

"Do you think you'll get the job?" Elizabeth asked.

"The lady I interviewed with said it's mine if I want it."

Elizabeth sipped her vodka cranberry drink, twisting her face in disgust. "This is *not* Grey Goose. Hey, you." She flagged down a busboy who was clearing a table across the bar. He turned and pointed to his chest as if to say, *me?* Elizabeth rolled her eyes and waved more aggressively. The young man approached hesitantly, leaving his tray full of dirty pint glasses behind. "This is not what I ordered." She held her drink in the air. "I asked for Grey Goose."

The boy took the drink but remained in place, uncertain how to proceed.

"Ask them to make it again?" Elizabeth said.

The busboy wheeled around and stalked toward the bar.

Astoria fought to remain expressionless, hiding her disdain for anyone who treated servers poorly. She wanted to close the deal and get out of that noisy bar so she could go back to the airport, find an empty bathroom, change out of her suit, and take a sink bath. "What sorority were you in at Belmont?" she asked.

Elizabeth brightened, clapping her hands. "Oh my gosh, Phi Mu! What were you?"

Astoria smiled, pleased with her accurate profiling. "I wasn't in a sorority in college," she said.

A different waiter—the one who'd taken their original order—returned with the revised drink. Elizabeth held the straw primly to her lips, sipped, then nodded approvingly, dismissing the waiter without offering gratitude or an apology for pretending the brand of vodka mattered when smothered in cranberry juice. In that moment, Astoria knew she and Elizabeth would never be friends. But she needed a safe, affordable place to live, even if only for a short time.

"Sometimes I wish I would have rushed," said Astoria, tilting her head to the side and feigning introspection to reinforce the lie. "So fun."

"Best time of my *life*." Elizabeth reached toward Astoria and patted the table as if to punctuate their newfound connection. "Two of my sorority sisters are still, like, my *best friends*. They work in the industry, too. You'll meet them if you move in with me. Rent is thirteen hundred a month. We'll split it down the middle, plus utilities. Is that doable?"

***

One Saturday morning, a few weeks into her new life in Nashville, Astoria teetered on the brink of exhaustion in the kitchen she'd co-rented with Elizabeth while waiting for the coffee to brew. Her brain and bones felt like concrete after the cross-country move, new job, and the culture shock of waking up in a new city.

Elizabeth scuffed into the tiny kitchen in her leopard-print house slippers. "Want to buy a couch?" she asked, slipping a West Elm catalog onto the counter between Astoria and the coffeepot.

Eyeing the glossy marketing piece, Astoria slid the carafe from the burner and poured a cup.

"We won't need an entire couch," Elizabeth said, talking fast and clapping the pads of her fingertips together. "My father already bought me the first half."

One-half of a white satin couch had been sitting in the apartment's living room since Astoria had moved in, a lone arm on one end and an open drop on the other where the next investment was supposed to lodge.

"It's modular furniture," Elizabeth explained, "so we can go in on whatever configuration we want for the other half."

Astoria flipped through the catalog, scanning the prices. The furniture was sleek and minimalist, unlike the frumpy brown set she'd grown up with, which was still lodged in her parents' living room. In middle school, she asked her mother about getting new furniture after returning home from her first sleepover. She and a gaggle of girls had spent the night watching movies at a classmate's, their peach fuzz legs sprawled across a wraparound blue velvet sofa that filled the living room, Pepsi cans tucked in cup holders hidden in flip-down cushions. Her parents' single-wide trailer couldn't accommodate such grandeur. Still, after seeing the plush comforts in other girls' homes, Astoria longed for her parents to upgrade their furniture before hosting her own sleepover.

"Let's talk about needs versus wants," her mother said, staring down at a sink full of dirty dishes. Suds clinging to her bony elbows, she pulled a plate from the dishwater and held it dripping in front of Astoria's face. "You need a plate because you need to eat, right?"

Wishing to step away from the lesson but knowing better, Astoria lifted her eyes to meet her mother's.

"You need to eat to survive, correct?" her mother reiterated, holding the plate closer.

Astoria nodded.

"Does it matter whether this plate has gold flowers or rainbows?"

Astoria shook her head no.

"That's right. Because no matter what it looks like, you can eat off it." She slipped the plate back into the sink and sighed, holding her wrist to her brow. "I wish we could get new furniture, too, Astoria. I wish we could build that big house your dad and I always talked about. But we have a roof over our heads, and a couch to sit on, and food to eat. Sometimes, life forces you to forget about what you want and be happy with what you have. Understand?"

Astoria nodded again, throwing her arms around her mother's waist. Her mom wrapped an arm around Astoria and squeezed. A few years later, Astoria witnessed her mother's body dissolve to bone on that same brown couch, the chemotherapy killing her faster than the cancer.

"These aren't even entire couches," Astoria said, holding the catalog between two fingers and shaking it toward Elizabeth like a dirty rag. "They're half-couches, and they cost more than my entire paycheck."

Elizabeth's mouth popped open. Astoria tossed the catalog onto the counter and shrugged defiantly. She sipped her coffee, leveling a stare over the mug's rim. Elizabeth snatched the catalog from the counter and stomped out of the kitchen, slippers slapping the floor as she went.

Despite early tensions with her new roommate, Astoria settled into Nashville along with the fall, soft and slow. As the evenings cooled, she explored her new surroundings by taking long walks after work. Walking was free, and she didn't get too lost if she kept to the same square block vicinity. The red brick sidewalks of Hillsboro Village teemed with Vanderbilt students fresh off summer break, their comings and goings positively charging the air with anticipation over the new season as they bopped in and out of the neighborhood bars, bistros, and little shops.

Elizabeth attended industry events most evenings, leaving Astoria to enjoy the quiet apartment. For her room, she'd bought an AM/FM alarm clock radio from Goodwill and placed it on an upturned box next to the air mattress she'd packed from Washington. Her plan was to sleep on the portable bed until she could afford to buy the real thing.

Some nights, she lay there listening to Lightning 100, the local radio station whose DJ promised, *"David Hall rocks y'all on Lightning 100"* before playing tracks from the likes of Justin Townes Earl, the Drive-By Truckers, and Gillian Welch. Astoria's mind drifted on the music, and she'd think of home and the last morning she spent with her father, Ace, before leaving Washington.

The memory was clear: while she'd crammed a few final belongings into her car, Ace had stood in the driveway, kicking at rocks, looking beaten by time and loss. He held a coffee cup in a gnarled hand; his back curved like a question mark from years of falling timber. He told her he loved her and knew she would do great things. An early fall breeze rustled the leaves of the poplar trees, sounding like a river in the sky.

Thinking of Ace intensified her longing for home and the guilt she felt for leaving him, but she clung to the image and sound of those trees rustling in the wind, and even on the saddest nights, it lulled her to sleep.

CHAPTER FOUR

After the professor had issued his edict and ended their relationship, Astoria was determined to prove him wrong by starting her illustrious career as an award-winning journalist without leaving home. She applied to newspapers up and down the Washington Coast. When her resumes and cover letters went unanswered, she finagled a meeting with the editor of the nearest regional daily by emailing him directly, saying she had an idea for tapping into the unrealized revenue potential of social media. *Might he be interested?*

It was only a meeting, arguably scheduled under false pretenses, but she was hellbent on turning it into a job opportunity. The newspaper didn't even have a Facebook page, so Astoria planned to pitch herself as a freelance digital journalist, hoping the editor would jump at the prospect of allowing young talent to help him conquer the digital age.

She'd never felt surer of her purpose than she was standing in the hallway outside the editor's office before her meeting, smelling ink and coffee wafting from the newsroom, listening to telephones ring and reporters discuss their plans to tackle the events of the day. The bustling, unscripted energy triggered her instincts—everything noteworthy happening in the world was filtering through that very place. *This is where I belong.*

The editor poked his head into the hallway and waved her into his office.

He slumped behind his desk. Astoria slowly lowered herself into a chair across from him. Stacks of manila folders teetered on the desk between them, a portal between two worlds. "Tell me about this social media program you offer," he said.

"At my college paper, we went beyond print to reach more students and tell stories from different angles through Facebook and Twitter—"

"Hold up," the editor said. "Did you *just* graduate from college?"

"In June." She pulled her resume from the Pee-Chee folder on her lap and slid it toward him. "And I believe I could help your paper achieve similar results if we—"

"Let me stop you right there." With great effort, the editor leaned forward over his bulbous belly, snatched up the resume, ran his eyes down its entirety, and tossed it back. "We aren't hiring right now. Hell, we've already laid off three reporters this year."

"What about your digital team?"

The man scoffed. His crusty eyebrows hovered over the rim of his wire glasses. "Where are you from?"

Astoria stiffened. "Small town near here."

"Which town?"

She exhaled, the fight draining out of her. "Aberdeen," she said.

The editor leaned onto his elbows and ran both hands over his balding crown. "Look. If you went off to college and learned all about social media, then you should try breaking into a market where people care about that stuff."

Astoria opened her mouth but said nothing, unsure what he was getting at.

"Go to New York. Chicago. Hell, even *The Times* up in Seattle might be hiring people to figure out all that Facebook crap. We get half our news from that desk these days, anyway. But you don't wanna stick around here."

Astoria blinked against the familiarity of a man banishing her from a place she believed she belonged. Cheeks flushing pink, she scanned the room for an answer. Her eyes landed on a red and blue Phillies pennant hanging on the wall above a framed Penn State college degree. "But you're not even from here," she said, desperation rattling her voice.

"What's your point?"

"Rural communities are dying. Don't you think social media could at least bring journalism online and tell stories about what's happening to the people in this area?"

"We are print journalists here," the man said, jabbing a finger toward Astoria as if she'd threatened his livelihood. "Always have been, and if I have anything to do with it, we always will be."

***

Those first weeks in Nashville felt like years, each day heavy with the stress of surviving off an empty bank account. The Account Girls never invited her to lunch. Every day, she watched as they stood from their desks, debating where to dine while checking their makeup in compact mirrors, then flitting off to lunch, chattering like little birds as they went. She felt like an outsider but was relieved at the same time. It would have been death to her reputation if she went to pay for a meal, only to have her debit card declined for everyone to see.

Anna Mae had shown her where the company provided free snacks to its employees in the kitchen, along with a wet bar and a keg, which usually ran dry by Thursday afternoon.

"Just mind your moderation," Anna Mae had instructed.

Astoria wasn't so much interested in the booze as she was in calculating how she might survive off the kitchen snack supply. Lunchtime would be lonely, but the free food brought relief.

She'd been embarrassed to take it at first. It reminded her of elementary school, marching single file with her classmates into the cafeteria, where they each picked up a plastic red tray then shuffled down the food line, stopping first at the milk station. The kids whose parents had given them a dime proudly slapped their coin on the milk lady's counter. The kids on the free milk program clung to their oversized red trays, eyes wide, while the milk lady, shrouded in a ring of harsh light, gave them a carton of processed calcium without a word or currency exchanged. If little Astoria didn't have the dime, she hugged her tray tight to her body and looked the milk lady straight in the eye. Nobody had much money—Astoria's parents included—but they'd raised her on that working-class edict you didn't take handouts. Because if you did, it meant you'd lost the war, even though everyone else was fighting it right alongside you.

But Astoria wasn't a kid anymore. Alone in the agency's kitchen, she glanced over her shoulder once, twice to make sure nobody was around, then hastily filled a coffee filter with pretzels, snatched a mealy apple from a fruit bowl, and smuggled her sustenance back to her desk.

She chewed these meals slowly, savoring the sweet apple and salty pretzels on her tongue, washing them down with a fizzy 7-Up. The free snacks tasted better than her pride, and they were cheaper, too.

Aside from the food supply and promise of a paycheck, Astoria found Corporate America one big snoozefest. The low lighting, scratchy carpet, beige walls, and marathon meetings had her feeling like some dark force had tied a big rope around her heart and was twisting it tighter with every billable hour.

One afternoon, while fighting to stay awake in a new project kickoff, she jotted down the following behavioral traits she observed as standard for achieving acceptance at the agency:

- *Arrive to meetings on-time; smile politely and nod along with whatever Henry Hunter and the Creatives say.*

- *Don't ask challenging questions—it frustrates the Account Girls.*

- *As a follow-up to the previous point, don't ask the Account Girls about their client's business goals. They get flustered. Avoid questions like, "What is your client trying to achieve?" - or - "Why are we doing this?"*

- *Don't ask anyone how they think social media should impact clients' businesses—this is your job—pretend like you know the answer.*

- *Respond with enthusiastic support to whatever solutions the Creative Team presents in meetings. Be careful how you ask follow-up questions; try not to sound like you're challenging their ideas.*

- *Project a sense of enthusiasm on your way to the next meeting.*

- *Learn the acronyms.*

Every day, sometimes every hour, she wondered, *is this all there is?*

She recalled how it felt to stand in the hallway of that newspaper office back home in Washington. But then she thought of her checking account's single digits, the latest round of overdraft fees pushing her deeper into the red, a reality punctuated by the pink envelopes she received in the mail from Sallie Mae, which she slipped into a shoebox in the back of her closet. She never opened those letters—didn't have to—she knew what they said.

***

Two months passed before three of the Account Girls—Lexi, Kayleigh, and Caroline—found time in their schedules to invite Astoria to lunch. Their cohort, Evie, was not invited.

They went to the Sunset Grill, an eatery tucked off bustling 21st Avenue in Hillsboro Village, notorious for its late-night menu among service industry folks, but the business crowd favored its wooden booth enclaves and ice-cold martinis for lunch. The latter came to dine and whisper about those on the uphill climb or downhill slide, their musings safe amidst the soundtrack of silverware clinking and ice cubes settling in glasses of sweet tea.

A lanky waiter with long, stringy hair and a button-down shirt concealing most of his tattoos showed the Account Girls and Astoria to their booth. Perched evenly around the table, the Account Girls ordered martinis and chicken Caesar salads without glancing at the menu. Astoria followed suit. The waiter returned promptly with their drinks as if they'd been ready-made.

"I just love this little neighborhood," said Lexi, holding her glass to the side and tossing her blonde curls over her shoulder like some 1920s Hollywood starlet. "The shops and old brick buildings are so quaint. Have you been to Hillsboro Village yet, Astoria?"

"Been here? I live here." Astoria said in a vaudevillian tone, swirling an index finger.

The girls stared.

Astoria straightened, dropping the act and her eyes. "I share an apartment here with a girl who works in the music industry."

"Aren't you the girl about town." Lexi pursed her lips, then sipped her cocktail.

"Make sure you get in good with your roommate," said Kayleigh. "Anyone with an industry hookup is a good connection to keep in this town."

Malnourished as she was, the alcohol worked fast, softening Astoria's senses and numbing her patience. "I imagine you'd both get along well with my roommate," she said.

"Let us know when she hooks you up with the backstage passes," said Lexi.

"Henry Hunter said you moved here all the way from Seattle?" Caroline asked, smiling warmly while the others scanned the restaurant.

"Not exactly."

Caroline waited.

"I'm from a small town in Washington that nobody's ever heard of. Near Aberdeen."

"What made you come to Nashville?"

"A mentor from college referred me to Anna Mae." Astoria issued this line just as she'd rehearsed it in her mind.

"How wonderful," said Caroline. "Lexi here went and got engaged to her mentor last month."

The bride-to-be preened.

Astoria choked on her martini at the mention of mentors and marriage, the alcohol burning her throat. "Come again?" she said, fighting through a cough.

"I was working as an assistant for a doctor down in Franklin," Lexi said, demurely tucking her chin to her shoulder.

"Only to discover he needed you to help him run his business *and* his entire life," Kayleigh interjected.

Lexi swatted at her, beaming proudly. "He needed help getting his practice off the ground. But yes, it did so happen we fell in love with one another in the process."

The three Account Girls swooned.

"But you don't work for him anymore?" Astoria asked.

Lexi waved a hand dismissively. "Lord, no. All that healthcare coding liked to have bored me straight to death. I found some old battle axe nurse and pulled her out of retirement. She runs that place like a dang CPA at tax time and keeps my man focused on his work, which gives me peace of mind, if you know what I mean."

The waiter brought their salads; he slid a pepper mill from the crook of his arm and set to grinding. He had the letters G-R-U-N-G-E-R-O-C-K tattooed on his knuckles. Astoria smiled, thinking of home.

"Do you think you'll invite Evie to your shower?" Kayleigh asked, flicking a hand at the waiter, signaling him to stop with the pepper. The waiter rolled his eyes and faded away from the table.

Lexi groaned. "I'm afraid she'll drink all of our booze."

"Do you think she's an alcoholic or just a pill head?"

"Come on, now, you two," Caroline said, but the girls carried on.

"Probably both," Lexi said as she slowly, deliberately, stirred her fork through her salad as if doing so required the utmost intention. "She acts drunk half the time. And that obnoxious cackle of hers is too much. I swear, all she does in meetings is sit there and laugh. Like, don't you have anything interesting to say?"

Astoria took a long drink of her martini.

"She swings that knockoff Coach bag around," said Kayleigh, "and you can hear all those pill bottles rattling inside."

Lexi stopped stirring her salad and raised her eyes contemplatively toward the ceiling. "I wonder if she has any Adderall. It's always helped me drop those last five pounds, you know? Might see if I can bum a few off her before my wedding."

"Not a bad idea," Kayleigh said. "At least she'll be good for something."

Both girls snickered.

"Y'all stop gossiping," said Caroline. "Astoria here will think that's all us southern gals know how to do."

Astoria glanced at the faces of her new co-workers as they poked at their calorically deficient lunches. She didn't know what they were talking about as far as Evie and pills and Adderall, and she didn't want to.

"I have a cousin who went to high school with her in Memphis," Lexi continued. "Her daddy is new money, and her family thinks their *you-know-what* doesn't stink. But the truth is, they're total trash."

This last word Lexi pronounced *tray-ush*, which Astoria found ironic, though it still made her wince.

A new waiter arrived with a basket of bread.

"No, no." Lexi waved off the waiter with her fork. "No carbs on the table."

"Oh, Lexi," said Caroline, "just don't look at them, and they won't make you fat."

Back at the office, Astoria slouched glassy-eyed at her desk. She'd done her share of day drinking with the professor, but she'd been too nervous to eat much with the Account Girls, and the two martinis she'd guzzled packed a punch.

After clearing her inbox of its three emails, she navigated to the Google Analytics tutorial bookmarked in her internet browser. Clicking mindlessly through the training modules, all she could think about was how she never wanted to go to lunch with those Account Girls again.

***

To survive the endless meetings that filled everyone's day at the agency, Astoria activated a plan: she spoke up twice to appear engaged, then slipped off to the restroom where she locked herself in the last stall and crouched on the closed toilet, knees to her chest. She waited until the last minute to return to the meetings so she might capitalize on 'next steps,' although the meetings rarely resulted in actionable clarity.

One Wednesday morning, while hiding in her stall, the main door of the bathroom whooshed open. Two voices entered, deep in debate. Astoria recognized them immediately—Lexi and Kayleigh were unpacking the gossip du jour—something about Caroline, the supply room, a locked door, and an allegation that one of the Creative Guys saw Hanz slip inside one afternoon shortly after Caroline herself had gone in.

Astoria recalled her lunch with the Account Girls and what they'd said about Evie. They'd feigned friendly with Caroline, but were now shredding her reputation like hyenas on a zebra. Scared of being caught eavesdropping, Astoria held her breath, hugging her knees tighter. When Kayleigh and Lexi finished debating whether Caroline and Hanz would do such a thing, they left, their whispers fading into the hallway.

Dizzy from holding her breath, Astoria stood and leaned against the wall, exhausted at the idea that she needed to engage with these women if she was to be successful in her new role.

***

When the office cleared out in the afternoons, Astoria would pass by Anna Mae's office to see if the door was open, and Anna Mae was inside. If she wasn't on the phone, Anna Mae always brightened when she spotted Astoria lurking.

"Astoria Lyons. Come on in here and tell me how you're doing."

Jazz music womp-womped from the CD player. Incense burned on a shelf next to Anna Mae's plants, emitting a thin tendril of smoke. A can of Diet Coke fizzled on the desk. Astoria would sit across from Anna Mae and listen and talk, sometimes until the cleaning crew came in and turned on all the overhead lights.

Anna Mae was a quintessential southern storyteller, spinning yarns of places, people, and culture so wild that Astoria always wondered what was real and what was an exaggeration, but she never asked. She loved hearing Anna Mae tell of growing up in Greenville, Mississippi, a progressive seed germinating in the vast Delta. The boomtown was once home to more authors and artists per capita than any other city in America. A group of old-money social activists bankrolled the place, atoning for their ancestors' sins as they crusaded for a more inclusive Mississippi.

"Greenville had some of the best blues clubs in the country, modern shopping downtown. It was quite a scene—a port city at the intersection of ideas and commerce," said Anna Mae.

"Is it still so vibrant?"

Anna Mae's mouth softened at the corners, and her eyes focused on something far away. "No," she said, shaking her head. "Manufacturing went away, and the world moved on, taking the rest of us with it, I suppose."

"That sounds familiar," Astoria said. "My hometown sprang up from the timber industry. When I was younger, there were small businesses, a couple of restaurants and stores, but by the time I left for college, the Feds had shut down the forests, and Main Street was empty."

"What do people do there now?"

"Drugs, mostly." Astoria shrugged.

"Isn't that interesting," said Anna Mae. "Seems to be a common theme in small towns across the country."

On the nights when Anna Mae wasn't in her office, Astoria would drive to the Opry Mills Outlet Mall, where she walked in circles until the stores closed and only the Olive Garden remained open. The mall's hallways were cold and otherworldly beneath shallow gray lighting. Astoria floated along, studying the outfits in the windows, halfheartedly scouting the clearance racks for sheath dresses she might buy when her paycheck came in—another excuse for delaying her student loan payments yet again. A plastic, sugary smell permeated the air while mainstream country music blasted from loudspeakers. She imagined all that manufactured chaos boring holes through her skull, melting her brain into a pool of mercury that was slowly trickling out of her body along with any sense of purpose she'd ever harbored for herself.

One particularly lonely Thursday night, she mustered up some courage and went for a drive instead of walking the mall.

Multiple interstates merge at various points around Nashville, meaning a driver can be hauling ass down I-40, I-440, and I-65 at the same time, but the road splits quickly, so if said driver is trying to head west on I-40, they'd better be in the correct lane, or they'll find themselves heading north on I-65 without blinking.

The iPhone had been on the market for a year, but Astoria couldn't afford new technology, so she relied on sets of directions she'd printed off Maps.com for her commute to and from work. Still, she got lost in this entangled transitory web every time she coaxed her Corolla onto the interstate, unable to push it past sixty without the engine overheating, zippy BMWs and oversized trucks passing her on the left and the right every time she hit the road, whether going to work or getting groceries.

That night, the tangled landscape of potholed lanes, exit signs, and off-ramps blurred around her until she realized she'd circled the entire city twice. On her second lap around the urban speed-way, she accepted she'd lost her bearings. She took the Rosa Parks exit for no reason other than name recognition, decelerated off the interstate, and turned left at the first stoplight.

Dusk was settling beneath the overpasses, charcoaling the edges of the city. Her car sputtered up a hill as she peered at a columned Greek Revival building—the state's capitol—perched stoically above her like some aristocrat judging the peasantry. At the next red light, a limestone clock tower shimmered gold in the setting sun. Down the street, a line of brick buildings leaned against one another like drunken old friends. The stoplight turned green. On another whim, Astoria eased the car left, her face soft-ening from stress to surprise when the dancing lights of Broadway came into view.

A strip of honky-tonks lined both sides of the street, their neon signs flashing in a gaudy cavalcade all the way down to the Cum-berland River. The scene unfolded before her as she drove slowly down the hill. She opened all the car's windows. High-charged music spilled out from the bars, the sound of fiddles floating up into the night.

White-haired tourists in thick-soled tennis shoes and blue jeans meandered past Tootsies, Roberts, Palisades Park, pausing on the sidewalk to listen to the bands through the open doorways, tapping their toes to the country-western songs. Young men with lanky arms, greasy hair, and holes in their jeans smoked cigarettes as they bopped along with the old-timers to the rhythmic pulse of the street.

Astoria drove to where the road ended at a stoplight at the bottom of the hill; the Cumberland River rolled on beyond. She recalled seeing this part of town, Broadway, on Maps.com; she'd noted the river was north, and her apartment was in the opposite direction. When the light changed, she flipped a U-turn and drove back up that frolicking, spirited street, holding an arm out the window and letting it float on the warm breeze.

The stress of the day peeled away, and something of hope sparked inside her. Perhaps Nashville wasn't the unattainably glamorous city the professor had made it out to be. Maybe, beyond the stuffy confines of Dixon-Richards and the artificial lighting of the Opry Mills Mall, it was a sleepy southern town, an unassuming place where a small-town girl like her might find space to make something of herself.

CHAPTER FIVE

Fall 2008

"New girl. Wanna go to lunch today?" Evie hoisted herself onto Astoria's desk and plopped an oversized hobo bag down next to her, the sound of pill bottles rattling from within. Astoria turned and glanced behind her to where Kayleigh and Lexi perched over a box of glass stones—wedding decorations—separating them by subtly nuanced shades of green.

Shortly after Astoria had accompanied the Account Girls to lunch, Kayleigh had announced that she, too, was engaged at a company-wide quarterly meeting. The floor had been abuzz with wedding chatter and event planning ever since.

Now, the brides-to-be were separating teal pieces of glass from seafoam green, a task they'd been diligently focused on since the mail boy delivered the decor in a package marked "URGENT" earlier that morning.

"I still can't believe they sent me the wrong colors," Lexi said, flicking a blonde tendril and pouting. "My colors are teal and coral, not teal and this weird green color."

Kayleigh held a smooth green piece up to her desk lamp. "I'll be able to use them in the vases at my couple's shower. It'll be dark. They'll add texture to the tablescape."

Astoria recalled what the Account Girls said about Evie at lunch. Whether there was any validity to their gossip, Astoria figured Evie's real offense was that she didn't even try to fit in. Didn't talk about her personal life at work. Didn't dress like the others. And now, sitting there on Astoria's desk, kicking her legs back and forth like a child, it was clear Evie didn't give a rat's ass about what they thought of her, either.

"Where to?" Astoria asked.

"The Video Guys and I are going to Arnold's."

"What's that?"

"It's a meat & three."

"A what?"

Evie hopped up off the desk, slinging her purse over her shoulder. "Girl. A meat-and-three. If you don't know, then you're coming."

Evie drove her Mercedes. One guy from the video production team—Jake—rode shotgun. He was notorious for always wearing a black jean jacket and his hair in a pompadour style. Astoria squeezed into the backseat between two other Video Guys, pinning her knees together and tugging at the hem of her shift dress, attempting to make herself smaller to make room.

"You're the new girl, right?" asked the guy to her left. His soft belly blinked out from the bottom of his Drive-By Truckers T-shirt. "My name's Todd."

Astoria smiled and nodded. "Astoria—right—nice to meet you."

The guy sitting to her right leaned forward and waved, introducing himself as Cody. His cropped hair, groomed beard, and pearl-snap shirt made him look like the Creative Guys, except with nerdish mannerisms. Astoria relaxed slightly.

In the passenger seat, Jake hammered his fists on the dashboard, then reared back and howled. Astoria, Todd, and Cody side-eyed one another in the back.

"Did you know there is a place where good ideas go to get fat and bloated and irrelevant, ladies and gents?" Jake said. "Not only is there such a miserable place, but we fucking work there!"

"What's going on?" Evie asked, accelerating onto the interstate. She cracked her window and lit a cigarette.

Astoria realized she hadn't seen anyone smoke in a car since she was a kid. Her mother would sneak a Lucky Strike on the drive home from the grocery store on the weekends. With Otis Redding on the radio, the lines softened on her mom's face as she lit that cigarette and rolled down the car windows. In those moments, the smell of smoke and fresh air mixing in the car and the wind blowing through their hair, her mother looked young and carefree. She seemed happy. Those cigarettes were a rare guilty pleasure for her mother, who often opined that only simple-minded people wasted all their money on booze and tobacco.

"I'm stealing a smoke," Jake said, fishing a cigarette from Evie's purse. He lit up. Exhaled. Explained. "All those creative fucks are trying to tell us how to make movies. They need to stick to making fucking billboards, you know?"

Todd leaned forward to chime in. "Yeah, like, I would never roll up on their precious creative space and tell them how to design bullshit banner ads that nobody wants to look at."

"Yeah, because they'd kick your ass," said Jake.

Astoria pulled her elbows into her ribs and pressed her knees tighter together. Cody leaned into her, their shoulders touching. "Sorry," he said. "Lots of pent-up emotion."

"It's okay," Astoria said, sharing a quick smile, their faces close.

Evie cackled and pressed harder on the gas. The scenery blurred past like watercolor brushstrokes.

They parked on the street and climbed out of the car, spreading out as they walked through an abandoned lot toward a squat red building with "ARNOLDS" painted in yellow block letters across the side. A line snaked out the door. A gray-haired black man in grease-stained coveralls leaned against the wall at the end, smoking a cigarette, his gnarled knuckles contrasting with the smooth white tube, like some mid-century painting. He narrowed his eyes at the group as they approached.

The Video Guys stopped hurling slurs at one another for the first time since they'd left the agency and stepped into line. The man took a pull and then exhaled, long and slow, the smoke hovering around his head like a gritty halo. Astoria made eye contact and nodded *hello* like she'd seen Ace greet fellow working men her entire life. The man tilted his head back and eyed her warily in her preppy shift dress.

The girls and the Video Guys shuffled along in line. Evie and Jake smoked another cigarette. Astoria prayed the guys wouldn't get worked up and start hollering about the Creative Team again. She wondered if the old man saw them all as a bunch of soft-handed brats. She realized it didn't matter, because even though she only had twenty-eight dollars left in her bank account, it was almost payday, and she now occupied a different world.

Once across the restaurant's threshold, Astoria smelled bacon, pie, mashed potatoes, and salty gravy, all mixed in a cacophony of cafeteria chaos. In the kitchen behind the counter, thick-armed women hollered "need mo' cobblah" at men in dirty aprons who, after wiping their biceps across their brows, lugged industrial-sized metal pans of peach cobbler up to the counter. Metal silverware clinked against plastic plates, adding to the hubbub. The lunch-goers pressed in close as they approached a stack of trays.

"Here," Evie said. "Take one of these." She handed Astoria a tray. "Then grab a plate and your silverware. Hand your plate over to the ladies when you see what you want to order."

The Video Guys let the ladies go first. Following Evie's lead, Astoria slid her tray along a set of metal rails while she peered behind a steamy glass window where vats of macaroni and cheese bubbled, pulled pork glistened, and collard greens simmered.

"You order one meat, and then you get three sides," Evie said over her shoulder as she step-paused down the line. "The brisket is to die for. Squash casserole. Bread pudding. Oh, my Lord, the bread pudding." Pointing at the food, Evie ticked off her recommendations. "And the sweet tea." Evie swiveled to face Astoria, hands up, as if addressing the most important issue of the day. "You gotta get the sweet tea."

Astoria surveyed the vast landscape of working man's food, calculating the calorie count of an average plate. A menu board hanging above the room said a 'meat and three' cost eight dollars and seventy-five cents. With the help of a to-go container, she could easily stretch one meal into two.

Carrying their loaded trays, the five co-workers waded among the diners, descending on a table for four. Evie pulled up an extra chair and perched over the group as if at the head of a banquet, her cackle flooding the room when the Video Guys made off-color comments. They settled into their meal, loading black-eyed peas onto forks and shoveling potatoes au gratin into their mouths. Astoria sipped unsweetened iced tea out of a red plastic cup.

"Astoria," Jake said. "That's an interesting name."

"It's where I was born back in Oregon."

"But you're from Washington, right?" Cody asked.

Astoria blushed, pleased he'd taken note. "That's right."

"Where in Washington?"

"Ever heard of a town called Aberdeen?"

"Hey. Wait a minute." Jake brightened, snapping his fingers. "Isn't that where Kurt Cobain is from?"

The co-workers gaped at Astoria.

"Winner, winner," she said.

"I thought Cobain grew up in a real shithole or something," said Todd, wondering aloud.

Evie slugged him on the shoulder. "Dude. You are such a dick sometimes."

"You're not wrong," Astoria said. "Aberdeen is an old logging and shipping port. But while Aberdeen is, in fact, a shithole, I'm from the next town over. And it's even smaller and poorer and shittier than the birthplace of grunge, if that gives you a sense of scale."

The Video Guys laughed, then shoveled more food into their mouths. Evie sipped her tea.

"I've always wanted to go out there," said Todd, trying to recover while a line of gravy snaked down his T-shirt. "Go west, young man, and all that."

"There's great lore in going west," said Cody. "It's such a timeless American trope. But I suppose if you're from there, you don't have anywhere to go if you want to find yourself. Is that why you came here?"

Astoria blushed again, this time more flustered than flattered. She ran her thumb up and down her glass, clearing lines in the condensation. The moment must have made Evie uncomfortable because she cackled again for no good reason.

"Maybe," Astoria said. "Mostly, I needed a job."

"Fair enough," said Cody. "Have you ever worked for an agency before?"

"No."

"Good," said Jake. "Means you're not an asshole yet."

"Well, you guys haven't worked for agencies before, and y'all are assholes." Evie rattled her tea glass in Jake's face.

"Aren't you funny?" Jake grabbed the back of Evie's head and played like he might smash her face into his tray of food.

"It's good that you're not agency scum," Cody said to Astoria, "but you gotta watch out for Hanz."

"The Creative Director?"

Cody nodded.

"Do tell." Astoria had received her fill of office gossip from the Account Girls, but she wanted to hear what Cody had to say about Hanz. During her first week, he'd invited her to an introductory one-on-one. For their meeting, he sat beside her at the massive table in the empty conference room, scooting his chair close, positioning his body perpendicular to hers, triggering her instincts. With eager energy, he asked about her background and complimented her social media prowess, even though she'd yet to contribute to a project, let alone prove herself. She left the conference room with a pit in her stomach; she'd seen those moves before.

"He tries to get with all the girls," Todd said.

Astoria grimaced. "You'd think he'd be past all that at his age."

"Seems all you young girls are titillated by the idea of an old scandal," said Jake.

"Hey, fucker," Evie cut in. "You know we're not like those other girls."

Jake waved her off. "Rumor going around says he's hooking up with Lexi from Accounts."

"Oh, who cares." Evie pushed her tray to the center of the table. Astoria noticed she hadn't taken a bite of food.

"I don't know if they hooked up or not," said Todd. "But I know Hanz gets pissed when those girls talk about their weddings in meetings."

"It *is* a bit much," said Cody.

Todd nodded. "It's like they didn't get their M-R-S degrees in college, so they're on a mission to find a guy at work."

"What's an M-R-S degree?" Astoria asked.

Evie giggled, placing a hand on Astoria's forearm. "Honey. An M-R-S Degree is the reason half of these girls go to college. Not for an education, but for a husband."

"I've never heard of that." Astoria wondered if people had accused her of such a thing when she was carrying on with the professor.

"Maybe it's a southern thing," Evie said.

"I don't understand how they get away with it." Cody tapped his fork against a leftover pile of potatoes. "We get those Friday emails from Henry Hunter about how important it is for us to track our time, but those girls fuck around with all that wedding stuff every day."

"And they're the ones running Accounts." Todd lifted a dish of banana pudding to his mouth and tilted the wobbly yellow dessert down his gullet as if to punctuate the situation's absurdity.

Evie shoved Todd's shoulder again. "Not *all* Account Girls are planning their weddings at work."

Jake threw his napkin on his plate. "I am full as a tick."

"My eyes were definitely bigger than my stomach," said Evie. "Now. Let's discuss where we're getting drinks after work."

CHAPTER SIX

They'd worked together for months before realizing Evie lived a mere half a mile from Astoria in the Belmont neighborhood. The first time Astoria went over to Evie's after work, she stood on the front walk, gaping up at the two-story Craftsman with its beveled glass windows, stone pillars, and sprawling front porch.

Evie sauntered onto the porch with her arms raised, the screen door slamming behind her. She held a frosty glass of Chardonnay in one hand and a smoldering cigarette in the other like a queen calling her subjects to court.

"Evie. You live in a mansion."

Evie rolled her wrist, waving her cigarette nonchalantly. "Never know what you'll find when you answer an ad on Craigslist. My roommate Lorenzo's dad owns it. The old man is loaded. Too bad his son is a disaster."

Astoria bounded up the steps and followed Evie over the threshold into a grand room with built-in cabinets and oak-coffered ceilings. Potted plants stretched across the windowsills. Mismatched furniture slouched about, with three couches forming a horseshoe around a coffee table. Spiral-bound notebooks and sheets of paper covered the table; a few had found their way to the floor. Some sheets were filled to the margins with penciled scribbles, while others held but one declarative statement written in red ink.

In the center of the room, a pock-faced man brooded in a camp chair, his face mere inches from an oversized television, his back to the coffee table and its documents. He had long black hair, like some rock 'n' roll relic from the '80s, wearing a black T-shirt, ripped jeans, and Converse sneakers. Gripping a video game controller with both hands, the man gazed blankly at the screen, clicking through a game where the characters ran from one bombed-out building to the next, throwing grenades and shooting automatic weapons at invisible enemies.

Evie stood over the man, holding her cigarette straight in the air, wine to the side. "Lorenzo," she said, but he remained hypnotized. "Hey! Lorenzo."

He startled to attention, blinking at the two girls. "Oh. Hey. Damnit, Evie, I told you not to smoke in the house."

Evie rolled her head and her eyes in a dramatic circle. "As if. You smoke weed in here all the time." She took a drag from her cigarette, blew a pillar of smoke to the ceiling, then nodded toward Astoria. "Lorenzo, this is that chick from Washington I told you about. The only girl from work who isn't a total bitch."

"Well, not at work anyway," Astoria said, grinning at Evie's positive review. "Evie says you work in the music industry?" Lorenzo looked at Astoria and scanned her from head to toe. She frowned. Shrugging, he refocused on the screen.

"I'm a songwriter," he said. Electronic warfare boomed and rat-a-tat-tatted from surround-sound speakers. The girls furrowed their brows at the papers scattered across the coffee table, then smirked at one another.

"And a guitar tech," Lorenzo added, his tone dark, eyes still fixed on his battle. Astoria wondered what caused him to be so surly, sitting there in his daddy's fancy house, playing video games at six o'clock in the evening.

"Lorenzo is a roadie," Evie said, narrowing her eyes at her roommate. "He just finished touring with Keith Urban. Isn't that right?"

Lorenzo didn't respond.

Evie smirked, turning to Astoria. "Shall we move to the front porch? I need some fresh air. But we gotta get you a drink first."

"Lorenzo's not so bad," Evie said as they padded back outside into the cooling evening. Bugs clicked softly in the trees. Astoria sank into a wicker chair. It creaked beneath her weight, a mildew smell floating up from the seat. Evie hopped backward onto the porch swing, kicking her legs and sailing back and forth. "I shouldn't give him such a hard time," she said. "He says he's bipolar, but it's hard to say."

"Oh?" Astoria arched her brows inquisitively.

Evie nodded. "Takes Adderall by the handful so he can focus. Smokes weed to balance that out. He's either high up or low down. You caught him on a down day. But he's lots of fun when he's in a good mood. Poor guy keeps writing songs, saying he's close to his first big hit, but he loses focus before he can finish anything, so he's stuck being a roadie."

"Isn't Adderall supposed to help people focus?"

"Who knows how it works if you take it with a handful of other pills."

Astoria recalled what Kayleigh and Lexi had said at lunch. She filed their gossip away in the back of her mind. She was relaxed, even happy, sitting on the front porch having a drink with Evie.

One week later, they returned to the front porch after work. Evie settled into her usual place on the massive swing, a box of wine on the floor.

"What happened to that wicker chair?" Astoria asked, dropping into a gold velvet rocker, landing closer to the ground than expected. "Oof."

"Wicker chair?"

"I sat in it the last time I was here. How do you *lose* furniture?"

Evie cackled, kicking the swing into motion. "I can't keep up with this place."

Astoria rolled from side to side in a futile attempt to elevate her position while trying not to spill her wine as she fought gravity. "You're gonna have to bring me refills."

"I came looking for you around lunchtime," said Evie.

Astoria hooked an elbow over one of the chair's wooden arms and clung there to keep from disappearing. "I was hiding in Anna Mae's office."

"I figured you'd gone to lunch with the Account Girls and Creatives."

"Lord," Astoria groaned. "You know they'd never invite me, and I'd do everything in my power not to go."

"New gig going that well, huh?" Evie lit a cigarette, the flame illuminating her nose and eyes, making her look angelic in its glow. Beyond the porch, lightning bugs flashed across the unkempt yard and the prim box shrubs lining the neighboring homes.

"I've only been here a few months, but I feel like I'm on autopilot," Astoria said. "It could be a fun job, but we spend all our energy talking about the work instead of *doing* the work. We go to the office, sit at identical desks, endure the same endless meetings. Only a few people produce anything tangible. It's like a bad sci-fi flick with those girls marching around using the same buzzwords in their matching dresses."

"Not me." Evie winked.

"Okay. You don't dress like a corporate clone. But you sit next to me in those meetings. It's supposed to be a creative agency, for crying out loud, but by the time six people have opined on what one of my stupid Facebook posts should say, I am the farthest thing from creatively inspired. I feel like my brain is atrophying."

"What would you do instead?"

"I wanted to be a journalist. Thought it would keep me entertained, you know? Chasing new stories. No two days the same. Travel."

"You'd be a great journalist," said Evie. "You're good at reading a room."

"That's a nice compliment, Evie. Thank you."

"So, explain how you ended up in a B-rate marketing agency halfway across the country."

Astoria thought about the professor. "I couldn't get a job with a paper or a magazine to save my life," she said after a pause. "I sent out hundreds of resumes and never got one callback. When this job came my way, it hurt to take it because I felt like I was giving up on myself, but I needed a paycheck ... I just don't want to be poor for the rest of my life."

"You think being poor would be worse than working for Henry Hunter and his cronies?"

Astoria considered Evie across the porch. "Did you grow up with money?"

"Yes," she said matter-of-factly. "Why?"

"Because only a rich kid would ask that." Astoria smiled to convey that she wanted to keep it light, but Evie's face fell, and her bottom lip quivered.

"I was only kidding, Evie."

"Being poor wouldn't be all that bad." Evie remained sullen for a moment, then brushed it off, brightening. "At least there's some eye candy around the shop."

"Like who?"

"Couple of the Video Guys have asked about you."

Astoria contemplated telling Evie about the professor, but decided it was too soon. Maybe she'd never tell Evie. Over time, it would be like he never even existed in her life.

"Well, I can't date someone we work with," she said.

"Says who?"

Astoria closed her eyes and shook her head. "I should expand my horizons before fishing in my own backyard. See what this town has to offer, you know?"

Evie raised a hand in the air like she was about to testify. "Astoria Lyons. I am one hundred percent here to spend whatever tickets I have left before my daddy can find a trust-fund recipient he deems suitable for his beloved pride, I mean, *daughter.* But fair warning: this is a dirty dick of a town for dating."

"That's horrible."

"Which part?" Evie chuckled darkly. "Take it from me or learn the hard way. This place teaches a girl to keep her expectations low and her hair high. You gotta set out knowing they ain't gonna call you back the next day, whether you hook up on the first night or after the first month."

"Sounds promising."

"But if you are looking to date someone a little more seriously and work is off-limits, Lorenzo has a few friends who aren't total dirtbags. You should come by and meet one of them sometime."

"Isn't Lorenzo like, a drug dealer?"

Evie waved her cigarette dismissively. "He's a jack-of-all-trades. Entrepreneurial, he likes to say. He picks up odd jobs when he's not on the road. Prides himself on not being a corporate shill like us."

The tweedy gentleman who lived next door stepped out onto his porch. Hands on hips, he peered over to where the girls were drinking beneath a cloud of Evie's cigarette smoke.

"If he's trying to look menacing, he'd better lose the cardigan," Astoria said under her breath.

Evie turned and waved at the man.

He shuffled down his front porch steps, opened the door to his Mercedes, and slipped inside.

"Old Mister Ryerson over there called the cops on us last night because we had some people over." Evie rolled her eyes. "Filed a noise complaint and told the cops we were smoking weed."

"Were you?"

"Not outside. Mean old bastard needs to mind his own business."

Mister Ryerson scowled at the girls over his steering wheel, then backed out of the driveway; his car puttered softly down the street.

****

After months of sleeping on an air mattress, Astoria withheld her student loan payment for the month and went online shopping for the real thing. A Craigslist post offered a new mattress set for only two hundred dollars. Astoria called the number listed and spoke to post's author; the man sounded surprised she'd called, promising her the mattresses were "clean."

"What do you mean, *clean?*" she asked.

"Full set—never been used. Pulled 'em off a truck yesterday." He offered delivery. "How about nine o'clock on Sunday?"

When the Lord's Day came, Astoria listened outside Elizabeth's closed bedroom door. Nothing sounded. Tiptoeing downstairs, she made coffee, then leaned against the kitchen counter, counting out the twenty-dollar bills she'd retrieved from the ATM the night before. When the clock on the stove flashed 9:00, she went outside to wait for the mattress man.

Right on time, a pearl-white Escalade with oversized wheels rolled into the parking lot. Astoria smiled and waved, but her heart sank at the sight of the two thin mattresses strapped to the top of the SUV with bungee cords. The car rolled to a stop at her feet. The tinted driver-side window rolled down, revealing a sunglassed man wearing thick gold chains atop an oversized white T-shirt.

"You the girl wanting the mattresses?" he asked.

Astoria nodded.

The man slid out of his car, unhooked the bungee cords, then deftly pulled both mattresses off the top of the car with one hand, landing them on their ends. He tilted them toward Astoria. "Two hundred dollars," he said.

"I have the cash." Astoria extended the wad of money.

The man took the cash, counted it, then slipped it into the pocket of his baggy jeans. The mattresses' pearlescent fabric billowed in the morning breeze.

"Want me to take 'em inside for you?" he asked.

"I can manage," Astoria said. "Thank you for delivering them."

"No problem."

Astoria offered a handshake. The man raised his eyebrows but accepted, then climbed back into his SUV and rolled out of the parking lot, the morning sun glinting off the Escalade's pearlescent paint. Astoria checked for movement at Elizabeth's bedroom window. If she could get the mattresses into her room without waking her roommate, nobody would ever know.

Each mattress was so flimsy that Astoria hauled both upstairs with little effort, stacking them on the floor in her empty room. Holding her face to the fabric, she sniffed, as if a scent might reveal something of origin. A faint smell implied they'd probably been sitting in a damp, dark truck, nothing more. She slowly lowered herself onto her new sleeping arrangement, laughing when the mattresses sang like a chorus of frogs beneath her weight.

Soft bumps sounded down the hallway.

Elizabeth was stirring.

***

Astoria and Evie celebrated paydays with cocktails and appetizers from the late-night menu at the Sunset Grill. A plate of nachos between them, they peered over their martini glasses at the couples on more amorous escapades.

"You think she's paying?" Evie nodded subtly across the room to where a souped-up blonde perched in a booth, stroking the thigh of her younger companion. The woman wore a low-cut dress revealing tanned leather décolletage stretched taut over perkily oversized breasts.

"You mean the tab or the kid?" Astoria asked.

Evie cackled. The other patrons looked up from their conversations with furrowed brows.

"Oh goodness," Evie said, carefully setting her drink on the table. "No wonder there's not a decent man in this town. They're either married, or all these old money crones are buying them up for the weekend."

"Or they're broke musicians, and neither of us are that desperate." Astoria had heard Elizabeth and her Music Row cohorts discussing how dating a musician in Nashville was a bad idea. She relayed this logic to Evie with the confidence of a long-time local.

"Speaking of decent men, Cody might come by tonight."

Astoria tilted her head and arched a brow. "Here?"

Evie nodded.

"Isn't that convenient? How, pray tell, did you manufacture such a miraculous encounter?"

"Oh, stop." Evie swatted at Astoria. "He's a nice guy. Don't act like there isn't chemistry between you two."

"A nice guy we *work* with."

"So?"

"I don't want to be the target of your cohorts' gossip ring."

"Who cares? Give 'em something to talk about."

"I'm good, thank you."

"*Are* you?"

"Are *you*?" Astoria shot back.

Evie scoffed. She drained her martini. Gripping the glass by the stem, she turned away. "Where is that waiter?"

"I didn't mean to be hurtful," Astoria said quietly. She wanted to press Evie for more, but Cody appeared at their table, a messenger bag slung over his shoulder.

"Am I late for the work session?" he asked.

Astoria crossed her arms.

Evie beamed brightly, her energy brightening. "Not at all," she purred. "We're about to order another round."

Over the next several weeks, Evie always had an excuse for why she couldn't join Astoria and Cody for drinks, leaving them to get to know one another and discover shared interests, like how they both had writing projects they wanted to start and how they couldn't afford drinks at the Sunset Grill every week. They swapped their martinis for espresso and began meeting at Fido, a coffeehouse down the street with high-backed wooden booths, warm lighting, and an endless stream of Vanderbilt students, which made for excellent people-watching.

Perched over their laptops, they nursed cappuccinos and hacked away at their projects. Cody wanted to write a sci-fi screenplay. Astoria was outlining a novel about a predatorial professor who loses his chance at tenure when he's outed by a gaggle of brave students whom he's had sexual encounters with throughout a school year.

"How's it going?" Cody asked.

"Horrible." Astoria grinned from behind her screen.

"Maybe you need a shot of vodka in your coffee?"

"Maybe I need to un-fuck my plot."

"Here's to trying." Cody raised his tiny ceramic cup.

They typed in silence, breaking periodically to discuss the struggle of translating ideas into words on the page. Sometimes, they talked about characters in television shows or movies, or inspiration they'd found in whatever book they were reading. Sometimes, they talked politics.

"It'll be cool to have a black man as President," Astoria said, "but surely there's a person of color with a more active voting record than Obama."

"What do you mean?" Cody asked.

"Obama had this way of voting 'present' instead of 'yes' or 'no' as a Senator. It's like he was a shadow man or something," she said.

Cody rolled his eyes. "Fox News tell you that?"

"I took a course on public speaking. We had to watch the debates. Hillary said Obama was *taking a pass*."

"That's an obvious assault tactic against a guy trying to usher in universal healthcare," he said.

"Why would the woman who wrote *It Takes a Village* oppose universal healthcare? Besides, do you really think universal healthcare is realistic? Financially? For a country this big?"

"I don't think we can avoid socialism. Technology will allow an elite class of visionaries to consolidate power and lead for the greater good. Why not let the smartest people in the world try to run things for a while?" Cody's voice rose as he spoke, his neck flushing red.

"You want someone else running your life?" she asked. "Making critical decisions about your health, your money? You're good with that?"

"The world's population isn't sustainable. People can't be trusted to act in the best interest of the common good anymore."

Astoria groaned and tilted sideways, feigning like she might fall out of the booth. "Why are men so obsessed with the idea that they can force the world to conform to *their* version of fair?"

"I suppose you'll tell me you have a superior approach."

Astoria straightened, turning serious. "I know better than to believe anybody who says they want to control my life in the interest of the greater good."

CHAPTER SEVEN

Friday night. Rain was coming, and the sky loomed starless outside the empty office where only janitorial staff remained, vacuuming and emptying garbage cans beneath bright white lights.

Astoria walked to her car across the deserted parking lot, thinking about how she'd lingered at the office, hoping Cody might find her and ask what she was doing that evening. She wasn't sure if she liked him enough to pursue a serious relationship, but she enjoyed his company and dreaded spending another Friday night alone. But by the time she worked up the nerve to walk over to his desk, he was gone.

Panicky disappointment crept in, triggering memories of the professor and that lingering feeling of rejection. She worried this nerdy dude she'd been hanging out with and letting herself think about during the day might be pursuing other interests; maybe *she* was the one who wasn't good enough for *him*.

The traffic on Briley flowed rhythmically, having thinned out since rush hour.

"Fine," Astoria said. If Cody saw her as nothing more than a Tuesday night hang, then that's how she would view him, too. Lightning 100 played Coldplay's "Viva la Vida" on the radio, and she decided that was exactly what she needed to do.

Her cell pinged with a text from Evie as she walked in the front door.

—Come drink wine? Lorenzo is having friends over.

Astoria stepped out of her heels while staring at the screen. Wiggling her toes on the cold linoleum, she imagined the cast of characters Lorenzo might count as friends. Fingers poised over the keypad, she was about to respond when Elizabeth popped out of the kitchen and squealed. "Hey!"

Astoria gasped, dropping her phone. "You scared me. Didn't know you were home."

"What are you doing tonight?" Elizabeth wore a black v-cut bodysuit with puffy lace sleeves and low-slung bedazzled jeans. "The girls are coming over for drinks before we go to an industry party on Demonbreun. Care to join?"

Astoria retrieved her phone from the floor, thinking Evie's invite was the perfect excuse to avoid Elizabeth and her music industry clique. But then she straightened and considered Elizabeth, all ramped up and ready to party. She thought about Cody and the sting she'd felt when she saw his empty desk, and how she'd never been invited to a Music Row gathering before. Maybe she needed to broaden her social circles beyond Fido and Evie's front porch.

"Sure," Astoria said. "Why not."

"I have clothes you can borrow if you want."

Astoria snapped her phone shut, blowing off Evie's text. "I have clothes."

They went to a bar on Demonbreun with sticky floors and perspiring walls, the kind of place where girls always drank for free as part of some promotional schtick. Elizabeth and her friends offered their IDs to the doorman and filed inside. Last in line, Astoria stepped into the hazy space, realizing the others had already dispersed. From the periphery, she scanned the crowd. Three men leaned against the bar, red-faced and sweaty, oversized in their jeans and sports coats. She thought of the pickled blood sausages they sold out of glass jars in country stores back home.

As for the women in the room, Astoria realized they belonged to one of two categories: younger and used to be younger. The former wore silk blouses, designer jeans, and flawless makeup; they bounced from group to group, yelping and dramatically embracing everyone they encountered. An air of exhaustion surrounded the older women, sitting in clusters in their polyester blouses, stretchy pants, and cakey makeup.

Alone on the perimeter, Astoria was tallying up her judgments when a short man with an auburn-colored beard held a cold beer bottle against her arm, causing her to jump.

"You look thirsty," he said, offering her the beer.

She accepted the drink.

He introduced himself and asked where she was from.

"Washington."

"Ah. Seattle? Cool." He nodded and launched into his story. He'd graduated from Belmont with a degree in music industry marketing. He'd scored a "killer" internship with a label and was "amped" when it turned full time.

"I dated a guy who graduated from Belmont once." Astoria lifted her beer to her lips but paused before taking a drink. "He was a real asshole."

"Never heard of him," the guy said, grinning. "What do you do for work?"

"Marketing."

"In what capacity?"

Astoria proudly explained her new role while the Belmont guy scanned the room, cutting her off mid-sentence. "I'm super interested in hearing more about what you do, but I gotta run and say hey to this guy I've been trying to network with for a while. You get it because you're in marketing, right?"

"For sure," she said, faking a smile and clutching her beer to her chest.

"Don't move one inch." The guy dipped past Astoria and disappeared into the crowd.

Once the alcohol kicked in, Astoria spent the evening meandering from group to group, boldly introducing herself to strangers, slinging snarky comments, and making people laugh before wandering off to find a new audience, confident in her newfound wit. At one point, the floor tilted, and the walls began to shift. Holding herself upright at the bar, she jolted at the press of another cold bottle against her arm—the bearded Belmont alum had reappeared with a peace offering.

Once again accepting the beer, she held it to her lips, but her stomach protested up into her throat. Swallowing her body's warnings, she forced herself to drink.

The guy leaned in, his breath hot on her ear. "Wanna get outta here?"

Astoria scanned the room but didn't see Elizabeth in the thinning crowd.

Yes, she nodded.

"You sure you wanna do this?" the Belmont guy asked after parking outside her apartment.

Astoria swayed in the passenger seat, thinking she ought to go upstairs to her bedroom and pass out, but an image of the professor flashed across what remained of her consciousness. In her state of impaired rationale, she decided it would be the ultimate revenge to hook up with a younger industry guy. She giggled.

"What's so funny?"

"I've never had a hookup," she said, fumbling with the door handle before to face the Belmont guy. "Let's go."

On the way upstairs, they kissed, hot and messy. Sliding across the walls and down the hallway, they stumbled into her room. He shut the door. They pulled at each other's clothes and fell onto the bed, laughing.

Laying beneath him, she sensed she was sinking to the bottom of a lake, drowning, until a sharp pain jolted her back into the room. She looked up at the guy, her eyes searching for his, but he turned his face to the side.

"What is wrong with your bed?" he asked, panting. A bead of sweat dropped from his forehead onto her face. "I can't fucking focus."

He went harder and faster, finally finishing. Then he stood and dressed.

Astoria turned onto her side, holding her knees to her chest. Her brain was blurry, her body pulsing, a silent siren.

He opened the bedroom door. The hallway light cast him in silhouette.

"Your bed is really weird," he said. Then he turned and left.

When Astoria woke the next morning, she felt bruised and sore. Sensing the day was moving on without her, she rolled off the mattress onto her hands and knees, focusing on the carpet biting into her palms instead of her need to vomit. Sweat dampened her temples. Planting her feet on the ground, she slowly pushed herself to stand, then opened her bedroom door and shuffled into the hallway. Elizabeth leaned against the bathroom doorframe as if she'd been waiting for Astoria all morning.

"Sounds like you had quite a night last night," she said.

Without looking at her roommate, Astoria staggered into the bathroom. She closed the door behind her, grabbed the edge of the toilet with both hands, and vomited into the bowl.

***

Having managed a shower but still enduring the shakes, Astoria hauled herself to church. She hadn't been since college, since the professor.

She'd never considered the denomination of the church she grew up attending with her mother. It was a modest one-room building hidden beneath a curtain of fir trees at the back of a meadow, a haven in the wild. Some viewed that little church as an institution, and they attended every Sunday without fail. But it was also a beacon where others sought emergency salvation on the fly, a place people quietly floated in and out of as they fumbled through life. A white cross anointed the steeple—the building's only moniker and, in Astoria's opinion, the only signage a church might need.

But in Nashville, all the churches featured prominent signs, even billboards, denoting which brand of religion one might find inside. Protestant, Baptist, Methodist, Methodist Episcopal, or Episcopal Anglican—Nashville had it all. Astoria didn't know where to start, so she started with what she knew: the church on the edge of Hillsboro Village, which she drove by every day on her way to work.

The Hillsboro Community Church of Christ towered at the neighborhood's edge in a grandiose brick building. Its billboard hovered above the Interstate, beckoning commuters and neigh-borhood residents alike: *Jesus is Alive! Morning Service at 11:00. Afternoon Service at 1:00.*

At 12:55 on her defiled Sunday, Astoria stepped into the church's brightly lit foyer. Ornate floral arrangements buttressed a set of double doors leading into a grand auditorium. Assuming the flowers were for a funeral and not a standard Lord's Day adornment, she turned to flee, but a woman placed a hand on her shoulder. Astoria turned to face a man and woman wearing matching chambray (him in a shirt and pressed khakis; her in a shirtdress and nude heels), beaming at her with identically blinding veneers, all shiny and clean and good. The man held a stack of clipboards. Astoria swallowed hard against the bile crawling up the back of her throat.

"Welcome to the Hillsboro Community Church of Christ. Is this your first time here?" the woman asked, her southern accent thick and sweet, so 'here' came out as *"hey-urrrr."* Nary a blonde hair strayed from her coiffed bob. A gold cross pendant dangled over the divot in her clavicle. A monster diamond ring twinkled on her left hand.

"I'm not sure if I'm supposed to be here," Astoria said. Her mind flashed to the night before—how the industry guy's car had smelled like expensive cologne. The moment he asked if she was sure she wanted him to come up, how she had led the way. Him standing in her room, then moving on top of her, inside of her. Seeing black. Her body hurting, then and now. She shook her head.

"Every soul who comes through these doors is supposed to be here," the man said, extending a clipboard toward Astoria. "And you're right on time for the afternoon service."

"This is my husband." The woman wrapped an arm around the man's waist, placing her other hand on his chest and introducing them using their family name. Hungover as she was, Astoria forgot it immediately.

"We're heading up the welcome wagon for the week, and we'd love it if you'd stay," said the man, still offering the clipboard.

Astoria peered beyond the matching couple and extravagant flower arrangements into the auditorium where people were shuffling into the rows of pews, taking their seats.

"Sure. Thank you." Astoria said, stepping toward the auditorium.

The woman snatched the clipboard from her husband and pressed it against Astoria's arm. "Before you go!" she said playfully, as if teasing Astoria for forgetting the most important thing. "We ask all our new guests to fill out a little informational card so we can support our community of parishioners. Go ahead and take it in with you. You can fill it out during the opening hymn."

Clipboard in hand, Astoria slipped into the auditorium, moving quickly as the congregation stood to sing. She stepped into an empty pew and held the clipboard at her waist, studying it instead of the hymn book. Swallowing against her nausea, she scanned the card: it sought her name, email address, and social media handles. *They're better marketers than we are.*

The preacher moved to the pulpit as the congregation sat. He cleared his throat into the microphone, then announced he wanted to address the topic of *truth*. "Please open your Bibles to Second Timothy, chapter three ... 'But mark this: There will be terrible times in the last days. People will be lovers of themselves, lovers of money ... without love, unforgiving, slanderous, without self-control ...always learning but never able to come to a knowledge of the truth.'"

The words hammered at Astoria's brain. After her one-night stand, she was supposed to feel modern, empowered, alive. Instead, she felt like she'd lost herself. Like she was still drowning. Also, like she might vomit again. She fished a pen from her purse and began filling out the card. The act of slowly, deliberately, writing her information was a brief distraction from the tears pooling in her eyes.

When the congregation rose to sing again, Astoria crept out of the auditorium, holding the door behind her until it clicked softly shut.

Following signs for the restrooms, she made her way down a long hallway. As she passed a doorway, a woman's giggle caught her by surprise. Peering through a crack in the door, she recognized the woman who'd greeted her leaning against a desk. A man—not the chambray husband—was leaning over her, whispering into her ear. The woman glanced over his shoulder and gasped; the man whipped around.

Astoria turned and ran down the hallway, out of the church, and into the brooding late fall day.

CHAPTER EIGHT

Winter 2008

Winter blew into Nashville like it had something to prove.
The northern jet stream scraped south, its icy hands ripping the last of the golden leaves from the trees, rendering the limbs bare and blanched to rattle against an apathetic sky. Darkness seeped into the corners of the office earlier and earlier, making it easy to stay late, work more. While the downshift into shorter days was lulling the world into hibernation, work ramped into a frenzy at the agency as the team prepared to pitch a new client.

From the front of the conference room, Henry Hunter announced they would pitch Old Hickory Workwear, one of Middle Tennessee's longstanding manufacturers, in two weeks.

The Creative Guys moaned.

"Another local client who doesn't understand marketing."

"What kind of workwear are we talking about?"

"Heavy-duty apparel for construction workers, mechanics, road work, things like that," said Henry Hunter.

"What about the timber and fishing industries?" Astoria asked. "It's not a well-known brand in the Pacific Northwest, but could we make it one?"

The Creative Guys cast sidelong glances at one another.

"We could make this a *real* brand," Henry Hunter continued. "Like Nike, but for workwear." He proceeded with the briefing, assigning roles, responsibilities, and due dates to each team member.

"Ms. Lyons," Henry Hunter said without looking at her. "Research how competitors show up online. Websites. Facebook. Twitter. How are they positioning their brands? What are they doing to attract customers? Anything else that stands out."

Astoria wrote diligent notes, excited for the chance to prove herself.

For the next two weeks, she immersed herself in the assignment. To avoid Elizabeth and her Music Row cohorts when they came over for cocktails, Astoria worked late at the office, scouring case studies on other marketing agencies' websites and researching the elements of successful digital marketing campaigns. One night, she drove thirty minutes east to Lebanon to explore a factory store where they sold all kinds of workwear, including Old Hickory.

Work became her salvation. Instead of returning to the Hillsboro Community Church of Christ, she hunched over her laptop in the empty office on Sunday afternoons, analyzing other workwear brands' websites and exploring how they told stories and promoted their products across social media. The Google Analytics courses she'd taken to pass the time when she first started came in handy as she analyzed keyword searches and whether people were interested in buying workwear online.

When her bank account ran dry, the Account Girls tried to loop the office into their episodic drama, or Elizabeth pressured her about buying furniture, work was an escape—the one place that would take what Astoria could offer. Amidst the fevered pace of the Old Hickory Workwear pitch, she realized she could out-hustle most of her peers. She saw this as a private victory but proof that she could make something of herself if she kept her head down and continued to grind.

The week before the pitch, the team languished through endless afternoon practice sessions where Henry Hunter grilled each person on the strategic approach, creative solution, and specific reasons Dixon-Richards was the best agency for the job. Everyone had a precise role and a tight script for the pitch, which they practiced until almost every team member had their parts down verbatim.

Evie was the appointed Account Lead. Astoria heard whispers that Henry Hunter selected her because none of the other Account Girls were interested in a workwear client. In the practice sessions, Evie struggled to remember Henry Hunter's buzzwords. He held the entire team hostage for hours while making Evie recite her talking points. The harder he pushed, the less effort she put forth.

One afternoon, while Henry Hunter and Evie were waging their battle of wills, Astoria escaped to Anna Mae's office. Sitting in her usual spot across the desk from her boss, she admitted she wouldn't mind the grueling pace of pitch prep if it didn't require her to spend hours with the Creative Guys.

"They're kind of elitists," she said, gauging Anna Mae's reaction. "They ignore what I say and carry on their conversations like I'm not even in the room. It's a power play or something."

"How's Evie doing?" Anna Mae asked.

Astoria shifted in her seat, crossing her legs to the side. "Okay, I guess."

Anna Mae pressed two fingers against her temple. "That's being generous, from what I'm hearing."

"Oh." Astoria picked at the pilled fabric of her sweater dress, not wanting to know what criticisms people might be issuing against her friend, even if they were valid.

"I took a risk in referring her here," said Anna Mae. "What did I know? Her father is a ruthless businessman. I figured the apple wouldn't fall far from the tree."

Astoria glanced up at the birds-of-war painting.

"But she seems to have taken a liking to you," said Anna Mae. She swiveled in her chair to face the painting. "Just as leadership here has taken notice of your contributions. Sometimes in business, helping the strays find their way back to the flock is as important as shepherding the entire herd." She looked at Astoria. "Do you understand?"

Astoria nodded. "I think Evie will deliver. But I'll do what I can."

After work, Astoria and Evie settled onto Evie's front porch. Evie sailed back and forth on the swing, wine glass raised like a torch, belting out, "... and I don't give a fuck about Old Hickory Workwearrrr..." in a throaty baritone that echoed down the empty street.

Astoria pursed her lips, irritated by Evie's indifference. "But I need you to care, Evie. I've worked so hard on this. It would be fun to win one, you know?"

Evie lowered her glass and stopped pumping her legs, the porch swing still creaking back and forth. "Look at you, trying all of a sudden. We're obviously going to kill it. I just like giving Henry Hunter something to worry about."

"You're making yourself a target."

"I know what I'm doing. He's a control freak—he needs to give up the ghost and accept that I'm never going to say exactly what he wants me to." Evie pawed around the bench in search of her cigarettes, but the pack had fallen to the ground.

Astoria was in awe of Evie's unflappability but also wished she knew how to make her lean in, even if only to prove they were both capable.

***

The clients—three of them—arrived ten minutes late. Two men wearing sports coats and jeans, one woman in a pencil skirt and silk blouse.

"Take your seats, and we'll get started with introductions," said Henry Hunter, smiling with such force that he appeared to be in pain or perhaps straining against some bodily betrayal. He walked each client to a chair and motioned for them to sit. Astoria sensed the clients' late arrival had him flustered.

The air was tense, making her even more nervous she'd say something wrong despite all their practice. When it was her turn to introduce herself, she made eye contact with each client and smiled politely, but her voice wavered. She was already sweating in her new dress, yet another ill-advised purchase she justified by telling herself it would ensure a strong performance.

"So, talk to us about what you're looking for in an agency partnership," Henry Hunter said to the CEO, the tall man seated next to him with graying hair and leathered skin; he reminded Astoria of John Wayne on *Rio Lobo*, a movie she'd seen countless times with Ace. Henry Hunter reclined in his chair, crossing his legs and clasping his hands behind his head like he was settling in for story time around a fire. Astoria recognized this as his practiced casual look; she felt embarrassed anyone would manufacture such a thing.

"Well, let's get one thing straight from the start," said the CEO. "I own and oversee the company, but Sarah here has been our marketing director for going on twelve years now." The man nodded toward the woman. "She's in charge of this relationship, so I'll let her answer."

Henry Hunter snapped forward in his chair like a kid caught sleeping in class.

"Of course," he said, shuffling through his papers as if searching for the separate set of notes he'd prepared in case he needed to address a woman. "We love appointing decision-makers from the outset. Sarah, is it? Have you worked with an agency before?"

She exchanged a knowing look with the CEO before smiling patiently at Henry Hunter.

"In fact, we've worked with two different agencies since I've been with Old Hickory," she said. "One here in town and one from Louisville."

"Great. So, you're familiar with how most agencies work?"

"Yes. I'm familiar with how agencies work."

Astoria wondered if that was how a woman became a marketing director—she allowed men like Henry Hunter to ask demeaning questions in a room full of people so he could feel in control, be in control. Meanwhile, as the woman, it was her job to sit there and smile while providing agreeable answers to obvious questions.

The clients requested to "keep the conversation casual," so the team didn't showcase their presentation as they'd rehearsed. However, the Creative Team insisted on walking the clients through their portion of the PowerPoint, doggedly injecting their opinion that Old Hickory should invest in a rebrand to make the company more palatable to a broader audience. The marketing director pushed back, saying she wanted to drive sales with their existing base.

The meeting droned on.

Astoria only spoke up once when the CEO asked about social media. "You guys can help us with Facebook and Twitter and all that?"

"Oh yes," said Henry Hunter. "We have a video team within our Creative Group, and Ms. Lyons down there is our social media expert."

Everyone turned to Astoria. She started sweating again. But she straightened, pressed her palms against the table, and took a deep breath.

"Well, I don't know if anyone is an expert on these channels," she said. "They're all so new."

Across the table, Henry Hunter held a fist to his mouth, glowering at her for going off-script. She was supposed to say *she was the expert*, projecting absolute confidence like they'd practiced. But reading the room, Astoria's instincts told her to be honest, even humble, with these clients.

"Maybe you can help us figure out how to reach more of our base audience through these new online channels," said the marketing director.

Astoria scanned the room to gauge whether she should continue speaking. Anna Mae nodded softly, so Astoria continued.

"We can help build a following on social media. But first, we'll want to understand where your primary audience wants to engage, then figure out your messaging strategy—does your audience care about brand, or are they mostly concerned with things like performance, durability, and price? If we can identify what matters most to them, we'll use those insights to inform what type of content they might want to consume from Old Hickory Workwear."

They hadn't rehearsed this part either, but she'd learned it from Google's free online tutorials, and nobody else was saying it, so she figured, *what the hell*.

"That Facebook stuff is foreign to a guy like me," said the CEO. He leaned forward onto his elbows. "But everything you're saying sounds right. We don't want to jump onto any bandwagon. We want everything y'all do for us to help drive our business."

"Of course," Henry Hunter said, extending an arm across the table as if cutting off the rest of the room to reclaim the clients' attention. "But it all starts with brand, which is what our Creative Team can do for you—build a brand audiences want to identify with."

"A brand people want to be seen wearing," said one of the Creative Guys. "Like how we all want to carry an iPhone because it shows we're into innovation."

"That's right," said Henry Hunter.

The CEO smirked. "I don't know if carrying an iPhone proves you're an innovator," he said. His team snickered as if they'd already discussed this. The CEO pulled a Blackberry from the pocket of his sports coat and deposited it on the table. Henry Hunter shot Astoria a quick scowl. She spent the remainder of the meeting wondering if she'd said all the wrong things.

After the meeting, Henry Hunter, Evie, and the Creative Team took the clients to lunch. But before departing, the marketing director made her way around the conference table to Astoria.

"It was nice to meet you," she said, offering a handshake. "I like what you said, and I think you can help us grow our social media presence. I'm looking forward to working with you."

"We would love the opportunity," Astoria said, returning a firm grip.

Eavesdropping nearby, Anna Mae beamed.

Henry Hunter and the team ushered the clients out of the conference room in a cloud of chatter.

"You did good, young lady," Anna Mae whispered to Astoria. "Let's go get us a drink."

***

In the dimly lit restaurant, elevator music mixed with the clink of silverware. Men in suits talked quietly across mahogany tables. Amidst the heady cologne, Astoria and Anna Mae found their way to a green leather booth.

Anna Mae ordered a glass of Chardonnay and a grilled chicken Caesar salad. Astoria followed suit, succumbing to the ritual of every southern woman's standard lunch order.

"So, how do you think that went?" Anna Mae asked.

A waiter brought their drinks.

"I'm not sure." Astoria smoothed the white linen napkin across her lap. "I didn't follow Hunter's script exactly, but I think the clients liked what we had to say?"

"You did great."

"Yeah?"

"Yes. We're here to celebrate! I know Henry likes things buttoned up, but you spoke convincingly on a topic the rest of us are still trying to figure out. Every time you talk about social media, I learn something new. Keep up the good work."

Astoria exhaled, dropping her shoulders. "I'm so relieved. Hunter kept shooting me the evil eye. I was so stressed."

The waiter brought their salads.

"Can you bring me another glass of Chardonnay when you have a second?" Anna Mae held up her half-drained glass.

"Yes, Ma'am." The waiter peeled away from the table.

"Might as well," said Anna Mae, shrugging guiltily.

Astoria sipped her wine, the alcohol flooding her bloodstream with hot release.

"Don't stress," said Anna Mae. "I wasn't as involved in that pitch as I would have liked, so you can blame me for any uncertainty you're feeling. Truth is, I'm spending a lot of my time fighting to keep Video under Production. This isn't widespread knowledge, but leadership is considering restructuring Video within Creative."

Astoria recalled lunch with the Video Guys and what they'd said about Creative encroaching on their territory. She was about to ask Anna Mae what it would mean for her role if Video shifted from Production to Creative when a tan man in a blue sports coat approached their table.

"Bless my eyes. Is that Anna Mae Alcott?" he asked.

Anna Mae brightened. "Hey, Cal. What brings you off Music Row?" She offered the man her cheek, which he kissed lightly. Astoria beamed at the formal gesture, finding it charming and refined.

"Had a meeting with my real estate guy," said Cal.

"You selling your place?"

"No, I'm looking to buy some land out in Cheatham County. A little getaway spot on the river. You ladies lunching or drinking or both?" He nodded at Astoria and smiled.

"Cal, this is Astoria Lyons. I hired her to teach me about digital marketing."

"Digital marketing, eh? We could use some help with that in the music industry."

"Cal owns a video production studio," said Anna Mae. "We used to make music videos together back in the '90s."

"Long time ago." The man ran a hand through his silver hair, brushing it off his forehead, but it immediately fell back across his eyebrows.

"Yeah, but who's counting," said Anna Mae, laughing into her wineglass, cheeks flushing red.

Astoria watched the cohorts closely; Anna Mae was flirting. With a shock, she realized this man, Cal, likely knew the professor. She found herself hoping Anna Mae would invite him to stick around for a drink.

Cal checked his watch. "Ladies, I'll leave you to your lunch. Astoria Lyons, it's been a pleasure. Anna Mae, always."

"We'll talk toon, Cal."

"How long have you known him?" Astoria asked once he'd walked away.

"Long time. We pioneered country music videos, Cal and me. We worked with Reba. Garth. Alan Jackson. All of 'em."

"No kidding?"

"God's honest truth. We were trailblazers."

"One of my mom's co-workers had a satellite dish. She recorded music videos from CMT and TNN on VHS tapes and lent them to us. We'd watch those videos over and over."

"You were probably watching some of my work."

Astoria remembered the hot summer afternoons she'd spent standing at her parents' television set, leaning close to the staticky screen and studying the permed hair, pearl-snap shirts, and high-waisted jeans of the country music stars.

"Those were fun times," said Anna Mae.

"Why'd you quit?"

Anna Mae considered her wine glass, slowly twirling it by the stem. "It's a cutthroat industry. After a certain point, you realize that a young man's game is no place for a woman."

Astoria thought about the re-org Anna Mae had mentioned before Cal approached the table. "So, this won't be your first rodeo if they take the Video team from you."

Anna Mae smiled sadly. "No. But don't you fret. You have such a bright future, and I'm hearing nothing but good things. You're already teaching us a lot about this digital stuff, and you just aced your first pitch!"

"Is it bad that I'm making it up as I go?" The wine had loosened her judgment, and the words flew out of her mouth before her brain could catch them.

Anna Mae chuckled. "You fake it until you make it, young lady. That's how you play the game. And sometimes, you learn how to play new games. But if you can figure out how to reinvent yourself, then you'll be okay."

The waiter reappeared, sliding Anna Mae's wine refill onto the table. He went to take her first glass, but Anna Mae held up a finger and dumped its remnants into the new one, filling it to the brim. The waiter smirked, took the empty, and left.

"But enough about work," said Anna Mae. "Will you be coming to the Christmas Party? It's a lot of fun."

"Sounds like it. The Account Girls seem excited."

Anna Mae smirked. "I'm sure they're busy shopping for their dresses."

"I must admit, Anna Mae, I cannot believe how much online shopping happens during the hours of nine-to-five."

"Don't mind them. You'll have fun at the party. We close the office for a day. You'll get a nice steak dinner at Merchant's downtown. Have you been there yet?"

Astoria shook her head no.

"After lunch, we end up at Tootsies or Paradise Park. There'll be a band. Probably an open bar."

"Sounds wild."

"It's a blast. Just don't get sloppy." Anna Mae raised her glass and winked.

CHAPTER NINE

Holiday 2008

It wasn't yet noon. Astoria leaned against the doorway of the Merchant's banquet hall, waiting for Evie to arrive. Dressed in their finest holiday attire, Dixon-Richards employees buzzed about, seeking the social security of their tribe. A small army of waitstaff hoisted trays of sparkling champagne flutes around the room, dipping in and out of the chattering cloisters. A waiter with chiseled biceps and a finely-trimmed mustache approached. "Can I get you something to drink, Miss?"

"This early?" Astoria asked.

"It's a holiday party, doll, why play prissy?"

"What are my options?"

The waiter shook his hands like he was praising the alcohol gods. "Everything."

Astoria froze; the waiter snatched a glass from a passing tray and shoved it into her hand. "Flag me down if you would like something else." He brushed past, off to his next task.

Minutes later, Evie blew into the room, donning her signature charcoal eyeliner and an oversized black fur coat.

"Well, well, well, if it isn't Elizabeth Taylor, fashionable late for the ball," Astoria said.

After hours of listening to the Account Girls debate which matching party outfits to wear (in the end, they agreed on green tartan plaid with gold accessories), Astoria and Evie forged their own pact to wear black.

Evie looked svelte in her dramatic coat, cigarette pants, and a v-cut blouse, revealing what she liked to call her *two greatest assets*. Astoria wore a silk sheath dress with a boatneck and a bow at the waist, which she couldn't afford but bought anyway from the Green Hills Mall.

"You look stunning," said Evie. "Very Hepburn. I should have loaned you my pearls. Then we really would have outclassed these bitches."

"Evie. You look downright sexy."

"I'm going to insert myself into as many of their photos as I possibly can." Evie shimmied out of her coat and handed it to the attendant. "And what, lovely, are *you* drinking?"

Astoria pointed at a tray of champagne bobbing past. Evie rolled her eyes, then snapped her fingers at yet another waiter. "We'll each have a glass of Veuve, please."

Lunch was served at one o'clock. Evie had commandeered the central banquet table, where she, Astoria, and the Video Guys held court. Cody sat next to Astoria.

"Are you having fun?" he asked.

"I've never imagined a company throwing a holiday party like this."

"Well, it is a tax write-off." Cody scanned the room. "So, it's not that altruistic."

Astoria frowned, but Cody took no notice. It seemed entitled, she thought, to indulge in the company's generosity while simultaneously trashing it.

"Well, I'm grateful either way," she said.

"Oh, for sure."

Cody lifted his lowball glass, and she lifted her flute.

"Cheers."

They ordered filet mignon, then passed around platters of mashed potatoes, marinated mushrooms, and smothered greens. Waiters reappeared again and again, sliding glasses of wine, scotch, coffee, whiskey, and beer onto the table.

"Can you take a picture of our table?" Evie shoved her digital camera toward a young waitress, who lethargically obliged. Astoria recognized the girl's defeated energy. She saw herself standing in her greasy black apron at the head of a booth full of her college peers, and she felt guilty for being on the other side of the apron, sitting there in her fancy dress, soused out of her senses so early in the day.

"Scoot closer," the waitress said, motioning for Astoria to move towards Cody.

Pulse quickening, Astoria slid her chair next to his. Playfully, he rolled his eyes, then put his arm around her. He smelled woodsy. She lifted her flute towards the camera and smiled, her cheeks burning red. Here she was—part of the group.

The alcohol sloshed around her brain, and the room blurred as her co-workers roared throughout the restaurant, the entire company making merry.

Someone clinked a spoon against a glass. The room hushed. All heads turned toward two white-haired gentlemen in gray suits, poised to address the room. "Sorry to interrupt all this fun," one of them said into a microphone, his mustache fluffing above his mouth as he spoke, the restaurant lights reflecting off his bald head. "For those who don't know me, I'm Gary Richards, and this is my business partner, George Dixon."

Dixon raised his tumbler.

The men spoke briefly about why they started the agency in the '60s and how they believed paid media was the future back then.

"You know, television ads. Full-page spreads in *The Tennessean* every Sunday ... but as you've probably heard, digital is the way forward ..."

"We want to thank you all your fine work. We truly believe we have the best talent in the region to take this agency to the next level. And now, we'll hear a few words from your fearless leaders, Henry Hunter and Mister Hanz."

The Creatives whistled and clapped at their tables.

"Woo-hoo," said the Account Girls.

Cody took a long drink while the other Video Guys looked on, stone-faced. Astoria searched for Anna Mae, surprised she hadn't joined Henry Hunter and Hanz at the microphone.

"We won't talk long," said Henry Hunter. "But we want to thank each of you for all your hard work and dedication this year. Accounts Team, where are you?"

The girls squealed and waved.

"There you are—Caroline, Kayleigh, Lexi. Evie, too. And Cassidy, who recently joined us from Chicago." Henry Hunter pointed to the Account Girls' table. "I see you. You're providing world-class account leadership. Keep it up."

Evie chugged her chardonnay.

"And the Creatives? Where are you?"

One of the Associate Creative Directors raised a fist straight into the air and bowed his head.

"Words don't do justice to the level of creativity coming out of this shop. Award-winning creative. That's what I'm seeing. And in 2009, we're going to produce even more."

The room erupted with applause and sharp whistles.

Across the table, Jake whispered something into Todd's ear. They chuckled, shaking their heads.

Astoria inventoried the restaurant, craning her neck, still unable to spot Anna Mae.

His freshly-gelled mohawk glistening beneath the lights, Hanz took the microphone and began recounting his career as a Creative, name-dropping all the agencies he'd worked for along the way, waving his glass of scotch around as he spoke, having already mentioned as an anecdotal aside in every conversation he'd been in that day how he was drinking aged Pappy van Winkle.

Jake banged both fists on the table, causing the silverware to rattle. "I gotta get the fuck out of here."

Evie placed a hand on his shoulder. "One more round, then Tootsies?"

Everyone nodded.

She flagged down a waiter.

On their way out of the restaurant, they passed a dimly lit bar. Astoria glanced over just in time to see Anna Mae sitting inside the wooden cavern with her legs crossed atop a barstool. Anna Mae was glowing, seemingly in the throes of a heart-to-heart with a gentleman in a blue sports coat and jeans. Astoria realized it was Cal, the man who'd said hello at lunch. Hoping the two old cohorts were recounting warm memories from better days, Astoria turned and fled to catch up with Evie and the Video Guys.

Cool air sharpened Astoria's senses as she stepped outside. The Broadway lights sparkled in the winter dusk. Tourists waited in lines outside of the honky-tonks, tapping their feet to the live music blasting from within.

Leaning into the chilly night, Astoria, Evie, and the Video Guys darted through the choked sidewalks as they crossed the street toward Tootsie's. At the bar's crowded entrance, Jake turned to the group and whipped a finger in a circle. "Let's go around back."

They skittered up a side street, turning down an alley between the bars and the Ryman Auditorium.

"Waylon and Willie used to come in this way when they would play the Ryman," Cody said, pointing to a gated entryway at the base of the infamous church-turned concert hall. "That leads into the Ryman. They'd pop over here into Tootsies to eat and drink and write songs."

"No kidding," Astoria said. "Don't you think it's ironic how pop culture idolizes those guys now, even though the industry treated them like outcasts back in the day?"

"For sure," Cody said, leading her down a set of stairs off the alley and through a heavy metal door. Southern rock and red lighting blasted their senses as they emerged into Tootsies' upstairs lair. The space held a bar, six creaky barstools, a small stage crammed with a full band, and an empty dance floor. Cody scanned the room as if looking for someone, then split from the group. Evie appeared in his place, sliding a cold Miller Lite into Astoria's hand.

"Drink 'em if you got 'em," Evie said, yelling above the music.

"I'm pretty drunk," Astoria yelled.

Evie smirked. "It's practically water."

The band launched into a hard-charging version of Steve Earle's "Guitar Town."

"We're dancing," Evie said. Without waiting for a response, she shimmied onto the floor. Astoria followed, bobbing up and down.

More agency folks filtered in. Soon, Dixon-Richards employees were packed in front of the stage, whooping, sweating, and spilling their drinks. The night blurred between the songs and the beers. Astoria sensed the room was tipping sideways when Evie grabbed her by the arm and spun her around to face the bar.

"Look." Evie pointed to where one Account Girl was bent over a barstool, shaking her ass in the air. Another gyrated against her cohort's backside, holding her dance partner's hip with one hand and a cocktail in the air with the other. Lurking nearby, the guys from the Creative Team, Hanz included, howled and whistled.

Inspired by the crowd, the girls faced each other and danced seductively, their legs intersecting, hands exploring. Then they kissed, open-mouthed and sloppy. The Creative Guys held their hands to their mouths, doubling over with laughter. A few raised their drinks high and cheered. Beyond the fray, the agency owners stood at the end of the bar, smoking cigars and staring into space in their fine gray suits.

"Total trash," Evie said, her voice cutting through the chaos.

Astoria remembered Anna Mae's directive not to get sloppy. "I think it's time to leave," she yelled into Evie's ear, alternately lifting her heels off the sticky floor.

Evie thumbed toward the exit. "Let's go to my place. Lorenzo said he can pick us up."

"Is he sober?" Astoria asked.

Evie rolled her eyes, then turned for the backdoor. Astoria followed.

A sharp wind greeted them as they stepped into the alley behind Tootsie's. Evie shoved her arms into her fur coat then lit a cigarette. Astoria shivered, quickly sobering in the fresh air, her sweaty dress damp and cold against her skin. Looking down the alley, her eyes adjusted to see Cody standing against the wall of the Ryman, his arm resting above the head of the newest Account Girl—Cassidy—the petite brunette with porcelain skin who'd moved to Nashville from Chicago and started working at Dixon-Richards at the beginning of the month. Cody beamed down at her. Doe-eyed, she smiled up at him.

Hair matted to her scalp and mascara smeared around her eyes, Astoria wrapped her arms around herself. Evie tapped her on the shoulder. "You ready?"

"Looks like we've lost one." Astoria nodded toward Cody and the new Account Girl.

Evie narrowed her eyes and took a deep pull from her cigarette before removing it and painting the sky with her exhale. She shook her head.

"The socialist and the sorority sister," Astoria said.

Evie cackled, the sound ricocheting down the alley. Cody and his newfound affection didn't notice. Evie held her wrist to her mouth, still laughing. "Shit, I gotta apologize for the misdirect on that one, honey. They talk a big game, but these guys never cease to disappoint me."

"Let's go," Astoria said.

Evie put her arm around Astoria's shoulders. They turned and walked down the dark alley, then out onto Broadway, where the neon lights flashed, and the rockers caressed their guitars as they sang for tips and dreams inside the honky-tonks.

***

Lorenzo picked them up in his Volvo station wagon; his eyes were dilated, but he delivered them safely home.

The girls staggered inside, complaining about their aching feet. In an unusually good mood, Lorenzo teased them for walking like a bunch of drunks. Ignoring him, they poured more wine, then reclaimed their ritual spots on the porch, drinking and shivering in their party clothes, Astoria sitting in yet another dilapidated secondhand chair. A soft drizzle blurred the streetlights and darkened the sidewalks.

"What's your hang-up with dating a co-worker, anyway?" Evie asked. "Not that it matters anymore."

Astoria sighed; the day of drinking had softened her discernment. And she trusted Evie now, so she started talking, revealing everything about the professor. How she'd fallen for him; how she wanted him to be the bridge between her working-class past and a future she couldn't imagine achieving on her own; how he'd broken her heart, then referred her to the job with Anna Mae; how she moved halfway across the country, dragging her bruised pride and broken heart with her. Astoria finished her story and glanced at Evie, nervous she'd overshared.

Evie grunted. "Guess it's good to know I'm not the only sad sack in Nashville."

"Your heart broken too, Evie?"

The girls looked at each other, recognizing for the first time the shared sadness in each other's eyes.

Evie choked out a laugh. "Where to start? At least you fell in love with a guy who had something going for him. Maybe if I'd have done that, my daddy would've approved.

"Chuck—that was his name. Chuck. He delivered beer to my favorite dive bar back in Memphis. I was living with my parents and working as a teller in a bank, and those were the longest days ever, you know? All my high school and college friends were throwing wedding showers, and there I was, counting the minutes until I was taking shots and shooting pool at Suds & Buds.

"Chuck was a beer distributor. Short. Chiseled. Big, thick arms and a bunch of dumb tattoos. Total redneck, you know?"

Astoria gaped at Evie. "Is that your type?"

"Girl. I can't say no to a sturdy little southern boy." Evie pressed her feet against the porch floor, setting the swing in motion.

"I watched Chuck haul kegs in and out of that bar for a month. Finally, I challenged him to a game of pool. He declined because he was on the clock. I love me a man with some discipline because Lord knows I ain't got none of my own. But Chuck wasn't working the next night, and he asked me to meet him for a game of darts. We started hanging out. And girrrl. This boy drove a jacked-up Chevy truck and lived in a trailer house on twenty acres out in the country. Can you imagine?"

"As a matter of fact, I can, Evie. That sounds like a carbon copy of my hometown."

Evie turned sad again, her lips quivering around her cigarette. She plucked it from her mouth, cupping it between her index and middle finger. "I loved the simplicity of it all. And I loved him." Her voice cracked. "We were going to get married. He told me he'd support me. I didn't even mind the idea of spending the rest of my life in some shitty old trailer on a beautiful piece of land."

She looked out on the damp street. The rain had cleared. Tissue-paper clouds sailed across the sky. The porch swing chains creaked.

"What happened, Evie?"

Evie sighed, her shoulders falling. "My father said no."

"What do you mean?"

"When Chuck asked my father for my hand in marriage, my father said *no*. Said it wouldn't work because Chuck and I had different upbringings."

"It's 2008, Evie. America finally elected a black man for President, for crying out loud. Surely you don't care about all that."

"I don't, but Chuck's pride couldn't handle it."

Astoria shook her head. "I still don't understand. You loved each other."

"It would've been nice if he'd have stuck around and fought for me. But maybe he knew me better than I know myself. Maybe I wouldn't have been content to play darts and barefoot it around a trailer forever."

"I dunno, Evie. I grew up in a single-wide trailer and had a pretty good time. If you look at it right, there's freedom in having nothing because you have nothing to lose."

Evie dabbed at the corner of her eyes with her wrist. She downed her wine, then deposited the glass onto the porch with a clatter.

"Anyway," she said, straightening herself, "like my daddy always says, *what can't be cured must be endured*. At least this town has plenty to keep me entertained while I lick my wounds."

"So, that's it?" Astoria asked.

"That's all there can be," Evie said.

Astoria was about to object, but a big, grumbling truck pulled into the driveway.

"What have we here?" Evie's demeanor shifted. Grinning, she hopped up from the swing.

Astoria furrowed her brow at the sudden transformation.

"Let's go see who it might be." Evie flicked her cigarette into the yard, plucked her wineglass from the porch, and grabbed Astoria by the arm, hauling them into the house in one fell swoop.

The living room was bright but empty. Astoria followed Evie into the kitchen. The backdoor stood wide open. Lorenzo shifted anxiously from foot to foot, narrating a blue streak to nobody while he waited for whoever had been driving the truck to come inside.

Astoria wondered what had gotten into Lorenzo—she'd never seen him frenzied beyond the rapid clicks of his game controller. She felt annoyed that he'd never been able to muster this level of energy when she and Evie were in the room, then pondered what substance he might have ingested to produce such a drastic personality shift. Suddenly, the day caught up with her, and she felt exhausted. "Evie, I think I need to head home."

"One more drink," Evie commanded, joining Lorenzo by the open door.

Too tired to argue, knowing she'd lose anyway, Astoria poured one last glass of wine. She glanced up just as the much-anticipated guest emerged from the darkness, stepping past Evie and Lorenzo and into the kitchen's warm yellow light. Stamping his feet, the man shook the rain off his jacket and pulled back the hood of his sweatshirt, revealing a straw-colored, floppy bowl cut that accentuated his craggy features, eyes like milk chocolate, and a sly, apple-cheek grin.

Holding the bottle of wine in one hand and her glass in the other, Astoria stared, dumbfounded. Time stopped on its axis, but the room spun around her like a record. In a flash of déjà vu, the scene was familiar. Seconds passed as minutes, like a song she'd heard somewhere before but couldn't name.

"Astoria Lyons?" Evie gestured dramatically, presenting the man. "This is Johnny Dalton."

Astoria wasn't fully aware of whether Evie had made the introduction or Lorenzo. Nor did she hear herself say, "I'm Johnny."

Evie bugged her eyes at Astoria, then cackled, snapping Astoria from her trance. Lorenzo laughed, too. Astoria blushed.

"I mean, it's nice to meet you, Johnny. We've been drinking all day." She raised the bottle and glass as proof. "And I mean ... hi ... I'm Astoria."

Evie slapped her palm to her face, shaking her head.

"It's nice to meet you," said Johnny Dalton, holding her with his eyes, but all she heard was the resounding sound of *yes* drumming in her ears. If Johnny Dalton was a drug, then Astoria Lyons was already hooked.

Operating from a different realm of consciousness, Lorenzo buzzed about the room. He picked up a cookbook, a cast iron pan, a dirty casserole dish from the sink, rattling on about how he would have made dinner, but he got too hungry so went out but couldn't decide what to eat, so he came home and ate a bag of Doritos, and, and, and, and, and, and. He rifled through a stack of mail, ripped open a junk drawer, then set to raving about how much shit Evie had packed into the house and how it was her fault he couldn't ever find anything.

Shaking his head in disbelief, Johnny turned to Astoria. "Got any more of that wine?" he asked, "or do we need to crack into this?" He offered the bottle he'd brought. "I dunno much about wine, but the guy at the store said it was good."

His accent was hillbilly southern, sidelong and sharp, like what you hear in the Appalachian Mountains where liquor is *likker*, and also homemade and clear. He was tall and visibly lanky, even in his faded blue jeans, sweatshirt, and canvas jacket. He leaned close to Astoria, placing the bottle of wine on the counter; she caught his scent of pine needles and fresh air.

"About time you came over to fix my porch light," Lorenzo said, slapping Johnny on the back while grinning at Astoria. "This guy's a regular Bob Villa."

"Johnny can fix anything," Evie swooned, searching the cupboards for a clean glass.

Johnny told Lorenzo to fetch him a Phillips head screwdriver from the junk drawer, then he set to task, fixing the porch light's electrical glitch in ten minutes. Next, Evie and Lorenzo asked him to look at their leaky kitchen faucet, which he did, taking intermittent sips of wine as he tightened a few screws. While the roommates raved about his handiwork, Astoria floated along on the periphery, studying him as he moved.

After completing the home repair favors, Johnny wiped his hands on a towel. "Wanna go sit and talk?" he said quietly to Astoria, hope creasing his brow as if she might say no.

She followed him into the living room. Lorenzo trailed behind them, quickly turning his attention to a stack of CDs on a bookshelf, chattering to himself while Evie stayed in the kitchen, checking her phone.

"Evie says you're from Washington?" Johnny asked, letting Astoria sit first.

"That's right." She settled in the middle of one couch to see where Johnny might land.

He eased in next to her. "Seattle?"

"No. A logging town further south."

"Your family in logging?"

"It's just my father now—" Her desire to play it cool broke through her intoxication, stopping her from over-explaining that her father spent most of his time resting in his recliner, having not worked since losing his business and taking disability in the '90s, leaving her mother to pick up the slack with two jobs until she got sick and died. "Are you from Nashville?"

"Nah. These Nashville guys are a bunch of city kids. Ain't that right, Lorenzo?"

"Hey," Lorenzo shot from across the room, where he was now alphabetizing his record collection. "We can't all be from the holler!"

Johnny shifted toward Astoria, his back to Lorenzo. "I grew up in northeast Tennessee in a place called Mountain City, although we call it 'the mountain.' Used to be my family worked in coal. They also dabbled in transport and distribution from time to time, if you know what I mean, but they're mostly woods loafers these days."

"Come again?"

"Woods loafers."

Astoria frowned.

"Mountain folk—hunt, fish, gather—try to go to town as little as possible."

"Oh," Astoria brightened. "Sounds like where I'm from. I've never heard that phrase before."

"Maybe it's a southern thing," said Johnny.

Astoria sipped her wine and smiled, her cheeks red.

"I like it," she said. "I think I'm a woods loafer at heart."

Holding a record sleeve in the air, Lorenzo made an off-color joke about Johnny liking to do a lot more than loaf in the woods.

"Why are you such a dumbass?" Johnny wadded a piece of paper from the coffee table into a ball and threw it at Lorenzo, who dodged it, howling with laughter.

Evie breezed through the living room, wineglass in hand. "You are a dumbass, Lorenzo," she said before slipping out the front door.

"Where's she goin?" Johnny asked.

Astoria jutted her chin towards the door. "Cigarette."

Johnny nodded. "Hey, Lorenzo, play that new bluegrass CD I brought you."

"I already lost it."

"It was bootleg, Lo. I could get in a whole lotta trouble."

"Maybe I sold it." Lorenzo chuckled like a deviant.

"Maybe you need your ass kicked," said Johnny.

"Who's the band?" Astoria asked.

"Hottest group in town right now. They have this burly front man—an East Kentucky boy—best thing to hit Nashville since Waylon and Willie. They play down at the Station Inn. We'll have to get you to one of their shows."

"Sounds like I have some catching up to do. You have connections in the music industry or something?"

"Lorenzo and I used to go on the road together, but I had to get outta that lifestyle. A buddy of mine still gets me bootleg albums before they're released from time to time, but mostly, I try to steer clear of the trendy fucks on Music Row."

"Good," Astoria said, thinking about her one-night stand and praying that Johnny didn't somehow know the Belmont guy. "My roommate is one of those, what did you call them, *trendy fucks*? Her co-workers always come over and share industry gossip—it's like a never-ending soap opera. Luckily, Evie lives within walking distance, so I can escape when I need to."

"You crossways with your roommate, are ya?"

"She's okay, just deep into that industry scene. Pretty shallow group, from what I can tell."

"That's saying a lot coming from someone who works in marketing," Johnny laughed. "I'm just kidding."

"If you only knew. If there were a pageant for mean girls, the ones Evie and I work with would slit one another's throats to steal the crown. What do you do for work?"

"I'm a civil engineer," he said. "Work for a firm here in town."

"So, you're the brains behind big buildings, or what?"

He shrugged. "Sort of. We do engineering, planning, environmental, landscape architecture. You know the pedestrian bridge downtown?"

Astoria nodded.

"That was a huge structural rehabilitation project we tackled ..."

While Johnny explained the technical details of the project, Astoria stole a sidelong glance at the man sitting next to her, the outline of his quads visible through his jeans. His fingernails were clipped but not manicured. He smelled fresh and looked clean, but also rugged. *Balanced,* she thought—*the perfect balance.*

"... I came to Nashville when I got out of high school and got a job as a roadie. That's when I crossed paths with Lo. Like you, I realized the music industry was no kind of place to waste my time, so I worked my way through undergrad, got an apprenticeship, and then my master's. Been working at this firm for a few years now. First one in my family to go to college."

"Me too," Astoria said.

"Aren't we the fools," he said, his grin softening his features.

Her cheeks felt hot, her head light. She admired Johnny Dalton, the engineer, and found herself fighting the urge to curl up next to him and snug in between his arm and torso, maybe rest her hand upon his chest.

She blinked.

It was time to leave.

Evie came in from the front porch. "Need a refill," she said.

"Evie. We'll have been drinking for twelve hours straight if we keep going."

Evie brightened at the suggestion. "I'm game if you are."

Astoria shook her head, then turned to Johnny, smiling. "It was nice to meet you."

"You can't leave," Lorenzo said, standing from his records.

"One more drink," Evie said.

Astoria moaned, pushing herself up from the couch. She steadied herself against her wobbly equilibrium. "I won't even be able to crawl home if I have another drink."

She slid between Johnny and the coffee table, her knees brushing his. Boldness rising within her, she stepped to the middle of the room, lifted her arms to the side, and spun slowly in a circle, her dress floating around her as she twirled across the floor. Evie and Lorenzo howled approvingly. At the door, she stopped and giggled.

"Do you always dance by yourself in the living room?" Lorenzo asked.

Watching her, Johnny rose from the couch; Astoria locked eyes with him and smiled. "Only on the good nights."

CHAPTER TEN

On the day before Christmas Eve, the office bustled with festive energy. People chatted in small groups all morning, drinking mimosas and sharing holiday plans. Someone turned up the volume on the surround sound, sending Bing Crosby crooning throughout the hallways. Even the Account Girls were friendly. As the noon hour approached, only a few folks remained at their desks, deleting emails or calling clients to wish them a Merry Christmas, although most had long since checked out.

Reclined with her feet propped on Astoria's desk, Evie flipped through the latest issue of *AdWeek*. Snapping the periodical closed, she tossed it aside and looked around the emptying office. "Are you sure you won't come home with me for Christmas?"

"It's okay," Astoria said. She refreshed her email. She wasn't expecting a message from anyone but had developed the habit as a nervous tic. "They said I haven't accrued enough time off yet. I don't want to push it."

Evie threw her hands in the air and rolled her eyes. "What would *they* do? Fire you? *Nobody* will even be around."

"Henry Hunter told Anna Mae it was company policy," Astoria said, shrugging. "I'll be fine. Promise."

"That's some Dickensian bullshit. Who are you, Bob Cratchit?"

"The office will be empty. I'll come in and drink coffee, steal a bottle of wine, then peel out in the afternoon. Elizabeth is in Illinois. I'll have the entire town to myself."

Evie slid her feet off the desk. "Suit yourself," she said, rising to leave. "Happy hour in Memphis starts at four o'clock sharp, if you change your mind."

"Merry Christmas, Evie."

"Merry Christmas, Astoria Lyons." Evie paused. "I keep forgetting. Did Johnny call you?"

Astoria tensed at the mention of his name. Thoughts of Johnny Dalton had dominated her mind in the week since she'd met him after the holiday party. "No," she said, not wanting to appear too eager. "Why?"

Evie shrugged, feigning nonchalance. "Because ... he asked me for your number the day after you two met at my place." She patted Astoria on the shoulder, then sauntered away.

"Evie! You can't leave me hanging."

"Let me know if you change your mind and wanna come to Memphis," she hollered, laughing as she drifted off to her holiday break.

***

No ghosts of Christmas past, present, or future haunted the office on Christmas Eve. Astoria padded about in her stocking feet, feeling awkward for coming into the empty office because she'd been told to.

She drank a pot of coffee and ate three granola bars while watching a DVD of *White Christmas* on her laptop. At ten minutes past noon, she packed up her things and selected two bottles of red wine from the agency's booze closet. She slid them, along with four apples, a handful of granola bars, and several bags of goldfish crackers, into her computer bag.

Once home, she uncorked a bottle of wine and settled in to watch *The Christmas Story* on TV. The Parker boys and their mother shouted Christmas carols as the Old Man commandeered the family Oldsmobile. She realized it wasn't the loneliness that had been nagging at her all day, but the idea that something was fundamentally wrong with her for being alone on Christmas Eve.

Why not swallow her pride and drive to Memphis?

Because payday wasn't for another week, and she couldn't afford the gas, that's why.

She wondered if being alone on such a holiday qualified her as some sort of sociopath. These self-critical thoughts ping-ponged about, absorbing her consciousness until her cellphone chimed with the sound of an incoming text, interrupting her identity crisis. *Ping!*

She side-eyed the clamshell phone on the floor next to the wine bottle.

What if it's him?

The green LED light blinked, *YES*. Excitement welling up inside her, she grabbed the phone, inhaled as she held it to her chest, then flipped it open. The professor's name appeared on the screen. Astoria gasped—hesitated—clicked to open the text.

—Thinking of you, Astoria Lyons. Wishing you the Merriest Christmas yet.

All those old feelings of shame, anger, self-loathing, and sadness surged to the forefront of her psyche. She snapped the phone shut, wanting to throw it across the room, but she leaned back and opened it again, clicking through the names on the screen until finding her target and hitting the call button. Four rings sounded before the call picked up, some twenty-five hundred miles away.

"Yello?"

"Merry Christmas, Ace."

"Merry Christmas, Daughter. You caught me right before I stepped out the door."

The sound of his voice pulled a lump into her throat.

"Where you off to?"

"Figure I might head down to the Elks. The garden club is hosting that Christmas Eve feast they put on every year. Probably be some good food down there."

"You figure Miss Wanda will have one of her famous pies for you tonight?" Astoria imagined her father smelling of Brut cologne, dressed in his finest pair of decades-old Levi's, a button-down flannel shirt, and an old grease-stained trucker hat with his logging company's logo embroidered on the front.

"You know? Your mother never did like her much. Can't argue she makes a good pie, though. Not that I should have any. It's not good for the diabetes."

"How *are* you feeling, Ace?"

"Old."

"Are you taking care of yourself?"

"I'm keeping my numbers down. My damn back hurts, so I don't get around like I'm supposed to, but I stay plenty busy."

They talked a while longer. Astoria assured him she was doing well at work. He assured her he was staying active.

"Sorry I didn't make it home for Christmas."

"You're not missing anything back here. You have anyone to spend the day with tomorrow?"

"A girl from work—I told you about Evie—she's hosting a big dinner party at her house."

"That'll be fun."

Astoria imagined the lie floating across the country, dissipating over some great frozen plain.

"I'm good, Ace. Things are good." She thought of her bank account and how she'd swiped the wine from work to have enough money to survive the holiday break.

"Keep working hard," he said. "You'll be making the big bucks here soon. You can fly your old man down to see you."

Astoria laughed. "You wouldn't get on an airplane if I paid you."

"Probably not."

"Merry Christmas, Ace."

"Tomorrow's Christmas. Call me then."

"Enjoy your pie."

"Ten-four."

***

Christmas Day covered Nashville in an icy dome. Astoria woke with a dry mouth and pounding head. Her hangovers always delivered a side of crippling anxiety, and she spent the day worrying she was the only person in the entire city spending the holiday alone.

A billboard near the interstate promoted a Christmas Day service at the Hillsboro Village Community Church. Astoria contemplated attending, but ever since her first visit, members of the church had been calling her, having captured her phone number on the information card she'd filled out and left in the pew. One woman invited Astoria over for dinner at her family's house, apologizing in advance for having six kids.

"You like kids, don't you?" the woman had asked.

A gentleman called Astoria a week later, introducing himself as an elder in the church and asking her if she might like to picnic with his family at their house on Percy Priest Lake some day after the service.

"I have two older sons," the man said. He asked Astoria if she had ever been married. Astoria wondered how he knew she was single. She politely declined the invitation to the kid-friendly dinner and the meetup on the lake, then began screening all calls with a 615-area code for fear the church wouldn't stop recruiting her.

It would have been nice to feel the warmth of a room full of people and sing hymns on Christmas Day, but she lounged on the couch beneath her laptop instead, half-heartedly clicking through Google Analytics courses. She thought about opening the outline of the novel she'd been working on, her writing habit having dissolved since Cody had stopped meeting up with her a few weeks before the holiday party. Closing her computer, she mindlessly scrolled television channels. Folded laundry. Washed the dishes piling up in the sink. Called Ace again. He reported rows of casseroles at the Elks dinner, a turkey, ham, and nineteen pies.

"Ended up taking a whole one home," he said.

Astoria washed a hand over her face. "Ace. Please don't eat it all at once and slip into a diabetic coma on Christmas."

"Nah."

The afternoon lingered, like time had forgotten it was in such a big hurry. Astoria considered uncorking the second bottle of wine, but she feared going into the evening with no alcohol in a town full of closed liquor stores. Instead, she zipped her coat to her chin, stole a pair of Elizabeth's leather gloves, and stepped out for a walk.

The thin light waned, daylight already giving way to dusk. Strolling through the Belmont neighborhood, its Craftsman homes and sprawling front porches adorned with cedar garlands and colorful lights, Astoria stole glances into warm-lit windows. Families laughed around Christmas trees, embraced loved ones, and gathered over meals. Turning down Evie and Lorenzo's block, she slowed past their house, hoping to see if Lorenzo might have some friends over, but it loomed dark and empty.

An icy rain dotted the sidewalks. She turned back toward Vanderbilt. Instead of strolling around the frozen lakes in Centennial Park, she walked north up Elliston Place, stopping beneath a neon sign buzzing red and green. Creatures were stirring, after all, in Rotier's Restaurant, a warm glow beckoning from behind the dingy windows.

Inside, the place smelled of fried meat and decades of spilled beer. Astoria removed her gloves and scuffed her Converse sneakers. *It's a Wonderful Life* played on a small television hanging in the corner. The black-and-white film contrasted with the neon beer signs adorning the walls. A plastic diorama showing a team of Budweiser horses pulling a stagecoach hung over a pool table. The scene reminded Astoria of home. As a child, she joined her parents down at the Elks Club on Saturday nights, where the whole town turned out for Bingo. The caller always held court in the great hall, a neon Pabst sign hanging behind him that read, "THIS IS THE PLACE." Astoria remembered liking the simple proclamation, how it was anchored in a promise and not distracted by the possibility of other options. She thought of how advertising somehow carried more meaning in a rural bingo hall in the early '90s than on a banner ad on some computer screen twenty years later. *Has everything lost its meaning?*

A gray-haired waitress wearing a clump of plastic holly pinned to her gray sweatshirt and silver bell earrings that jingled shuffled up to the hostess station. "Sit anywhere you want," she said, her voice raspy.

"Thank you." Astoria chose a booth a respectable distance from the lone man drinking dark liquor at the bar, although he paid her no mind. They were the only patrons at Rotier's on Christmas night.

The waitress appeared, earrings jingling, notepad at the ready. "Whaddya have, Hon?"

"Miller Lite and a side of fried pickles?"

"That it?"

"Yes, thank you."

The waitress turned and hollered, "fried pickles," to an invisible cook behind an opening in the wood-paneled wall.

The beer came in an ice-cold bottle, the fried pickles in a brown paper bag, grease-soaked at the bottom. Astoria dipped the pickles into a plastic cup of ranch while, on the television, mean old Mister Potter was planning George Bailey's financial ruin. Four beers later, the movie ended, and the old man at the bar had left. Figuring the waitress and cook were ready to get on with their evenings, Astoria wiped her greasy fingers on a paper napkin and threw it in the paper bag.

At the hostess station, she handed the waitress the bill and cash, including a twenty-five percent tip. "Merry Christmas," she said.

"Merry Christmas, honey. Get home safe," said the waitress, offering a tired smile.

Astoria stepped out into the cold. The night sky hung like a blanket. Floating through the empty streets, Astoria wondered if she'd moved across the country to make something of herself only to become a phantom. But then she thought of Johnny Dalton, and on that holiest night, she clung to hope that he would call. Shouldering the loneliness, she walked herself home.

CHAPTER ELEVEN

New Year 2009

January seeped in, dank and dark. Fighting to stay awake at her desk, Astoria silently bemoaned that it was just past four o'clock and the afternoon had already faded to black outside the windows. She'd only been in Nashville five months, but deep in her lonely season, it felt like much longer.

Evie didn't return to work after the holiday—not immediately. She emailed in sick for a week, claiming complications from food poisoning, but the Account Girls whispered otherwise. Glancing over her shoulder, Astoria watched them; she wondered why nobody ever whispered about Kayleigh and Lexi's little make-out session at the Christmas party.

"What do you think of this sash for my shower?" Kayleigh asked, pointing to her computer screen. Lexi and Cassidy, Cody's new fling, peered over Kayleigh's shoulder. "I might do pearls," Kayleigh said, not giving her peers a chance to answer. "I'm worried diamonds will be too jazzy with the lace and the sash."

"Oooh," Lexi purred. "What about a bolero?"

Caroline cut in from across the desk pod. "Kayleigh, have we billed for the second round of banner ads or not?"

"Oh my *god*," Kayleigh said. "We should have billed for that last month. I have had this conversation so many times. What is *wrong* with accounting?" She rolled her eyes but returned to her online shopping. "The boleros are cute, but I can't cover up my arms. I love my arms."

"You do have great arms," said Cassidy.

"Oh my god, you look so skinny," said Lexi.

Kayleigh beamed. "I know. I haven't been eating at all."

Astoria's phone pinged. Still eavesdropping on the girls' wedding talk, she mindlessly rifled through the new tote she'd bought over break, extracted her mobile, and flipped it open, not recognizing the number on the screen.

—Hey, Astoria. This is Johnny. I met you over at Evie's a few weeks ago? I was wondering if you might want to go hiking this Saturday. We're supposed to get some sunshine.

Clutching the phone in both hands, Astoria held it to her face, rereading the message, the Account Girls and their absurdities fading into the background.

***

The mid-winter day was a diamond. A strong front had moved in from the north, pushing out the dank cloud cover, leaving behind bluebird skies and a piercing silver sun.

Astoria stood peeking out her kitchen window when Johnny's big truck roared into her apartment's parking lot at 10:00 a.m., right on time. Being her first proper date—with Johnny or any other man—she told herself to play it cool. They were going hiking, and she wanted to appear easygoing, so she'd fastened her hair into a loose ponytail and wore a pair of blue jeans, a long-sleeved T-shirt, and her Chuck Taylors. After some deliberation, she dabbed on a light layer of foundation to even out the dark crescent moons hanging beneath her eyes.

Astoria scurried outside, where the truck idled loudly, and ripped open the passenger door, unable to hide her excitement.

"Right on time," she said, pulling herself up into the truck and bouncing into the seat.

"Them shoes gonna make it up the mountain?" Johnny asked, jutting his chin towards her footwear.

"Oh, I-uh, I wear these everywhere," she said, her anticipation popping like a balloon, the feeling replaced with soft shame as she noted his Merrell hiking boots.

"Suit yourself."

Something whimpered in the backseat as Johnny shifted the truck into gear. Astoria turned, coming face to face with the inquiring snout of a hound sniffing at her between the gaps in a metal grate.

"Who is this?" She reached through and stroked the dog's silky ears.

"That's Duke."

At the sound of his name, Duke lunged against the barrier, landing his tongue across her cheek.

Astoria laughed. "He's coming with us?"

"Duke never gets left behind."

After rumbling through the stop-and-go congestion of West End, the city fell away, and they cruised down Highway 100. Their energy was upbeat until Johnny asked Astoria if she was hungry.

"I already ate," she said quickly, although it was a lie. She'd been too excited to think of food. Also, she was scraping the dredges of her bank account, sure to overdraft in the coming week, if she hadn't already, and was terrified she might attempt to pay for a meal only to have her card declined in front of this man she already wanted to spend more time with.

"You ain't one of those girls who never eats, are you?"

"I eat a lot. I'm just not hungry right now." She laughed nervously.

"Suit yourself. I was thinking of taking you to the Loveless Café for biscuits, but you probably wouldn't eat none of them, anyway."

"I like biscuits," she said, facing to the passenger window.

"Let's roll into this Publix and at least grab some snacks." Johnny steered the big truck into a sprawling strip mall parking lot, crowded with Saturday morning traffic.

Astoria followed him into the store, wishing she had checked her bank account that morning to see if she could afford a bottle of water. Since November, she'd stopped checking her balance online because she didn't want to face her inevitable overdraft charges. She found it easier and less depressing to look away.

Standing in the checkout line, she clutched a bottle of water and an energy bar to her chest with both hands.

"Throw your stuff up here," Johnny said. "Least I can do is buy you a PowerBar."

Astoria shrugged like it was no big deal, but her palms were sweating, her heart racing. Placing her items next to his on the belt, she stepped back, exhaling, hoping he couldn't sense her relief.

They parked at a trailhead on the Natchez Trace Parkway. Astoria feigned interest in the maps at the Forest Service signage station while Johnny sat on his tailgate, eating a sandwich. Still kenneled in the truck, Duke whined and scratched at the window. Astoria turned from the map and squinted at the searing blue sky. The air was brisk, but the sun warmed her face. Johny hopped off the tailgate and tossed his sandwich wrapper into a nearby trash can.

"Ready?" he asked.

Astoria's stomach grumbled loudly; she coughed to mask the sound.

They set off down a forested trail, quickly settling into a rhythm. The bright sky above contrasted with the shadows pooled beneath the canopy of trees. Glittering dust particles danced across rays of sunlight. Brown leaves covered the ground. With Johnny leading the way, she studied his wiry frame moving ahead of her, stirring up earthy scents as they walked, an air of strength in his height and broad shoulders. Duke ran ahead of them until he was out of sight, then returned on a dead sprint minutes later.

As they moved along in silence, Astoria began obsessing over her finances, worrying she'd already blown it by acting uptight about breakfast.

"How was growing up in Aberdeen?" Johnny asked, disrupting her mental meltdown.

"I grew up about forty minutes outside Aberdeen," Astoria said, "just south of the Olympic Peninsula. Way out there."

"Sounds perfect."

"It suited me."

"So, is it dumb to ask if you knew Kurt Cobain growing up?"

Astoria smiled. "You knew?"

"Nashville prides itself on not getting too crazy over famous people," Johnny said. "I figured you might get tired of people asking about it."

"Luckily, I'm not even famous by proxy." Astoria laughed. "My roommate told me about that, how it's the status quo to leave famous people to go about their lives here. Of course, she thinks she's the ultimate handler of the stars."

"You said your roommate was a little extra."

"That's one way of putting it. She and her girlfriends act like they invented Country Music, but I doubt they even know who Patsy Cline is."

Johnny chuckled, then fell silent.

"I didn't know Cobain," she said. "I was young when he died. Growing up, we all knew his name, but people in Aberdeen still act surprised that someone so average made it so big."

"Funny—I can't imagine anyone ever describing the lead singer of Nirvana as average."

"I think people struggle to see the world beyond themselves, you know? Aren't many people in my hometown brave enough to realize their full potential, so they can't fathom how someone else could muster up the courage."

They walked on, the forest chirping, sighing, and shifting around them.

"Sounds like your mom isn't around much. Is that right?" Johnny asked.

Silence stretched out between them.

"Cancer," Astoria finally said. "She died of cancer."

Johnny stopped on the trail and turned to her, eyes wide. "Oh, dang. I'm sorry. I thought—"

She waved a hand and shook her head, encouraging him onward, which he obliged.

"I was a freshman in high school when she got sick. Senior when she died." Astoria spoke slowly over the lump in her throat. When she first started seeing the professor, he'd encouraged her to process her mother's death by seeing a counselor at the student health center. When she didn't immediately follow his advice or seek professional help, he told her she had to accept the loss as a fact and move on instead of wallowing in her suffering. But there on the trail with Johnny, all the emotions she'd been ignoring flooded to the surface. Head down, her vision blurred as her sadness spilled over.

"I didn't mean to pry," Johnny said.

"It's okay." She laughed, but it came out sounding like a sob; she dabbed her tears with her sleeve. "Good impression for a first date, huh?"

"Nothing to hide here."

Duke thundered back toward them. He ran two circles around Astoria's legs, then leaped up, landing his paws on her chest and licking her face. Astoria threw her head back and laughed, sunlight catching her face.

"Besides, I think you've already won over this damn dog. Git down off 'er, Duke."

The hound dropped back onto all fours and sprinted away. They moved on, bent at the waist and slowing as they climbed the trail up and out of the forest.

"My people carry a lot of sadness," Johnny said after a time, somewhat quietly, as if to himself.

"Yeah?"

"My momma and daddy got divorced when I was young, and my momma and I moved around a lot. We counted it out once, and we'd moved sixteen times before I even graduated high school."

"You moved *sixteen times?*" Astoria asked, her question sounding more judgmental than she'd intended.

"Couldn't make up our minds, I guess. Momma found a spot she finally approved of when my daddy bought her a little house up in the mountains where I'm from." Johnny's tone was upbeat, tinged with a grin, as if he'd spent his entire life making light of the situation.

Astoria felt guilty for judging after Johnny had extended such grace to her moments prior. Still, she couldn't comprehend such an unstable upbringing; she thought about how expensive it would be to move so often.

"Another thing you gotta know about my people," Johnny said, his voice low and steady, "is they like to drink."

"That's a relief," Astoria said, not fully considering what he was telling her. "Nobody wants to hang out with a bunch of teeto-talers."

"Yeah, well, it's nothing for my kin to sit around and drink beer all day on a Saturday and then right on into Sunday."

Astoria thought of the professor and his WASP-y ways. From what she'd learned, he'd grown up with a housekeeper. His family spent holidays and summers at their vacation home on a white sandy beach in Florida. Even as adults, he and his siblings wore matching pajama sets on Christmas mornings, an annual tradition captured in photographs the professor displayed in frames around his apartment. In more formal photos, his mother wore pearls, and his father wore V-neck sweaters over pinstripe button-downs. Astoria often worried about what the professor's family might think of her should they ever meet.

"Your family sounds like fun," she said to Johnny. "Nothing wrong with having a few drinks on the weekend."

Johnny walked on.

"Who am I kidding?" Astoria said, anxious to fill the silence. "I'm at the point where I easily finish a bottle of wine by myself any given weeknight." She laughed, but Johnny stayed silent.

At the top of the hill, a meadow unfolded. A 'No Trespassing' sign marked the trail's end on a tilted fencepost. A sun-bleached picnic table waited next to the post, offering something of a consolation prize.

"Do you want to sit and rest for a second?" Johnny moved toward the picnic table. "Ain't gonna lie. I'm gassed. Don't get much exercise sitting at a computer all day."

They each took a bench—Johnny facing the table while Astoria extended her legs, sitting perpendicular to him. Duke trotted into the meadow, but Johnny whistled, and the hound returned to the table, circling three times before collapsing beneath it in the shade.

"It's weird, isn't it? Sitting in an office all day?" Astoria squinted over at Johnny; the sun reflecting off his blonde hair. "Makes me feel like I'm barely alive."

"New job going that good, huh?"

"It's not my dream job, but I'm glad for the paycheck, I guess."

"You know, I've never had a dream job. I don't mind working hard, but I don't want to be cooped up in an office in a city all day." Mirroring her, he extended his legs on the bench and lay down to face the sky. "My end goal is to save up enough cash so I can build me a cabin back home on the mountain and leave all this behind," he said.

Astoria reclined on her bench, too, crossing her arms over her face against the sun. She contemplated telling him she'd wanted to become a reporter and travel the world and how she gave up on all that when the professor referred her to the job in Nashville.

"It's funny," she said. "All we ever heard growing up from teachers and the like was we needed to leave our small towns if we wanted to be successful, but then you get out into the world and realize their definition of 'success' doesn't mean freedom or even happiness. It's just playing by somebody else's rules."

Johnny remained silent for a pause. "You think you'll go home to Washington?"

"There's not much left for me back there," she said. "But I'm not sure the corporate world is right for me either."

"If only you could find yourself some middle ground," he said.

Peeking out from under her arms, she saw he was smiling at her. She grinned back at him. They lay across from each other on their benches, soaking in the winter day. She felt a peace settle between the man resting a few feet from her, his dog on the ground between them, the meadow beyond. Her mind was drifting on the magic of their newness together and the perfect moment when Johnny asked if they should get a move on. She rose slowly, stretching her arms skyward and smiling as if waking from a dream

"You need to stay here and take a nap?" he asked. "I can send Duke back for ya."

She laughed. "He probably wants to leave me here so he can reclaim his spot in the front seat."

They rustled themselves back onto the trail, their resting place still bathed in sunlight at the meadow's edge.

On their descent, instead of returning the way they came, they took a spur following a shallow stream where clear water glimmered over flat limestone. The land flattened out at the bottom of the hill, and the stream skirted a green pasture, where they happened upon an elderly man and woman.

The woman sat in a camp chair with a crocheted blanket wrapped around her shoulders and an open book resting in her lap. She held her face to the sky, her eyes closed to the sun. Downstream, the man stood at an easel, preparing oil paints and brushes for his canvas upon which he'd already sketched the lines of a landscape. The man smiled at Johnny and Astoria with wrinkled eyes. They nodded a quiet hello in return.

Shadows grew along the edges of the field. The river babbled softly. The earth sighed, waiting for the next season to surge forth.

The trail circled back to the parking lot. Too soon, they were in Johnny's big truck, driving back to the city. Astoria felt the peace of the day slipping away.

The sun raced west ahead of them, setting the faces of the limestone cliffs on fire. Golden light dappled across the dashboard. Duke slept in the back seat. Patty Griffin sang "Oh, Heavenly Day" on the radio. Staring out the passenger window, Astoria swallowed hard against the fleeting moment. She wanted it to last forever.

Johnny rolled his window down and lit a cigarette. They rode back into town.

CHAPTER TWELVE

The screen door flew open, banging against the wall of the house. Evie burst forth, waving her overstuffed Louis Vuitton weekender bag in the air as she bounced down the front porch steps. From the driver's seat of the rental car, Astoria shuddered against her hangover.

Anna Mae had met her at the Enterprise rental lot earlier that morning to book the car on the corporate card because neither Astoria nor Evie could swing it with their abysmal credit scores and shallow bank accounts.

"You'd better keep it between ten and two on this trip, Missy," said Anna Mae, handing Astoria the keys as Astoria tried not to vomit. Anna Mae laughed. "I'm teasing. I got full coverage. But you're the only one listed as a driver, so don't let Evie get behind the wheel."

"Girl. It has been too long!" Evie said now, hopping into the SUV. She shoved her bag over her shoulder into the backseat. "Have you been hanging out with Johnny?"

Astoria groaned. "Evie, I am so hungover." She explained how, the night prior, she and Johnny had consumed pitchers of margaritas beneath twinkle lights at the Rosepepper Cantina, a funky Mexican joint in East Nashville.

Pitchers.

How many? She'd lost count.

Had she eaten? She couldn't recall.

The last thing she remembered was passing out next to Johnny on his couch, both fully clothed. It was the first time she'd been to his house, although they'd spent several weeks eating and drinking their way across East Nashville. They'd listened to bluegrass and drank red wine at the Family Wash. She'd fallen off a barstool on her way to feed the jukebox at the seedy Red Door Tavern. He treated her to French cuisine and fine wine over candlelight at a romantic eatery called Margot's. If there had been a spare night unencumbered by work, she'd spent it with him.

"You okay to drive?" Evie asked.

"I have to. You're not listed on the car."

Evie rolled her eyes. "I think it's okay to bypass the rules if you're going to puke on the steering wheel. Let's swing by a Rite Aid and get some Pedialyte. But you ain't getting off that easy. I need details."

After stopping at a pharmacy for electrolytes and securing a greasy breakfast from Sonic, the girls settled into the rhythm of their road trip. Interstate 24 stretched southeast like a scar across the belly of the country. Parched hills peeled away from the road, the stark landscape looming lifeless in the winter sun as they passed exit signs for towns like Bell Buckle and Manchester.

Evie wiped her fingers on a napkin, balled it into the fast-food bag, then tossed the entire package on the floor. "Alright," she said. "Tell me everything."

"He's great, Evie. I owe you and Lorenzo for introducing me to him."

"Girl. I knew you'd hit it off. Are you guys hanging out every night?"

"Pretty much. Drinking, too. It's killing me, but we're having so much fun."

"Have you guys hooked up?"

"He hasn't even made a move yet. I linger, but he just gives me a hug, and we go our separate ways."

"Oh girl, that's how you do it if you want it to last. There's always so much pressure to hook up, but the second you do, the guy bolts. Total double-standard."

"I guess it's nice to take it slow," Astoria said half-heartedly. She'd already fallen for Johnny—she wanted more than a hug—but she worried about how she'd made the first move with the professor, telling herself not to force anything this time.

"What about you, Evie? What happened over the holidays? You disappeared on me. Someone said you were bad sick?"

Evie pulled a pack of cigarettes and a lighter from her purse.

"I don't think we're supposed to smoke in here."

"Oh, Lord." Evie shoved her paraphernalia back into her bag. "Is this how it's gonna be the entire trip? Let a girl have some fun, will ya?"

Raising her eyebrows, Astoria glanced at Evie. "I don't think Henry Hunter assigned us that responsibility this week."

The girls laughed.

"No, I wasn't sick over Christmas." Evie shimmied her shoulders. "A hot little number has come into my life, too."

"Evie! Why didn't you tell me?"

"Girl. I haven't even seen you for more than a month. I've been spinning like a damned tornado. I met this guy, Pierce, through some of my high school friends at a house party before Christmas. You really missed out by not coming home with me. Anyway, he's from an old family in Memphis. And by old family, I mean *old money*. His parents sent him away to boarding school when he was a kid, so I didn't know him, but my father knows of his family. We hit it off and went on a little New Year's bender. Ended up drinking our faces off at the casinos in Tunica for four days. It wasn't until

Tuesday when I sobered up enough to realize I was supposed to be in Nashville on Monday." Evie cackled.

Astoria tightened her grip on the steering wheel as she processed Evie's story. "Weren't you worried about getting fired? The Account Girls were talking."

"Let 'em talk. They can't fire me for being sick. And honey, after the amount of champagne we drank, I promise you, I *was* sick for a while. Besides, there's so much more to life than dragging our fabulous asses into that sad office and having to lick Henry Hunter's loafers every day."

Astoria thought about how showing up and playing nice had become a requirement, at least in her own life, if she wanted to keep her paycheck.

"None of it matters anyway," Evie said. "Because if Pierce and I get married, Henry Hunter will be the one kissing my ass."

"How so?"

"Pierce Mathers' family owns a printing press and a coffee company—big businesses in Memphis and Nashville—been around since the Civil War. When I say his grandmother is old money, honey, I mean she probably owns the copyright to the phrase."

Astoria was about to ask Evie where all this marriage talk was coming from when her cell phone rang. Clutching a coffee cup against the steering wheel with one hand, she retrieved the phone with her other, pulling it from the new tote she couldn't afford but bought anyway during the holiday break. She grunted at the name on the screen. "It's Elizabeth."

"What's that uppity bitch want?"

Astoria shrugged, flipping open the phone and pinning it between her shoulder and ear. "What's up?" she asked.

"I just got off the phone with our landlord." Elizabeth's voice was shrill, her rage pouring through the receiver.

"And?"

"Your rent check bounced."

Astoria felt the leather tote bag pressing against her calf. She tried to focus on the apathetic horizon, panic clouding her mind.

"That can't be," she said. "I looked at my account yesterday, and the check had posted."

"Well, you'd better check again because the landlord said it *bounced.*"

"I'm so sorry. I —"

"I don't want to hear it," Elizabeth hissed. "I don't even know if I can trust you. I mean, do I need to kick you out?"

Tears flooded Astoria's vision; she blinked to see the road.

Wide-eyed in the passenger seat, Evie mouthed, *"What the fuck?"*

"I'm so ashamed," Astoria said quietly, though Evie could hear every word. "I bought some things for my trip that might have caused me to overdraft. I wasn't raised to think this is okay, you know?"

Elizabeth snorted.

"It's not like I bounce checks all the time."

"I wish I believed you."

The road blurred. Evie waited. Astoria felt like she was separating from her body, rising up and away. After a long, painful pause, she found her words. "I'm driving to Atlanta right now. Let me get to the hotel and check my account."

"You'd better call our landlord."

"I'm gonna call my bank, and then —"

"It's Sunday," Elizabeth said. "The bank is closed. You need to call our landlord."

"What's his number?"

Astoria relayed the digits to Evie, who scrambled to find a pen in her purse and then write them on her fast-food bag.

"I can't tell you how sorry I am," Astoria said.

The line went dead.

The landlord was more annoyed than angry.

"I can't apologize enough," Astoria said. "The check was posted as pending, and I assumed it had gone through. I'm traveling for work but will check when we get off the road to see what happened."

"Yeah, you let me know what you find out," the landlord said. "But you shouldn't rent a place you can't afford."

After hanging up with the landlord, Astoria sobbed for several miles.

"Honey, pull the car over," said Evie, repeating the directive like a lullaby.

Astoria kept on sobbing—fat, hot alligator tears rolling down her face.

"At least slow down," Evie said. "You're gonna get a damned ticket, which will only make matters worse."

Astoria blinked at the speedometer and, seeing she was pushing ninety-five, eased her foot off the gas.

"Listen here," Evie said. "Just because your roommate doesn't have to worry about bouncing checks doesn't mean she gets to be cruel to someone who does."

"I'm so embarrassed," Astoria said, choking on snot and tears.

"Why? Because you wish you had more money than you do?" Evie cracked her window and pulled the cigarettes back out of her purse. She slipped one out of the package and lit it. "Join the club," she said before exhaling a thick stream of smoke. "But you ain't gonna be embarrassed on account of me. I am the overdraft *queen*. My daddy covers my ass when I fuck up, but that's nothing I did right. I was born lucky. That's all."

Evie extended the cigarette across the console. Astoria cracked her window, accepted Evie's offering, held it between her lips, then took a long, blood-softening pull. Tears continued rolling down her face, but the hit of nicotine softened her nerves. "Thank you." She handed the cigarette back to Evie.

Lightning 100 crackled on the radio, fading out of reception as the girls drove farther toward Atlanta.

Despite Evie's assurances, Astoria's stomach remained in her throat as she and Evie coasted into the porte cochere of the Hilton Garden Inn, where the Dixon-Richards team would stay for the week. They pulled in behind a taxi, groaning when they saw Hanz and his white hair emerge from the backseat, then gasping as the Creative Director extended his hand to extricate Lexi.

"Oh, my 'Lanta," Evie said. "Even if the rumors aren't true, they certainly aren't working to prove 'em otherwise. How on earth did they get here in a taxi? Did they fly?"

Astoria remembered the whispers in the bathroom and how Lexi, who spent most of her workdays planning her upcoming wedding, had said *Caroline* was carrying on with Hanz.

Was Lexi inspiring a rumor to throw the scent off the trail of her misdeeds?

Was she trying to one-up Caroline?

Or was she clocking her last hurrah before getting married?

It was all so tawdry for a group of people who feigned prestige.

"I cannot believe we have to associate with these people," Astoria said, but then she remembered the bounced rent check, and she felt guilty for judging anyone else that day. Exhausted from her hangover and the stress and the drive, she killed the ignition, then peeled herself out of the car. Turning to grab her tote bag and cell phone, she paused as something caught her attention from the middle of the driver's seat—a round, dark mark, like the eye of an evil monster staring up at her.

She stared back, her mind racing.

Was it there when we picked up the car?

Did I eat chocolate?

Had I spilled coffee?

Her pelvis cramped. She held a hand to her abdomen. Bending over, she contorted to check between her legs, discovering another stain identical in color and size to the one now soaked deep into the fibers of the driver seat. Color draining from her face, she checked the stained seat again, then looked across the car to where Evie stood, eyes wide.

"Evie. I ... I can't—"

Before Astoria could finish, Evie was standing next to her.

"Give me the keys," Evie said softly, placing a hand on Astoria's shoulder and slipping them from her grasp. Astoria looked to where Hanz and Lexi were still unloading their bags from the trunk of the cab.

"This never happened because I'm going to take care of it," Evie said. "Hustle, now. Beat those two into the hotel. Find the bathroom. It'll be down the hall from the lobby. Do you know what I'm saying?"

Astoria nodded.

"Good," Evie said. "Go wait for me. I will come, and I will get you. This never happened."

Astoria snatched up her tote and shuffled, peg-legged, into the hotel through the sliding doors, keeping her head down and ignoring Lexi and Hanz's greetings as they trailed behind. Zipping past the front desk, she found the restroom down the hall from the lobby, just as Evie had promised.

The peach and mauve wallpaper, tiled floor, and elevator music imparted a bygone promise of commercial happiness. Astoria walked to the end of the room and stood before a floor-to-ceiling mirror; a girl with tired eyes and splotchy skin stared back at her.

"I want to die," she whispered, her mind jumping to a story she'd once heard where a man hung himself from a bathroom shower rod in a cheap motel, but she figured it was too complex an engineering feat with too many chances to opt out. Evie probably had several bottles of pills inside her purse that she might access, but what if Evie caught her rummaging through her purse, especially now that she knew about Astoria's financial woes. She'd already caused enough stress—Evie didn't deserve the burden of discovering a co-worker passed out in a shared hotel room on some boondoggle of a work trip.

Astoria was still at the mirror, feeling the wet spot grow stickier between her legs and considering her options, when Evie burst into the bathroom, holding both of their overnight bags over her head like trophies.

"Our room is ready," she boomed triumphantly. She'd assumed her own role in the proverbial driver's seat and was in total control. "I've gotten us checked in, and don't even worry about the car. It's taken care of. Everything is okay."

Astoria turned to face Evie. "Everything's not okay," she whispered. She covered her face with her hands and sobbed. Evie dropped the bags and stalked across the peach tiles, grabbing Astoria by the wrists and prying them away.

"You get to decide what this looks like. Do you understand?" Evie said, searching Astoria with her eyes, silently pleading, encouraging, promising. "If you decide this isn't a big deal, then it's not a big deal. You'll look back one day, and it will be like this never even happened."

Astoria blinked at Evie, their faces mere inches apart. Evie shook Astoria's wrists once more, released them, then gathered the bags. She turned back and haughtily rolled a shoulder. "Let's go."

***

The agency team had dinner reservations with the client for six o'clock. Astoria lay in the fetal position on one bed in the hotel room, staring at the TV. Fastening her earrings in the mirror, Evie glanced at Astoria. "Cramps still giving you fits?"

Astoria nodded yes. "Thanks for covering for me." She wondered if Evie sensed her hopelessness.

"Of course." Evie flipped her hair over her shoulder, then turned and grinned. "One mention of menstruation to Henry Hunter, and nobody will ask another question." She cackled.

Astoria couldn't help but smile.

"But Sarah will be disappointed," Evie said. "You're like, her favorite, so you're coming to dinner with us the rest of the week."

"Okay, Evie. I'll be there."

After running enough hot water to steam up the bathroom, Astoria stepped into the porcelain tub and stood in the shower stream, hoping it might drown out her shame. She lathered and scrubbed her arms, torso, and between her thighs, over and over, as if she might wash away the past twenty-four hours. She sat in the tub for a time, letting the water rain down on her, finding comfort in its warmth. Studying her pruned fingertips, she decided she felt better and reached for a towel.

Sitting cross-legged on the hotel bed in her boxer shorts and T-shirt, she dried her hair while flipping through the channels on the television. Out in the hall, drunk people shrieked and stumbled, thudding along the wall.

Unfolding herself from the bed, Astoria padded to the door, opened it slowly, and poked her head outside. At the end of the hallway, Lexi fumbled with the keycard to her room. Bracing himself against the doorframe, Hanz swayed, laughing. After several failed attempts, Lexi mastered the electronic lock, grabbed the Creative Director by the collar of his pearl-snap shirt, and pulled him inside. The door slammed shut behind them.

Astoria retreated, closing her own door softly behind her. She climbed back onto the bed and hugged her knees to her chest, contemplating what she'd seen. *At least we all have our issues,* she told herself, although she felt a renewed sense of hopelessness knowing that a few doors down, a married man and an engaged woman were ruining multiple people's lives, including their own.

Her cell lay on the bed next to her. Despite promising herself she wouldn't be too aggressive this time, she gave into the urge for a distraction, for connection. She grabbed the phone, flipped it open, and dialed.

"Hello?" Johnny's sharp accent cut through the miles.

"Hey, Johnny. It's Astoria."

"Oh. Hey." He sounded unenthused. If Astoria didn't know any better, she might even say annoyed.

"I hope it's okay I'm calling?"

"Yeah. Sure. What's up?"

"I, uh ... Evie went out for dinner. I felt like staying in after driving all day, you know?"

Silence poured through the line. Astoria panicked. "And I, uh, wanted to thank you for dinner and drinks last night. Well, mostly drinks."

"For sure," Johnny said. "Glad you got to experience the Rosepepper."

"It was great. Although I don't think I should consume an entire pitcher of margaritas before a road trip ever again." She forced a laugh.

"Felt a little rough today, did ya?"

"I'm still hungover."

"That's no good."

"Were you *not* hungover?" She recalled how he'd drank two margaritas for each of hers.

"I was moving slow this morning," he said. "Nothing a little hair of the dog couldn't help."

"You drank again today?" She laughed again, hoping not to sound judgmental while ignoring her better judgment.

"It's Sunday," he said. "Might as well."

"You're hardcore."

More silence.

She took a deep breath, summoning her courage. "I was thinking about you, so I wanted to call."

"Oh." He sounded surprised. "I'm glad you did. Maybe, uh, maybe come over for dinner some night when you get back?"

"I'd love to," she said.

"You have a good night down there in Atlanta."

"Goodnight, Johnny."

Astoria ended the call. Clutching the phone in both hands, she held it to her lips. On the day she'd lost all hope in herself, she'd regained a glimmer of something she might hold on to.

She was asleep by the time Evie got back from dinner.

***

Evie and Lexi had been co-managing the Old Hickory Workwear account, but when Evie hadn't returned to work after Christmas, Henry Hunter demoted her, appointing Lexi as director. He assigned Astoria and Evie to spend their week in Atlanta standing on a concrete floor in Old Hickory Workwear's trade booth, handing out brochures and collecting email addresses of prospective retailers attending market. Meanwhile, Hanz, Lexi, and Henry Hunter accompanied the clients to catered lunches and off-site meetups.

The hours dragged while Astoria silently bemoaned her life, whereas Evie was a natural salesperson. Her curves brought the male buyers to the booth, and her personality kept them there, chatting flirtatiously until the men asked for *her* contact information, at which point she handed them a pamphlet. Evie didn't chide Astoria for her low energy. Instead, she activated her charm and carried the days.

On her breaks, Astoria walked the convention hall. For miles, vendors peddled their wares out of glossy booths. Workwear filled one floor; home construction materials filled another; home decor and furniture filled yet another. Wandering past all the manufactured objects, the nose-burning smell of chemicals and plastic filling the air, she thought of her simple upbringing. Her family's home couldn't accommodate much more than a kitchen table, a couch, and a recliner—the same furniture her parents had owned for thirty years—its small closets allowed for a few changes of clothes per season. They didn't own much, but in the early years of her youth, she believed they had a lot.

Strolling through the massive market, Astoria realized how the American economy had grown from a garden of commercial desire instead of pastoral need. And here she was, groping aimlessly around the heart of that big machine.

Thursday finally arrived—one more day until they could go home. In the afternoon, Astoria sat in one metal folding chair with her feet propped on another, flipping through a copy of *People Magazine* Evie had bought. Absorbed in a story about Amy Winehouse, the troubled British singer who had taken the world by storm with her "Back to Black" album, Astoria startled to hear a man state her name.

"*Mizz* Lyons."

She looked up to see the sharp creases of Henry Hunter's slacks staring at her. Fists on hips, he surveyed the booth.

"Where's Evie?" he asked.

Jumping to her feet, Astoria looked left and right, feigning surprise, as if only now aware of her cohort's absence, even though Evie said she was stepping out for a cigarette and maybe a cocktail at a bar down the block.

"She ran to the bathroom," Astoria said, rolling the magazine into a cylinder.

"I see." Henry Hunter squinted at her. He was always squinting at people, holding their insecurities in his steely gaze. But Astoria was too tired to care about his stupid mind games. All she wanted was for Friday (payday) to come so her rent check would clear, and she could climb into a booth with Johnny, get lost in his brown eyes, and drown in a pint.

"I trust this week has treated you well?" Henry Hunter asked.

Astoria thought of Elizabeth's voice hissing through the phone, the bounced check, and the red spot in the rental car.

"We've had a good week," she said.

"You've been subdued at the client dinners."

"I figure it's best to let the pros do the talking." Astoria shrugged, eyes darting across the neighboring booths, praying Evie magically reappear.

"Is that so?" Henry Hunter cocked his head to the side.

"Evie will be right back."

Henry Hunter narrowed his eyes again. "I need to talk to you, too."

"Oh?" Astoria gripped the magazine tighter.

"I need to inform you that as of today, Anna Mae is no longer with Dixon-Richards."

Astoria's mouth popped open. "What?"

"Another opportunity has come her way, and we wish her the best." Henry Hunter folded his arms across his chest and smiled thinly. Astoria doubted the validity of either claim.

He continued. "I know she only recently hired you, and this change might come as a shock after you moved here from Oregon, was it?"

"Close."

"But there's no need to worry. We are betting big on social media at Dixon-Richards, so you have a place here, but we don't know if that's with the Creative Team as a copywriter or how we might accommodate you because you're not really a writer."

Astoria's throat tightened. The convention hall buzzed around her. A wild instinct told her to throw the magazine in Henry Hunter's face, run out of the teeming concrete market, and haul ass back to Washington.

"We are impressed with how you've tackled Google Analytics," he said, "so we're considering calling you a *digital strategist* and putting you in more of a support role for the Account Team. Leave the writing to the pros, right?"

Astoria imagined herself as a stack of papers scattering in the wind. She didn't know what to let go of or hang onto.

"Miss Lyons?"

"So, I would report to you?" she asked. The thought terrified her, but she imagined the professor calling, saying he'd heard about Anna Mae, and would Astoria be coming home? She couldn't bear to admit such a fast defeat. Besides, she needed the paycheck.

"Correct." Henry Hunter checked the status of his cufflinks. "This is an incredible opportunity for someone like yourself who is starting out in the industry. But I have sensed some tension between you and the Account Girls. If you can apply yourself and build relationships with them, you'll find you have a promising future with Dixon-Richards."

They eyed one another across the booth.

Exhaustion sloshed about Astoria's mind, drowning her ambitions. She'd already been applying herself at work, and she wasn't necessarily on bad terms with the Account Girls, she just didn't play the role of fake best friend.

"I see how I might better support Accounts," she said, her voice robotic.

Henry Hunter set his fists on his hips and squared his shoulders, nodding. "I think you could be a great resource for the ladies.

They're a hard-working group. By taking a more strategic approach, you can help them with competitive analysis, consumer research, and staying on top of digital trends. Is this something you're interested in?"

An ear-piercing cackle sounded across the hall. Astoria and Henry Hunter looked to where Evie was squeezing the arms of a contractor in a nearby booth. Henry Hunter clenched his jaw. Astoria wanted to laugh at the absurdity of it all, but she thought about the bounced rent check. She thought about Johnny. She envisioned being a career woman with a successful partner, making a life for herself in the city, escaping with Johnny to his mountain from time to time.

"Yes. Of course," she said. "I'm interested."

"We'll talk logistics back in Nashville." Henry Hunter turned to leave, then paused, nodding toward Evie. "Tell your friend to get back to work."

After their shift, Astoria and Evie bought Banquet Beer tallboys at a convenience store on their walk back to the hotel. Sitting on their beds, they rubbed their feet and drank from the oversized cans.

"I still can't believe they pushed Anna Mae out," Astoria said. "The signs were there, but I'm still shocked. She *just* hired me."

Evie took four long gulps, her throat flexing in and out, then she burped, low and loud. "Henry Hunter is a corporate shill," she said. "He is not to be trusted."

Astoria thought about Henry Hunter's offer. She didn't trust him, but she was in no position to decline the opportunity. "I cannot imagine what Anna Mae is feeling right now. I'm sad she hasn't called me."

"She probably can't." Evie fished her cigarettes out of her purse and popped one out of the pack, rolling it between her thumb and forefinger.

"Why not?" Astoria asked.

"Whether they fired her, or she has another job somewhere else, I'm sure they made her sign a no-contact clause."

"Really?"

"It's standard. Doesn't mean you can't contact her, though." Evie jabbed the cigarette toward Astoria, punctuating her point. "Give it a week, then get the scoop. Maybe she's going somewhere amazing and can get both of us jobs."

Astoria groaned. "I don't want to work with the Account Girls."

"Hey. I'm an Account Girl."

"You know what pisses me off the most?"

"What's that?"

"Those girls can get away with anything. They can embarrass themselves at the company Christmas party—"

"In front of the founders, no less." Evie stabbed her cigarette toward Astoria again.

"They can carry on with the Creative Director on a client-funded work trip—"

"Both committing acts of infidelity."

"No less." Astoria jabbed a finger back toward Evie. "And yet, because they know how to play the game and will do whatever Henry Hunter tells them to, they're his gold standard. Meanwhile, I gotta eat a shit sandwich and try to fit into their club, or I'm screwed."

"Why do you think that?" Evie asked.

Astoria balked at Evie's incredulity, but then she thought about everything Evie had seen—how much Evie now knew about her situation. A deep sense of relief flooded her chest, and she burst into laughter. "Oh, Evie. May I always be so lucky to draw from your well of eternal optimism."

***

Dusk was falling, softening the lines of the city and painting the sky purple as Astoria and Evie idled in downtown Atlanta's choked traffic. Cars puttered, bumper to bumper, as if they might never move again. The girls sighed and shifted in their seats. Orange streetlights cast a sepia glow on Astoria's face, deepening the shadows beneath her eyes. During the week, Evie had found a place to get the rental car detailed. They'd done a fair job of removing the blood spot, so only a faint blemish remained. "Like it never happened," Evie said, echoing her bathroom pep talk.

Instead of listening to the radio as they crawled northbound, they re-hashed the news of Anna Mae's departure and the newly discovered details surrounding the affair between Hanz and Lexi.

"Everyone pretends like nothing is going on," said Astoria. "But you can feel the tension when they walk in the room. It's so awkward."

"I mean, Hanz could be her father," said Evie. "I wonder if he has a wrinkly ass."

Astoria groaned.

"Or a flappy old ball sack."

Astoria screamed, banging her fists against the steering wheel. "Evie. Stop. That's all I'll be able to think about the next time I see him."

"All you'll be able to think about is that wrinkly old ball sack." Evie rapidly slapped the dashboard. "Thwap-thwap-thwap-thwap-thwap."

The girls howled through the night.

Lightning 100 had just crackled back within range when Astoria saw red and blue lights flashing in her rearview mirror. A cop emerged onto the interstate from his hiding place behind an overpass pillar.

"Fuck. Fuck. Fuck," Astoria said. The speed limit was 70—the speedometer read eighty-five.

"Don't hit your brakes," Evie barked.

Astoria let her foot off the gas.

"No. Don't slow down. Take a deep breath. Check your blind spot, but don't use your blinker. Now, hurry and get in front of this car to our right."

Astoria romped on the accelerator and, without signaling, slipped into the long line of traffic in the adjacent lane.

"Yes. Now, ease off," Evie said.

After a moment, the squad car sped past, lights spinning.

"Stay here for a bit."

"Holy shit, Evie, I don't know what I'd do without you."

"Honey, I've had my fair share of running from the cops." She rolled down the window and lit another cigarette.

CHAPTER THIRTEEN

Face inches from the mirror, her tongue pressed against her top lip, Astoria wiggled the mascara wand through her eyelashes, pulling it up and away like the woman at the Dillard's makeup counter had demonstrated.

After her second rent check had cleared, she'd gone straight to the Green Hills Mall, where she bought makeup and a new party dress to prove that she deserved to look pretty and wear nice things like the other girls parading about Nashville.

"You're going to East Nashville again?" Elizabeth asked, appearing in the doorway of the bathroom.

"I am." Astoria stuck the wand into its tube and then looked at her roommate in the mirror.

"But we're celebrating my birthday tonight," Elizabeth said, crossing her arms. "I planned this weeks ago."

Elizabeth hadn't uttered more than a 'hello' to Astoria since she'd returned from Atlanta, so Astoria assumed she wasn't invited to the birthday bash on Broadway.

"I guess I forgot," Astoria lied. "Are you going to celebrate on your actual birthday as well?"

"The girls and I are going to brunch."

"I'll join you for brunch, then?"

"We've already made a reservation for ten. Not sure we can fit another."

"I see." Astoria gave herself one last look, fluffing her hair with her fingers. "Let me know if someone drops out for brunch on Sunday, and I'll join you."

Glowering, Elizabeth held her ground. Astoria slipped past and trotted down the stairs. Instead of bopping out the door, she crept into the kitchen, pulled one of Elizabeth's beers from the fridge, poured it into a plastic to-go cup, and left the empty on the counter.

***

She'd been to Johnny's house before—the night she almost drowned in pitchers of margaritas at the Rosepepper. Due to her tequila-induced memory loss, she had to ask him for directions again. It all sounded simple enough. But as she cruised past block after block of postage stamp houses with overgrown lots and crooked mailboxes, Astoria realized she had no idea where she was or needed to be. It was 2009. The iPhone had been on the market for two years, but she couldn't afford such groundbreaking technology with its navigation capabilities, and she didn't have a printer at the apartment, so couldn't print directions from Maps .com.

With the windows down, she drove slowly, studying the neighborhood. The air smelled like tires. Pickup trucks rusted in driveways. Brick ranchers sprawled behind splotchy brown yards. Pitbulls lounged behind chain-link fences. On one block, a ramshackle flop house slouched in a dandelion lot next door to a refurbished Craftsman style home with an exotic garden and wrought iron fencing. Two young boys rode bikes down the middle of the street toward her car. They swerved onto the sidewalk and waved, grinning at Astoria as they passed. She waved back.

When Astoria first started driving over to East Nashville to go on dates with Johnny, Elizabeth had warned her to be careful.

"Why?"

"It's, you know, ghetto," Elizabeth said.

Astoria shrugged. She didn't know.

But driving around the eastside in the waning light, she realized her roommate's caution was more a symptom of sheltered midwestern elitism than reality. East Nashville was raw, honest, unassuming—a neighborhood where people didn't have much, but they made the most of what they had. She felt at ease cruising the streets, hoping to find a house she recognized in this new place that was gritty enough to feel like home.

After stopping to call for directions twice, Astoria nosed her way to Johnny's house on Riverside Drive. A cropped lawn hemmed in a white brick cottage with a limestone chimney and black shutters. Johnny's big truck sat in the driveway. The house glowed from within.

Johnny greeted her at the door with a kitchen towel draped over his shoulder. "Welcome back to the Riverside Riviera," he said, holding the screen open for her. Astoria stepped across the threshold into the warm home, the smell of savory, herbaceous food cooking flooding her senses.

"I'm still prepping dinner. Care to join me?" Johnny asked, gently guiding her by the elbow. The rich smells, the warm room, and his touch made her lightheaded. She followed him, floating, into the next room where an assembly line of garlic, bell peppers, and cutting boards covered the counters.

"You want beer or wine?"

"Whatever you're drinking," Astoria said.

He poured her a glass of wine from an open bottle of red and handed it to her. Their fingertips touched, and her body buzzed.

Johnny took up a knife and positioned himself at the cutting board. "You find your way alright?" he asked.

"I took a nice tour of the neighborhood."

"Ah. You could have called me."

"I'm used to getting lost."

"Yeah?"

"But I always seem to end up where I'm supposed to be." They locked eyes, and Astoria smiled. "Better watch what you're doing with that knife," she said, jutting her chin toward the cutting board.

Johnny chuckled, looking back to his task. He fingered three garlic cloves into a row and slivered them horizontally, then sprinkled the translucent shards across a pan of cubed sweet potatoes. "Let me get these home fries in the oven, and I'll give you the grand tour."

"You mean now that I'm sober enough to remember it?" Astoria laughed.

"Now that I'm sober enough to walk," he said.

The house was laid out in a perfect square with a circular flow: the living room and kitchen were located at the front, anchored by a grand limestone hearth; the dining room and bedroom were situated at the back, and a bathroom was positioned in between. Off the dining room, a glass-enclosed sunroom overlooked the backyard, making it feel like a treehouse.

In the kitchen, a set of doors opened to a stairway leading up to a bedroom loft. Johnny had decorated it with an antique rug, a reading chair, bookshelves, and a series of floating pipes he'd fashioned into an open-concept closet.

"This is my little bedchamber," he said.

Astoria noted the mattresses stacked on top of the hardwood floor.

"I like your style."

"I spend a lot of time hitting up garage sales and thrift shops."

Astoria made a mental note of this; she assumed he made a decent living as an engineer but appreciated his frugality.

"I do a lot of shopping on Craigslist myself," she said, recalling the mattress salesman. "But garage sales might be more trustworthy."

"The Eastside has great garage sales on the weekends. We'll go sometime."

Astoria stifled her smile, but her heart raced at the suggestion they might spend more time together.

"Let's go see Duke," said Johnny.

She followed him downstairs, then through a pantry and down into the basement. On one wall, shiny metal wrenches, pliers, and hammers hung across a giant pegboard. Metal toolboxes waited on a worktable like soldiers in formation. Gas cans, weed eaters, and two chainsaws lined the floor. Astoria inhaled deeply, the familiar smells of diesel fuel and dirt reminding her of home. She found the orderly nature of the dark, earthy basement, with its array of machines and tools, and the man who kept them in such precise order immensely attractive.

In the backyard, Johnny pointed out three raised garden beds and a stone fire pit he'd built. The space was calm until Duke launched out from the shrubs, sprinting toward Astoria. He jumped up, landing his paws against her chest. She stumbled backward.

"Duke!" Johnny scolded, grabbing the dog's collar. Duke fought back, lunging and sniffing. Astoria bent down and cupped Duke's floppy ears in her hands; he lunged once more, sweeping his foamy tongue across her face. Johnny jerked on the collar again, pulling Duke backward and releasing him. The dog bolted into the house. Johnny apologized before returning to his raised beds, describing what he wanted to plant once spring came.

The light shifted from purple to gray. Astoria examined the man as he talked of gardening, walking around shoeless in the dirt, his wispy straw hair imparting a boyishness, his presence strong and tall.

"The dirt here ain't much good for growin' things." He picked up a clod and crumbled it in his hand. "I'll probably stick to tomatoes, cucumbers, maybe peppers for canning some homemade chow-chow."

"I'm a little jealous," she said.

"How's that?"

"I want something like this—how you've carved out this perfect life for yourself here in the city, but somehow it still feels like we're in the country."

"Just takes time, is all."

"I've wondered how I might stay close to where I came from but also have a career and build a life for myself. I didn't know how to find that middle ground, you know? But here you are."

Johnny looked at his garden beds and pulled at a strip of hair with his thumb and forefinger. "You'll get there someday."

She wanted him to say something different, to tell her she didn't need to go any further, that he'd be her middle ground, help her achieve that perfect balance. If only she could have this man and his home—a garden in the backyard, a rich meal warming up the house, a partner to discuss the days with—she would survive the likes of Henry Hunter and the Account Girls. *Could he do that for her? Help her forge her path?* She didn't say these things; she just smiled and nodded when he suggested they go back upstairs.

After dinner and too much wine, she helped him wash the dishes and clean the kitchen, then drove home with the windows down and the radio up, her belly full and head swimming. Justin Townes Earle sang "Can't Hardly Wait" on Lightning 100. The loud music and the cool night air sharpened her senses, though her heart had taken flight. Pulse throbbing in her ears, she felt euphoric, fueled by the moments she'd spent with Johnny in his home, the whole time knowing she never wanted to leave.

CHAPTER FOURTEEN

One drizzly late-winter morning, Astoria hoisted her tote over her shoulder and trudged into the office. A dirty-sweet smell accosted her as she heaved open the oversized glass doors and stepped into the lobby.

Sniffing the air, she recognized the scent of bleach and something underlying that she couldn't identify. Beyond the reception area, yellow caution tape stretched the length of the hallway, cordoning off the men's and women's bathrooms.

Astoria paused at the front desk and asked the admin what was happening just as the phone rang. Without offering an answer, the girl raised a finger and picked up the receiver.

Astoria rolled her eyes and lumbered onward, following the yellow tape the length of the office, beyond the restrooms, and out onto the floor, where it extended to a supply closet across the room. A series of white splotches marked a corresponding trail in the carpet. On the floor, people huddled in small groups, whispering and glancing over their shoulders, a frenetic energy pulsating throughout.

Henry Hunter had reassigned Astoria to sit with the Account Girls after her lateral promotion (she'd received a new job description and a title change but no salary adjustment) and Anna Mae's unforeseen exit. Most days, when she arrived at the office, she kept her head down, slid into her chair, made a show of plugging in her headphones, and tried to disappear into her work. But some days, she had to pass through a toll booth of toxic chatter to reach her desk, and on that caution tape Thursday, the Account Girls were holding court.

Arms crossed at the helm of the pod, Kayleigh was leading the inquisition with Caroline and Cassidy flanking her. The three women eyed Astoria as she approached. Lexi glanced up from her desk outside the circle, her eyes red and ringed with dark circles, which she'd failed to hide beneath charcoal liner.

"What's going on?" Astoria asked.

Lexi looked back to her computer.

"Apparently, somebody had themselves a little free-for-all here at the office last night," Kayleigh said.

"Yeah?" Astoria asked, continuing toward her desk.

Kayleigh shifted her stance, blocking the path. "Yes," she said, hissing like a snake. "And not only did they drain the wet bar, but they seem to have encountered some issues between all that booze and the restroom."

Astoria's face turned from annoyed to amazed, her eyes popping wide. The nature of the underlying smell registered, and she snorted, suppressing a laugh.

"You think this is funny?" Kayleigh asked.

"That somebody threw themselves a wild party and then shit themselves all over the office? Yeah, I think it's a little funny."

"Not only that," Caroline chimed in. "They got into the supply closet and tried to—"

"Clean up their shit?" Astoria blurted, laughing again.

Caroline nodded, horror distorting her face. "They spilled bleach all over."

Astoria looked back to the trail of white splotches across the carpet.

"And where were you last night?" Kayleigh asked.

Snapping out of her humorous state, Astoria narrowed her eyes at the Account Girl. "At home, working on the pitch."

This was partially true. She had worked on the pitch the night before, but from her usual spot on Johnny's couch, the same place she spent most weeknights drinking and working until the wine blurred her vision and jumbled her sentences. She and Johnny had even cracked into a third bottle of wine, but she wasn't about to let on how hungover she was.

"And what about your friend?" Kayleigh nodded towards Evie's desk. "Any idea where she was last night?"

Astoria hadn't seen Evie since Atlanta. Evie never responded anymore when Astoria texted to see if she wanted to drink wine on her front porch or if Evie wanted to meet up for drinks on the eastside. She called in sick multiple times every week. When she did drag herself into the office, it was never before 10:00 a.m., and her hair was always a ratty mess, her eyeliner smeared, looking like she hadn't taken a proper shower in days. Her teammates couldn't get her to return an email, text, or call. When Evie was at work and in meetings, she spoke louder and more maniacally than before. She disappeared around eleven-thirty for lunch, but never with the Video Guys or Astoria. Not that they lunched together anymore anyway—they'd all stopped hanging out after Cody started dating an Account Girl. None of that mattered to Astoria, though. She needed a paycheck and wanted Johnny to see she was a hard-working professional, so she maintained a low profile, did her job, and lived for the moment they could reconnect over a cocktail at the end of every day.

Astoria shrugged off the insinuatory question. "Wherever Evie was last night, I promise she wouldn't be here if she were looking for a good time. No matter what kind of shit was gonna go down."

"She's been spending all that time with Pierce Mathers," Lexi said, sparking to life at her desk. "I knew him at Belmont. Total cokehead. He got kicked out of the university for selling drugs."

"Like you've never done coke," said Kayleigh.

Lexi shrugged. "It's different if you take a little hit at a party. But this guy was sloppy. One day, he rolled into class looking like he'd eaten a powdered donut."

The Account Girls laughed.

"Can we get to work now?" Astoria pushed past Kayleigh, dropping her bag on her desk with a thud. "No use talking shit when we're already walking in it."

***

Later that night, Astoria dragged a chair from Johnny's dining room into his kitchen and sat, nursing a tumbler of bourbon and relaying the day's drama while he made dinner.

"I understand somebody shit themselves after drinking all the booze at your office," he said, "but where does the bleach come in?" He stood barefoot, holding a fleshy chicken upright on a cutting board and rubbing it down with olive oil, salt and pepper, and sprigs of sage and rosemary. A beer can waited open in a nearby baking pan.

"Nobody is entirely sure, but the culprit either destroyed the entire bathroom and tracked their mess out into the office, or they messed themselves on the way to the bathroom. Either way, the shitbird in question made a mess between the bathroom and the supply closet. They found the bleach, then spilled it all over the office in their drunken stupor, presumably attempting to cover their tracks."

"That stinks," said Johnny.

"At least the puns have been good today."

"You think Evie had something to do with it?"

She paused, contemplating, but shook her head no. "Why would Evie party in an office she hates? Unless she's out to destroy the place."

"Shit on her career."

"I don't think it was Evie, but those girls are doing everything they can to keep her name in the mix. The power of suggestion, you know? And she wasn't there to defend herself today or any damn day. I'm surprised they haven't fired her yet."

Johnny whistled softly, positioning the chicken over the beer can, talking as he worked. "Lorenzo says this guy she's gone and shacked up with all of a sudden is bad news."

Astoria shifted in her chair, crossing her arms and legs. She'd been engaging in her own share of shacking up with Johnny; she wondered if he felt like they were moving too fast. But, having decided Johnny was her ticket to making something of herself, she'd ignored any niggling insecurities about the rapidity of her pursuit. She stared at the naked chicken, its veiny wings hanging limp as Johnny slipped the hollowed cavity over the can.

"That's what the Account Girls are saying about Pierce, too," Astoria said slowly. "A couple of them went to college with him. They're saying he's a cokehead."

"Coke. Pills. You name it," Johnny said. "Not that Lorenzo is one to talk. But I hate this for Evie. She's a nice girl." Johnny opened the oven, settled the chicken on the top rack, then washed his hands.

"Wanna take Duke for a walk after dinner?" he asked. "Be good to get some fresh air after such a crappy day."

Astoria raised her glass and laughed. "Good one. A walk sounds great, but I don't have a coat."

"I got one you can borrow."

Out in the living room, Duke scratched at the door.

"Besides," said Johnny, "that crazy dog already heard us talking about going for a walk. There ain't no turning back now."

***

Streetlights glowed sallow over the empty roads. Sitting tall in the front seat between Astoria and Johnny, Duke pressed his nose to the windshield, panting excitedly and steaming up the glass. They coasted past simple brick ranch homes resting beneath thick power lines, then under a railroad trestle onto a one-lane switchback road, the truck's headlights searching through the dark.

"Where are we?" Astoria asked.

Johnny eased the truck to a stop on a service road and cut the engine, killing the lights.

"We're in Shelby Bottoms," he whispered.

"Why are we whispering?"

"Because we don't want the Po-Po to get us."

"Serious?" she asked.

"No," Johnny said, louder now. "But the wild dogs might!"

She sensed him grinning through the darkness. He opened his door and bailed out of the truck, Duke following close behind.

"You're horrible," she said, fumbling for the door handle. Outside the truck, she moved slowly, groping through blackness as she stumbled toward the sound of Johnny laughing and Duke whimpering. The canopy of trees yielded no light.

"What?" Johnny asked, feigning innocence. "There are wild dogs in Shelby Bottoms. Be quiet or they'll come for us."

"I don't believe you." She slapped at his shoulder. He wrapped his arm around her, pulling her into his warm body. Duke pulled them both forward through the dark. At the top of a rise, the forest gave way to a grass plain that unfolded into rolling hills. The night sky hung like a curtain across a stage, its rhinestones glittering in the dark.

"Look at that," said Astoria.

"Thought it might be nice out here."

"Is this a golf course?"

"Yep. Shelby Bottoms."

"Are we supposed to be out here?"

"We'll be okay as long as Duke doesn't drop a deuce on the green."

Astoria laughed. Johnny unclipped the dog from his leash. The hound broke into a sprint, stretching his legs as he raced across the fairway, his silhouette fading to shadow. Johnny and Astoria followed, bumping against one another as they walked.

"I like how good you are with dogs," she said.

"Did you grow up with dogs?"

"I did, but they were animals, not pets. They were always getting attacked by wildlife or hit by a log truck. Ace had to put a few out of their misery."

"I understand. Ain't nobody back home got the money to spend on a vet. My daddy gives me hell for even letting Duke in the house."

Astoria gazed at the man walking next to her. He was handsome, but what she found the most attractive was he understood where and who she came from.

Once they reached the putting green, Johnny pointed across the Cumberland River where the Broadway lights danced like they were putting on a show for two.

"Ohhh," Astoria said, eyes bright, feeling like the night, the city, and the glittering sky all belonged to them.

Johnny took Astoria's face in his hands, pulled her in, and kissed her. His mouth was hot and wet, contrasting with the cool air on her temples. They stepped back, grinning at one another. She tucked herself back into the space between his arm and torso—a perfect fit.

CHAPTER FIFTEEN

Spring 2009

Spring burst forth, the lush trees throbbing green, their white buds swelling towards anthesis. The sweet smell of honeysuckle filled the air, making the evenings heady and sensual as the heat pressed in. It wasn't yet the summer solstice, but the concrete sidewalks steamed across East Nashville in the late afternoons, humidity laying thick on people's skin whenever they stepped outside.

Astoria and Johnny were riding east to see his family for the weekend. The truck's thermostat short-circuited to three zeroes once the temperature passed one hundred and seventeen degrees. Duke panted in the backseat. Astoria rested her elbow on the passenger door, cradling her head in her hand. The heat and the bottle of wine from the night before made her thoughts like heatwaves on the horizon, warped and glistening, appearing then dissolving. She needed electrolytes and a nap.

My people are real country.

That's what Johnny had said to her when they took their first hike on that sunny winter day a few months prior, although it felt like a lifetime. She thought she'd known what he'd meant; she had contrived comfort from the idea that Johnny's people would be the Appalachian version of the Pacific Northwest loggers and mountain folk she came from.

"It'll be cooler up on the mountain," Johnny said.

He was always promising everything would be better on the mountain.

And he was right—at least about the temperature.

Low-rolling hills of silver grass gave way to looming rock faces and jagged cliffs as they traveled east. The temperature gauge came back to life once they exited the interstate, registering eighty-six degrees as they climbed a switchback road into a darker, damper, hidden world.

Johnny's truck stirred up a cloud of dust when they pulled into a sprawling gravel lot. The space served as a front yard for a string of clapboard houses squatting in a tattered row along the base of a black mountain.

Built as company housing for miners in the 1930s, the mining company sold the homes at auction when it pulled out of the region in the late '90s. With no local jobs, most people couldn't afford mortgages, so they left, too. But Johnny's father had always been frugal, and he purchased one house for Johnny's mother; he also secured a nearby lot of land with a freshwater spring where he lodged his own trailer house. The state acquired the remaining homes, turning them into subsidized housing for people who came and went with the seasons.

Greasy recliners, broken down washing machines, dirty toys, and University of Tennessee flags littered the lot and porches. Johnny's mother grew red geraniums in Yuban cans and plastic buckets on her porch, the ruby gems sparkling amidst the otherwise bleak scene.

Johnny's mother and father were fixtures at the old mill camp, as it was known. His place was a humble beacon of consistency and strength, like a shift watch diligently doing his duty from the periphery. Hers was a gathering spot where locals came to gossip and drink in the afternoons before the party carried over into the parking lot, where they notoriously raged long into the night.

Astoria and Johnny stayed with Johnny's father when they visited the mountain. He placed extra quilts on their bed and stuck wildflowers in a Mason jar on the nightstand. He always kept the door to his trailer locked, but he'd given Astoria a key so that, as the party surged every weekend, filling the gravel lot and flowing from one home to the next until three or four in the morning, she could escape to the single-wide trailer until Johnny came stumbling in, the sour stench of booze oozing from his pores.

When Astoria and Johnny pulled into the old mill camp that day, two dishwater-blonde girls splashed naked Barbie dolls around the bowl of a deconstructed bird bath, which lay at an angle on the ground, only a murky pool of water available for play. Nearby, two men knelt over a soot-covered engine, their silver tools flashing in the sunlight as they tinkered. Several other men served as project managers of sorts, drinking beer and offering unsolicited advice to the mechanics. The men stared as the big truck rolled to a dusty stop. Upon realizing the driver's identity, they raised their beers, hollering salutations.

Johnny and Astoria climbed out of the truck; Duke bailed out behind them. He sprinted behind the line of houses and up the mountain where he would spend the weekend chasing rodents and deer, and Astoria couldn't imagine what else. Johnny opened the tailgate and pulled a cooler to its edge, fishing two Coors Lites out of the ice and offering one to Astoria. She accepted the can, the cold in her palm sharpening her dulled wits. Before Johnny could close the cooler lid, she reached up, slipping her free hand inside and dragging her fingers through the icy water.

"Why don't you go on into Momma's and see what the women are up to," Johnny said as he moved off to join the men.

Astoria remained with her arm inside the cooler, gripping ice cubes and standing there, waiting, as they dissolved between her fingers. She watched Johnny merge back into his other world, slapping the men's backs, laughing, seamlessly code-switching into this place Astoria thought would be familiar but found so foreign.

Inside his mother's house, four women, including Johnny's mother, sat around the kitchen table drinking beers; three others leaned against the yellow Formica counter. The chatter ceased when Astoria entered.

"Y'all finally get here?" Johnny's mother asked.

Astoria smiled. "Nice to see you again." She searched each face, unsuccessfully seeking a connection.

"Anyway," Johnny's mother said, refocusing the group on whatever they'd been discussing before Astoria had entered. "I heard he got arrested for possession again. But this time, he was carrying a pistol that wasn't his."

"Lord," said a woman with short, flippy blonde hair, wearing an oversized blue T-shirt with Cookie Monster on the front and red-and-black checkered pajama pants.

"What a fool," said another.

"That's a felony," Johnny's mother continued. "With them other charges he already has, he's looking at doing even more time."

"It's that Lyles girl he's been running with," said a woman seated at the table with her back to Astoria. She had spiky red hair accented with black tips and wore a pink camisole, revealing a large blue butterfly tattoo between her shoulder blades. The body art seemed to fly up and away whenever she leaned forward. "Ain't no good ever come from anyone who took up with them Lyles girls."

"Entire family is bad news," said the woman in the Cookie Monster shirt.

Astoria scanned the kitchen. Its almond-colored appliances, fruit magnets on the fridge, ceramic bear cookie jar, and yellow linoleum floors were artifacts she recognized from her childhood. They reminded her of home, but nothing about this place or its people was warm or welcoming.

"Where is it you're from again?" Johnny's mother asked, speaking to Astoria now. The women turned and sized her up. Astoria brightened, happy to be acknowledged. "Washington."

"Washington?" the woman with the butterfly tattoo said with a snort. "Isn't that by California?"

"Sort of," Astoria said.

The women blinked at her, then returned to gossiping about the Lyles Family.

"Somma them Lyles moved out that way for mining jobs after the mill closed. New Mexico, maybe."

Astoria slipped back outside.

Around midnight, Astoria slouched in a camp chair at the edge of the gravel lot, a severe case of hiccups rocking her core, having consumed nothing but beer since they'd arrived. She needed food.

A party crowd had been gathering since late afternoon. People socialized on all the front porches, men's laughter and women's shrieks one-two punching through the night. Music blared from a truck's radio. When a popular dance song came on, women poured down from the porches, whooping as they gathered in a dance circle, bobbing up and down to the beat.

The circle opened, revealing one of the women from inside the house earlier, who stood bent forward at the waist, twerking her rear in the air. Another woman stepped up and gyrated from behind. The crowd cheered them on until the woman in front dipped her head too low and, losing the war with gravity, toppled over onto her back, splaying out across the gravel lot. Rolling from side to side, she laughed up into the night. Two men emerged from the darkness and bent over the woman, each grabbing one of her forearms and pulling her upright. She staggered sideways, her legs giving out, and she dropped again.

Astoria pushed herself up from the camp chair and turned toward the trailer house. A single lightbulb shone over the front door, illuminating the simple structure like a beacon in the darkness, promising peace beyond the fray. Passing by Johnny's mother's house, Astoria startled to see the two blonde girls sitting next to one another on a wooden bench on the porch.

"Shouldn't you be in bed?" she asked, squinting at the girls through the porous light, then glancing around for anyone resembling a parent.

The girls stared at her, their blonde hair haloes and giant eyes looking extraterrestrial beneath the thin light from the front room window. The youngest girl lifted her Barbie and twisted it toward Astoria, making the doll dance. Then, she held the doll's face over one of the red geraniums as if she hoped it might at least experience something beautiful that night.

A deep longing pulled at Astoria from within, urging her to wrap the girls in her arms, stroke their pretty heads, read them a book while they splashed in a rose-smelling bath, then put them to bed in a clean, quiet room with pink wallpaper and a wall hammock full of stuffed animals. But she couldn't do any of those things, and even if she tended to the girls, it would only be for one night, leaving them to fend for themselves the rest of their lives. She turned away. Stumbling through the darkness, she told herself she was building a different life with Johnny in Nashville, a better life, a world away.

***

Back in the soft but mind-numbing confines of the office, Astoria returned to her desk after a meeting to discover a letter waiting for her. The shimmery-cream stationery felt heavy and expensive in her hands. Someone had written *Miss Lyons* across the envelope in impeccable cursive. She scanned the office for signs of who might have delivered the note, then delicately opened it.

RSVP! The invitation commanded in embossed gold script. Astoria ran her fingers along the letters' curves and silky cardstock. She glanced at the Account Girls, wondering if there had been a mistake, perhaps some sort of joke. They carried on undisturbed, intently hammering away at their laptops.

Evie happened to be at work that day; she caught Astoria's eye and shot her an inquisitive look. *What's up?*

Astoria shrugged, waving off her friend. She lowered into her desk chair and slipped the invitation onto her lap, studying its contents.

The future Mr. and Mrs. Lexi and Braxton Langston Hewitt cordially invite you to a Couple's Shower at the Riverwood Mansion on Saturday, May 23, 2009, at six o'clock in the evening. Please RSVP by May 1.
The couple is registered at Sur La Table, West Elm, and Williams and Sonoma.
Let's celebrate love!

Astoria's stomach clenched as she clicked around the online registries. The cheapest gift was a pair of brass measuring cups, which cost $28. She purchased them with the idea to also purchase a set of mixing bowls, spatulas, and maybe a brownie mix from Walmart to round out the gift. She never mentioned the invitation to Evie, but she did immediately RSVP for herself and a plus one. It felt nice to be included.

Two weeks after the invitations went out, Lexi sent a follow-up email to her co-workers on the invite list. Recipients included the Account Girls minus Evie, the entire Creative Team, Administrators, Astoria, and Cody. The subject line read:

"Couple's Shower Update: Dress to Impress!"

The email instructed attendees to *"dress for derby"* by flaunting their best seersucker and ascots.

"Oh, how fun," said one of the Account Girls seconds after the email pinged into the select recipients' inboxes. She began telling the others about her experience at the Kentucky Derby and how she'd worn the cutest pink hat with black and white feathers.

Bugging her eyes, Astoria tried to catch Evie's attention from across the pod, but Evie appeared half asleep, nodding back and forth in front of her laptop. Astoria wished they could sit on Evie's front porch, drink too much wine, and laugh about the absurdity of issuing a dress code for a couple's shower. Astoria hadn't even heard of a couple's shower before moving to Nashville, and she didn't have a derby dress or a feathered hat, nor could she imagine where to find such a thing.

***

After stalking the Opry Mills Outlet mall for two hours, checking price tags on seersucker sports coats, and looking for ascots, Astoria accepted that derby dressings were beyond her budget. But the J.Crew Factory store had a 50% off sale, so she settled on a blue button-down shirt embroidered with little yellow pineapples for Johnny and a matching blue and yellow-striped dress for herself. She also bought a denim headband, which she planned to affix with a yellow silk flower and some fabric glue.

Good enough, she told herself.

Johnny was enjoying his nightly dose of beer and ESPN when Astoria walked into his living room.

"Where you been?" he asked. "I was gonna make dinner, but didn't know if you were coming."

"Aww, you missed me?" She deposited her tote and the J.Crew shopping bag on her end of the couch.

"I figured you'd gone and ran away with them computer boys you's always talking about."

"The odds are good, but the goods are odd!" She extracted the shirt from the shopping bag. "I needed to swing by Opry Mills for something to wear to that wedding shower, and I bought this for you." She held up the shirt by its shoulders.

Johnny grunted out a dark little laugh. "What on earth makes you think I'd wear that?"

Astoria dropped the shirt to her waist and pouted. "I know it's absurd, Johnny, but they have a dress code for this party. And if we're gonna go, we might as well play along."

"Let's not go then. You hate your co-workers."

Disheartened, Astoria looked at the crisp cotton fabric in her hands. "Johnny. You know I have to go," she said, withholding that she also wanted to go.

"But I don't," he said.

"Please don't make me go alone. I RSVP'd for a plus one."

"Why does it matter? You don't do anything but talk shit about these people."

She wadded up the shirt and threw it at him, but it unfurled mid-flight, landing at his side.

"I go to the mountain with you every weekend so you can party with the same people you've known since high school."

Johnny held her in his sad brown eyes, looking hurt for a moment, but then a dark knowing flashed across his face. He blew a snort of air out of his nose and nodded, tossing the shirt further away from him toward the other end of the couch. "I won't ask you to go next time," he said, his voice quiet.

"That's not what I want," Astoria said, hoping to hide the lie. "I'm trying to make it at this job, so I need to play the game and go to this shower. Can't you support me here?"

He stared at the television.

The conversation was over.

She crammed the shirt back into the shopping bag, then sulked into the kitchen and poured a glass of wine.

Walking into the Couple's Shower, Astoria righted her headband and wiped at the strands of hair sticking to her neck. Sweat soaking the silk lining of her new dress, it hung heavy against her skin. She reached out to grab Johnny's hand, but he dodged her in his blue jeans and short-sleeve button-down. She pulled back, wringing her hands at her waist.

***

The Riverwood Mansion towered before them, its white Gothic columns, tall green shutters, and iron railings projecting centuries of opulence. Head down, Johnny climbed the steps. She scurried after him. He paused at the door. "There'd better be an open bar," he said.

Astoria forced a smile, lip gloss sticking to her teeth.

They stepped into a roaring room. Men were laughing, clapping one another's shoulders as they leaned in to deliver punch lines. Women huddled demurely in groups, scanning the crowd and whispering behind cocktail glasses. A statuesque ice sculpture dripped onto a buffet table laden with cucumber sandwiches, miniature crab cakes, stuffed mushrooms, and crudité. Giant crystal vases loaded with heady lilies, pink and peach roses, and fluttery hydrangeas loomed throughout. All the flowers, gauzy pastel dresses, and pink khaki shorts made the party look like an adult Easter egg hunt.

"There's the gift table." Astoria nodded to one side of the room, where Kayleigh stood beaming alongside a spread of packages.

"The bar's back there," said Johnny, moving away as he spoke.

"Grab me a drink?" Astoria asked, but he was either out of earshot or too thirsty to acknowledge her request.

Astoria greeted Kayleigh, holding the oversized gift bag before her like a peace offering. The Account Girl had elected to wear a sherbet-colored sheath dress and a black hat with a long, thin feather soaring off the side. The orange-and-black ensemble gave stronger Halloween vibes than springtime couture. Kayleigh's hat made Astoria feel like she ought to curtsy, but she slid the gift onto the table instead.

"Hold up." Kayleigh lifted a clipboard and pen from the table. "What registry did you purchase from?"

"What?"

"What registry did you purchase from? Lexi doesn't want duplicates, so we need to keep track in case people didn't update the registry at checkout."

"Oh. Uhm. Williams & Sonoma, I think. But also, Walmart." Astoria laughed nervously. *What was it with southern women and clipboards?*

Kayleigh scowled.

Lexi appeared at the table, her foundation pooling in orangey blotches across her milky white cheeks and forehead. Astoria thought of the Salvador Dalí painting, "The Persistence of Memory." The professor had a knockoff print of it hanging in his living room. Astoria leaned close to Lexi, staring at the makeup melting down her face, but then caught herself and stepped back, shaking her head; the heat was making her dizzy.

"What are you doing here with a date?" Lexi hissed.

Astoria looked behind her, wondering who Lexi was scolding. "Me?" she asked, realizing nobody was nearby. "I RSVP'd for two. My boyfriend is over there somewhere." She thumbed toward the bar.

Like a child about to throw a tantrum, Lexi straightened her fists at her sides and puffed out her cheeks. "I promised the groomsmen there would be single girls at this shower."

"But I'm not single," said Astoria.

Cody appeared, breaking the tension. "I don't know what to do with this." He shoved a present wrapped in silver paper and a bouffant bow between Astoria, Kayleigh, and Lexi.

Kayleigh took the gift and nestled it among a pile of matching packages. "How does this look, Lexi?"

"Lovely. It's all so lovely. How are the registries evening out?" Lexi and Kayleigh reviewed the clipboard in earnest.

Astoria side-eyed Cody. It had been months since she'd been close enough to smell him. His boy musk made her even lighter in the head. He wore khakis, shiny black shoes, and a black button-down shirt. Not the southern gentleman Lexi may have been hoping for when she developed her guest list, but Astoria thought he'd cleaned up nice all the same.

"What registry is your gift from, Cody?" Kayleigh asked.

Cody's eyes popped wide. "What's that now?"

Kayleigh rolled her eyes. "Ask Cassidy to tell me later."

Cody turned to Astoria as if to escape. "Where's your drink?" He leaned in and whispered under his breath. "You're not gonna survive this without one."

Astoria stiffened. "But look at you," she said, raising her nose in the air. "Who would've guessed you'd be right in your element?"

Whatever good mood Cody may have harbored drained from his face.

Just then, near the front door, a crash. All heads turned toward the commotion.

"What the hell!" a man shouted.

A vase fell to the ground, shattering, its contents ejecting like floral spears across a parquet battlefield. Somewhere near the chaos, a woman was cackling. The entire guest list gawked at a bulbous, red-faced man flopping about the floor, smashing the flowers beneath him. Bent at the waist, Evie straddled the man, her magenta ascot hanging askew over one ear. Holding a glass of wine in one hand, she tugged at the man with the other, struggling to pull him upright and laughing like a maniac while he flailed amidst the flowers, broken glass, and water.

From across the room, Astoria studied Pierce Mathers. He was making such a fuss, thrashing about for so long that she wondered if it was all an act, if he was actually enjoying holding the audience captive.

Finally, he cooperated with Evie and sat upright, his belly ballooning over his water-stained khakis. He was laughing too, his cheeks red, like a window into the chemicals burning inside his body. He ran a set of sausage fingers through his blonde combover. Astoria shuddered at the thought of this man touching anyone, let alone her friend.

Evie helped Pierce Mathers to his feet.

"That vase knocked over my drink," he said, his brutish voice filling the room. He brushed foliage off his pants.

"Get out!" Lexi roared. Amidst all the chaos, Astoria hadn't noticed the Account Girl move toward the entrance, but now Lexi stood between the crowd and the party crashers, seething, eyes on fire, pointing toward the door.

Pierce laughed, leaning into Evie, who was gulping her chardonnay. He thumbed in Lexi's direction. "Is this the bride-to-be who's fucking that old guy?"

The crowd gasped.

Evie spit out her wine, springtime yellow particles glimmering in a pretty rainbow across the room. "Pierce!"

One of the Creative Guys moved to Lexi's side, commanding Evie and her guest to leave immediately. A deep maroon blush crawled up from Evie's neck into her cheeks. She scanned the room, eyes landing on Astoria. They held each other's gaze until Astoria looked away.

"Big loss," Pierce said. "Probably don't even have a free bar. Let's go."

But Evie didn't move. She just stood there, staring at Astoria as if waiting for something to happen in her favor. The crowd murmured. Finally, she turned and followed Pierce Mathers out the front door. The Creative Guy put his arm around a sobbing Lexi, thick black mascara snakes running down her face.

"Who was that?" Johnny said, startling Astoria from behind. She turned and grabbed his wrist with both hands.

"Pierce Mathers—the guy Evie's been dating," she said.

"No. Not him. Who was the guy flirting with you? He some boyfriend from work?"

Astoria dropped Johnny's wrist and frowned. "Seriously, Johnny? After that debacle, you're worried about one of my co-workers?"

"Seemed like he was into you is all. For the record, Mathers wasn't wrong. These cheap bastards only give you two drink tickets, then it's a cash bar."

"You couldn't spare a ticket for me?"

Johnny handed her his glass of bourbon.

She took a long drink, then shoved the tumbler back into his hand.

"I needed that," she said.

Another crash sounded near the bar. Another man hollered. "You sonofabitch!"

"What now?" asked Johnny.

Once again, the crowd turned, this time to see the father-of-the-bride pulling the boy-faced groom, Braxton Langston Hewitt, up and away from where he had Hanz, the Creative Director, pinned to the ground and was pummeling away, his white shock of hair flopping like a fish with each blow.

Johnny snickered like the whole thing was one big, dark comedy. "Can we get the hell outta here now?" he said.

Astoria remained in place, mouth hanging open, eyes wide. Johnny grabbed her by the hand and pulled her behind him; she followed, and they ran out the front door into the sultry night.

CHAPTER SIXTEEN

Summer 2009

Crescent moons of sweat darkening her yellow sheath dress, Astoria gripped the steering wheel, holding her elbows away from her body. She needed to escape the heat. Her car's air conditioner protested as if it wasn't cut out for the southern summer, either. With the windows down and hot air blasting, she pushed the engine to sixty. She was going to be late for lunch with Anna Mae.

Astoria had called a week prior; Anna Mae answered immediately.

"I've been hoping you might reach out," said Anna Mae. "I feel so poorly about dragging you all the way down here just to disappear like that. I hope you understand I couldn't initiate contact based on the agreement they had me sign."

"Then let me be the one to insist we meet for lunch," Astoria said. "I miss you and am starved for your eternal wisdom."

They agreed to meet at the Mad Hatter in Germantown.

"Far enough away from the office that we should be safe, although you never know in this town," said Anna Mae.

Inside its historic brick building, the Mad Hatter was miraculously dark and cool beneath the lazy ceiling fans and stone walls.

A genteel crowd of southerners wearing linen and seersucker sipped iced tea laced with orange and cinnamon. They spoke in hushed tones over wedge salads and crab cakes. Silverware clinked against fine china. Anna Mae waved from a table near the back. She raised her arms and stood as Astoria approached. The two embraced, joyously rocking back and forth.

"I was worried you'd never want to see me again," said Anna Mae as they sat, scooting in their chairs.

"Why would you think that?"

"I didn't know if you might have written me off for leaving you to fend for yourself."

"Did you leave, though?" Astoria asked. "Sorry to cut to the chase, but Evie and I have been dying to know what really happened."

Anna Mae smoothed a hand across the white tablecloth and smiled sadly. "Not by choice, Astoria. Not by choice."

"Oh." Astoria fiddled with her cutlery set.

"Don't you worry about me. The Universe never closes one door without opening another."

"What are you doing these days?"

"Do you remember my friend, Cal? I introduced you to him last winter when we went to lunch?"

Astoria nodded and smiled, remembering seeing them at the Christmas party.

"Turns out, you're never too old to get the band back together. All these up-and-coming singers need digital content to promote themselves online and bypass traditional publishing routes. So, we're giving the kids what they want. I'm wearing a million hats, and we're making it up as we go. Cal still has some contracts with the big labels, which keeps the lights on. But I feel alive again, like I have something left to give."

"I'm so happy for you," Astoria said. "Think you'll need a writer?"

"We may someday. But in the meantime, Henry Hunter promised me he would promote you to a social strategist role. Did he make good on his promise?"

"He did." Astoria squinted at Anna Mae. "I didn't realize that was your doing. I thought it was Henry Hunter's way of bringing more people under his control."

Anna Mae pursed her lips and arched an eyebrow. "Well, that may have had something to do with it. But the leadership there sees how talented you are. Hanz wouldn't allow you to be his copywriter because he didn't hire you. I insisted they put you to work as a strategist rather than shove you in a corner and have you scrolling Facebook all day."

The waiter brought their salads and wine.

"Speaking of Hanz. Did you hear?" Astoria asked.

"Hear what?"

"We all knew he was having an affair with one of the Account Girls, right?"

After three sequential gulps, Anna Mae set her glass on the table and pressed her fingers against its base, taking her time to respond. "I'd better not speak about what I may or may not presume to know."

"Fine. You can still be professional, but I'm going to dish." Astoria leaned in, speaking rapidly. "Evie showed up with her boyfriend at Lexi's bridal shower, sauced to the gills. They knocked over a massive flower arrangement and made a big scene, and then Evie's boyfriend announced to everyone that the bride was sleeping with Hanz. Then, the groom hauled off and punched Hanz in the face!"

Anna Mae gasped. Diners at nearby tables turned their heads ever so slightly, like sharks adjusting their fins towards the faintest whiff of blood. "No," said Anna Mae.

"Yes!" Astoria was speaking loudly now. "And then, last week, Hanz melted down in front of the Old Hickory Workwear clients.

Yelled at them for not approving his TV spots. The clients said they don't want to invest in television anymore. They want to invest in digital. Hanz said they wouldn't know good Creative if they caught it in bed with their wife, which is ironic coming from him. Regardless, they asked him to leave. Now everyone's saying they might fire us."

Anna Mae pressed both palms against the table. "Astoria Lyons. Tell me you're pulling my leg."

Astoria shook her head. "We're having a big meeting about it this afternoon—the entire agency." She pulled her phone from her purse and checked the time. "Speaking of, I'm gonna have to cut out of here soon."

"I'm so sorry I brought you into such a circus."

"Do you think I should stick around?"

"In this economic climate, I think you need to get a few solid years under your belt."

Astoria tossed her phone back in her bag and slouched in her chair, as if defeated.

"Just keep your head down and work hard," said Anna Mae. "You know how to do this. Put in the time and earn experience you can leverage for your next big break."

Astoria sighed. "Figured you'd say that."

***

The agency-wide meeting was at one o'clock. At five minutes past, Astoria crept into the packed auditorium. People huddled in groups, nervously whispering and glancing around the room. Head down, she slid along the back wall until she encountered Evie and the Video Guys. Even Cody was there, leaning casually with his arms crossed, sans girlfriend. The Video Guys nodded hello. Astoria waved. Evie stiffened.

Astoria slid into place at the edge of the group and inhaled, exhaled, but Evie's cold shoulder and the room's frenetic energy had her heart racing.

At the podium, Henry Hunter cleared his throat. "Alright. Take your seats and settle in."

The crowd buzzed.

One of the Creative Guys popped two fingers between his lips and whistled. People shuffled to their chairs, the chatter like a wave going out.

"Thank you," said Henry Hunter. He scanned the audience. "These are never easy announcements."

The room held its breath.

"And these are never easy days. We're announcing that, as of next month, we will no longer be Old Hickory Workwear's preferred marketing partner."

Murmurs rippled throughout the staff.

From her tiptoes, Astoria strained to get a look at the Account Girls sitting along the front row. Kayleigh had an arm draped around Lexi, whose face was hidden in her hands, golden ringlets hanging down.

Henry Hunter continued. "We asked our clients at Old Hickory if they will be issuing a new RFP. We expressed our desire to participate if they do. They are discussing whether they will bring their marketing in-house or continue partnering with an agency."

The Video Guys whispered to one another. Astoria realized they stood taller than usual, chests out, carrying themselves with an air of bravado.

"And as some of you know," said Henry Hunter, "when we lose a client, we sometimes lose pieces of our team, too. Because of this, we've had to part ways with the Creative Lead on the account. Hanz has been an incredible mentor in this organization. I value him as a business partner and a colleague, and I know many of you have benefitted from serving under him as well."

Gasps erupted across the crowd, but the Video Guys snorted into their hands, turning into one another's shoulders to muffle their laughter. Nearby staff glowered at them.

"Will there be more layoffs?" someone shouted from the audience.

Henry Hunter squinted in the direction of the question. "We can't say for sure right now. We are doing everything within our power to keep this amazing team together until we can get more business."

Back at their desks, Kayleigh reigned over the pod, seething and ranting. "I cannot lose my job right now, y'all. I'd have to edit my employment status in our engagement announcement in *The Tennessean,* and I'd like to die before I endure that level of embarrassment."

Lexi sobbed at her desk. Astoria thought about the couple's shower, the hazardous waste incident at the office, the rumors about Hanz having an affair, and how Lexi was always part of the chatter, suggesting possible culprits, casting blame. Astoria remembered what she'd seen in the hotel hallway in Atlanta—and now Hanz was gone, a client lost, the agency's finances on thin ice. She wondered which part of all the upheaval was causing Lexi's tears.

***

At the bottom of a gorge in midtown Nashville, a gravel parking lot sprawled beneath an overpass, bordered by abandoned warehouses and rusting train tracks. Locally referred to as "The Gulch," this abandoned wasteland was full of shadows and unknowns in the dark—a good place to get drugs or mugged, or both. But it was also home to the Station Inn, a squat cinderblock building where patrons paid five dollars cash at the door for a night of live bluegrass, two-dollar cold beers, and popcorn served in oversized coffee filters.

Johnny parked his big truck on the sidewalk behind the Station Inn.

"This is where the band usually parks," he said.

"Didn't know I was rolling VIP." Astoria smirked. "You gonna tell 'em you parked with the band, so you don't have to pay the cover?"

Gravel crunched beneath their feet as they walked across the barren lot. A line of people snaked down the sidewalk, waiting to get in. Johnny whistled low and slow. "Looks like word is getting out about these guys. Their lead singer is that eastern Kentucky boy I was telling you about; the one who has written all the number one country songs in town."

"But we're seeing him with a bluegrass band tonight?"

"Right."

After waiting in line for thirty minutes, they reached the door, where a stubby woman with curly red hair and beady eyes barked, "Cash only!" when patrons tried to hand her a debit card. Some dug deep into wallets, pockets, and purses, scrounging for quarters and dimes, while others shuffled away, staring blankly in dismay.

"That ol' gal runs this place," Johnny said, holding his cash at the ready. "Doesn't take shit offa nobody."

"Have fun, kids," the woman said as she stamped Astoria and Johnny's hands, decades of cigarettes in her voice. She reminded Astoria of the Elks Lodge back home. The woman waved them on. "Next!"

Inside the Station Inn, bare lightbulbs cast a pallid glow across metal folding chairs crammed into the small space. The low ceiling and cement floors imparted a garage band aura. A small stage waited empty behind hot show lights. At the back of the house, bartenders loaded beer bottles into large metal ice chests. Popcorn kernels sizzled and snapped behind the plastic doors of an old-timey machine.

"I love this place," Astoria said.

Johnny scanned the crowd. "Buckle up. These guys are gonna blow your mind. Go grab those two chairs there near the front." He pointed. "I'll get us some cold beers."

"And popcorn?"

"And popcorn."

There wasn't an opener, but every seat was full an hour before the show. An overflow crowd leaned shoulder-to-shoulder against the back wall. At 8:30, the woman who'd taken their cash cover hung a sign on the front door reading, *"Sorry Suckers - Sold Out."*

"This is why we had to get here early," Johnny said.

Astoria shoved a handful of popcorn into her mouth, then swigged her beer. "Best dinner ever."

Ping! A text announced its arrival from inside her tote. Setting set her popcorn and beer on the ground, she wiped her greasy fingers on her jean shorts, then retrieved her phone.

"You forget to cancel your other hot date?" Johnny asked.

Astoria flipped it open: Cody's name waited on the screen.

—Heard anything?

Astoria cupped a hand around the device.

Johnny shifted towards her, peering. "What the hell's a guy doing texting you when you're out with me?"

"Oh, stop." Astoria waved him away. "It's Cody from work. You met him at the shower, remember?"

"Trendy fuck. I remember he was creeping on you, but you didn't introduce me to him."

Astoria rolled her eyes, but she worried Johnny had sniffed out her chemistry with Cody, which she'd told herself never existed in the first place after he'd started dating an Account Girl.

"He's asking if I've heard anything about the layoffs, and he was not creeping on me at the shower. His girlfriend was there. Will it bother you if I text him back?" Astoria shoved Johnny's shoulder playfully, then held the phone before his face, hoping it would earn his trust.

Glowering, he leaned away.

—All quiet on the western front, she texted.

After hitting send, she snapped the phone shut and powered it down.

"Sorry. Everyone's stressed." She nuzzled Johnny's shoulder. "Nothing a little cold beer and junk food can't help."

"You damn near ate all the popcorn."

"Stress eating," she said, shrugging.

"Think those layoffs are gonna impact you?"

"No idea," Astoria said. She dropped the phone into her purse and retrieved her beer from the floor, relieved by the change in subject. "My roommate asked me the same thing. Except she was screeching about how I won't be able to make rent. I think she's more stressed about it than I am."

The rent check memory pinballed across Astoria's mind. She'd never told Johnny about her money struggles, and she didn't intend to.

Johnny rested his right foot atop his left knee and draped his arm across the back of Astoria's chair. "You could move in with me," he said, making it sound like a casual suggestion.

"Are you being serious?"

"Why not? You practically live at my place anyway. At least this way, I can get some money out of ya." Johnny snickered.

Astoria elbowed his arm off the back of her chair.

"You know I'm just foolin," he said.

"I'd pay rent, though, right? I don't want you to think I'd take something for nothing."

"I'll give you a break from what you're paying now. Make sure it works so you can get ahead. And if you get laid off, I guess I found me a full-time maid."

Four people stepped onto the stage. The crowd whistled and clapped. A short man with a receding hairline tuned a banjo while a lanky giraffe-like gentleman plunked at a stand-up bass. A pensive-looking fellow in waxed denim jeans and a button-down shirt tuned his guitar. The fourth bandmate, a slight woman with short brown hair giving minivan mom vibes, ran a bow across a violin.

"Elizabeth will be so pissed," Astoria half-whispered, grinning widely.

"Come again?"

"Nothing."

"Get ready," Johnny said. "It's about to get wild."

Finally, a bear of a man in a tattered cowboy hat stepped onto the stage. The hat concealed the top half of his face; a matted beard covered the rest. Balancing his guitar atop his thick middle, he fastened a leather strap to the bottom of the guitar, then nodded to his band. Instruments held at the ready, like cavalry about to fire, the other members nodded back.

The crowd inhaled.

Then, the man from eastern Kentucky opened his mouth, and what came out in one singular exhalation was neither singing nor talking but howling and wailing, crying and praising—all other utterances encompassing the brutal beauty of living and dying — as if something trapped deep inside him was trying to claw its way out from where it hovered at the heart of eternal truth. For three hours, the crowd clung to the edge of their folding chairs as that gnarled voice transported them through time and space to an atomically minute pinpoint place where the source of all light glimmers in the darkness, reminding them what it is to love, to hurt, and to reel. The crowd had paid to hear some live music, but what they got in return was a spiritual awakening.

After the band left the stage, and the lights of the Station Inn buzzed on, nobody moved from their seats or rushed the exits. They blinked, glancing about the room, trying to process what they'd heard and seen.

"How has nobody heard of this guy?" Astoria asked.

"He's not exactly the profile they're looking for on Music Row," said Johnny.

They locked eyes and grinned.

"Trendy fucks," they said.

CHAPTER SEVENTEEN

It was Evie's last day at the agency. Thick gray clouds hovered over the office park, threatening to unleash a summer downpour. Inside, the office hummed, its white noise punctuated by the tic-tic-tic typing of those choosing productivity over lethargy.

The Creatives were gone, likely crouched in some dive bar, salivating over their impending brilliance as they scratched out the next award-winning campaign idea on a napkin, each envisioning himself the next Don Draper.

The Account Girls had been in high spirits in the morning, prancing about the floor and laughing louder and more disingenuously than usual at their inside jokes and entitled assertions. But a three-martini lunch celebrating Evie's departure (yet another event to which Evie wasn't invited) had rendered them sleepy. Now, they slouched at their desks, shopping online or clicking aimlessly through their inboxes.

The only haste came from Evie rustling through her desk, her blonde hair in a ratty heap atop her head. She dropped thick files of paperwork into a wastebasket without reviewing their contents. When she ripped open a desk drawer, pill bottles rolled to the front. She grabbed the orange plastic containers by the handful and tossed them into her purse.

Astoria blinked at a consumer trends report, scanning the same information over and over, unable to focus. Her thoughts were on Evie—her sadness anchored in the guttural pain of losing sometime in real-time. Shame gnawed at her psyche. She'd left Evie to twist in the wind in front of everyone at the shower. Was it any surprise she was now blowing away?

"Everything is working out perfectly." That's what Evie had told Astoria when she'd phoned a week prior to announce she and Pierce Mathers were moving to Memphis, sounding frantic and forcedly optimistic. They were engaged. He was buying them a house back in Memphis (*or maybe his grandmother was?*), and he was going to work for a law firm there (*or maybe it was an accounting firm?*). Whenever Evie explained her plans, the details skittered around like a Jesus bug on a lake. Astoria didn't press for clarification. She knew that sometimes the truth doesn't need explaining because it's hiding in plain sight.

Now, Evie hefted a box onto one hip and her purse over the opposite shoulder.

"Need any help?" Astoria asked.

"I won't have to make another trip if you can grab this last box."

Astoria hustled over to Evie's desk. It was fully stripped, the stark expanse of Formica making Astoria feel even more forlorn.

"Chop-chop, Lyons. Time to get the hell outta here."

The Account Girls rolled their eyes.

Evie cackled.

Each carrying a box on her hip, they shuffled across the concrete parking lot.

"At least it's not raining," Astoria said.

Evie dopped her box and purse on the ground, opened her car's backdoor, and kneeled on the backseat, her rump bobbing in the air as she shoved loose piles of clothes onto other stacks of belongings to make room. Mounds of Louis Vuitton weekender bags, clothes, lamps, shoes, picture frames, and Lord knows what else filled the car—all of Evie's lovely things in their disheveled piles conveyed a desperate sense of haste.

Standing there watching Evie throw her belongings across the backseat, Astoria knew this was what running looked like. She felt a pang of concern—false guilt, perhaps—knowing that Pierce Mathers was what Evie was running to.

Evie extracted herself from the car. Astoria's face must have telegraphed her feelings, because Evie cackled nervously. "It looks a mess because we're going to buy all-new when we get to Memphis," she said.

"When are you leaving?" Astoria wanted to invite Evie to lunch one last time if only to make herself feel better.

"I think tonight."

Astoria toed the ground. "Are you sure you want to leave?"

Evie cackled again, then crammed the office boxes into the backseat. "I've been sure since the day I moved to this pretentious town."

Slamming the backdoor, Evie turned to Astoria and extended her arms. "It's been a trip, lady. Give me a hug."

They embraced, light and quick.

"I'll see ya again," Evie said, flashing a smile. Then she opened the front door and slipped into the driver's seat.

The moment was blinding. Astoria wanted to say a hundred things. "Take care of yourself, Evie," was all she could manage.

"That's Pierce's job now." Evie cackled one last time. "*You* take care of *yourself.*"

Like a little kid making a promise, Astoria shook her head yes. Arms at her side, sadness in her heart, she watched Evie drive away.

The light faded to gray as Astoria packed away her belongings for the day. Driving home with the streetlights glowing orange on Briley Parkway, Astoria flicked on the wipers as rain began to fall.

***

Hell hath no fury like a Type-A Millennial whose plans have changed without her consent. Which is to say: Elizabeth didn't receive the news well when Astoria revealed she was moving out. In their apartment's kitchen, she clenched Astoria's 30-day notice letter in her fist.

"You haven't even been dating this guy for a year, and you're moving in with him?" she screeched.

Astoria reminded herself to stay calm, her face registering no emotion, while Elizabeth continued seething, her eyes wide, pupils dilated, prim lips twitching. Astoria motioned to the letter as if submitting a piece of evidence for a jury.

"I'll pay through the end of next month, so you have time to find someone, and you can keep the security deposit."

"Trashy."

Astoria swayed backward as if the slur were a physical blow. "I beg your pardon?"

Elizabeth waved the letter in the air. "Moving in with a guy this quick is a trashy thing to do."

Unable to make eye contact and burning with shame, Astoria heaved her overnight bag over her shoulder. "I'll pay through the end of next month, but I'll move my things this weekend."

"What things?" Elizabeth scoffed.

Astoria turned and fled, closing the front door lightly behind her, hot tears streaming down her cheeks.

***

"I made room for ya," Johnny said.

Astoria peered into the empty closet in the downstairs bedroom—the space barely three feet wide and two feet deep. She turned to Johnny and frowned, uncertain if he was joking.

"But where will I put my clothes?"

He snorted. "How much stuff do you have?"

Thinking better than to answer, she faced the closet again. "Guess I can downsize."

Aside from the limited closet space, she settled into life with Johnny and Duke in the cottage on Riverside Drive. In the mornings, birdsong filled the backyard. Johnny brought her cups of coffee in bed. Chatter from the morning news floated up to her from the television downstairs while Duke snoozed at her feet.

Their days were filled with alarm clocks, commutes, meetings, making dinner plans via email, quitting times, and that soft, everyday soft release of leaving the workday behind. Slanted golden rectangles of light stretched across the wooden floors in the afternoons. Astoria loved returning home, taking off her heels and nylons, and standing barefoot within the warm shapes as they moved across the floor.

On weeknights, Johnny cooked hearty meals, which they shared, and then they chatted on the front porch, sipping glasses of wine, sometimes cocktails, while watching the low riders rumble down Riverside Drive, the bass from their radios thumping like an anthem through the gritty streets.

They took walks in Shelby Bottoms beneath the stars. Nodded along to bluegrass bands at the Station Inn. Snacked on popcorn and cried at indie films at the Belcourt Theatre. Ate fried bologna sandwiches and drank ice-cold beers while listening to the country bands playing the Tennessee waltz at Robert's on Sundays before the tourists roused themselves onto Broadway for the day.

They drank to survive the weeknights and celebrate the weekends. Hunted for treasures at garage sales across East Nashville. Hiked the Cumberland Plateau. He made roaring fires to keep them warm in the winter. She luxuriated in the sunroom, reading books and studying the light as it moved through the trees. They ate good food to make the everyday more palatable, found security in tracking their paychecks, punctuated the mundane with concerts or a night on the town, and found nourishment in the warmth of waking up next to someone whose scent they'd come to know better than their own.

A year passed.

Aside from the hangovers, life was simple. Ignoring the energy required to endure those endless weekends on the mountain, Astoria found plenty of reasons to find peace and contentment in the day-to-day. She figured they were happy.

CHAPTER EIGHTEEN

Spring 2010

The last day in April fell on a Friday. Johnny stood before the TV, worrying his fingers down a patch of stringy hair as he watched the evening news. He'd wanted to leave for the mountain as soon as they got home from work.

"They're issuing warnings for flash flooding," he said. "I don't think it's wise to get on the roads."

Appearing in the doorway between the living room and kitchen, Astoria fought the urge to smile. She and Johnny had been on a bender, having spent the past three weekends on the mountain, binge-drinking then and every night in between. Her fingers and face were bloated. She was sorely behind at work. She'd never carried extra weight, but all her trendy shift dresses barely fit around her thickening middle. The last thing she wanted to do was endure another weekend drinking for survival on the mountain while simultaneously feeling like she was killing herself. She needed water, a salad, and a nap.

"Darn," she said, "probably smart to wait it out."

"Reckon so. We'll see how things are looking in the morning."

Much to her relief, conditions only deteriorated overnight.

"You're probably used to rain like this in Washington," Johnny said as they huddled on the basement landing the following day, peering down to where four inches of flood water glowered back at them like a patient monster, alive and growing. Long seams rolled across the placid surface. "But I ain't never seen it rain this hard for this long."

"Channel Five is saying the Cumberland might jump its banks. How is that even possible?"

"We're a good two miles from the river."

"Are we safe here?"

"No tellin. Think you can help me move my tools and equipment to higher ground?"

"Whatever you need me to do."

They spent the morning lugging the lawn mower, power saws, and toolboxes up from the basement into the dining room and kitchen, filling the house with the scent of diesel fuel and oil.

"Smells like the saw shops I grew up going to with Ace," Astoria said.

"Maybe we ought to keep all this up here for good? Convert the dining room to my man cave."

"Go for it," she said, calling his bluff.

Johnny laughed.

Outside, between the banks of earth and sky, an oceanic river flowed over Middle Tennessee.

They loaded into the truck in the rain-soaked afternoon and drove around, assessing the damage with the windshield wipers slapping out a rhythm, creating a soundtrack for the day.

The Cumberland had jumped its banks, flooding all of downtown and restricting access to East Nashville from the east, west, and south. Red and blue lights flashed at intersections where police blockades rerouted traffic.

As they cruised down Riverside Drive towards Shelby Bottoms, Astoria rubbernecked at the men, women, and kids bucking sandbags across front porches. Some families loaded belongings in their cars.

"Where can they go?" Astoria asked.

"Probably try to head north."

When they neared the train trestle marking the entrance to Shelby Bottoms, a scowling NPD officer waved for them to turn around. Chocolate-milk-colored water lapped at the river's newfound banks at the bottom of the park.

"Let's go have a look at downtown," Johnny said. "Then we should probably get back to the house." He waved at the officer, who slid his hands beneath his flak jacket and glowered back.

On the radio, somber voices talked about a rising death toll. The waters rose too fast, they said. People got caught in their cars on the way to dinner. An elderly couple drowned in their home. The total number of dead and missing was unclear.

They made it as far as the interstate on-ramps at Shelby Street. People from the neighborhood had pulled their cars onto the sidewalks and parked. A small crowd gathered at an intersection at the top of a rise. Men surveyed the scene in silence, arms crossed. Three young women and an elder chattered and pointed, shifting babies on their hips.

Following the crowd, Johnny parked halfway on the sidewalk, and they climbed out of the truck and trekked to the top of the hill; he whistled at the sight of downtown Nashville up to its knees in brown water. Sirens flashed across the horizon. Helicopters whirred overhead.

"I wonder if those old buildings are ruined," Astoria said.

"No telling, but it's gonna take a while for anyone to even get in there and see. They've blocked off the entire freeway." Johnny pointed north to where I-65 stretched empty into the brooding sky. "Something this big is gonna change everything," he said.

"What do you mean?" Astoria asked.

"They're already working on that new convention center. A disaster this big will bring in federal funds. You watch. It'll be good for business, but everything is going to change."

CHAPTER NINETEEN

Summer 2010

Henry Hunter spent a year looking for Hanz's replacement. "We don't want to settle for just any Creative Director," he said, repeating the mantra at agency-wide meetings. "We want someone who will take us to the next level."

Dixon and Richards, the old-timers who owned the agency, appeared more frequently than they had when Astoria first started. Stooped in their wrinkled skin, they shuffled around the work floor, grumbling to themselves, never speaking to their employees, even though the good little workers always held their breath whenever the old men passed, like little kids seeking validation.

One afternoon, Henry Hunter appeared on the floor, the Creative Team flanking him, their chests full and proud, eyes steeled in confidence, imparting a sense of victory. Henry Hunter cleared his throat and raised his hands. "Excuse me, if I may."

The Account Girls blinked up from their laptops.

"Sorry to interrupt like this, but we couldn't wait any longer. We've found our candidate. He comes from a Big Six agency and has global brand experience. He's moving here from L.A. and is a *pro*—the likes this town hasn't seen before."

The Account Girls squealed and clapped. The Creative Team slapped one another on the back.

While Henry Hunter continued, Astoria scanned the floor, looking for an ally to connect with over the absurdity of the moment. Finding only blank faces, she thought of Evie and felt the heavy pull of missing someone she loved. Evie was the closest thing to a best friend she'd ever had, and in that moment, Astoria felt the depth of her loss. She wondered how long she might endure working alongside people she loathed. But then she thought of Johnny. In a world full of Account Girls and Creative Guys, shapeshifters like Cody, she told herself she and Johnny were different. She could survive anything with him by her side.

***

Nashville began quaking with a sudden uptick in energy—an invisible buildup of friction and force that was moving so fast it was about to explode. Ever since those floodwaters receded, developers had been pouring into town. Johnny's firm tripled its workload. Many nights, he stayed late at the office or took clients to dinner, texting Astoria his status on her commute home.

The dizzying chaos of renovations, new construction, and alleged historic preservation efforts unfolded from downtown to Opry Mills and every neighborhood in between, even those untouched by flooding.

Trendy bars and eateries sprang up in once-empty gravel lots; many were extensions of flagship locales in New York, Austin, and LA. But small businesses appeared too, and it was at one such haunt where Astoria and the Video Guys resumed their ritual of Thursday Night Pints. They liked this new joint, aptly named The Village Pub, because it was a no-frills place to drink cold beer and eat pretzels, and the owner (a rare East Nashville native) allowed smoking on the spacious outdoor patio.

On an oppressively sticky evening in the heart of happy hour, they settled in with their pints around their usual table.

Jake cupped a hand over his cigarette and flicked his lighter, the tip of the cigarette flashing orange as he inhaled. He pulled the cigarette out of his mouth and exhaled a stream of smoke across the hazy porch. "I love this place."

"Give me one of those," said Todd.

Jake tossed him the pack of American Spirits.

Todd examined the yellow package longingly. "None of these new bars will even let you smoke outside anymore," he said. "You guys notice how most of these new places opening around town all look the same?"

"My boyfriend and I were just talking about that," Astoria said. "White tile. Exposed beams. Lots of industrial metal. Farm-to-table menu. It's like some global corporation issued its blueprint for appearing authentic."

"But no smoking," said Todd.

"Right. Corporate policy." Jake tapped his cigarette against an ashtray. "I read the new Music City Center is going to cost something like six-hundred-and-twenty-million dollars."

Astoria studied the foamy bubbles in her beer, deciding to withhold that Johnny's firm was involved in that massive downtown project.

"Will they use the money the city got from the flood?" asked Todd.

"No," said Cody, shaking his head matter-of-factly. "Council approved that City Center before the flood even hit. The mayor has been hard-charging for this new convention center for a long time so they can lure more convention tourism dollars to town."

Astoria sipped her beer, eyeing Cody as he spoke. His attendance at these happy hours depended on his girlfriend's mood at work. If Cassidy was bubbly and chatty with the other girls at the office, Astoria knew Cody wouldn't join them. But if Cassidy slammed her notebook on her desk and refused to engage in the day's gossip with the other Account Girls, Astoria would bet money she'd see Cody on the porch, laughing along and talking shit about the Creatives like he'd never missed a beat, like nothing had changed. But the energy was different when he was present—Astoria and the Video Guys chose their words carefully, and an air of uneasiness permeated the group. They still told stories and aired their grievances using general terms, but nobody spoke about the Account Girls.

Now, Astoria listened to Cody wax on about the convention center. He was a chameleon, seamlessly shifting from one world to the next, harboring no loyalty to either. She hated him for it.

The Video Guys were debating the merits of Nashville becoming the epicenter of corporate tourism when Astoria noticed a familiar figure standing at the edge of the porch holding a pint. "Don't all look at once," she whispered, "but we have company."

In unison, they turned to see the new Creative Director standing on the patio, short with wide-set eyes and a groomed beard, smirking as he surveyed the scene. Even on the pub's laid-back patio, the young man twitched with aggressive energy, ready to dominate the conversation in his waxed denim jeans and slip-on Vans, his short-sleeve shirt buttoned to the top.

"Who in the hell invited him?" Jake said, hissing through his teeth. A blue vein bulged at his temple.

They all looked to Cody.

He raised his hands in surrender. "It wasn't me."

Another group of co-workers—three developers and the agency's disgruntled IT director—stepped out onto the patio, their pints dripping beer.

"I did invite them," Cody said, nodding toward the tech guys. "But they're cool."

All heads snapped back to where the new Creative Director stood blocking the tech guys' path onto the patio. Unaccustomed to anyone from Creative or Accounts ever acknowledging their existence, the techies shifted nervously, taking long drinks from their beers.

Jake crossed his arms and slouched back in his chair. "That guy is the driest of fucks."

Cody leaned forward, chin tucked, voice low. "I've been trying to avoid him because I keep hearing about what a dick he is, you know? But we were in the kitchen this morning, and he introduced himself, then asked me if I *SUP.*"

"SUP?" Jake asked. "The fuck is that?"

"Stand-up paddle boarding," said Cody. "It seemed like he only introduced himself because he wanted to brag about it."

"Is that what's on top of his Jeep?" Astoria asked. She nodded toward the parking lot where the Creative Director had parked his army-green Jeep Wrangler at the front, making the vehicle visible to all pub patrons drinking inside and out. An oversized white surfboard lay strapped to the top.

"I thought it was a surfboard," Cody said. "But where would you surf in Nashville?"

"Look at those fucking California plates," said Jake.

Todd tapped a forefinger on the table's edge. "You know how they're all saying he's from L.A., like it's a big deal and anyone should give a shit? A little birdie in H.R. told me he's actually from New Jersey."

"Originally?" Astoria asked. "Or he never lived in L.A.?"

"He's originally from Jersey but claims he's *from* L.A. He worked at a global agency there, but only for like, half a year."

They snickered.

"Captain Hollywood," said Jake.

Cody choked on a gulp of beer; the others howled.

A silver 1970s Challenger thumped down McGavock Pike. Astoria felt the base from the car's stereo rumble up her chair. Their beer pints shuddered on the table. Across the street from the pub, a tendril of smoke crawled up from the chimney of a mint green restaurant (which was also the owner's house), Bailey & Cato, one of East Nashville's oldest meat & threes. It offered daily specials, including catfish and cornbread on Tuesdays and pork shoulder and smothered greens on Sundays. Two houses down, a gray-haired old man rested on a sagging front porch, swatting at flies and accepting the day as it came. Unkempt mounds of grass and kudzu lined the street.

Still talking to the tech crew, Captain Hollywood motioned to the neighborhood as if he were a developer envisioning his next acquisition. "You know, this place could be cool if it were a little more like L.A.," he said, loud enough for all on the porch to hear. "Venice Beach, maybe."

Grabbing his pint glass, Jake tipped its contents down his throat, then slammed it onto the table, knocking over Cody's half-finished beer. Without pausing or apologizing, Jake stood, kicking his chair out behind him; he dropped a wadded ten-dollar bill on the table, then stomped away, knocking shoulders with Captain Hollywood before marching down the porch steps. Oblivious to the offensive nature of his elitist posture or perhaps propelled by it, the Creative Director approached their table.

"Mind if I join?" he asked.

"Why would you move to a new city just to change it?" The words flew from Astoria's mouth before the Creative Director had fully settled into Jake's chair.

He squinted at her, smiling condescendingly. "Maybe you need to expand your horizons to see this place needs some work. I can't believe how many people at this agency have never left Nashville."

"I'm not even from here," Astoria said.

"Well, then, you have no say in the matter." The Creative Director picked up a menu and held it in front of his face, effectively ending the conversation.

Astoria looked to Cody for backup, but he ignored her, feigning a sudden interest in the happenings on the street beyond the patio. Todd studied his feet. Astoria wanted to get up and stomp away like Jake, but the Creative Director had put her in her place, so she remained there, wallowing in embarrassment, sweat dripping off her elbows. She realized there were countless other Captain Hollywoods in the world, and they were coming for Nashville in droves.

CHAPTER TWENTY

Her face against the passenger window, she closed her eyes to the landscape blurring past, making her hangover-induced nausea even worse.

Scenes from the weekend replayed across her mind. From the moment they'd arrived at the mountain, Johnny had once again morphed from a mild-mannered engineer into a brazen drunkard who didn't care whether Astoria was along for the ride or not.

Twenty people set out on a series of four-wheelers and side-by-sides through backwoods trails, drinking beers from nine in the morning until all hours of the night. It wasn't yet eight o'clock in the evening when, clinging to Johnny's middle, Astoria vomited off the side of their machine while he gunned the accelerator. Johnny dropped her off at his father's trailer, then motored back into the wild night where he'd surely passed a Mason jar around a fire, slurring over the same stories he'd already told a hundred times.

He tricked me, she thought, but her conscience chimed in, and she wondered if she were the trickster in her sheath dresses and her corporate job. She didn't fit in with Johnny and his family on the mountain, but she didn't fit in at Dixon-Richards either.

She wondered what Johnny expected from her between their life in Nashville and the weekends spent drinking on the mountain. *Did he see how she was losing herself as she failed to code-switch across the different worlds? Or was he preoccupied with swapping in and out his own roles? And how could they ever truly find one another if they spent all this time trying to be anyone but themselves?*

Maybe that's what she'd found attractive in him in the first place: he knew how to transition into any environment seamlessly, and he did so with such prowess that she knew she was learning from a master.

Lifting her face off the window, she squinted out the windshield and blurted out the single thought ping-ponging around her brain. "I wish we didn't drink so much when we go to the mountain."

"So, don't drink." He lit a cigarette, turned up the radio, and they rode for a while. Duke slept in the backseat. After a long silence, Johnny added, "My family doesn't drink like that every night. Only when I come home 'cause they're happy to see me."

Astoria wanted to cry and vomit at the same time—anything to offload the weight of Johnny's lie and her truth. Shutting her eyes, she slid down in the seat, fighting the panic rising inside her, screaming that she was backsliding away from anything positive she'd set out to achieve.

***

Henry Hunter's office door was closed. Astoria paused, listened, knocked.

"Yes?" He said, sounding annoyed.

She opened the door and poked her head inside. He'd emailed, telling her to come to his office at 1:30. She'd obliged, and now he remained focused on his computer, glancing between keyboard and screen as he hammered out a correspondence. Hesitantly, Astoria entered and took her place on the single plastic chair. She waited. Henry Hunter arched an eyebrow as his fingers flew across the keyboard. Tick-tick-tick-tick. He would make her wait as long as he wanted.

Astoria drummed her pen on her notebook. Henry Hunter hit the return button with gusto, then looked up, brightening, as if only now realizing she was in the room. He leaned forward, clasping his hands atop the desk.

"Miss Lyons. How are things going between you and the new Creative Director?"

"Fine." She gripped her pen and faked a smile, her stomach tightening as she recalled the day before when Captain Hollywood had dressed her down in a meeting. Astoria had been clicking through a PowerPoint showing how digital ads with a clear call-to-action outperformed more creatively expressive ads when Captain Hollywood interrupted, asking how many campaigns she'd worked on in her career.

"I've never worked in marketing until now," she'd said, her cheeks burning.

"I rest my case," said Captain Hollywood. "How about you go research campaigns from Ogilvy and Wieden, then get back to me on impactful work."

"But these results are from *our* work. I don't see how campaigns other agencies have produced for other clients apply to what we're discussing here."

Captain Hollywood and his creative counterparts snickered.

Now, sitting across the desk from Henry Hunter, Astoria assumed he'd heard about the exchange. Was Henry Hunter enjoying leftovers? Or was he genuinely interested in hearing her side?

"He's certainly bringing a lot of opinions to the table," she said.

"He's an incredible talent. We're lucky to have someone with his level of experience because this agency has a lot to learn." Henry Hunter clapped his hands. "Speaking of, I wanted to brief you on a new business opportunity with the mayor's office."

"Oh?" she said, surprised at the sudden change in topic.

"They need to understand how Nashville citizens feel about this new convention center and its costs and to see if people are talking about it online."

"My boyfriend's engineering firm is involved with that."

Henry Hunter brightened. For the first time since Astoria had started working at Dixon-Richards, he seemed interested in what she had to say.

"Do you know anyone over there who I might want to talk to?" he asked.

Astoria wished she could stuff her words back in her mouth; she wanted to keep Henry Hunter as far away from her personal life as possible, so she played dumb. "At the mayor's office?"

Henry Hunter's face and shoulders fell, the hope draining out of him just as fast as it had appeared. "As I was saying, the new convention center is an enormous project, and they need to understand current citizen perception to inform future messaging."

Astoria scribbled in her notebook. "Do they need a survey or just social listening?"

"Likely both."

"Interesting."

"But there's a catch." Henry Hunter turned his computer monitor around, sharing the project brief on the screen. Astoria scooted to the edge of her chair and leaned forward.

"The convention center is already under contract, and the mayor is coming up for re-election."

"Okay?"

"You have thirty days to do your research and get a clear understanding of stakeholder perceptions. You'll need to run a channel analysis, do some social listening, probably a focus group, and recommend a messaging strategy."

Astoria blinked, processing the amount of work she'd need to accomplish on such a tight timeline. "Who else is going to work on this project?"

Henry Hunter grinned broadly now, repositioning his screen away from Astoria. "Why, Miss Lyons, you're our digital strategist. This might be your big break."

Driving home with the windows down, the air conditioning whistling the tiniest thread of reprieve, hot air funneling around her, Astoria organized the new project in her mind. She would break the work into three ten-day sprints: qualitative research would come first, followed by quantitative analysis, and then data synthesis and recommendations. It was a great challenge.

"Guess who else gets to work on the convention center?" Astoria said, greeting Johnny when he got home that evening. His firm was still struggling to keep pace with its tidal wave of projects. He worked late most nights, coming home looking tired, dark circles ringing his eyes, his features pronouncedly gaunt.

"Who?" he asked flatly, dropping his leather briefcase on a bench by the door.

Astoria frowned. "Me, obviously."

Johnny washed a hand over his face. "What on earth would you guys be doing for the convention center?"

Astoria crossed her arms and jutted out her chin; Johnny loved rattling off some technical engineering jargon but was quick to roll his eyes whenever she talked about her projects.

"We have a contract with the mayor's office. They want us to do some consumer research to gauge public opinion on the whole thing."

"Probably best you don't let on that we're connected if you're working on that type of project," he said, moving toward the kitchen to fix a drink.

Astoria's face fell. "Did you have a bad day or something?"

"No," he said over his shoulder, still walking away. "I just don't think it's wise to mix business with pleasure is all."

She recalled the moment, a few hours prior, when she'd thought the same thing in her meeting with Henry Hunter, which somehow made Johnny's response even more offensive.

***

Motivated to succeed, she found discipline like a drug, and work became her new addiction. From the time she arrived at the office to the minutes before shutting her laptop and climbing into bed, all she did was work.

When Johnny worked late, spent an evening down at Five Points with Lorenzo and the boys, or took off for the mountain on the weekends, Astoria stayed home and put in the hours. She and Johnny still cooked dinners together and enjoyed the Antique Roadshow on Monday nights, but when it came to the roar of the bar at 2:00 a.m. or those long weekends on the mountain, their lives were quickly unfolding in separate realms. She told herself that maintaining some autonomy in a relationship was healthy; maybe this project was their saving grace. They could work hard, he would play hard, and they would both be happy.

One Thursday evening, Astoria was working from the couch when Johnny handed her a bowl of pinto beans and cornbread.

"Thanks," she said, taking the dish but keeping her eyes on the laptop screen.

"You're putting in more hours than I am," he said, adjusting the dish towel on his shoulder.

"We've done so much research that we have too much data. I'm worried I won't have time to work through it all before this first presentation to the mayor." She balanced the bowl atop a pile of notebooks on the end table. "Which is why I can't come to the mountain with you this weekend."

Johnny pinched at his hair. "No surprise there, I reckon."

She smiled up at him. "I can't blow this."

"Maybe you're trying too hard. I mean, it ain't like you're the one constructing the building."

Astoria squinted up at him.

"What do you want me to say to that, Johnny? That you're a genius who conjures entire buildings from your great mind? Or, how about this? My job is so irrelevant; maybe you should just marry me and make it so I don't even have to work. How about that?"

He slipped the towel off his shoulder and flicked it in the air. "You're getting all worked up over nothing. All I was saying is those trendy fucks you work with ain't putting in weekends."

"Which is why this is my big break. My co-workers can party all they want, but they won't outwork me."

"Suit yourself."

CHAPTER TWENTY-ONE

She woke to the sound of Johnny's phone pinging downstairs, where he always left it plugged in on the kitchen counter overnight. Her tongue lolled dry in her mouth as she lay in bed, blinking between the mysterious layers of sleep and awake, the text notification and her need for water pulling her toward consciousness. Johnny snored loudly next to her. She slipped out from under the covers, then crept down to the kitchen.

Standing at the sink, she stared out the kitchen window while filling a glass with water. A car, indistinguishable in the dark, drove slowly down Riverside Drive. Rising onto her toes, Astoria leaned toward the pane and watched the headlights float through the night. Turning off the faucet, she wondered what the person behind the wheel might be up to, driving around at this hour.

The cell phone pinged again.

The clock on the stove read 2:34.

Staring at the phone, she chugged the entire glass and placed it on the counter, careful not to make a sound, then picked up the device. The screen's light illuminated the kitchen. Adrenaline racing, she cupped her hands around the little computer and waited, watching the stairs leading to the bedroom, listening.

The house hummed around her. She squinted at the text app showing three new messages, calculating how accessing Johnny's phone without his knowledge and reading his texts might cross a

Rubicon in their relationship. But then she thought about how her and Johnny's lives were spinning down different paths. *Had they already drifted too far apart?* With the unread texts beckoning, she tapped the screen.

"Lu." The person behind the texts had a name, but all prior communication history either didn't exist or had been deleted.

2:10 a.m.

You out tonight?

2:12 a.m.

Would be fun to meet up.

2:34 a.m.

Guess that green Camry is still in your driveway. Maybe next time.

Heart racing, she glanced out the kitchen window. *Who is Lu?*

The following day, Astoria stood dripping on the bathroom rug after her shower. She wiped condensation from the mirror and studied her puffy eyes. After reading Johnny's text messages, she couldn't go back to sleep. Time passed tortuously slowly.

Serves you right, she told herself.

Her mind raced around how she might broach the issue with Johnny. Deciding there was no way around it but straight through, she secured the towel around her chest and tip-toed into the living room, where Johnny was drinking coffee and watching the morning news.

"Hey," she said.

His eyes stayed fixed on the TV.

"Uhm ... I was getting a glass of water last night ... err ... this morning, I guess, and your phone was blowing up at, like, two-thirty? I thought maybe it was an emergency or something because it was so late, you know? So, I checked it."

Johnny snapped to attention, suddenly disinterested in the television. "You checked my phone?" Duke had been sleeping next to Johnny; his ears perked, and he lifted his head at the sharpness in Johnny's voice.

Astoria counterpunched. "Who is Lu?"

Johnny slammed his coffee cup on the side table, its contents sloshing onto the lamp.

"I can't believe this," he said, rising and stalking out of the living room toward the bathroom, his shoulder brushing Astoria's as he passed. She trailed behind him.

"Who is Lu?" she asked again.

Johnny wheeled around to face her, rage in his eyes.

"*Lucas* is a guy from work," he said.

"And he's texting you to hang out at two in the morning?" Water streamed from the ends of Astoria's hair down her shoulders. She fastened the towel tighter around her.

"He's hung out with me and the guys a few times down at Five Points. He's got a drinking problem."

"So, he's in good company," she said.

Johnny turned and stalked into the bathroom, kicking the door shut behind him.

That night, after Johnny had gone to bed, Astoria was on her way upstairs when she heard his phone ping again. Her conscience chimed in, and she realized it would be insecure to resume her snooping. Doing so would prove their relationship was on rocky ground. But despite all rationales, she tiptoed back downstairs, hovered over the phone, took a deep breath, and touched the screen. It lit up, showing a lock icon. Password now required.

***

Summer burned through the south. In the mornings, curtains of steam draped the city, mingling with ghostly vapors rising from the ground, the smell of wet dog and dank water permeating the air. The highways sizzled against the horizon, blurring orange and hazy in the afternoons. The relentless heat kept people indoors while air conditioning units whirred, chugged, and hummed across the empty neighborhoods.

In the Riverside cottage, Johnny insisted the thermostat stay at seventy-five degrees to keep the electricity bill low, explaining in technical terms how the home was constructed to stay cool in the summer and warm in the winter. Astoria stopped listening about halfway through Johnny's lecture, but having resumed paying her student loan bills after years of dodging telephone calls from collectors, she couldn't argue with frugality. She sweated, and she worked.

One Friday night, instead of coming home, packing his bag, and heading for the mountain, Johnny poured himself a glass of wine and settled into the couch. On the opposite end, Astoria pecked away at the big report she'd been preparing for the mayor, which she was scheduled to present on Monday morning. Having just finished her research, she needed to distill her findings into recommended next steps, which meant synthesizing hundreds of pages of data into a ten-slide presentation. She was drowning in information and half-baked conclusions and trying not to panic.

"Aren't you going to the mountain this weekend?" she asked Johnny.

"Nah. Gonna hit the lake tomorrow instead."

"What lake?" Astoria furrowed her brow at Johnny. "I didn't realize you knew anyone with a boat."

"Got invited out to Percy Priest with the guys."

She wanted to ask if the midnight text machine, Lucas, would be there, but fear blocked her throat. She glanced at Johnny; he sipped his wine.

"Is Lorenzo going?" she asked.

"Nah. He's on the road."

She swallowed hard.

"Can I come?" she asked.

"Don't you have work to do?" Johnny swirled the wine around in his glass.

"I've killed it this week on my project. I don't want to jinx myself, but I feel ahead of my timeline." She smiled to cover the lie.

"Good for you."

On the television, an injury law commercial promised viewers they deserved to be paid. Duke flopped back and forth on the ground, scratching his back against the jute rug.

Astoria focused on her breathing, but her chest felt tight. "Do you not want me to come?"

"Come if you want," he said, his face blank.

Astoria nodded.

"You ain't gonna know anyone," he added.

"But it'll be fun to spend a day together. Between work and travel, we've been like two ships passing in the night."

Johnny sipped his wine.

Astoria picked crumbs out of her laptop's keyboard, her thoughts exploding like fireworks probing a dark sky for answers.

***

Party Cove was a renowned bay on Percy Priest Lake where the 'in crowd' motored to drink, swim, see, and be seen. From sunup to sundown, tanned bodies in bikinis and bathing trunks bobbed across the mercurial surface, floating on inflatable toys and foam noodles, forming a loose circumference around a long line of boats anchored in a row.

The moment she climbed aboard the ski boat belonging to Johnny's friend, Astoria regretted inviting herself along for the day. Johnny's three friends had invited three girls to join them. They all worked together in the music industry. The girls launched into insider gossip; Johnny knew all the details, slipping seamlessly into the scene. Astoria tried to laugh along at first but quickly realized it made no difference whether she feigned interest in their stories—*why bother pretending?* She fashioned her beach towel into a little nest on the back bench seat, tugged her swimsuit out of her bum, and settled in, determined to enjoy the day.

After idling out of the wake zone, they raced straight to Party Cove and docked next to a pontoon blasting "Toxic" by Britney Spears from roof-mounted speakers. A crowd mingled on the pontoon's deck. Girls wearing string bikinis held red solo cups in the air and popped their hips to the beat. Three men with beer bellies stood around a grill, watching hot dogs sizzle in the heat.

Johnny's industry friends grabbed beers from a blue cooler and scrambled over the back of the boat into the water. Holding a silver can in each hand, Johnny paused on the swim platform before jumping in. He turned, squinting at Astoria where she was still sitting cross-legged on her towel. "Ain't you coming?" he asked.

Glancing toward the pontoon, she scanned the crowded porch for familiar faces, worrying she might run into the Belmont guy or, worse, Elizabeth. "Think I'm gonna chill in here for a bit," she said. "Get some sun."

"Suit yourself." He hopped into the water, holding both cans high in the air.

After retrieving her own beer from the cooler, Astoria lay down across the bench seat, resting her head against the warm leather.

She could still see the crowd on the pontoon, but they couldn't see her. People came and went, the girls dancing and pawing at one another as they laughed and looked about to see who was watching. Guys flexed as they tipped their beer cans high in the air and poured translucent golden streams into their mouths.

Astoria tried not to think about work. She drank one beer, then another, telling herself it was good to relax and play. Her body baking in the sun, she was mentally inventorying what she needed to accomplish upon returning home when something on the periphery caught her eye—a drunk girl stumbling across the pontoon's deck, grasping at the boat's railing to steady herself, her white bikini hung loosely across her starved frame. The girl swayed against the railing, her eyelids fluttering as she fought to maintain balance. The men at the grill smirked, then two stepped toward her. One man put his arm around her, and she fell against him, almost spilling his beer as he squatted to hold her up. The other man supported her on the opposite side. Together, they carried the girl out of view.

Scrambling to her feet, Astoria watched the men coordinate efforts and pass the drunk girl onto a neighboring cabin cruiser as if she were as light and inconsequential as a floatie, then haul her into the interior. Scenarios spun like a roulette wheel around Astoria's mind. The fastest way for her to get to the girl in the white bikini was to jump in and swim two boats over. She was kicking off her flip-flops when she heard a familiar voice carrying across the water. Looking up, she saw Elizabeth and her industry friends file onto the roof of the pontoon boat, where people were taking turns sliding into the lake.

Astoria dropped to her hands and knees. The slide ran off the other side of the pontoon. From her vantage point, hiding on the floor of the ski boat, Astoria couldn't see whether Elizabeth and her friends were still on the roof or in the water. She waited, listening for the splash of bodies and the girls' chatter to die out.

Crawling to the starboard side of her boat, she grabbed the top rail and, in one swift movement, hauled herself up and over the edge, splashing sideways into the lake like a big tuna tossed overboard.

The water, warm and dark, shimmered with minerals. Arms flashing white with each stroke, she doggy paddled away from the flotilla until she spotted Johnny and his friends floating in a circle, talking with the three industry girls and one more—a redhead—Astoria had never seen before. She swam towards them, and Johnny stiffened as she approached, as if a fishing line had caught him and was fixin' to pull him out of the water. The new girl with curly red hair bobbed next to him.

"What label did you say you were with now, Lucy?" asked one of Johnny's friends.

Blood roared in Astoria's ears. Her pulse hammered loudly, and she had to fight to stay afloat, eyes darting between Johnny and the redhead. The girl was all moon-faced and smiley; he remained stiff, but his eyes softened when they landed on her.

Lucy, *or was it Lu?*

"Anyone need a beer?" Johnny asked. His friends raised their empty cans in the air. He swam back toward the boat, returning minutes later with a one-armed sidestroke, pinning several beers to his broad chest with his other arm. The girls squealed as the cans popped out of his grasp and floated around him. They lunged at Johnny and the cans like a game of whack-a-mole, retrieving the beers before they sunk to the bottom of the lake. Still treading water, Astoria watched, stomach clenched, as Johnny handed a beer to the redhead.

The girl thanked him with a lingering smile.

"I got you," Johnny said.

Their sunburns were glowing deep red when Johnny and his friends loaded the boat onto its trailer at the marina. Astoria waited outside Johnny's truck while the industry girls—the three from the boat and the newcomer, Lucy, who was apparently joining the group—hovered nearby, padding towels across their tanned torsos and discussing where to go next.

"Let's go to Hooters!" one of them squealed.

Astoria rolled her eyes. She heard Johnny open the driver's side door; the truck engine roared to life. She knocked on the passenger window. Johnny returned a look of mock confusion.

"Unlock the door?" Astoria said, motioning with her hands. A moment passed, and he obliged. Astoria pulled herself up into the passenger seat.

"We're not going to Hooters, are we?" she asked.

"You are a dang wet blanket," he said. "You never want to have fun."

His words took the air out of Astoria, partially because she knew they were true. It was her fault she was insecure and preoccupied with work and scared to hang around people from the music industry. She was fighting through her beer buzz to find the right response when Johnny put his truck in gear and ripped out of the parking lot, tailing his friends and the industry girls, who had all piled into the truck pulling the boat. The little caravan sped out of the marina parking lot.

Astoria's head and body throbbed as they barreled down the road. The sun had zapped her energy, and the day's steady diet of lite beer had drained her of electrolytes. She was so tired; she felt like she couldn't hold on to the pieces of her life as they were flying out the window and scattering across the highway behind her.

"Please, let's go home, Johnny. I'm so tired, and I have work to do."

"You're the one who had to come," he snapped.

The truck drifted between the white and yellow lines.

Astoria didn't have the energy to worry about Johnny's driving ability after drinking in the sun all day; she looked vacantly out the windshield as the light faded from orange to gray, her stomach still clenched.

"Have you been friends with those girls for a long time, or did you just meet them today?"

"We've run in the same crowds off and on," Johnny said.

She wanted to ask about Lucy but recalled how mad Johnny had become when she'd checked his phone and pressed him about the texts from *Lu*, and he was already plenty mad. The question lingered like a sickness in her throat.

Hooters was a blur of white tank tops, blaring televisions, and sticky orange countertops. The industry girls and Johnny's friends had secured a picnic table on the patio.

"I'm going to the bathroom," Astoria said.

Without acknowledging her, Johnny moved through the buzzing restaurant.

After sitting on the toilet for several minutes, skin throbbing, Astoria finished her business then went out, stopping at the bar, which gave her a clear view of the patio. She climbed onto a stool and plopped her purse atop the counter.

"Whatcha drinking?" the bartender asked. Her orange shorts matched her skin.

"Glass of water and a margarita?" Astoria slurred the last word, so it came out sounding like *mar-greee-tuh*. The bartender slid a glass of water toward her. Perching atop her elbows, Astoria dropped her head over the straw and sucked down the entire glass while squinting at a gray-haired man sitting to her left.

"You okay?" he asked.

"I will be." Astoria slurped the remaining water through the ice.

After watching Astoria from the other end of the bar for a time, the bartender returned with her drink. "You wanted salt, right?"

"I *need* salt." Astoria wrapped her hands around the frosty margarita glass and sucked greedily on that straw, too, intermittently turning to spy on the patio from her barstool. The four industry girls sat on one side of the table. Johnny and his three friends laughed shoulder to shoulder on the other, with Johnny and the redhead, Lucy, directly across from one another. The sun had turned Johnny's skin reddish-brown. He looked happy. Astoria's heart seized.

A waitress arrived at the picnic table with two pitchers of beer and a tray of food, perking Johnny, his friends, and the girls to attention.

"Ready to cash out?" the bartender asked.

Astoria startled, looking to her glass, surprised it was already empty.

"One more," she said, retrieving her debit card and slapping it on the bar. The bartender paused, then took the card, returning minutes later with the bill and one more margarita.

Astoria scribbled an incoherent tip on the receipt, grabbed her drink, and slid off the barstool, stumbling into the man beside her. "Careful now," the man said, his voice warm and kind as he caught her. A tighter grip seized her opposite forearm, and she looked to see Johnny standing there, burning red. He yanked her upright, spilling her drink.

"Well, well, well, where'd you come from?" she said drunkenly.

"What is your problem?" he said, spittle flying from his lips.

"Apparently, it's that I'm not some basic industry bitch named Lucy." She slurred this, too, spilling more of her drink as she jerked her arm away from Johnny's grasp.

The man at the bar raised his eyebrows and turned away, retreating to his own business.

Johnny's eyes flashed dark. He leaned in close.

"Stop fucking around. Come eat some food so we can get out of here." He turned and stalked outside.

"I didn't want to come here in the first place," she called after him.

Out on the patio, red plastic baskets full of chicken bones and a few sticky wings, crumpled napkins, and little cups of ranch dressing covered the picnic table. Astoria skulked behind Johnny. She dragged a nearby chair to the head of the picnic table, positioning herself between Johnny and Lucy, and plopped into it. The industry girls smirked into their beers.

"Want some wings?" Lucy lifted a basket like a peace offering.

Astoria gave a shitty fake smile and dropped her chin to her shoulder, feigning demure. She picked up her empty margarita glass and sucked loudly on the straw. Lucy balked toward her friends and set the basket back on the table. Johnny stared blankly at Astoria, then shook his head.

Astoria burned, feeling unwelcome while still clinging to obstinance. She forced overtly fake smiles at the industry girls as they prattled on. A voice inside her screamed she deserved to be there. She wanted to stand up, stamp her feet, and holler that she and Johnny were soul mates, that they understood one another in a way nobody else ever would. But she couldn't find the courage, so she chewed on the ice from her drink.

Staring at the baskets of bones and goopy poultry joints littering the table, she realized she hadn't eaten more than a banana for breakfast, and her mouth watered. She could feel the sugary tequila drink going to war with the cesspool of light beer in her stomach.

The patio steamed.

Johnny and his friends laughed at everything the girls said.

Squinting, Astoria gripped the arms of her chair as a vile, sour taste crept up the back of her throat. The cavalry was about to charge.

Instinct told her to run to the bathroom, but choking back that first heave, she looked at the industry girls sitting so close to her and figured they deserved whatever fate the evening might have in store for them. Pressing both hands against the table, Astoria stood, steadying herself against the burn in her eyes and the poison churning up from deep within her belly.

The bile came in a steady stream, like water out of a fire hydrant, except burning poisonous as it surged up her esophagus, shooting out her nose and mouth and washing across the table.

The girls jumped up, screaming in unison, while the stream kept coming. At one point, between rounds, Astoria paused and took account, impressed by how much liquid had erupted from her and was now flowing between the pints of beer, soaking into the napkins. Her refuse dripped between the table boards and washed onto the girls' tan legs while they shrieked and scrambled to climb over the bench.

One of Johnny's friends clenched his lips tight, fighting the urge to wretch, but the volume and the stench overwhelmed him. Trapped on the seat between Johnny and the other bros, he turned, aiming his emittance behind the bench, but ended up puking down the back of the guy sitting next to him.

Wild-eyed, Johnny looked at Astoria like he was ready to wrestle her to the ground and tape her mouth shut if that's what it took to get her to stop vomiting all over his perfect afternoon. She smirked at him, then looked straight at the redhead, who was wiping her legs with a napkin, horror distorting her face. Astoria cleared the corners of her mouth with her forefinger and thumb.

"Looks like it's time to go," she said.

***

Astoria woke by herself, starfished across the mattress in the downstairs bedroom. The alarm clock on the nightstand read 10:45. An accounting of the work she hadn't done the day before flooded her mind. Then she remembered.

The long day at the lake.

The redhead: Lucy.

The scene she'd caused at Hooters.

Her mouth felt like she'd eaten a handful of cat litter. Her guts turned. More than a wicked hangover, she felt an existential awareness that she'd slipped out of orbit and was spiraling farther and farther from this perfect life she was so close to achieving.

Rolling onto her side, she pulled her knees to her chest and closed her eyes against the light. Her head throbbed, and she remembered the looks on the faces of the music industry girls as they raced to escape her projectile bile. She thought of Johnny and how it had felt to watch him, like he was inside a movie, floating in a chocolate milk lake, staring so warmly at the girl named Lucy. More hurt flooded in, along with panic.

How far had it gone?

What was to become of them?

Of her?

How could she show face around Johnny's friends ever again? Would he even allow her the chance?

A lawnmower sputtered to life in the backyard. Johnny was already up and tackling Sunday chores, sweating out his hangover in the backyard, undoubtedly soothing it with another beer for breakfast. She pushed herself upright, but the room spun. Circles of white light flashed behind her eyes. She collapsed back onto the bed. It was going to be a long day.

Having kept down a cup of coffee and a piece of dry toast, she sat on the bed in the downstairs bedroom with her computer on her lap, staring at the screen and fighting the urge to run into the bathroom when another wave of nausea hit.

The sound of water running in the kitchen. A pause. A glass clinked against the sink.

Holding her breath, Astoria listened, trying to telegraph Johnny's movements through the house. From what she could remember, the ride home the night before had been silent. They hadn't spoken a word to one another since.

His footfalls sounded like he was heading toward the front door.

Astoria called out, "Johnny?"

Silence.

Her heart was racing; blood coursed through her ears. She sensed him standing in the living room, waiting. "Can you come in here for a second?"

He appeared in the doorway, annoyance pinching his face. "What?"

Even from ten feet away, she smelled the stench of sour beer oozing from his pores. He always stank of stale beer the mornings after he'd tied one on.

"I'm sorry for last night," she said, her eyes probing his for a connection. "Everything feels out of control."

Stone-faced, he said nothing.

Dropping her shoulders, she sat taller, lengthening her posture. "I'm trying to say I want to take a break from drinking."

"So, stop drinking."

"Well ... I was hoping we'd stop together. A detox break, you know?"

He snorted. "I'm not the one with the problem. I can stop drinking whenever I want."

He turned and stalked away.

The front door slammed shut.

Astoria dropped her face into her hands. Her body shuddered against another bout of nausea.

CHAPTER TWENTY-TWO

Henry Hunter insisted they use his new iPad to present to the mayor. "Email me your presentation," he told Astoria, patting his sleek new tablet. "I'll drive from here."

The company had purchased iPads for select agency members—namely the Creative and Accounts Teams—and they carried the minicomputers from meeting to meeting, unfolding black felt covers from the devices with great pomp and circumstance, furrowing their brows at the screens, tap-tap-tapping with fervor as if about to launch the next shuttle into space.

However, in the mayor's conference room, minutes before their scheduled start time, Henry Hunter couldn't connect his iPad to the public sector's outdated technology. He shook USB cords in their ports and fiddled with remotes while their client—the city employee who had hired them—paced about the room, wringing her hands as the mayor and members of his cabinet exchanged glances. A few minutes turned into ten. Sweating out her lingering hangover, her mind as blank as the projector screen looming over the room, Astoria swallowed against the growing tension.

"We're going to have to wing it," Henry Hunter said under his breath.

Astoria's mouth popped open as she'd never heard him utter such a thing in the two years she'd been at Dixon-Richards.

"Let's use your laptop to present," he said. "I'll follow along on my iPad."

Dumbfounded, she pulled her laptop from her tote. They were now fifteen minutes behind schedule. The recessed lighting burned hot, pulling out little beads of sweat along her hairline. Her MacBook wasn't compatible with any of the outdated plugins, either. She couldn't connect her computer to the internet because of a firewall. As the technical difficulties dragged on, the mayor conferred with an aide. His cell rang, and he took the call.

Face more ashen by the minute, their client flitted from person to person, demanding they surrender their laptops so she could test every port. Someone offered to transfer the presentation to their government-issued machine with a flash drive. After an exchange of directions—*now click on that folder, then click on the file named 'final presentation'*—they loaded the presentation onto a sturdy Hewlett Packard, and the introductory slide flashed on the screen.

Henry Hunter introduced himself, then gave Astoria the floor. He paced to the back of the room, leaned against the wall, and folded his arms. She was on her own.

Astoria faced her audience. She introduced herself, scanning for a smile or encouraging nod, but her audience remained fixated on their laptops, clicking and typing. Sitting at the opposite end, the mayor said something to his aide. Astoria continued.

Throughout the presentation, she fumbled her words and tripped over her thoughts, struggling to draw conclusions from the run-on sentences on the slides. The mayor scrolled through his phone. Someone incessantly clicked a pen. Others nodded along, forcing pained smiles and silently urging her to get it together. After sweating through the first ten slides, she read directly off the last five, flipping through them as fast as possible. A slide saying, "Any Questions?" appeared on the screen, surprising her.

"So, uh, are there any questions?" she stammered.

People exchanged glances; someone scoffed through their nose.

It was over.

She wanted to run from the room, find a balcony, and jump.

"Thank you, Miss Lyons, you've brought us a lot to think about," said the mayor. He swiveled his chair toward the woman who had hired Dixon-Richards. "I expect next time we'll have a clear roadmap for how we will proceed?"

The woman nodded, rapidly explaining the way forward as if her words might erase the dark cloud hanging over the room. Astoria toed the floor, paranoid the stench of shame was seeping from her every pore.

***

At home that night, she nursed a glass of bourbon on the front porch while sweating out her misery.

Heat waves radiated up from Riverside Drive. Cars floated by like mirages, their wheels sounding gooey, as if sticking to the asphalt. Leaves hung limp and withering in the brutal season. Astoria imagined the day, her relationship, her career, her life as thin sheets of rice paper hanging on a line; she saw them incinerating, one by one.

The mechanical jingle of a cell phone startled her from her self-loathing. Assuming it was Henry Hunter calling to read her the riot act after her botched presentation, she left the phone to ring on the arm of the wooden bench and took another sip of bourbon. The liquid was cold, but the alcohol flooded her bloodstream. Immediately, the phone rang again.

"Damnit," she said, grabbing the device, catching herself as she read the name on the screen then answered.

"Ace?"

"Heya, kid."

The last time they'd spoken, she'd been drinking all day with Johnny and his people on the mountain. She'd felt ashamed as she lied to her father, slurring her words and saying life was great. She'd cut the call short. Now, here she was, drinking again and most certainly about to lie again, too.

"How you makin' it down there?" asked Ace. "Fox News says it's one-hundred and seven degrees in Nashville today."

"It's hot."

"How are things between you and Johnny?"

Astoria thought of the empty house and how Johnny had texted earlier to say he was grabbing beers with the guys after work. "They're okay."

"When you gonna bring him home to meet your old man?"

"Soon."

They talked about the haying season and how Ace was helping the neighbors put up their summer crops, and they would help him in return. He asked about work. Choking back tears, she said it was going great, then admitted she'd fumbled her presentation to the mayor.

"I know I can do better," she said.

"Go easy on yourself," said Ace. "The cream always rises. Sometimes, you just gotta work at it until you get it right."

Astoria ended the call. The evening sizzled around her. A cicada whirred in a tree, its electric siren sounding a drawn-out alarm. She held up the tumbler and studied the amber liquid sliding around the ice cubes. Then, in one swift motion, she tossed the drink across the porch railing and onto the grass.

***

After the abysmal meeting with the mayor, she assumed word would spread among the Account Girls, and she'd have to endure their whispers and judgmental glances all summer. But to her surprise, she received an email from Caroline one morning.

"Care to join a few of us for lunch today? We're going to drink margaritas at Chuy's. Meet us in the parking lot at 11:30."

She still felt out of place sitting at the table with the Account Girls as they complained about their clients and waved off the free baskets of chips the waiters offered. She had little to add when the lunchtime chatter shifted to weddings and honeymoons or which neighborhoods had the most idyllic starter homes, but Astoria smiled and nodded politely, grateful to her peers for the invitation and their grace.

A week later, Lexi invited Astoria to a crawfish boil at her newlywed home, a renovated historic Craftsman in the Twelve-South Neighborhood. Johnny had gone to see his family for the weekend, so Astoria went alone.

She'd wanted to mingle among the men in pastel polo shirts and khaki shorts, the women floating about in breezy sundresses, but found herself lingering on the periphery, uncertain what to do with her hands and shifting insecurely from foot to foot as the other guests laughed and drank in clusters around a crystalline blue swimming pool. After forcing a smile for one hour and consuming one beer, she skirted the crowd, making her way toward a gate in the fence. Lexi appeared from out of nowhere, placing a dainty hand on Astoria's arm.

"You're not leaving so soon?" she asked, sincerity in her voice.

"Oh, I-uh, I need to get back to work. We're presenting to the mayor again in a week, and it's make-or-break at this point."

Lexi scrunched her mouth into a little pout and leaned in as if to share a secret. "I heard you suffered a bit of a flop the first time around. But you have another shot, right?"

Astoria's cheeks flushed. They'd known all along. She nodded. "Thank you again for having me, Lexi. Your home is lovely."

"You must come again. We love to entertain."

Driving home across the broiling city, Astoria sweated as the air conditioning fought to keep up with the heat. She rolled down the windows and, with hot air funneling around her, focused on what she wanted to accomplish. Determined to redeem herself with the mayor, she'd returned to those long, sober evenings working from home. Night after night, with Nashville Public Television on mute and Duke snuggled next to her, she'd perfected the roadmap the mayor had requested. Johnny rarely came home after work, so she ate turkey sandwiches over her laptop and sipped unsweet iced tea by the gallon. The idea of failing again lingered at the front of her mind, motivating her to stay focused and prove herself this time. She couldn't help but wonder why she'd been so quick to throw it all away for one disastrous day on the lake.

***

Back in the marbled hallways of Nashville City Hall, Astoria focused on her breathing in the conference room where she'd first bombed. Her PowerPoint presentation glowed on the massive screen. For four counts, she inhaled through her nose, then exhaled through her mouth, steadying her mind on how she wanted the meeting to go. It was three o'clock.

"The mayor will be here at three-thirty," the client said, clutching her pearls near the door.

Astoria nodded. "Perfect." Keep breathing, she told herself.

"Ready?" Henry Hunter stepped next to her, his posture and energy as rigid as the stick Astoria assumed remained full-time lodged up his ass. He checked his cufflinks.

"Just like we practiced," she said.

"Let's do our work justice this time, shall we?"

The mayor was thirty minutes late. Astoria figured it was payback for the disastrous previous meeting, but she remained unshaken. The second the mayor assumed his throne at the head of the table, she didn't wait for the other suits to look up. Instead, she clapped her hands and started in.

"Good afternoon," she said, voice steady, projecting confidence. "It's nice to see you again. We have our executive summary of research to share today. More importantly, we have a roadmap for how the city can successfully engage its stakeholders, per your request."

She didn't look at her slides as she spoke. Merely clicked the remote, maintained eye contact with every person seated around the table, and offered her perspective with genuine enthusiasm. For thirty minutes, Astoria held the room. The men and women in blue suits took notes and nodded along as she spoke.

"If we allocate budget for these recommendations, would your agency be able to handle the work?" the mayor asked.

"We're ready when you are," she said.

"This is your day," Henry Hunter told her as they rode the elevator to the parking garage. He straightened his cufflinks again, his face stoic. Astoria beamed at the ground. She wanted to pump her fists and whoop victoriously but nodded modestly instead.

"I worked hard for this," she said. "It feels good."

CHAPTER TWENTY-THREE

Fall 2010

Labor Day gave way to crisp mornings and golden afternoons. The earth exhaled, its cool evening breezes softening the memories of the brutal southern summer. As if in celebration, trees burst into red, orange, and green swaths across the quaint neighborhoods where Nashvillians spent their evenings on front porches, waving at neighbors and carrying themselves with joyful ease, having survived that burning season.

Following Astoria's final presentation to the mayor, the city awarded Dixon-Richards an extended contract, positioning the agency to meet its revenue goals for the year.

They threw a party at the office.

In his speech to the agency, Henry Hunter commended Astoria for her efforts and the Creative Team's contributions, having designed the PowerPoint presentation. This sort of thing would have set Astoria off in the past, but she smirked at the silliness of it all. She'd made herself proud.

Riding the momentum of success, Astoria poured herself into her job. It was good timing, she decided, as Johnny's firm had projects lined up out the door, and he spent many nights at The Palm for work dinners.

"I'd love to join," she said. "I'll just listen in; it would be great research."

He snorted through his nose. "Nothing we discuss is even remotely relevant to marketing."

They made love occasionally, which Astoria didn't mind. She worked, exercised, attended happy hours with her own cohorts and clients, and relished her quiet time at home with Duke when Johnny was gone to the mountain on the weekends. She told herself she and Johnny had settled into the dependable rhythm of an established relationship.

Still, she worried. Every day, she worried.

The tide had gone out on their date nights; they never went out together. Rarely ate dinner or watched the Antiques Roadshow on Monday nights. She traipsed downstairs in the mornings and poured her own coffee. Read herself to sleep most nights, alone in their bed.

To rekindle their fire, she solicited the *Nashville Scene's* concert calendar for something fun they might do as a couple. Their favorite bluegrass band was playing at the Station Inn on an upcoming Saturday night.

"Can we go?" she asked Johnny.

"Sure," he said, "if nothing else is going on."

"It's a date."

***

When the day of the concert arrived, Astoria leaned against the bathroom door frame while Johnny smoothed two fingers across the mustache he'd been growing as he studied himself in the mirror. He'd been out at the bars the night before; Astoria had been asleep when he got home. Over coffee, he announced he was going to the Vanderbilt football game with some buddies. Now he leaned closer to the glass, inspecting both sides of his face.

"What time will you be home?" she asked.

"Dunno." Without looking at her, he turned and squeezed past, fleeing into the living room. She followed close behind.

"We're still going to the concert tonight, right?"

"Oh," he said, realization flashed across his face, revealing he'd forgotten. "Yeah. I mean, if I get back in time."

"The game is at noon," Astoria said, speaking slowly while her mind raced. "We won't need to get to the Station Inn until five or six. Can you make it happen?"

Johnny zipped himself into an all-weather vest.

"Johnny," Astoria said, searching him with pleading eyes. "Are we going to the concert or not?"

"I said yeah, if I get back in time. I swear to God, Astoria, you get fixated on shit like a damn rabid dog and you don't let go."

"We've been talking about going for weeks."

"But I never said I was going for sure."

Dumbfounded, her mouth hung open and her mind tripped over everything they had discussed regarding the concert.

"I'm going to be late," Johnny said. He kissed her dryly on the forehead as he breezed toward the door. "I'll keep ya posted."

It was nine o'clock.

Astoria drank more coffee and scrolled Facebook. She cleaned the kitchen. Swept the floors. Pieced together an outfit to wear to the concert. All the while, her mind fired like a pinball machine. She decided a walk would quell the panic she felt rising inside of her.

The sky was blinding blue, the air cool. Straining against his leash, Duke pulled Astoria down East Nashville's broken sidewalks to Shelby Bottoms. Astoria realized every day could be great if she didn't have to battle a hangover. Despite feeling great physically, she worried about how little time she and Johnny had spent together the past few months.

Could their relationship sustain divergent lifestyles? Maybe couples were happy to live like this. After all, variety is the spice of life. Surely, he saw how hard she was working. Surely, he saw she could learn to handle her booze and be a better person. Surely, he still loved her.

These thoughts spun around her mind as she dropped into Shelby Bottoms Greenway. She walked past the turnout where they'd parked the night they trekked across the golf course and took in the Broadway lights. They'd invested so much time in one another. *Wasn't that worth something?*

The sun was on the downhill slide of its arc when Duke refused to go any further, imploring Astoria with tired eyes.

"You ready to turn back?"

The dog plodded off the trail and collapsed in a patch of shade.

"Gonna be a long walk home if I have to carry you," she said. Duke rested his head on his paws. "Okay, we can rest for a minute. We've been out for a while. Johnny will probably be waiting for us when we get home."

On the return trip, Duke stopped every quarter-of-a-mile to lie down and rest, each time glancing up at Astoria as if to say, *what's the rush?*

"No rush," she admitted, allowing the dog his time, hoping the rest breaks would compound and move the day along so Johnny's game and time with the guys would be old news by the time she and Duke dragged themselves across the threshold.

But when they shuffled up to the cottage on Riverside Drive, Johnny's truck wasn't in the driveway. Astoria's pulse sounded in her ears. It was four o'clock.

She showered, then decided on a nap, imagining Johnny would come home and tease her for sleeping the day away. She crawled into bed in the downstairs bedroom. Duke jumped up next to her, spun in three tight circles, and dropped into the crook of her legs. They fell asleep; the day fading around them.

She woke, disoriented in the darkness. For a moment, it felt like she was spinning through the deepest pocket of the universe, weightless and placeless and irrelevant. Her mind turned over like a stubborn engine while she blinked, finally realizing she was home, having rested in the downstairs bedroom, and she'd been waiting all day to hear from Johnny. Eyes adjusted, she registered the outline of Duke's knobby head, mere inches from hers. The house was quiet; empty. It was late.

She checked her phone. Six o'clock. No new texts.

The door at the Station Inn would be open by now. Cash in hand, people would be waiting in line, excited for the show, talking about the lead singer and how amazing he was, and how they couldn't believe he didn't have a big record label deal.

Astoria typed out a text.

—Are we going to the concert?

She hit send.

Phone in-hand, she slipped out of bed and floated through the house, turning on lights, then the television, willing the place back to life in hopes the brightness and noise would drive out the sense of desperation swallowing her whole.

Two hours later, Johnny replied.

—Doesn't look like it.

She called him.

No answer.

She swallowed hard, then called again.

Still no answer.

Tears spilled from her eyes.

—That's all I get?

He texted back immediately.

—Yep.

The panic she'd been avoiding all day was crashing down around her, knocking time out of its rhythm and gravity off its weighted plane. The house she loved as her home, its yellow-painted walls, the bed upstairs where she and Johnny had first made love, all the forks and plates and wine glasses they'd touched over meals and conversations and lingering stares, the couch where they'd laughed and napped and dined—all objects and space and associated meaning were floating in disarray amongst the lies she'd told herself this was her way forward, that if she just worked hard enough, she could make it all work and make something of herself, too.

Choking on her sobs, she clutched her phone to her mouth and wailed. Stumbling to the liquor cabinet, she spun the cap off a bottle of vodka, then took a long pull. The clear liquid burned as it snaked down her throat. She dragged a wrist across her snotty nose and blubbered some more. Still holding her phone, she called the only person she could think to reach out to.

"Astoria Lyons. Whachu doin' calling me on a Saturday night?" Anna Mae's accent came through thick as Mississippi mud, a load dose of relief against the onslaught of panic.

"I—I'm so sorry to bother you."

"Oh, honey. What is wrong? Are you okay?"

"No." Talking through her tears, Astoria explained about the game, the concert, how things hadn't been going so great, the redhead named Lucy, how Johnny had not come home.

"That sonofabitch. Where are you?"

"At the house."

"Well, shoot. I'm down in Oxford for the weekend."

Astoria apologized again for disturbing Anna Mae's evening.

"I wish I was there. I'd come and get you in a heartbeat. But you cannot stay in that house, you understand me?"

"Yes."

"Do you have a girlfriend you can stay with?"

"Not since Evie left." The thought of losing her friend made Astoria cry harder.

"Listen to me. Get you a hotel room. Do you have enough for one night?"

"I think so."

"Let me call around and see what I can't do. Okay?"

Astoria whimpered. "Okay."

"What kind of bottle are you drinking out of?" Anna Mae asked.

"Vodka," Astoria said, mostly surprised but also a little ashamed Anna Mae had so accurately profiled the situation.

"Well, don't drink the whole thing. That'll only make it worse."

***

An online search revealed that the La Quinta Inn by the airport had rooms for $79 a night. Astoria shoved her laptop and the bottle of vodka into her tote, then drove straight to the hotel to check-in.

"You okay, honey?" asked the woman working the desk. She wore a blue polyester shirt with pink flowers on it, reminding Astoria of the wallpaper her mother had pasted to her bedroom walls when she was a child.

"No," Astoria said, offering her debit card. "I just need a safe place to cry for a night."

"You're safe here," the woman said. Instead of taking the card, she took Astoria's wrist in her warm, crepe-skinned hand and gave it a little squeeze. "Our rooms are clean and cheap, and you can cry as loud as you need to."

Astoria sniffled over a laugh. "Thank you."

Sitting cross-legged on the hotel bed, Astoria took another pull from her dwindling vodka supply and called Johnny one more time. It was 12:45 a.m. To her surprise, he answered. Music thumped through the earpiece, revealing the party happening around him, but Johnny waited, silent.

"Where are you?" Astoria's words echoed in the empty room.

"I'm out," he said, barely audible.

She waited.

"Why are you doing this to me?"

Forever, she waited.

"Are you at least coming home?" she asked.

"Not tonight," he said, his voice slicing through the airwaves now.

The line went dead.

Astoria slid off the bed and onto her hands and knees on the floor, where she sobbed and dry-heaved and screamed. Someone in the next room banged against the wall. Raising onto her knees, Astoria threw her phone toward the sound of the fist and wailed against the cruel pain consuming her. Hot tears streaming down her face, she pulled herself back onto the bed, grabbed the vodka bottle from the nightstand, and chugged the last of its contents before collapsing into darkness.

***

In the morning, after vomiting the previous night's vodka dinner into the toilet, Astoria staggered out to the single-dose coffee maker on the desk. Hands shaking, she ripped open the coffee pod. While the little machine gurgled, she poked her head through curtains and met the new day. Church traffic floated down Briley Parkway, slow and soothingly steady. She thought of all the nights

Johnny had spent out at Five Points. The late-night texts pinging his cell phone. The redhead from the lake. How much effort it took for her to endure those long weekends on the mountain with Johnny's family.

What did I think was going to happen?

She'd arranged her life in a neat little line. Established a relationship with a man who had figured out how to balance his rural upbringing with life in the modern world. Was on the cusp of achieving success with her career. Had a closet full of pretty dresses, a nice home, parties to attend, and someone to come home to at the end of every day.

Recalling the heartless tenor of Johnny's voice on the phone the night before, she was about to take her first sip of coffee when someone knocked on the door, startling Astoria from her thoughts.

"Housekeeping."

The alarm clock by the bed read twelve-thirty. Checkout was at 11:00.

Hastily, she dressed, shoved the empty vodka bottle into the trash bin, gathered her phone and tote, and opened the door. Two women waited in the hallway: one tall and broad-shouldered, the other small and round. They wore their hair back in tight, efficient buns, the smell of laundry detergent wafting off their crisp blue uniforms. Astoria ducked past the women, mumbling an apology as she dragged her hangover out into the day.

Back on Riverside Drive, the air inside the home was cold and stale. Standing in the living room, Astoria waited for the silence to tell her something when she heard a rustling in the bathroom. She crept into the hallway, reached out, and pushed open the bathroom door. Johnny sat with his back to the wall, arm draped around the toilet bowl, bead bobbing up and down. Daylight streamed through the window behind him, leaving his face in shadows.

"What happened?" she asked.

Johnny looked up at her, revealing a sick grimace, as if everything was funny, or might somehow turn laughable someday, although his blonde mustache hanging limp and sad around his mouth conveyed otherwise. A gurgle issued from deep in his throat, and he shot forward, retching into the toilet. After finishing, he leaned back against the wall and winced.

"Are you okay?"

He closed his eyes and shook his head no.

"Are we over?" Her voice ticked high, betraying her desire to sound unbroken.

He nodded yes, then leaned forward again, his face disappearing as he vomited into the bowl.

Her car was suddenly the only place she could exist that was hers. Sobbing, she drove around East Nashville, the road blurring through her tears as waves of rejection crashed over her, her mind racing across all her failed efforts. Dragging a wrist across the snot pooling on her upper lip, she choked out one more sob then forced a deep inhale: she needed to plot her next move, so she drove toward Bongo Java, the coffee shop at Five Points with free Wi-Fi.

After parking, she wailed some more into the steering wheel. A young man happening past bent down and rapped on her window, asking if she needed help. Shaking her head no, she waved him on, the blip of embarrassment spurring her to pull it together: get coffee, eat food, make a plan.

She climbed out of the car, slammed the door behind her, and squinted against the sun, scanning the neighborhood as if the light of day might reveal something of the previous night's sins.

The bars had opened their doors to the Sunday crowd, those midday risers seeking to soothe their hangovers from the night before with greasy food and a strong cocktail. Astoria pictured Johnny smoking a cigarette at a high-top table inside Three Crow, laughing through the haze and staring across a table with his deep brown eyes at the redhead before they stumbled down the sidewalk with their arms wrapped around one another to Red Door, where they would have drank some more and laughed into one another's necks before leaving together. *And then where'd they go?*

Shuddering against all the possible answers, she turned toward Bongo Java. A tall, gaunt man with midnight skin bearing layers of shabby clothes eyed her as he loped down the street in a pair of house slippers, thin as onion skins. A single tooth punctuated his wide, mad grin, and his stark white hair stood on end like he'd been electrocuted. The man slowed as he drew near. Astoria expected him to ask for money or a cup of coffee. Instead, he lifted his cracked palms toward the sky, tipped his head back, then snapped it forward, dipping his face close to hers.

"You cain't quit Jesus!" he screamed, the high-pitched proclamation floating up and over Five Points like a murder of crows.

Astoria stepped back as if forced by a gust of wind.

The man laughed and staggered sideways, then pranced jauntily down the street.

Her phone was ringing in her bag.

With the oracle's message still clanging in her ears, she fished for the device while turning in the direction the man had gone, but he was nowhere to be seen. She looked up and down the empty street once more, then checked her phone. An unknown number with a 615-area code flashed across the screen.

"Hello?"

"Astoria Lyons?"

"Yes."

"This is Martha Cline. I'm an old friend of Anna Mae's. She says you're looking for a place to rent?"

"I—uhm—yes, I think I am."

"I have a place that just came open. It's one side of a duplex in Lockeland Springs. I usually sub-let on short-term agreements to musicians and the like, but Anna Mae says you might be interested in something longer? Rent is eight hundred and fifty dollars a month, and I'd love if you could commit to a year lease. Can you make a deposit covering the first and last month's rent?"

A siren sounded in her mind. The down payment would clean her out. She'd have to return to surviving off pretzels, Diet Coke, and mealy apples from the office.

"I can cover that," she said.

"Then I won't run your credit score. And what about furniture? Anna Mae said you might could use some help?"

Astoria winced at the familiar sting of shame for not having enough, not *being* enough, but in the presence of this stranger's kindness, she summoned the strength to own her truth.

"I gotta tell you, Martha Cline, I need *a lot* of help."

"Oh, honey. Don't we all?" Martha Cline laughed. "You'll help me by taking some furniture off my hands. You wouldn't believe what people leave behind in my rentals—some of these kids must have rich parents. I rented an apartment to a girl who worked in the music industry, and she left an embroidered white couch and matching chairs. Beautiful, but they're crowding up my storage unit. If you can haul them, they're yours."

A car approached. Still clutching the phone to her ear, Astoria stepped out of the street and onto the sidewalk. The crystalline sky was sharpening to blue overhead while the day unfolded around her, bristling with risk, opportunity, sadness, and hope—whatever she chose to make of it.

CHAPTER TWENTY-FOUR

Winter 2010

In the weeks between Johnny breaking up and Astoria moving out, they orbited around one another in the cottage on Riverside Drive like the sun and the moon, Duke pacing anxiously from room to room.

When it came time to move into her new place, Johnny agreed to help haul her belongings from his house, along with Martha Cline's secondhand furniture, to her new duplex apartment in Lockeland Springs.

"Whatever we can do to expedite the process," Astoria said.

"Don't make it ugly," said Johnny.

They stared each other down. She wanted to ask him why; she wanted him to tell her what the redhead had that she didn't.

"It's already ugly," Astoria said. "Let's just get it over with."

"You're the one who is moving out," said Johnny.

"Because *you* said we were over, Johnny. Don't you remember?"

Ever since the night Johnny hadn't come home, Astoria replayed the sequence of events over and over in her mind, wondering how many of the details she'd exacerbated and whether they'd still be together if she hadn't peppered him with questions while he was vomiting into the toilet. She agonized over the role she'd played in the demise of their relationship until it felt like her brain had turned inside out.

"Guess it doesn't matter now," he said.

"How convenient." Astoria wanted to press the issue—ask him why he was spinning the truth and messing with her head. But she needed him to help her move, so she let it go.

***

Lockeland Springs was an upscale historic area of East Nashville where pristinely refurbished Craftsman homes nestled behind manicured lawns, wispy gardens, and wrought iron fences.

It was a quintessential American neighborhood. During the warmer months, neighbors basked on their front porches in the heady evenings, sipping cocktails and chatting while children colored the sidewalks with neon chalk. Even in the dead of winter, parents walked groups of children to the nearby school every morning, the wee ones bundled up in thick coats and brightly colored hats, their bright chatter imparting a sense of nostalgic optimism and goodness Astoria realized she'd never seen except in movies.

She moved into the east-facing unit of Martha Cline's duplex, in an old Craftsman house that had been flipped into two dwellings. The apartment was laid out shotgun-style, with the living room leading to the dining room and kitchen, and a little hallway leading to the bathroom and bedroom in the back. A musty smell seeped up from the basement when it rained or the humidity ran high, but Astoria didn't mind.

She clustered the furniture from Martha Cline in a close grouping in her living room and covered the walls with concert posters she swiped from bulletin boards in bars across town, imparting a bohemian vibe in a space she quickly fell in love with because it was all hers. In the afternoons, golden sunlight poured through the tall windows. Astoria sat cross-legged on the floor, basking in the warmth of the slanted, shimmery rays, letting the light wash over her while praying it was still within her and that she might still make something of herself.

The rational part of her brain knew why her relationship with Johnny didn't work, but her heart remained broken, her ego bruised. Beyond work, she spent her time licking her wounds in solitude, losing hours scrolling Facebook and sleeping away her weekends. After a few weeks of grieving, she forced herself to get out of the house and take a walk one afternoon instead of zoning out in front of the television.

She began taking a different route every day after work, studying the beautiful homes as she strolled, eyeing the neighbors who greeted one another as they came and went, seemingly having bonded over the shared trait of having kids. Astoria waved cordially from the other side of the street, then carried on while the locals leaned in, whispering to one another, inquiring who was the new girl always walking around the neighborhood.

She settled into a disciplined routine, cooking sweet potatoes, broccoli, and chicken legs for dinner on weeknights and saving the leftovers for lunch the next day. She stopped drinking at home and turned down invitations to happy hours at work. Feeling a resurgence of energy and mental clarity, she read herself to sleep at night and jogged around Shelby Bottoms in the mornings.

Instead of shopping or drinking on the weekends, she pulled out her writing notebooks and revisited the idea for the novel she'd tinkered with when she first moved to town. After plotting the outline on index cards, she spread them across her dining room floor. Sunlight danced across the ink and paper. Kneeling over the cards in the light, she took in the meager room around her and felt the peace of a simple life. She was carrying her rent and covering her bills and had next to nothing at the end of each paycheck, but there was freedom in living lean and clean.

***

After securing the contract with the mayor's office, the agency went on a winning streak with new business. More work allowed them to hire more people on the Creative and Video teams—newcomers Henry Hunter recruited from Chicago and New York. This fresh batch of agency kids was talented and aggressive. They challenged the Account Girls to step up and do their jobs, and even though they reported to Captain Hollywood, they went toe-to-toe with him in meetings, questioning his direction and pushing him for rationale.

"Why would we produce a long-form commercial when we can make a series of thirty-second YouTube spots for less money?" asked a junior associate creative director.

"Because I'm the goddamned Creative Director, and I said so." Captain Hollywood slammed a fist on the conference room table, then rose from his chair, kicking it backward and swiping his leather-bound notebook off the desk in a single motion. He stomped out of the room. Those remaining at the table looked at one another, eyes wide, then burst into laughter once Captain Hollywood was out of earshot.

These new co-workers invited Astoria out on the weekends. It had been cleansing to practice such rigid discipline across those first months alone, but loneliness had seeped into the long days of solitude in her apartment, and she figured she deserved to have a little fun.

The Video Guys ran with this new crowd, too; they gathered in smoke-filled dive bars like the Edgefield to watch SEC football, shoot pool, or throw darts, drinking until day blurred into night, and their little posse scattered like spiders to other bars, bedrooms, or parts unknown.

Astoria drank too much and subsequently overspent on these nights out, feeling carefree and having fun as part of the crowd. She began splurging on groceries because, *fuck it*, it felt good. Bought new shift dresses. Savored the dopamine high of carrying a shopping bag out the sparkling glass doors of a retail store. Resumed skipping her student loan payments, dragging her cell-phone bill past payment until shutoff. After a few months of falling back into these bad habits, Sallie Mae started calling again. Astoria had been down this road before—something needed to change.

***

Astoria glanced up from her laptop to see Henry Hunter, Captain Hollywood, and two juniors from the Creative Team saunter onto the floor, slapping each other on the back and laughing. They were returning from an afternoon at the shooting range with one of the agency's new clients. Apparently, shooting guns was the new version of playing golf for relationship-building activities. Astoria hadn't mentioned she'd been handling firearms since Ace had prepared her for a hunter's safety course when she was in the fourth grade. She knew Henry Hunter and Captain Hollywood would find such information threatening, and it wouldn't buy her an invitation anyway, so she kept her mouth shut.

Astoria's performance review with Henry Hunter was in three days. Her stomach twisted as he wrapped an arm around Captain Hollywood's shoulders, squeezing him like they'd won the

Panhellenic ass-grabbing championship. Seeking distraction, she fired up the Tinder app on her iPhone.

Online dating was a fun distraction at first—something to keep her from moping around her apartment, wondering what Johnny was doing, or worse, driving by his house after being out at the bars all night. But the Tinder dates proved interesting at best. Young men bought her dinner and asked about her interests. One invited her to attend church with him for their second outing. She declined. Another asked if she wanted to hook up after their first encounter over beers.

She accepted this offer.

After they finished at his apartment, she dressed silently and left, her body feeling empty and her emotions numb, knowing she'd never text or see him again.

She went home and deleted the app, only to reinstall it a few weeks later after spotting Johnny driving around East Nashville with Lucy, the redhead, riding shotgun in his truck. Online dating was a helpful distraction from those haunting questions about how she'd failed to achieve the perfect life with Johnny. Window shopping on her phone for dates even allowed her to tune out Captain Hollywood in meetings. He would fly off on one of his tirades while she swiped left, left, left, right, left, right.

In one Tinder profile, a big-bellied white boy in a UT baseball cap held a fish up to the camera—*swipe left*. In another, an olive-skinned man wearing a pinstripe suit, his long hair slicked back, held his hand over his heart, smiling in a way he intended to be charming. *Swipe left.* In yet another profile, a black guy posed in his bathroom mirror, his selfie exposing all he had to offer south of his washboard abs, his face hidden behind an orb of white from the flash. Astoria swiped left on that one, too. But she swiped right and matched with a guy from Alabama. He was a blonde, clean-cut, stocky man in his mid-30s. His profile said he liked college football, his family, Jesus, and he worked in real estate.

For their date, they met at Dino's, a hipster dive on Gallatin Road. Astoria arrived five minutes late, bursting through the front door, her heart jackhammering in her ears. She spotted her date standing at the bar; he'd already ordered a beer. She tapped him on the shoulder, said his name, and when he turned around, she flashed her best *look how fun and dynamic I am* smile. He gave her a casual side-hug; he smelled of leather and vanilla.

They stole glances at one another from across a chipped Formica table. Christmas lights flashed around the windows. A life-size cardboard cutout of Dolly Parton grinned down from the wall. Astoria folded a napkin in half, finding eye contact awkward but listening intently as the Alabama man told her about his big family and how he was staunchly conservative but not racist.

"I'm into all kinds," he said, laughing.

Something about the comment gave Astoria pause. "And you work in real estate?" she asked.

"Sort of. I sell manufactured homes. It's easier to say real estate."

She flagged the half-truth for later examination. She was tired of men who were too weak to handle their truth.

After drinking three beers each and sharing a basket of fries, they stepped out into the cooling night.

"You're alright," he said, watching his yellow cab pull up to the curb. Turning to face Astoria, he grasped her forearm, pulled her into him, and kissed her. His mouth was hot on hers; the kiss was electric and wet.

"Let's hang out again," he said before slipping into the cab.

The date went well, Astoria decided while dabbing moisture cream around her eyes and getting ready for bed. But something nagged at her as she continued texting with the Alabama guy throughout the week.

He texted one night while Astoria was brushing her teeth:

—So, are you into anything?

—You mean tonight? Nah. Getting ready for bed.

—That wasn't what I meant ...

Silencing her phone, she placed it face down on the nightstand she'd scored from Goodwill and climbed beneath the covers, pulling her duvet over her head. She'd already made plans to meet the Alabama boy again the following evening; the thought floated like a loose balloon across her mind all night.

The next day, he texted around lunchtime. Astoria was eating an apple and a bag of potato chips at her desk.

—One thing I should tell you before we hang out again. I have sex with men. I'm not gay. I just like how it feels.

Apple in one hand, she gawked at her phone in the other. Like an eighth-grade girl with a hot secret, she scanned the office, wanting to run and show somebody the text, but Evie was long gone. She had no one to confide in. After a moment, she realized the man's admission wasn't hers to share, anyway. She responded:

—Thank you for being upfront and honest. You seem like a good person, and I enjoyed hanging out, but we're on different paths. I wish you the best.

*****

At home that night, she stood before her fridge, peering in at the empty shelves, when her phone sounded with another text.
Ping!

Worrying it might be the Alabama guy following up to tell her she was small-minded and prude, she pulled her phone from the back pocket of her jeans.

Johnny.

—Cold beers and fried pickles sound good right about now.

The fridge hummed, its door hanging open.

Clutching the phone in both hands, she held it close to her face and typed her response.

—Where do you want to meet?

CHAPTER TWENTY-FIVE

Tall oak trees galloped against the darkening sky outside the conference room windows—a storm was brewing. The scene reminded Astoria of an old-timey cartoon from her youth, where black-and-white trees danced and sang behind a big-eyed girl who was running from a creepy, old, bearded man, and the forest animals saved the girl in the end.

She waited alone at the oversized table, wondering how many people had been involved in the creation, production, and approval of those weird old cartoons as the first rain of fall spattered across the glass.

Henry Hunter burst into the room, projecting his usual air of supreme busyness. Jaw set, he marched to the chair opposite Astoria, dropped a thick file of papers onto the desk, sat, stretched his lips into a thin smile, and launched into it.

"Astoria Lyons, remind me who hired you."

"Anna Mae Alcott," she said.

"Ah, yes." He flipped open the file and scanned its contents, methodically turning each page over before examining the next. "And you've been with the company for how long?"

"Just over two years." She leaned forward to try and get a peek at what he was reading.

"Why didn't you receive a review last year?"

"Because you were out of town, and we never rescheduled."

"Ah," said Henry Hunter, doubtfully arching his brow.

Astoria dropped her shoulders and sat taller to appear more confident.

"You started as our social media person?" asked Henry Hunter.

"Correct."

"But then you shifted into more of a digital strategist role."

"That's right. When Anna Mae left, you offered me that opportunity."

"But it was a new role for you, yes?"

"Right."

"Who has mentored you in that role over these past couple of years?"

Astoria froze, unsure what he was getting at.

"You might say I've been learning as I go. I took Google Analytics and AdWords courses. And I'm interested in taking a 4A's course in digital brand strategy up in New York. That's something I was hoping to talk to you about today."

"We can get to that." Henry Hunter tapped the papers back into the manila folder. "First, let's discuss compensation. Are you expecting a raise?"

The question caught Astoria by surprise. She had intended to ask for a raise but wanted to highlight her contributions to the agency first. He'd gotten the jump on her.

"I was hoping we could discuss my salary," she said, speaking slowly, deliberately, sensing he was playing an angle. "I've helped the new business team bring in three new accounts this past year, and my efforts with the mayor's project led to a retainer—"

"Let me stop you right there." Henry Hunter's mouth turned up slightly at the corners, and his eyes narrowed. "Miss Lyons, I know you've been working on building relationships with the team here, but I still get feedback that you can be difficult to work with. And frankly, I saw it firsthand with the mayor's project."

"Difficult, *how*?" she asked, her voice pitching high.

"Right there." Henry Hunter pointed at her. "It's your tone."

"You're telling me the tone of my voice is why I'm difficult to work with?"

He gestured toward the manila file. "The fact of the matter is, Miss Lyons, you're not worth more money. You need to build rapport with your team, not to mention work on your presentation skills ..."

Shame roared through Astoria's mind, drowning out Henry Hunter's words. Somewhere in the oceanic recesses of her psyche, a bell tolled. She tried to stop the thought from coming, but it surged forward, and the memory of the professor telling her she wasn't enough docked right into her cerebrum before she even realized it was in port. Fat alligator tears flooded her eyes; she blinked against them with all her might, but they fell anyway.

"You needn't react like this," said Henry Hunter, pursing his lips.

Astoria pressed her fingertips to her temples, inhaled deep, then chuckled on the exhale.

"It's all so absurd," she said, wiping at her tears. "All of it. That I am even here is absurd." She slumped back in her chair and threw her up hands, choking on another laugh. "But at least you're honest. At least nobody is left guessing. Turns out, I should have just planned my wedding at my desk for the past year. I mean, I would have gotten farther faster by doing less, right?"

"Why, Miss Lyons," said Henry Hunter, the smirk creeping back across his face. "I didn't realize you were getting married."

***

Wide awake in bed at three-thirty in the morning, she stared at the street outside her bedroom window. For the hundredth time, she thought about how confident she'd felt going into her meeting with Henry Hunter, locked and loaded with proof points for why she deserved more—more money, a more prestigious title, more respect.

But he'd been ready.

Ever the opponent, it seemed like he'd planned the entire encounter, like he knew Astoria had worked hard and thought the world owed her something in return. Like he'd been waiting for the opportunity to show her the world didn't owe her a thing.

Astoria propped her pillows against the wall behind her and pushed herself upright. Outside, the street sat empty, pensive, as if waiting to see how she would choose to respond.

How do I beat this? she wondered. *How do I flip this whole thing on its head and turn this pain into a win?*

Instead of hating Henry Hunter, she considered perhaps she owed him a bit of gratitude. No matter how many hours, nights, or weekends she dedicated to some corporate job, the world didn't care and would never care—it was just a stupid job. Henry Hunter was showing her she could give everything to Corporate America, and it would never fully reciprocate, just like Johnny had shown her that even love doesn't owe you anything in return.

She realized it was a fool's plight to give everything to a job or even a relationship and expect the same amount of energy or reward in return. She pondered what her life might look like if she reinvested her time and energy into things that made her feel happy, alive, free. Sliding her pillows off the wall, she lay down again, closed her eyes, and imagined traveling the world with nothing but a backpack, free from the weight of shift dresses and heels. She envisioned writing stories for adventure magazines, returning home after time abroad, spending time in her forests and fields, having dinners with Ace, volunteering at the local Elks in her hometown.

Doubt flooded her mind, causing her to question how she might afford to live so unconventionally, how she might make money as a writer, *how, how, how, how, how?* Shaking her head against the onslaught of questions, she inhaled deeply, then imagined all the questions flying out of her brain like bats, disappearing into the darkness.

For now, it was the ultimate fantasy—a counter-lifestyle to the corporate grind—and she floated on this vision of freedom and fulfillment until sleep found her once again.

***

She gave it a couple of days. Smiled pleasantly at her co-workers waiting for coffee in the mornings. Nodded agreeably with the Creatives in meetings, offering no alternative ideas or opinions. Laughed along with the Account Girls. Entered her timecard at the end of every day. Marched in and out of the office like a good soldier.

Henry Hunter caught her in the hallway as the team filed out of a meeting one afternoon. "Ms. Lyons, you seem to be having a good day," he said.

"Why not?" She flashed her most disingenuous smile and walked on.

Two weeks after Henry Hunter had tried to define her worth with his words, Astoria arrived at the office at 8:30 a.m., knowing only the finance and HR folks would be around.

Sure enough, the HR Director was perched at her desk behind stacks of manila folders. A bright blue sky glowed through the window behind her. Astoria knocked.

"Astoria Lyons, what a surprise! What can I help you with this morning? I'm sorry I never have more time to connect with you, especially after Anna Mae left, but I guess that's been a while."

Astoria entered and sat on the edge of a chair while the Director wrote the date and Astoria's name on the top of a yellow notepad.

"I'm here to give my notice," Astoria said.

"Oh?" The HR director shoved her glasses up the bridge of her nose and blinked behind her thick lenses. "Do you have another offer?"

"No." Astoria summoned the line she'd decided on. "I want to keep growing my skill set and build my confidence, but I'm looking for a different environment."

The HR Director tapped her pen on her notepad, then leveled her eyes at Astoria. "Does this have anything to do with certain members of the Creative Team?"

Astoria froze, wondering if the HR lead had received other complaints about Captain Hollywood and his cronies or if the complaints had been *from* Captain Hollywood *about* Astoria.

"I feel like my time here has come," Astoria continued, speaking slowly. "I'm proud of how I've helped the business development team bring in new accounts ..." She rattled off her contributions to the company, the same ones she'd prepared for Henry Hunter.

"Your contributions haven't gone unnoticed. You are a valued employee here."

"Yes," Astoria countered, "but there is a disparity between being *told* that I'm valued and being shown ... and I don't feel like I can bridge that gap. It feels like the healthiest thing for my overall well-being is to *grow* elsewhere."

"But you don't know where you're going yet, correct?"

Astoria bit her lower lip.

"How about this?" the HR director scribbled something on her notepad. "Give me notice of your intent to depart at the end of the year. This way, the end is in sight, but you can buy some time and figure out your next move. Thoughts?"

"Oh." Astoria blinked. She hadn't thought to give more than the standard two weeks.

"It's a pro move. Plus, you'll get healthcare for another forty-five-ish days. We'll pay out your unused vacation time, and you can enjoy a nice long holiday. Good timing." The woman winked.

Astoria nodded slowly, processing the proposition.

"But we won't announce this, not even to Henry Hunter, until December, okay? Stays between us." The HR Director circled 'Dec 1' on her notepad and dropped her pen on the desk, then leaned back in her chair. "For what it's worth, you're not the only one struggling with the culture here. Stay on the high road and don't look back."

"Thank you for this," Astoria said. "Thank you for helping me."

Outside, the wind pulled golden leaves from the trees, twirling them in a ribbon across the sky.

***

A thick layer of dust covered her desk; the stench of a rotten apple wafted up from within a drawer. The Account Girls buzzed about the pod, debating how they might best coordinate tartan plaid outfits for the upcoming holiday party.

Astoria clicked the blue "SUBMIT" button, launching one more application into the online abyss. Applying for jobs gave her a sense of agency, even though she wasn't sure she wanted any of the jobs she was applying to.

A company-wide email from Henry Hunter appeared in her inbox:

"Miss Lyons is pursuing opportunities beyond Dixon-Richards. Join us in wishing her the best when you see her around the office."

The Account Girls stiffened. Kayleigh whispered something to Lexi; they glanced over their shoulders. Astoria waved big like Evie might have done. Kayleigh sneered, but Lexi pouted her lips and held her thumb in the air, pointing it down.

Astoria nodded appreciatively, a little pang of missed opportunities burning her in the chest. But then she thought about Evie and was flooded with a deep sense of longing for her friend. She recalled how Evie had saved her that day in Atlanta, helping her hold her head high in the face of uncertainty. Evie had taught her not to worry about what other people thought and how to plow ahead. Even in her absence, she was still helping Astoria carry on.

CHAPTER TWENTY-SIX

Holiday 2010

The plane sank through the atmospheric layer of clouds, bouncing down onto the SEA-TAC tarmac. Astoria pressed her nose to the window as they taxied. The Olympic Mountains brooded on the horizon, shimmering metallic in the afternoon sun. She smiled at the familiar scene, then rested her head back against the seat. After two years, it felt good to be home.

Ace's old Ford idled in the arrivals port, gray smoke funneling from the exhaust. A security agent stood at the driver's side window, hollering and flailing at the No Parking signs posted in ten-foot intervals down the length of the bay. "I said, you can't wait here this long. Do you hear me?"

Ace grinned at his daughter through the windshield as she approached.

"You haven't gotten a Christmas tree yet?" Astoria said as they bounced down the highway. Ace shifted gears, and the old truck responded begrudgingly. The cab smelled like diesel and coffee. Astoria inhaled deeply, feeling at once whole and home.

"Think we need a tree this year?" Ace asked.

Astoria knitted her brow at him across the bench seat. "I haven't been home in two years, Ace. We're getting a tree."

Ace nodded at the windshield, one hand resting on the wheel. "Think we should go on down to the Elks on Christmas Eve?"

"Only if Miss Wanda is down there," Astoria smirked, but Ace drove on unphased.

"Glad you're home."

***

Astoria scanned her mother's kitchen, grief and longing flooding her senses. Ace wasn't much for housekeeping—the place smelled like bacon grease and dirty laundry instead of lemony bleach. Time, loss, and grime made what was once a safe and affirming space feel surreal and far away. Astoria gripped both arms as if holding onto herself as she stood on the chipped yellow linoleum, noting the faded goldenrod countertops, processing where she was, where she'd been, and who she was becoming.

She plucked an orange-and-white-daisy-painted glass from a cupboard; it was coated with a dusty film. A coffee cup rested upside down on the draining board. She placed the glass in the sink and examined the cup—*was it the only one Ace had used in the years she'd been away?*—when he stepped in from the hallway.

"You about ready?" he asked.

"Sure thing, Ace, just give me a second to find some work clothes."

"No rush." He shuffled toward the front door.

In her childhood bedroom, Astoria pulled a pair of steel-toed work boots from the back of the closet. She rolled up her Levi's and worked her socked feet inside, the dusty old leather resisting as she tried not to think about the generations of spiders lurking within. Ace's truck rumbled in the driveway. She hustled down the hall, buttoning her red-and-black checkered flannel as she went.

They drove into the mountains behind their land to harvest a Christmas tree and cut a half-chord of firewood.

Ace chopped while Astoria tossed the pieces into the truck bed. He swung the axe onto a massive round and groaned as the blade cracked the wood in two. He set the head of the axe on the chopping block and leaned onto the handle, grimacing in pain. Thick lines of sweat ran down his temples.

"Your back hurt?" she asked.

"Just need to rest here a second."

She squat-carried a chunk of wood to the truck and heaved it into the bed. Sweat soaking her own back, she placed her hands against the truck and extended her legs behind her, stretching her calves, hamstring, spine, and neck, then straightened, reaching both arms toward the sky. The air clung damp and cool to her cheeks. Salty ocean air floated on the breeze. Fog hung like a garland across the surrounding firs. Her gloves were sticky with sap. Her body ached. *This,* she thought, *is what it is to be alive.*

They drove back into town with the Christmas tree strapped between the pile of wood and the cab. Astoria took in the frumpy houses and muddy streets. Single strands of colored lights lined rooftops and doorways; other homes lurked dark, looking cold.

"What happened to the Miller place?" she asked as they passed a burned-out trailer, its charred walls still standing like an everyday American Acropolis.

"That youngest boy of theirs was running a homemade meth lab, and it exploded on him," said Ace.

"Hillbilly heroin."

"That what they calling it these days?"

"He was a grade below me," Astoria said, craning her neck to study the burn scene.

"Cheap poison is eating these kids alive."

At the outskirts of town, Ace guided the truck up a gravel drive toward a brown ranch-style home with a tendril of smoke curling up from the chimney. He honked the horn as he backed the truck onto the cement carport beneath a crooked metal awning.

The front door opened, and a gnarled woman peeked out from behind it, her remaining gray hair a meager pile of frizz atop her head, making her look like a helpless baby bird. She stood behind a walker, her shoulders and back slumped forward like the inside of a question mark. Astoria stared in shock, recognizing the old woman while registering what time had done to her.

"Ol' Dot can't see anymore," Ace said.

"Can't see at all?"

Ace shook his head.

Astoria swallowed against her thickening throat. Dorothy Wallace had been a centrifugal force in Astoria's small town for longer than Astoria had been alive. From church potlucks to high school sporting events, Dot's smiling eyes and booming laugh were the trademarks of a successful community gathering.

"Run on up there and ask where she wants us to unload this so it's easy for her to get to."

Astoria looked at her father apprehensively, but he took no notice.

Wet grass squished beneath Astoria's boots as she approached the house. Throat still thick with emotion, she called out, her voice cracking. "Hey, Miss Dot."

"Who's that?" asked Dorothy Wallace, her face searching but eyes not registering.

"It's me, Astoria Lyons." Astoria hopped up the cement steps to the front door. Moss covered the steps and grew out from under the home's shingled siding. "I'm here with Ace. We brought you some firewood."

Lines fell away from the old woman's face as she brightened, joy erasing uncertainty. She extended a papery hand, and Astoria took it between hers, warm and soft, surprised at how comforting it was to touch someone, to simply hold their hand.

"Oh, Astoria Lyons. I pray for you every day."

Astoria's face flushed hot; tears streamed down her cheeks.

"I pray for all you young people who have left our little town. I can't see you too well, but I'm sure happy to hear your voice."

Still holding Dorothy's hand, Astoria wiped a shoulder across her cheek. "I'm happy to see you, Miss Dot. Feels good to be home."

Back in the truck, having unloaded the wood and stacked it in a tight pile on the back patio, Ace turned up the heater as they bounced away from the house. Miss Dot remained in her doorway, clinging to her walker with one hand and waving goodbye with the other. Tears still spilling, Astoria watched as the old woman faded from view in the side mirror.

"Know what would be fun?" said Ace.

Astoria laughed at her father's propensity to dodge sadness. "What's that?"

"How about we go down to the café and get something to eat?"

"Sounds great, Ace." Astoria dragged her fingertips across her eyelids. "I just wasn't expecting Miss Mart to be so old. It's been so long since I've seen her."

"She's pushing ninety. She always loved all you kids."

"This town has been dying for a long time," Astoria said, "but when you see it up close ..."

The trees flashed by in strokes of green as the truck roared down the highway.

Ace squinted out the windshield. "We're not all dead yet."

Astoria nodded and laughed. "Food sounds good, Ace. I might need a cold beer, too."

***

On Christmas Eve, Astoria sat beside Ace and Miss Wanda at the Elks Lodge Christmas dinner, laughing at her father's ability to simultaneously allow and ignore the pie lady's overt advances. Other old timers from her hometown—gray-haired men and women she'd known her entire life—gave hugs, telling her they missed her, and they knew Ace was proud of her for making it in the big city, and *did she think she'd ever move home?*

A little bird-lady with tired skin and sharp eyes grabbed Astoria's hand, pressed a bill into it, then wrapped a wiry arm around Astoria's neck and pulled her in close.

"I can't stick around to chat," the woman said into her ear, "it'll make me too sad because you remind me too much of your momma, but I'm glad you came home to see your dad for Christmas." She released Astoria and slipped away.

Astoria examined the bill in her palm—one hundred dollars—and thought about the woman, well past retirement age, still working at the local store full-time, likely making less money than Astoria, *but look at how much she had to give*.

***

One rainy afternoon during that disorienting stretch between Christmas and New Year's, Astoria lay on her twin bed in her childhood room reading a book when she realized a glass of wine would elevate the experience, so she padded down the hallway into the kitchen. The house was quiet, the television dark. Ace lay in his recliner in the living room.

Only peppery dredges remained in the bottle of Cabernet she'd purchased at the local Thriftway, so she poked through the fridge, looking for a cold beer.

"Think you'll stay in Nashville a while longer?" Ace asked.

Astoria jumped. "Shit, Ace, you scared me."

"I was just restin' my eyes, but I wasn't asleep," he said.

"Sure ya' weren't." Laughing, she peered into the fridge again, avoiding answering his question as she searched the shelves.

Ace stared up at the ceiling from his chair, his fingers interlaced across his belly. "I know there's not much for you around here, but it's good to have you home."

A pang of melancholy tugged at her. In the short time she'd been home, she hadn't felt lonely, hadn't woken up hungover, and had laughed with people she loved. She thought of her hometown, its soggy old buildings cratering in on themselves amidst the dust-filled windows, dark storefronts, and empty streets. Torn between two worlds and uncertain of which direction to take her life, she hadn't told Ace she'd quit her job, or about the resumes she'd been sending out to agencies around the country and how they went unanswered, or how Sallie Mae was always calling and how much the idea of being broke again scared her.

"I don't know what I'm gonna do, Ace." Empty-handed, she shut the refrigerator and slipped back down the dark hallway; the walls feeling closer than ever.

***

Ace built a bonfire in the backyard on New Year's Eve. One of his friends stopped by, and the old men sat around the fire, volleying stories from their logging days back and forth across the flames. Astoria sipped wine and laughed along, having heard the tales countless times before. Embers glowed, the fire danced, and the stars shone.

"You're doing right by your mom," Ace said after his friend left.

Mesmerized by the fire, she wrapped her hands around the mug she was using as a wineglass.

Ace lifted his face to the sky. "I wish I could've given her more. But she would've been real proud of how you're doing out there on your own."

An image of her mother's skeletal frame deflating into itself as the cancer took over flashed through Astoria's mind. But she didn't want to dwell on her mother's death, so she pushed the thought away and joined Ace in staring up at the flood of stars. She thought of the agency with its scratchy carpet, dim lighting, and sea of identical desks. She wondered how many nights she'd spent staring at her computer screen instead of the vast expanse, infinitely greater than the melodramas of Corporate America and everyday life.

***

In her bedroom, she pawed through the stack of dresses that had remained folded in her duffle bag during her time home, wondering why she'd even packed them. Her red-eye flight back to Nashville left that night.

What if I came home? Found a simple job with an hourly wage? Would that prove them all right, that I'm never going to make anything of myself? The professor. The Account Girls. Henry Hunter ... even Johnny.

"Something's ringing out here," Ace hollered from the living room, knocking her mind off its hamster wheel.

"Probably telemarketers," she yelled back, fearing it was more likely Sallie Mae calling to tell her she was ninety days past due on her student loan payments and her account would go to collections if she didn't make a payment immediately. Astoria shuffled down the hall into the living room and checked the number flashing on the screen.

"New York?" She thought to screen the call, but Ace was sitting there watching her. "Hello?"

"Astoria Lyons?" a young man asked through the airwaves.

"Yes." Her pulse quickened, assuming the man was a debt collector.

"Hope I'm not catching you at a bad time. I'm a recruiter with a marketing agency in New York. You applied for a strategist role with us?"

"Oh. Right." Her mind rustled through the countless jobs she'd applied for in cities she never wanted to live in—Chicago, Seattle, Los Angeles. There was big, and then there was too big: she couldn't recall applying for one in New York.

"We have a satellite office in Nashville and are looking for a digital strategy director. While I understand if you're looking to shift into a bigger market, I was wondering if you might be interested in at least learning more about the opportunity we have down there?"

Avoiding eye contact with Ace, she slipped back down the hallway. "I, uhm, I'm interested in learning more."

The man explained it was his job to find people with the right experience who were also a good fit for his agency. "This position is director-level … you'll be working with global brands. A woman named Jessica Jones runs our Nashville agency. She's one of our company's most dynamic up-and-coming leaders. You'll learn a lot from her, but I must warn you: she demands excellence from her team. Does this sound like something you'd be interested in pursuing?"

Astoria could hear Ace shuffling from his chair into the kitchen. She closed her bedroom door lightly behind her.

"Absolutely," she said. Her pulse, or perhaps her ego, throbbed in her ears; it felt good to be wanted. The recruiter continued his pitch.

"I promise you will love our Nashville team. They're tight knit. Work hard, play hard. But before I pass you onto the next phase, Astoria, I need to ask, what are your salary requirements?"

Astoria stated the amount she had intended to ask Henry Hunter for.

The recruiter sighed.

"Look, Astoria. I'm not supposed to do this, but you need to tell me you expect double that amount because that's where the pay range for this job *starts*. But I didn't tell you this. Understand?"

"Oh," she said, face burning red. "Yes."

"So, Astoria," the recruiter paused, "I need to ask what your salary requirements are?"

Calculating the increase in her head, her voice caught as she uttered the revised salary request.

"Perfect," he said, "that's within range of what we've allocated for this role."

CHAPTER TWENTY-SEVEN

Winter 2011

Deep winter in the south—trees shivered naked while the sun bore a white hole in the gray sky. Astoria had found comfort in the drizzly forests of home, but Nashville's teeth-rattling frigidity was invigorating in its own right—a blank slate.

Exhausted after the first week at her new job, Astoria floated through her front door on Friday evening, kicked off her shoes, shed her tights and sweater dress, and climbed into sweatpants and a fleece. At her kitchen stove, she willed a pot of water to boil so she could pour a cup of tea and burrow beneath a pile of blankets on the couch. Even with the furnace set at 70 degrees, icicle formations splayed intricate patterns around the edges of the single-paned windows.

She'd barely settled in when her phone rang. Astoria squealed to see Anna Mae's name on the screen. She answered: "You'll never guess who just finished her first week at her new job with a global marketing agency."

"No kidding," said Anna Mae. "Congratulations are in order! I heard you left Dixon-Richards. Finally, time to recognize your worth?"

"Anna Mae, it has been a long couple of years."

"You've come a long way, young lady."

Astoria thought about how broke she'd been when she first moved to town and met Anna Mae, her life as stable as a wet cardboard box. She was still struggling to pay her student loans, but with this new paycheck, her finances were sure to improve, and she felt like she'd at least fortified her positioning.

"I still have a long way to go," Astoria said. "Thanks for giving me a shot when you hired me at Dixon-Richards. Feels like a lifetime ago."

"I have some big news of my own to share," Anna Mae said gleefully. "I'm moving to Mississippi next month."

"What on earth? Why?"

"I accepted a role with the Yoknapatawpha Arts Council in Oxford."

"Come again?"

"I know. It's a mouthful."

"But why are you leaving Nashville? Things are booming here."

"People keep telling me I'm crazy to leave. Our video business is doing okay. There's plenty of work to go around, but this town has no creative heart left. I want to live in a place that still has some soul. And at this point, my life gets to be about more than making money."

"Aren't you lucky," Astoria said, noticing the crystalline formations edging the window behind the couch. She pressed a finger to the glass, the delicate shapes dissolving at her touch. "If I'm honest, I had reservations about taking another corporate job and staying down here."

"Tell me about that."

"I went home for Christmas. It felt good. Sort of like what you're saying about Mississippi. Nobody has much, but plenty of folks still have what matters."

"Then what are you doing?"

"I don't know. Trying to make money and climb that corporate ladder. Isn't that how you make it in America?" Astoria laughed.

Anna Mae was silent. When she finally spoke, her words came through as sharp directives. "I hope you understand you get to define what success looks like. And I hope you factor happiness into the equation. A job or relationship won't make you happy. You have to figure out how to do that for yourself. But I understand being young, maybe even a little broke, and needing a paycheck."

"A *little* broke?" Astoria snorted. "Say, on another note, have you heard from Evie? She called me out of the blue several months ago. Pierce was yelling in the background the entire time. Evie had to lock herself in the bathroom just so she could talk. I asked if she was okay, and she laughed me off. But nothing about it seemed funny."

"I take it you haven't heard anything since then?"

The knowing tone of Anna Mae's question made Astoria wince.

"No."

"That good-for-nothing Pierce Mathers got thrown in damned *prison* for trafficking drugs in and out of doctor's offices across Tennessee. Oxycodone or something. Have you heard of this? Apparently, it's more addictive than crack cocaine."

"Prison?"

"The big house."

"What happened to Evie?"

"I haven't talked to her," said Anna Mae. "I've called her parents' house, but nobody will answer. All this information is coming through the grapevine. If you recall, her father and I share some common acquaintances. It's a mess, but you know Evie. She'll put on a big smile and make it all okay."

"Did she get in trouble, too?"

"From what I'm hearing, they gave her the opportunity to dodge legal implications if she enrolled in a treatment program."

"Rehab?"

"Something like that."

"Maybe it's the best thing that could have happened, all things considered?" Astoria thought back to Evie's oversized purse rattling with pill bottles every time she moved. "She was always good at pretending like everything was okay."

"I suppose that's an art we all have to master from time to time," said Anna Mae. "You're going to be great in this new job. Go get some more experience, but don't lose track of yourself. It's never too late to make yourself happy."

***

Aside from its location in a downtown high-rise, Astoria's new office looked a lot like Dixon-Richards: open-floor seating, Formica desks, scratchy carpet, an open bar. The agency's executives had their own offices, and these had windows, so people could see who was being reprimanded, promoted, raising hell, or issuing a complaint.

As at Dixon-Richards, the account leads were all women; however, all similarities between Astoria's prior Account cohorts and her new peers ended at gender. The latter clocked long hours on behalf of their clients, pored over financials, read industry reports, and pushed their creative counterparts to deliver better work on each project. When Astoria joined the team, they told her she needed to provide stronger briefs. She appreciated the direct feedback.

"Do you all have your MBAs or something?" Astoria asked an Account Director after an agency-wide review of accounts.

"Most of us do, yes," said the woman, a tall blonde who strictly wore power suits and heels, even on casual Fridays.

The recruiter had told Astoria the agency worked hard and played hard. She'd only been on the job two weeks when she found herself working past seven o'clock for the fourth night in a row. Astoria, the Account Leads, and their creative counterparts were dug in at their desks, a competitive tension having settled among them to see who would give up first.

"This is dumb," a mousey brunette finally said. "I've been staring at this spreadsheet for the past two hours, and I don't know where they expect me to find more budget for a retargeting campaign, and I need a fucking drink."

"It's about damn time," said the Associate Creative Director.

The co-workers slammed their laptops shut, slipped them into leather totes, pushed their chairs into their desks, and donned their pea coats and parkas. Astoria leaned forward, squinting at her computer screen.

"Hurry up, New Girl," barked the blonde account lead; she'd donned an electric pink suit and a black blouse that day. "This train is leaving the station, and you'd better be on it."

After that, Astoria never waited for an invitation. On nights when her new teammates trudged down to the nearest dive bar, she joined, happy to be included, although the conversation often defaulted into the same grumblings about the boss, Jessica Jones, whom everyone called Jones.

The Account Leads complained that Jones was more addicted to work than they were; the Creatives lamented how she expected them to work weekends. Astoria listened but said nothing. She was still new to the team but knew Jones was exacting, unwilling to settle for anything less than excellent. From Astoria's perspective, Jessica Jones was light-years ahead of Henry Hunter because she didn't play mind games, didn't operate by dominating the front of the boardroom; she praised her team in public, trained them in the trenches, and was the first to arrive at the office and the last to leave. Jessica Jones had high expectations, and Astoria sensed she was a leader who would celebrate anyone bold enough to meet them.

On a rowdy Friday night, after putting in a week of twelve-hour days, Astoria and her co-workers drank their way through two happy hours downtown, then bar-hopped over to East Nashville, where they ran into the Video Guys from Dixon-Richards smoking cigarettes and shooting pool at a smoke-filled sports bar.

Jake spotted Astoria from across the room. "Hey! We miss you!" Astoria ran to him, and they embraced.

"Who are they?" Jake asked, jutting his chin over her shoulder.

"My new team."

"Any of 'em single?"

Astoria rolled her eyes. "Good to know nothing has changed over there, Jake."

"Bring them over. We'll make room."

Astoria directed her new world to merge with her old. The Video Guys quickly engaged with her new gaggle of female co-workers, and she felt special for facilitating the camaraderie. She spent the evening laughing, guzzling bottles of cold beer, and eyeing the door, wondering if Cody might join. As the hours wore on, her pride wore off, and she tapped Jake's shoulder, shouting into his ear.

"Where is Cody? He still too good to hang out with you guys?"

"You don't know?" Jake yelled above the fray.

Astoria knitted her brow and shook her head.

"Cody moved to Brooklyn."

"What?"

"Big drama at the agency. You know he was seeing that Account Girl, Cassidy?"

Astoria shrugged like she didn't care.

"Cody didn't even tell her he was moving. She didn't find out until they sent out that bullshit email they always send when someone leaves. Said he received an opportunity he couldn't pass up. You know how they always spin it to make it sound like no one in their right mind would leave ..."

Jake continued ranting about Dixon-Richards while Astoria nodded along, pretending to listen, the chaotic bar with its TVs, neon lights, and loud music somehow bringing her disillusionment into focus.

After the group disbanded, Astoria stumbled home alone through East Nashville's icy streets, white clouds of breath puffing ahead of her. Stars blinked overhead. Instead of savoring the pristine winter night, she was lost in her angry mind, obsessing over the news of Cody's departure, wondering how he could leave without even saying goodbye.

Fumbling through her tote, she retrieved her cell and texted as she walked, typing out a litany of insults she wanted to send.

—Off to join the Comrades in Brooklyn?

Delete.

—Easiest to cut and run, huh?

Delete.

—Brooklyn? Could you be any more cliché?

Delete.

—Turns out you're as vapid as the rest of them.

Right as she hit send, her toe caught a lip of broken sidewalk, propelling her body, bag, and cell phone in all directions. Her mind went black until the pavement shocked her into a new realm of consciousness.

Pain shot through her knees and hips. She became acutely aware of the cold concrete, gritty against her cheek and hands. She lay on her stomach, splayed out cartoonishly like a crime scene sketch in a bad movie. Shifting her torso left, then right, she jostled her legs, flailing about until she began laughing at her own absurdity.

Back on her feet, she pressed her fingers against the holes in her tights, then examined her fingertips, black with blood beneath the streetlight. Someone flipped a switch somewhere within the recesses of the nearest Craftsman home, and the porch light flooded the front yard. Astoria spotted her cell phone shining in the grass a few feet away. She crept into the yard, retrieved it, collected her bag from the sidewalk, then hobbled home.

The following morning, she woke to a mean hangover. Her left knee was bloodied and bruised, but most of her pain was self-inflicted with too much beer, no food, and no water. Outside, the sunny winter day beckoned. Wounded, she wasted the day in bed watching Mad Men on her laptop. She'd never had the money for cable television, but with her additional income, she splurged on a monthly Netflix subscription. Binging its programming from bed while stalking Johnny on social media had become a secret gluttonous indulgence.

Well past noon, she dragged herself into the living room and peered out her front window. Two children wrapped in bulky coats rode their bikes down the sidewalk, their parents strolling close behind, big smiles plastered across their faces.

Ping! Astoria's phone chimed from within her tote, where she had discarded it next to the front door when she'd finally stumbled over the threshold in the early morning hours.

Cody's name flashed on the screen. Astoria cringed, having forgotten the drunken text until now. Braced for embarrassment, she tapped on Cody's name and read his reply.

—I wish you the best, Astoria.

She snorted, feeling Cody's smugness coursing through the screen and into the room, mocking her throbbing knee and brutal hangover and self-loathing and quiet, musty apartment. But standing there, the wood floor cold against her bare feet, last night's makeup smeared across her face, she realized it didn't matter if he was mocking her or if his response was sincere. He'd moved on. She was the one dwelling on the misery of old mistakes and unproductive habits.

Out on the sidewalk, the children squealed, and the parents laughed.

Astoria closed her blinds and went back to bed.

CHAPTER TWENTY-EIGHT

Spring 2011

Half-empty Chinese food containers littered the conference room table. The smell of their fried dinner lingered, smudges of pink sweet-and-sour sauce having long since congealed on paper plates.

Slouched in her chair, Astoria checked the time on her phone. 9:15 p.m.

She yawned, stretching her arms overhead.

"You still with me?" asked Jessica Jones.

Astoria slapped her fingertips against her cheeks, then pushed herself upright. "Oh yeah. Going strong."

"Think you can make it to ten?"

"For sure."

Astoria and Jones had hunkered down in the conference room for two days, researching, hammering at their laptops, and jumping up to sketch their thoughts on a whiteboard as they compiled a new business pitch, slide by slide.

After drunk texting Cody, Astoria's mortification lingered for days. She'd needed something to focus on, so volunteered to support Jessica Jones on another pitch, which they won. Through working closely on that project, Astoria realized Jones was genuine—she simply wanted to kick ass and win. Perhaps all the shit-talking came from people who were jealous or intimidated.

"She's a workaholic," Astoria's co-workers complained at happy hours. "Just because she doesn't have kids or a boyfriend or a life doesn't mean the rest of us should suffer."

"I think she's an incredible leader," Astoria said, earning doubtful sneers and wickedly angled brows from her cohorts. "I like how she tells us what's happening and why she's making big decisions."

"She's certainly taking you under her wing," said one of the Account Directors. The group scrutinized Astoria over their drinks.

"I know what it takes to win new business," Astoria said, staring back, then taking a long drink from her pint, daring them to say more.

She began opting out of the office happy hours, instead putting in even more time at her desk and doubling down on the quality of her work. The effort piled up, catching Jones's attention and garnering Astoria more opportunities. Once again, work consumed her life. Except this time, she felt like it might pay off.

"It's funny how the actual work starts once five o'clock hits and all the meetings are over," Astoria said, cracking open the extra fortune cookie.

"The meeting culture was off the charts at P&G," said Jones. "It's something I've been trying to wrangle here, yet here we are."

Astoria read her fortune, exhaustion blurring the tiny words on the strip of paper.

Jones had kicked off her red-soled Louboutin shoes and sat with her legs tucked into her chair. She wore a black pencil skirt and a sleeveless white blouse, showing off her chiseled brown arms. With her bleached hair cropped tight to her scalp, her high cheekbones imparted a strength, which she backed up with her business savvy.

"How long were you at Procter & Gamble?" Astoria asked.

"Seven years. Seven long years."

"In Chicago?"

"Chi-town." Jones bobbed her head up and down.

"How do you like working on the agency side?"

"It's less focused than working for one company, but I'm enjoying how there is always a new challenge to tackle."

"Did you always want to work for a marketing agency?" asked Jones.

"No." Astoria shook her head against the recollection of her past life. "I wanted to be a journalist, but when I finished undergrad in 2008, all the magazines and newspapers were shuttering, and I couldn't land a job."

"Bad timing."

"I needed a paycheck. So, here I am."

"And how do you feel about it?" Jones tilted her head to the side, exposing her slender neck.

"It's a job. I love to work, and there's power in that. But there are days I wake up wondering if I want to dedicate so much energy for someone else's benefit, you know? It feels like there's always someone higher up the chain waiting to tell me I'm not worth a raise or a promotion."

Jones smirked. "You're talking to a black woman in advertising."

Astoria lowered her eyes, feeling a pang of guilt in considering Jones must have endured countless Henry Hunters along her journey.

"But look, that's the game," Jones said, slipping her feet off the chair and leaning forward. "It's a cutthroat world, so you gotta be clear on your purpose so when you get knocked on your ass, *because you are going to get knocked on your ass*, you're not too disoriented when you get back up. What's your goal?"

Astoria shrugged. "I feel like I've been in the passenger seat of my life for years, and I don't even know where the car is headed."

"But who's driving, huh? We're nobody's victim, Lyons, you or me."

Astoria balled the fortune paper in her fingers and flicked it toward the to-go containers.

Jones reached out, placing her hand on the desk. "You can go anywhere you want in life. But first, you must be clear about where you want to go, and you gotta accept that nobody else is gonna take you there. You're in the driver's seat. It's that simple."

"Is it?" Astoria grimaced. "I feel like I'll never even own my own car though—metaphorically, you know? When you start out working class, it's like you're riding backseat your entire life."

Jones tossed her hands in the air. "Then get out of the damned car and *run*, sis."

Astoria laughed.

"Look at it this way," Jones continued. "Every person on this earth endures hardships to varying degrees. But you can't let that distract you from what you want to do with *your life*. I married my college sweetheart, and he was a fine-ass black man." She closed her eyes and waved a hand in the air as if tracing a memory of his frame.

"Ran his own brokerage firm. We owned a beautiful home in one of Chicago's most desirable neighborhoods. Season tickets to Broadway. Valet at the country club. A big circle of fancy friends with no kids and plenty of expendable income. I was on a career track straight to the top with P&G. But when I found my husband fucking another man in a pair of my Louboutin's, it knocked me on my ass so hard that by the time I picked myself back up, none of that stuff looked the same anymore, because none of it ever belonged to me. You know?"

"Holy shit, Jones. I had no idea."

"People acquire a lifestyle for the image, for the ego, but rarely do they sell their souls to the cars and the mortgages and the fake friends because they're being true to themselves. They do it because they think *that's what they're supposed to do.* That was the one lesson my ex-husband taught me: it takes some big balls to do what you want instead of what you think you're supposed to. But at least he learned to be true to himself."

"You mean you forgive him?"

Jones smiled sadly, then shrugged. "I will. Eventually. But in the meantime, I'm saving every penny from my divorce settlement to invest in my own agency."

"Jones! That's brilliant."

Jones grinned. "My daddy was the first black cardiologist in Tennessee. My momma was the first black woman to graduate from her nursing program at Vanderbilt. I'll be the first black woman to run her own digital marketing agency in Nashville."

"Of course, your parents are badass, Jones. Why am I not surprised?"

"We aim high, and we meet our mark. You can get there, Lyons. Figure out how high you want to aim. Stop whining about this working-class bullshit. That ain't your shackle. Like you said, it's your strength."

Astoria locked eyes with Jones and nodded. "Thank you."

Jones popped a hand on the table. "Let's go through the data one more time and make sure we're not missing anything, then get the hell out of here."

"Let's do it."

***

It was only 10:15 a.m., and Astoria had already consumed six cups of coffee. An unfinished chocolate chip cookie sat on her desk. Over-caffeinated but still zapped of energy, she grabbed her phone and slunk down in her chair. Screen inches from her face, she opened the Tinder app.

After her first experiences with online dating, she'd been hesitant to start again, but the girls at the office seemed to make a game of it. When they landed a date, they came to the office the next day and told of horror stories, snooze fests, and evenings spent with pleasant gentlemen who treated them to lovely dinners, then never texted again. Online dating kept them busy in the evenings and gave them something to talk about at the next happy hour.

Astoria expected nothing to come from it. But she was tired. And bored. And needed quick dopamine hits to survive her grueling workload. So, she went window shopping. Not for love but for the shallow thrill of seeing who she might match with. For every ten swipes left, she swiped right once, rarely connecting. The experience initially delivered cheap entertainment but always left her questioning whether she was attractive or even worth dating.

Ping! The text jolted her out of her swipe-induced trance. Johnny's name appeared on the screen.

—What are you into these days?

He always seemed to reach out when she was exhausted at work or feeling poorly about herself after a short-lived tryst with a disinterested man. He would invite her out for drinks or over for dinner. They'd hook up. She'd get her hopes up and ask if he ever thought they might get back together.

Probably not, he would say before fading away for another month or two. It was a toxic cycle, but it was easy, not to mention addictive, and Astoria told herself she didn't have time for anything else.

—Working my ass off, she replied. We've been at it for two weekends straight.

—Sounds like somebody needs a steak dinner.

—I'll bring the wine?

—Deal.

Don't sleep with him. Don't sleep with him. Don't sleep with him. She recited this as she drove to Johnny's house.

***

After a steak dinner and a bottle of wine, she woke up in his bed the next morning with Duke curled against her legs. The familiarity was comforting at first, but as the new day's light revealed the room, it also brought her hangover and disappointment into clear view. She had to be at the office no later than eight o'clock to polish up a presentation, so she slipped quietly out of bed and drove across East Nashville back to the forgiving comfort of her own space.

In the shower, she scrubbed her skin raw with a loofah, watching her torso turn a mean red while thinking about what Jones said about being in the driver's seat of her own life and wondering why she kept driving down the same old roads.

CHAPTER TWENTY-NINE

Summer 2012

In rural Tennessee, kudzu vines smothered the land, rendering it unrecognizable, its ecosystem forever changed. Meanwhile, a different invasive species was spreading across Music City. Young socialites were moving in droves from California, New Jersey, and Ohio, colonizing the social scene with a cannibalistic, selfie-obsessed energy.

These newcomers funded the festivals that popped up every weekend, always centered around drinking as if alcoholism was the only remaining cultural offering the country had left. Brewfests, beer and booze fests, beer, bourbon, and bacon festivals—countless sponsored gatherings materialized on any given Saturday in gravel lots across town, Nashville's once distinct neighborhoods now imparting a monotonous spirit of debauchery.

Troops of young women paraded about, wearing maxi dresses in the summer and long sweaters, skinny jeans, and knee-high boots in the fall and winter. Regardless of the season, young men wore khaki shorts and polo shirts—practical uniforms conducive to binge drinking and average personalities. Whether at festivals or in bars, these socialites gathered in gendered clusters, as if at a middle school dance, until the second or third round of drinks hit, after which the crowd integrated into one slurring blur.

Astoria's co-workers always knew of the latest happenings. They kindly invited her to join, and for the first time in her adult life, she could afford to spend forty dollars on a couple of beers, but now that she had money, it seemed too great a waste.

"I can't this weekend. Maybe next time!"

Along with these polite declinations, Astoria spent the summer playing a game with herself that she called "needs vs. wants."

The rules were simple: before spending any money, she had to answer whether the expense was a genuine need or a want. If it was the latter, she had to decline the purchase. For example, if she wanted to go out on the town with her co-workers but really just needed to release stress, she declined the invite and walked around Shelby Bottoms instead. To get out of the house on weekends, she still went to the Mall at Green Hills, where she walked in circles, enjoying the free air conditioning and window shopping. However, she adhered to her self-imposed rule of looking but not buying all the things she wanted but did not need. More extreme, she ate every dried bean and grain of rice from her pantry before allowing herself to buy more groceries—needs vs. wants.

After three months of playing this game, she paid off one of her student loans. Three more remained, but she enjoyed the thrill of achievement, anyway.

One negative consequence of all this disciplined prudence was that it rendered Astoria depressingly isolated, like when she'd first moved to town. Her coworkers had stopped inviting her to join them after she had declined so many times. It didn't bother her much while in the throes of her self-imposed savings challenge, but having achieved this milestone, she longed for contact with the outside world.

Installed on her couch one Saturday afternoon, she peeked out her living room window to see people strolling down the sidewalk and children playing in the streets. Her back and legs were sweaty; she needed to shower. See people. Be human.

An hour later, hair still wet but clean and piled into a messy bun atop her head, she stepped out into the sauna of a southern summer. Cotton dress clinging to her back, she strolled along, greeting neighbors and smiling at children as they chalked pictures of the sun and flowers on the sidewalks. She walked past the Lockeland Springs fire department, its burly inhabitants relaxing in white wooden rockers on the front porch. They waved at her, and she waved back.

At the intersection of 16th and Woodland Street, people sipped rosé around café tables around an old brick building. As if overnight, a restaurant had bloomed. Waitstaff floated in and out the front door, greeting customers by name, refilling water glasses, and rattling off daily specials. Inside, patrons nursed cocktails at a long wooden bar. Moved by the breezy mood of the afternoon, Astoria power-walked back to her apartment, grabbed her wallet, then hustled down to this new community gathering spot.

Thus, a cozy neighborhood eatery became Astoria's social outlet. She treated herself to a drink at the bar on Saturday afternoons. Cocktails cost eight dollars; she allowed herself two if she made it in time for happy hour. The bartenders and waitstaff all lived in East Nashville. They remembered their patrons' names and the details of their lives, sliding appetizer samples around the bar as they buzzed back and forth from the kitchen.

Neighbors soon came to know one another—Astoria included—as regulars. An older female couple punctuated their worldly stories with hearty laughter. A struggling songwriter spun his turquoise rings nervously around his fingers as he agonized over his creative endeavors. A divorcé's mascara ran while she cried into her wine.

Astoria was the quiet girl, initially self-conscious in her loneliness. But the staff and neighbors were kind, and once a week, she would stroll into the warmly lit restaurant, climb onto a barstool, talk and laugh, and feel connected to this glimmer of community.

After her two-drink minimum, she walked around the neighborhood, taking in the Craftsman homes with their cozy front porches and enchanting gardens. Fireflies twinkled across the manicured yards. The scent of magnolia hung heavy in the air. People lounged in wicker chairs, the clink of cocktail glasses punctuating their muted musings. The firefighters on the night shift at the fire hall smoked cigarettes and eased back and forth in their rocking chairs. All those good Southerners taking in the night and returning neighborly waves to Astoria as she passed, walking herself home.

***

A knock at her bedroom window ripped Astoria from the dead of sleep.

"It's me, Johnny. Don't shoot!"

Astoria lay in bed, blinking, wondering if she was still asleep and dreaming. Johnny rapped at the window again.

"What the hell," she growled, flopping out of bed. She stumbled toward the window and peeked through the blinds. Sure enough, there he was beneath the streetlight, teetering drunk and grinning sheepishly as if confident she'd find his late-night antics cute. Astoria pulled the cord, zipping the blinds open.

"What do you want?" she yelled.

"Let me in," he said, a lilt in his voice.

Astoria put her hands on her hips, glaring down to where he swayed beneath her. "Go around. You're going to wake the neighbors."

She met him and his oozing stench of booze at the front door.

"What the hell, Johnny?"

"I cain't make it home," he said.

"You want a hookup."

"What's wrong with that?" He giggled, stumbling in past her.

She turned, crossing her arms but not shutting the door. "It's not happening."

"Why not?"

"Because it's been a mistake every time, and I'm done making mistakes."

He smirked, swaying in place. "You at least got a drink for a man?"

"Doesn't appear you need another drink."

"C'mon." He raised his hands in surrender. "It'll knock me out, so's I won't pester you none."

She fished a bottle of beer from the recesses of her fridge, then watched him drink it as they sat across from one another at the kitchen table.

"This new?" he asked, rapping his knuckles on the table.

"Craigslist," she said.

"It's nice."

Astoria rubbed her eyes. "Why do you keep coming back, Johnny? Why, after all this time, can't you let us *both* leave well enough alone?"

He jiggled the edge of the table, suddenly interested in its construction.

"We had something pretty good, didn't we?" she asked, staring him down. "Could've made a great life together? It's like you didn't want to be with me, but you don't want to let me go, either."

Silence stretched between them.

Finally, Johnny spoke, determinedly slurring through his drunkenness.

"I was ten when my momma and daddy split. Never knew who was coming through my momma's backdoor or where my daddy was sleeping. Lots of people in and out, in and out, and I was always looking over my shoulder. I watched grown-ass adults hurt one another so many times like it was all they knew, and I made a promise to myself that I'd never trust anyone. Not my family. Not nobody. Only myself. And I've held that promise to this day."

Astoria registered the weight of Johnny's story—a lifetime of unaddressed pain and sadness that she couldn't change, fix, or take away. "Good Lord, Johnny. That's the saddest thing I've ever heard."

She spread a sheet on the couch and directed Johnny to lie down, then covered him with a blanket. She wasn't halfway down the hallway to her bedroom when she heard him snoring away.

Back in bed, she clutched her knees to her chest, allowing herself to weep for the broken boy who'd grown into a man with a sad story until a lightness washed over her. Wiping at her tears, she choked out a little laugh as the bitterness and grievances she'd harbored for Johnny, the professor, and even herself dissipated, allowing space for the peace of forgiveness to settle in.

***

The evening was so humid it felt like the air was perspiring all over Astoria instead of the other way around. Perched on her apartment stoop, she tapped Anna Mae's name on her fancy new iPhone, returning the call she'd missed from her old boss.

"I have a job for you," Anna Mae said, sounding giddy on the other end of the line.

"I'm listening."

"We got a grant from the state. I'm launching a website that promotes Mississippi artists, and I need you to create content for me. I can even *pay you.* Interested?"

Astoria's pulse quickened.

Bugs whirred in the trees.

"Sounds intriguing. What kind of content?"

"First, I need you to interview a textile designer who's making jeans from Mississippi cotton—I need this story pretty fast, so you'll interview him over the phone. Then, I'll send you to Clarksdale to cover a blues musician who runs a juke joint there. You'll recognize him. He's renowned in blues circles and has even acted in a few movies ..."

Astoria thought about the pitch they were working on at the agency, how Jones and the team would expect her to spend the next few weekends at the office, and how exhausted she was.

"Count me in," she said.

"I'm so thrilled. You'll be great. Maybe after you finish in Clarksdale, you can go up to Memphis and see Evie?"

Astoria paused, looking out at the steam rising from the street. "I'm not sure Evie wants to see me. I've texted her a few times, but she won't respond."

"Well," Anna Mae's voice dropped. "She got out of rehab last week and is back with her parents now. She may feel embarrassed, but I think knowing people still care would do her good."

"Tell me where to go."

***

To deliver at work and manage a freelance writing gig, she worked until eight or nine every night, skipped lunches, staved off the booze, and ignored Johnny's texts. But Jones pushed back when

Astoria announced she couldn't work an upcoming weekend because she'd be out of town.

"I know you'll get the work done, Lyons, but we need you around to practice for the pitch."

"I'll deliver the content strategy two days early. That'll get the Creatives started sooner than expected, and we can practice on Friday."

"Nobody will like that schedule," said Jones.

"They'll like not having to work this weekend."

Jones raised her hands in concession.

"We can sell it to them," Astoria said. "That's what we do."

***

Heading west out of Nashville, the rolling hills of Middle Tennessee flatten into the vast bottomlands of the Mississippi Delta. Astoria drove with the windows down, studying the scraggly crops withering beneath a thankless sky. Muddy fields waited, thick and deep, their parched surface concealing centuries of sins. The land felt haunted.

Sunday morning in Clarksdale, Astoria turned onto a deserted Main Street, driving slowly past empty storefronts and lifeless buildings, following her new phone's directions to an old two-story warehouse covered in a million bits of chipping white paint—allegedly home to a hopping juke joint. A brown recliner sat in repose on the front porch, stained by people and time. She parked, climbed out of her car, and scanned the scene. A dog barked. Music was playing somewhere down the block; Astoria recognized Hank Williams' whisky tenor eerily lonesoming through the town.

She locked her car, climbed the warehouse's front steps, and crossed the porch. When she opened the door, lively blues beats and icy air conditioning blasted her in the face. She stepped over the threshold and paused, letting her eyes adjust to the low lighting and neon signs. A stage sat empty but illuminated. Astoria spotted a jukebox beyond a line of pool tables. Behind the bar, a petite brunette with wild curly hair grooved as she washed pint glasses, handing them to a tall, thin man to dry. Dish towel at the ready, he turned toward the newcomer.

"Can I help you?" he asked, his voice thick and warm.

Even from across the room, Astoria could see his eyes dancing. Starstruck, she licked her lips so she could speak. "My name is Astoria Lyons. I'm with the Yoknap ... uh ... the Arts Council?"

"Ah, yeah!" The man whipped his towel in the air, snapping it playfully at the woman. "This young lady is here to get me outta these kitchen chores!"

The woman pulled her soapy hand from the dishwater and flicked it at the man, waving him away. "Get on outta here," she said. "Weren't helping me none anyway."

Astoria sat across from the blues man at a high-top table in the empty bar. His bony knees jutted out from each side of his barstool. The brunette—his wife—brought them unsweetened iced tea, a red plastic basket of tamales, and two paper plates.

"I didn't realize tamales were a southern thing," Astoria said, readying her pen over her yellow notepad.

"They're not." The man picked up the basket and slid a tamale onto his plate. "The Mexican folks sell 'em alongside the road to make money, but us Southerners always figure we can cook better than anybody else, so we stole the concept."

Astoria laughed.

"I take it you're not from the South, then?" the man asked. "You one of them new cool kids who moved to Nashville?"

"Definitely not cool, but I guess you could say I am a quiet transplant."

The blues man bobbed his head knowingly. "Where you from?"

"Small town in Washington state."

"Small-town girl up and left town, eh?"

"Something like that."

"Pretty sure there's a blues song in that old story. Especially if you was running from something."

"Just myself."

"Nah. What's a nice girl like you got to run from?"

Astoria blushed. "You know how it is—they say you'll never amount to anything if you never leave your small town. So, I left."

"Well, Clarksdale is a small town." Grinning, he held out his hands as if presenting the scene to her. "I was born and raised here, but I ain't done half bad."

"So, how'd you do it?" she asked. "How'd you go find all your success and then make your way back home?"

The man tipped his head back, closed his eyes, and inhaled, nostrils flaring. Opening his eyes again, he beamed, like he was about to share the secret of the universe.

"You know, I've always been clear on my principles," he said. "But when I was out there cutting up on the road, you might say I drifted over that double yellow line a time or two. No matter how hungover or hurting I was from the night before, I'd get up early in the morning and sit at the front of my tour bus to watch the sunrise. Those mile markers on the highway always spoke to me. They'd lull me into a trance as they ticked past, and I'd think about what kind of man I wanted to be and what I stood for. I was living in L.A., on the road mostly, but I realized I needed to use my principles as my mile markers if I was gonna find my way back home."

"So, what were they, your principles?"

"My faith in God, of course. Family. Community—giving back to this humble little place that made me. Honoring my creative spirit and sharing my gift of music in hopes I can give more than I take. Basic stuff if you think about it, and none of it requires moving somewhere new, driving a fancy car, or even living uptown to achieve it."

Astoria looked up from her notepad. "But your life hasn't been basic. You just starred in a major Hollywood movie."

He wagged a finger in the air and laughed, closed mouth, while chewing a bite of tamale.

"Isn't that the interesting part?" he said after swallowing. "I've enjoyed seasons of success throughout my life, but for a long time, I felt like I was playing someone else's game. It wasn't until I got real honest with who I was and who I wanted to be that things started clicking for me. I owned a house and a life in one of the richest neighborhoods—a place I couldn't have imagined as a kid. Then, I woke up one day and sold it and everything that came with it. Walked away a free man admitting there was nothing special inside of Hollywood and everything special inside of me as long as I kept that God light shining. And yeah, you could say life's been pretty good ever since."

After the interview, the blues man gave Astoria a tour around town in his rust-bruised baby blue Ford pickup. Back at the juke joint, his wife asked Astoria one more time if she was sure she couldn't stay for dinner, then handed Astoria a brown paper sack of tamales for the road. Arms wrapped around one another, the bluesman and his wife waved goodbye from the slanted front porch, telling Astoria to come back soon and stay for the live music next time.

It was a ninety-minute drive north to Memphis. At the risk of interrupting suppertime, Astoria pressed on.

***

The address Anna Mae gave her over the phone led to a neighborhood of grand brick homes featuring Southern Gothic columns, wrought-iron balconies, and porte cocheres.

A circular driveway paved a grand entrance to Evie's parents' house. Pruned shrubs lined the property, and wisteria vines scaled the front of the two-story home. Astoria counted six paned windows across the first floor and four across the top, each with black shutters that contrasted sharply against the white brick.

Peering up through her windshield, she imagined Evie standing atop the home's grand staircase for homecoming or prom, rolling her eyes and dying for a smoke as she succumbed to her role as a debutante. Astoria climbed out of the car. The delta air clung to her skin, but something pricked at the back of her neck, and she sensed someone was watching her as she ascended the front steps, rang the doorbell, then scanned the lush surroundings.

Waited.

Waited.

She could hear people shuffling within the home, so she rang the doorbell again.

Eventually, the door cracked open; a mousy woman with maroon-dyed hair peered out from behind it. "May I help you?" The woman's beady eyes and thin, o-shaped lips appeared fixed in perpetual shock. She wore a white blouse, blue slacks, Tori Burch flats, and an embroidered apron tied around her waist. The smell of buttery meat roasting in the oven wafted out from behind her.

"Sorry if I'm interrupting dinner," Astoria said quickly, sensing the woman might slam the door. "Is Evie home?"

The woman stepped forward. Fists clenched, she rose onto her tiptoes, peering toward the car in the driveway. "Who are you?" she demanded, dropping back and glaring up at Astoria.

"I'm her friend, Astoria Lyons. We worked together in Nashville."

The woman crossed her arms and sniffed, jutting her nose in the air. "Evie's not here. We're about to eat." She turned to retreat, but Astoria stepped forward.

"Wait," Astoria said, pressing a hand to the door.

The woman flinched, crouching and raising an arm as if expecting a strike, a small squeak escaping her. Astoria stepped back and raised her hands in surrender. She glanced down at her cutoff shorts, tank top, and worn Chuck Taylors, then at the woman in her apron and luxury brands, her pinched face. Beneath the polish, Astoria saw no trace of Evie's strength, only a woman who'd never claimed her power. Astoria thought of her friend, and she softened.

"I only wanted to see her," Astoria said, smiling sadly. "See if she was okay."

The woman stepped back inside and began closing the door.

"Can you at least tell her I came by?" Astoria pleaded. "Please tell her that Astoria Lyons came to see her. Tell her I miss her, and I love her, and I never would have made it if it hadn't been for her."

The woman paused, her mouth reforming into that surprised little o-shape. Astoria felt annoyed now, imagining Evie sitting on the front porch back in Nashville, cigarette in hand, laughing about how her mother was born without a backbone. "You'd better tell her, lady," Astoria said sharply.

The woman didn't respond.

Astoria threw her hands in the air and rolled her eyes like Evie might have done. "Do the right thing for once and tell her, will ya?" She turned and trotted down the steps, leaving Evie's mother standing there looking perfectly shocked in her apron.

Before slipping into her car, Astoria glanced up, thinking she saw a curtain twitch in an upstairs window. She waited, watching. A man joined Evie's mother at the door. After briefly conferring, he stepped forward and glared down at Astoria, shoulders squared, hands on his hips, as if ready to go to battle to protect his empire. Astoria smiled at the window, flipped the man the bird, then dropped behind the wheel. She fired up the engine, squealing her tires as she pulled away, honking her horn the length of the driveway and out of the neighborhood. She could hear Evie cackling all the way back to Nashville.

CHAPTER THIRTY

Fall 2013

A stack of pizza boxes beckoned to Astoria from where they sat on the agency's kitchen counter, all but pillaged by her co-workers.

Ravenous, she devoured one of the last remaining pieces without shame, chomping a cold mouthful and breathing deeply through her nose while refilling her wineglass. Padding back to her desk, Jones hollered from her office. "Wanna look at our deck one last time, then get out of here?"

"Be right there," Astoria said. "Gonna check my email and shotgun this wine first."

"Grab me a glass, will ya?"

Astoria gave a thumbs-up. They would fly to New York the next day for a new business pitch. In partnership with the NYC office, they were chasing a full-service retainer with an international hotel brand slated to break ground on a new property in Nashville. Astoria and Jones would arrive a day early, meet their counterparts, practice their presentation, and then get a good night's rest before their 9:00 showing.

Astoria fired up her computer and took another bite of pizza. A lone email waited at the top of her inbox.

Henry Hunter.

Her first thought was to hit *delete*, but curiosity got the better of her, and she clicked it open.

"Miss Lyons. I heard that you and your firm are competing for some work in New York. Playing in the big leagues, aren't you? Congratulations, you earned it."

A piece of mushroom fell onto her lap. She flicked it into the garbage. Glancing back to the screen, she dragged the email into the trash, then hustled into the kitchen to pour Jones a glass of wine before sitting down to review their pitch deck one more time.

***

In the glass-enclosed conference room, the president of the New York office walked the team through the presentation. His people had merged the Nashville office's work into the NYC template, turning Astoria and Jones's twenty-slide deck into a jumbled, incoherent mess double the original size.

Astoria sat at the back of the room, watching Jones faking a smile in the front. When the slide titled "Your Team" flashed on the screen, showing only New York personnel in their matching black turtlenecks, the two women locked eyes across the room. Nashville personnel were listed as "Supporting Resources" on the following slide.

Jones knocked on the table.

"Hold up, now," she said. "Talk to me about how you intend to allocate resources to this account."

"The new property will be in Nashville, but the client is headquartered in New York," the president gestured broadly as he spoke, as if Jones didn't realize the geographical difference between the two locales. "Naturally, we'll lead the business from here, but we'll depend on your team's local insights for our go-to-market efforts, especially for any real-time requests that hit hard and fast."

Jones chuckled. "Naturally."

The New York president smiled greasily. "Shall we continue?"

The city blared, smoking and seizing around Jones and Astoria as they walked to their hotel that evening. Somewhere in a more romantic pocket across the city, leaves flashed golden in the soft evening sun, but between the skyscrapers, the light was gray, and the hot, thick air tasted like rotten food.

"This is total bullshit," Astoria said.

Jones waved a hand dismissively, her face expressionless. "I can't do anything but offer our full support. This guy is going to be the agency's next CEO. Not the person you want for your enemy."

"What?" Astoria stopped walking, mouth agape at the woman she so admired. Jones kept walking, pedestrian commuters filling in the growing space between them.

"Catch up, Lyons, or else you'll fall too far behind."

Astoria trotted forward.

"Sometimes you do what it takes to play the game," Jones said once Astoria fell back in alongside her. They strolled on in silence for another city block, the city and its inhabitants showing no concern for their corporate power struggle.

"I get it. The entire team gets it," Astoria finally said. "Nashville might deliver some of the best work, but New York will always step in and take over. We know our place."

"Let's kill it tomorrow," said Jones.

"Deal."

***

The team sat fresh-faced in matching black suiting around a mahogany table in a lush conference room with low lighting and luxurious blue velvet carpet. Astoria waited for her turn to present to the group of pinstriped executives. She thought about how, if they won the business, she'd spend years of her life expending all her energy to promote a five-star hotel she could never afford to stay at. But there was no time for irony—she focused on performing, charming the clients with a bright, fake smile, and laughing along with her New York cohorts as they raved about their newfound love of hot chicken and country music.

***

"Let's have a toast," said the New York president, raising a glass of champagne back in the agency's glass tower. "To winning new business. Nashville ladies, you're in too," he said, glancing down at Jones.

"To winning!" the team cheered.

Astoria flexed her swollen fingers, unsure when she'd last gone a day without alcohol. She wanted to go home, drink a gallon of water, and sleep for a week.

"Dinner is at seven," the president announced. "Drink up, then we'll make our way downstairs. Nashville, keep close to your New York counterparts so you don't get lost."

Music and chatter bounced off the restaurant's blood-red walls. The New York colleagues volleyed accolades across the table for things they'd said during the pitch, indulging in the brilliance of ideas not their own.

Jaw tight from fake-smiling all day, Astoria twiddled her stir stick around in her frosty martini glass, the olives and vodka tasting acrid following the champagne she'd had at the office. She thought about the blues man she'd met in Mississippi, how kind he was in his white T-shirt and blue jeans, washing dishes with his wife and enjoying a quiet Sunday in a ghost town on the Mississippi Delta. Visions of white mile markers spun through her mind—*values as guideposts*.

The room suddenly felt too small, the air too stuffy as the alcohol mixed with her exhaustion, stirring her emotions. She wanted to escape the forced friendliness, flee the restaurant, fight her way out of the teeming city, and run west, forever west, until she could remember what it was like to feel well-rested, inspired, and free.

"Want to keep walking for a bit?" Jones asked as they stepped out onto the sidewalk, leaving their New York cohorts inside the restaurant where they'd washed down wedge salads with cocktails and steaks with wine. A sharp wind pushed at their backs, the city turning on its nightlife as if millions of people simultaneously flipped a switch. Jones stopped to peer into a window display at Bergdorf Goodman.

"Oooh," she said, pressing a fingertip to the glass, pointing at a Tom Ford clutch. "Call me Misses Ford because that has my name all over it."

"How much does a bag like that cost? Eleven hundred?"

"Probably," said Jones, the window lighting illuminating her cheekbones. "Might be a little excessive for me these days, but a girl can dream."

They floated away from the glittering display.

"I didn't want to drink tonight," Astoria said, flexing her fingers again.

"What if you climb onto the wagon tomorrow, and we have one more drink at the Plaza's champagne bar?"

"The Plaza, as in, *the* Plaza Hotel?"

"What other plaza do you think I would drag you into?"

"I'm not feeling that fancy right now," Astoria said.

"Fancy schmancy, Lyons. One drink."

"You're a bad influence."

"You need to learn how to have a little fun."

Inside the Plaza, mountains of ornate flower displays crowded the lobby. Gold-inlay gleamed in the marble floors; white pillars stretched toward the heavens. Crossing the threshold, Astoria paused, tilting her head back, eyes wide, sensing she ought not to proceed further.

"Follow me." Jones stuck out her chest and strutted through the lobby in her black leather skirt. Astoria scampered along behind, clutching her work tote to her side. As they entered a grand ballroom, a man in a black tuxedo approached as if to cut them off.

"May I help you?" He stood in the women's path, his pointy noise raised like a baton, white-gloved hands clasped at his waist. Astoria froze, ready to retreat to their overpriced and undersized hotel for the evening.

"No," Jones said, sidestepping the man and forging on without missing a beat. "We're bopping in for last call."

Eyes still wide like she knew they were doing something they shouldn't be, Astoria bypassed the man on the opposite side.

"Which bar?" he asked, spinning around in their wake.

"Why, the champagne bar," Jones said, stopping abruptly and spinning to face him. Her energy remained bright and open, but she smiled through clenched teeth. "It's not yet eleven, is it?"

The man straightened and turned his little nose up even further. "You're correct. The champagne bar should still be open."

"Perfect." Jones turned and sauntered towards a bar tucked in the corner of the grand room, where she and Astoria climbed onto pink velvet barstools. While Jones studied the champagne menu, Astoria ogled the floor-to-ceiling gold curtains, sparkling chandeliers, and green plants luxuriating between table settings. Intimate cloisters of white silk chairs dotted the great room, appearing reserved for only the most refined clientele. Astoria worried she wasn't supposed to be there, that someone would soon appear, raise a doubtful brow in her direction, and ask them to leave. Jones checked the time on her phone, then drummed her fingers on the bar. "You suppose that uppity maître d tipped off the rest of the staff?"

A bartender in a black leather vest emerged from the darkened recesses of the hotel.

"Champagne, ladies?"

Astoria checked her phone. It was 10:50 p.m.

"We'll have two glasses of the Krug Grand Cuvée," said Jones, flashing a *try me* smile. She dropped the menu as the bartender faded away, then shifted to face Astoria. "So! You've never been to *the Plaza*."

"It's a little above my pay grade."

"Don't say things like that," Jones said. "That's other people's bullshit you'll start believing if you're not careful. You know you can probably negotiate for a promotion if we win this hotel business."

"You think?"

"I don't think. I *know*. Little more money. Bigger title—*if* that's something you're interested in."

"I'm always interested in more money." Astoria smoothed her hand across the marble bar. "But I don't know how long I can last in the agency world without losing myself."

"But you bring great energy to the team and seem to enjoy yourself?"

"I like the work. But I hate that, no matter what agency I'm with, there will always be some corporate head in a suit who takes credit for other people's efforts. It's like they're bottom feeders who have somehow slithered to the top. And what are we doing, pouring our lives into this job so some wealthy serpents can get rich destroying another American city with a fancy new hotel I'll never be able to afford to stay in?" Astoria's voice echoed through the Plaza.

"Well," Jones snapped her fingers, "Astoria Lyons is fired up in New York City tonight."

"Ladies?" The bartender reappeared, placing two flutes of golden bubbly atop white napkins and sliding them across the bar. "Are we going to close this out?"

"We might need another round." Jones extended her credit card to the bartender. Glowering, he snatched it and retreated to whatever cleanup duties he'd been scrubbing against before these latecomers had ruined his plans for closing.

"Look. I get what you're saying," said Jones. "Lord knows I get it, but maybe you should invest your energy in changing the game."

"How so?"

"Who's to say you won't start your own gig someday? Ride this until it runs out. Learn all you can. Figure out how to do it better, then go work for yourself if you don't like working for the man ... or the woman." Jones tilted her glass toward Astoria.

"I love working for you," Astoria said. "You've taught me so much."

"Yes, and now I'm going to teach you how to negotiate for this promotion."

"Will you hire me when your agency is up and running?"

"You'll be my first call."

They clinked glasses; the sound floated across the plush hotel.

***

At her dining room table, Astoria logged into her bank account and refreshed the page twice to ensure she was reading her latest paycheck deposit correctly. The dollar amount stood out, bold on the screen. A month after the agency won the account with the luxury hotel chain, Jones coached Astoria on negotiating for a promotion, landing her more money than she'd ever imagined making. It covered rent, student loans, and bills, and she wouldn't even have to wait until the fifteenth of the month to pay them all.

She thought of Henry Hunter and how he'd told her she wasn't worth more money. It occurred to her she shouldn't need a paycheck or Henry Hunter's approval to validate her worth. The extra money brought relief, but even in the moment, it was a fleeting feeling. She could pay her bills now and have plenty of money left to spend, but doing so meant she had to endure the rest of her days within the corporate hierarchy. That was the exchange: her life for the paycheck.

Is this all there is, then? Working. Partying. Find a tolerable relationship with an equally damaged person who finds you equally tolerable. Become a job title. Make enough money until you can pay off your debt so you can buy more things.

She recalled the professor's edict—*you have to go make something of yourself.*

Her account balance loomed on the screen in bold black numbers; she stared at it, wondering what her life would look like if she built it around what made her feel the most alive, inspired, and free.

She considered her surroundings, savoring her apartment with its secondhand furnishings, golden light streaming through the tall windows and bubbling across the wood floors. The simplicity of the space and its natural lighting brought her peace, and in the silence, a vision sparked in her mind. With a little more discipline, her new paycheck might help her achieve financial stability. From there, all she needed was courage to achieve a life on her own terms.

CHAPTER THIRTY-ONE

Winter 2014

Every morning, an old man who lived in a dilapidated house in Lockeland Springs sat on a set of broken cement steps in front of his mangy yard, flashing a toothless grin to the neighbors out for their morning exercise or walking their children to school. People stopped to talk; they'd ask the man about his sciatica, comment on the weather, agree that the children were getting big as he chortled along, his eyes dancing.

Then, one morning, he was gone.

Astoria wondered if his health had faltered. Perhaps his heart had drummed its last beat. That's what happened to Dorothy Wallace the year prior. While Astoria was arguing over the flow of a PowerPoint with her cohorts in New York, the matriarch of her hometown passed quietly, alone in her country home. Ace was the one who found her when he took her a load of firewood.

"Miss Dot kicked the bucket," he'd told Astoria over the phone.

Astoria couldn't speak; fat tears squeezed out the corners of her eyes, and she feared that if she opened her mouth, she wouldn't be able to hold back her sobs.

"She sure loved you," said Ace.

"I know, Ace," Astoria finally said, choking over her words. "I loved her, too."

Astoria didn't make it home for the funeral. The team needed her at the office; they were grinding on another pitch.

Astoria assumed the old man from her neighborhood had passed away until she read on the Lockeland Springs Community Facebook page that he'd gone to live with his daughter in Antioch. A neighbor had inquired about the old man's whereabouts on the online forum; someone responded, saying they'd spoken to the old man's daughter the day they moved him out. People speculated that the family needed the money from the house. Others commented they hoped he was comfortable, cared for, and with people who would at least wave back should they encounter him sitting on a porch or set of steps in the soft morning light.

Like a soul leaving a body, the old man's crooked house with its faded siding and single-paned windows disappeared. Astoria didn't see the men operating the machines that demolished the home or the steel teeth of heavy machinery that chewed up the clumps of yellow daffodils dotting the yard. The old cement steps, the little walkway that led to the front porch, the grassy lot—all rendered back into the earth like they'd never existed.

As if erected overnight, a super-sized duplex appeared, swallowing up the lot where the old white Craftsman had sat amidst its untidy yard. The new two-story, side-by-side condominiums dominated the space, filling the lot from front to back, erasing all lawns, and towering over the neighboring houses like a rich-kid bully who wanted the natives to know it was a new hood now. Each unit sold for half a million dollars to buyers swayed by the modern marble countertops and brass fixtures.

Every time she walked around the neighborhood, Astoria saw another old house demolished, its gray-haired residents and tired front porches erased by modernity. Razing old Craftsman homes and replacing them with two or three condominiums became the norm across Lockeland Springs, Inglewood, Woodlawn Neighbors, Riverside Village—every East Nashville borough.

Grass yards gave way to modern front doors, which opened directly onto the newly paved sidewalks.

But the eastside wasn't the only place seeing change. In the same way that floodwaters climb rapidly inch by inch, all of Nashville was morphing from an easygoing southern city with gritty, historic charm into a pristinely polished, glittering 'experience.' Door by door, house by house, building by building, block by block, old Nashville was being replaced by a commercialized performance manufactured to perfection.

In neighborhoods where songwriters, young people, and the lifelong impoverished had rented modest homes for as little as $450 a month, shiny new pet-friendly apartment complexes were charging $1750 for studios with open floor plans and granite countertops. Young men in designer jeans walking designer dogs replaced old men on front porches. In the afternoons, when most folks had to steal away for a thirty-minute lunch break, these newcomers lounged poolside next to their model-thin girlfriends. Locals wondered how anyone could afford to live in such luxury while enjoying weekday afternoons at the pool.

Commuters suddenly needed to leave home 30 minutes earlier to get to work on time. Astoria's coworkers lamented how traffic seemed to be getting increasingly worse as they congregated around the coffee pot in the mornings. They observed the cranes from their office windows and heard the dynamite blasts as little men and big machines bore into the ground, ripping out old brick buildings and replacing them with sparkling high-rises.

Overnight, Broadway turned from a kitschy little row of honky-tonks with elderly tourists in thick-soled shoes into a wannabe rollercoaster ride of a Vegas strip. The city barricaded the sidewalks to keep the hordes of bachelorettes off the streets, herding them like cattle in a pen. Live music and cold beer made this new generation of tourists forget their Midwest manners. On any weeknight, you'd see a soccer mom vomiting on her new cowboy boots outside of Tootsies or a married father of three with a receding hairline nuzzling the shoulder of a voluptuous twenty-something at the Wildhorse Saloon.

Bachelorette parties flooded the city. Troupes of overfed young women poured into town wearing matching spray tans and co-ordinated outfits, morphing what was traditionally a single night of celebration into a marathon weekend of binge drinking and debauchery. Under the guise of live music and entertainment, they came to drink, scream, take selfies, and make out with frat bros or convention dads—after drinking for ten hours straight, it really didn't matter which. National media called Nashville the "*it city*" for tourism, while the locals bemoaned their newfound marathon commutes and cringed at the never-ending swell of locusts.

CHAPTER THIRTY-TWO

Spring 2015

The days passed as images flickering on a static screen: meetings, laptops, emails, heated debates in conference rooms, late-night takeout dinners at the office, PowerPoints, project estimates, proposals.

Astoria worked. Every waking hour, she worked, dropping every dollar that didn't go to bills into savings. She opted out of happy hours and spent her weekends on the road, traveling the south on assignment for Anna Mae.

"Why can't you come in on Saturday?" asked an Account Lead one frazzled Thursday.

"I'm going to Louisiana—it's a previous engagement I can't get out of," Astoria said, shrugging. "But I already turned in my work. Y'all call me if you have questions. I'm happy to support from the road."

She pulled late nights during the week, then set out on Friday evenings to interview painters, musicians, potters, and artists across charming nooks and crannies of the south where she met endearing, everyday characters who resembled her own everyday people from back home.

To meet her deadlines with Anna Mae, Astoria set to work upon returning home late on Sunday nights. Brewing a pot of coffee, she'd set to work at her kitchen table, comparing her notes to the photographs she'd captured and fleshing out a story she hoped would make people feel something positive.

Fueled by the people she'd met and the inspiration she'd found in her travels, she would drag her exhausted ass into the office on a few hours of sleep on Monday mornings and start the cycle again.

"I can't imagine how you're managing all this travel," Anna Mae said during one of their weekly phone calls. "I know you're working hard at your agency job. You sure you're not pushing yourself too hard?"

"I like to think of it as if you're paying me to travel the south and hangout with rockstars every weekend."

Anna Mae chuckled. "Sounds like a hell of a gig when you put it that way."

"It's the best gig ever."

"Say, you'll never guess who I heard from."

"Oh?" Astoria said nonchalantly, somehow knowing in her bones that Anna Mae was about to say the professor's name.

"He's no longer at the university and is looking for work. Says he's moving back south with his fiancée; she was a student of his. Can you believe it?"

Astoria shook her head, feeling nothing but gratitude for how far she'd traveled to arrive at that very moment. "In fact, Anna Mae, I can. Bless his little heart."

***

Astoria rapped on the doorframe of Jones's office. "Mind if I come in?"

"What's shakin', Lyons?" Jones said without looking up from her desk.

Astoria shut the door behind her.

"Is it that kind of meeting?" Jones asked, turning serious.

Astoria's heart raced as she sat, balancing on the edge of a chair, leaning into the silence stretching between them like a crutch.

"Out with it."

Astoria sighed. "Remember when you told me to get clear on what I wanted my life to look like?"

Jones knitted her brow. "Vaguely."

"I've been thinking about my next move ..."

"So, *it is* that kind of meeting."

Astoria nodded.

"Alright then, Lyons. What's your plan?"

"I'm burned out."

Jones considered this for a pause. "You're one of the few people who can keep up with me. Didn't think you could do it at first, but you surprised me. What do you think you're gonna do?"

"People need content ..."

"And?"

"And I need my days to be full of something other than emails and PowerPoint."

Jones waited.

"I want to work for myself, and I think I can make a living producing content."

"Journalism's dead, Lyons."

Astoria snorted. "Don't I know it. But I'm not talking about journalism, I'm talking about creating content for brands."

Jones leaned back in her chair, propping her elbows on the armrests and interlacing her fingers atop her torso. "I know you're good at living lean, but it's more difficult than you realize to go from a decent salary to the poorhouse."

"I hate the idea of being broke again, but I keep thinking about that story you told me about when you were in Chicago, how you and your ex-husband had all the things in the world, and you said that, even though it was a hurtful mess, you admired him for having the courage to be true to himself."

A grimace flickered across Jones's face. "Did I say that?"

"Something like that," Astoria said, smiling softly. "Look, I know that if I don't take a leap and start being true to all the invisible aspects of myself, I will spend the rest of my life just plodding through a deadweight existence like some*thing* and not some*one*. But when it comes to generating income, I know how to hustle, and I know businesses need more than copy; they need images, stories, even video."

"That's a lot of content for one person to produce."

Astoria waved her iPhone in the air. "Not really."

"Touché. You've clearly got enough hustle in you to figure it out."

Astoria smoothed her dress across her thighs as she collected her thoughts. "It's funny how, when we're starting out, people tell us to leave home, pursue a career, make something of ourselves, but nobody tells us to start with what makes us feel the most alive. Guess we gotta figure that out on our own."

The room hummed.

Astoria continued.

"Everyone needs a paycheck, but I'd rather die than spend the rest of my life in a cubicle. I want the freedom of working for myself, finding inspiration out in the world, not answering to a New York suit who can't even write his own PowerPoint, you know?"

"I do," said Jones. She dragged two fingertip across her eyelids. "Lord knows I do. So, do you have a timeline in mind, or are you figuring it out as you go?"

"I have a client in Mississippi and a lead on some work up in Seattle with a tourism group who will pay me to travel and write."

Jones waited.

"But it might take me a couple of months to get my plan together."

"Give it a year, Lyons. Keep your side hustle. Keep running circles around this place. Stash your cash. You'll know when you're ready."

Astoria frowned at the idea of enduring another year at such a breakneck pace. "You're probably right," she said. "I can do it."

"I'm always right." Jones sat up and leaned over the desk, grinning. "And you're going to thrive, Lyons. If your options are to sink or swim, you'll find a way to fly."

"Thank you, Jones, for everything."

"I'm not done with you yet, and you'd better say 'yes' when my agency needs your help. But," Jones lifted her palms to the ceiling and nodded, "you are welcome."

CHAPTER THIRTY-THREE

Summer 2016

Instead of hosting a yard sale, Astoria threw a moving sale and invited people straight into her apartment.

Strangers milled about the living room, picking through stacks of pots, pans, kitchen utensils, all those shift dresses and heels she'd purchased over the years, and a few knick-knacks, all of which she'd merchandised in neat stacks.

"Everything goes," she wrote on Facebook Marketplace, although she stowed her boxes of books, blue jeans, T-shirts, the AM/FM radio, air mattress, and her Chuck Taylors in her bedroom—these were the things she would carry forward.

"How much do you want for this couch?" asked a young woman in running shorts and an oversized Vanderbilt T-shirt, running her hand over the arm of the white embroidered fabric.

"How much are you looking to spend?" Astoria said.

The young woman's face flushed red. "I just moved here for college, and I have about three hundred dollars for my entire apartment, which currently has an air mattress on the floor. I'm using an upturned laundry basket for a dinner table."

"Ingenious," Astoria said. "I always used a box. How about this: give me a hundred bucks for the couch and anything else you can take out of here."

"Seriously?"

"Take it all."

"Think the couch will fit in my Subaru?"

"No, but I might have a solution."

Phone in hand, Astoria stepped onto her stoop and placed a call. While it rang, she noticed the leaves on the trees were already turning gold along the edges.

Johnny's southern twang came through loud and clear when he answered. "What's up?"

"I'm accepting your offer to help move some stuff out of my apartment."

Johnny was quiet; ESPN blared in the background.

"You offered," she said. "I need help moving a couch across town."

"Didn't I already help you move that couch once?"

"Yes, and you're going to help me move it again."

In the end, the Vandy student took the couch, a desk chair, ironing board, a Crock-pot and set of pint glasses, some battered concert posters, a pair of brown knee-high boots, and an old brass lamp.

"Are you sure you don't want more money for all of this stuff?" the young woman asked, slamming the back door of her Subaru, rattling the contents within.

"Pay it forward someday," Astoria said. "We'll be over with your couch after a while."

The young woman lived in Hillsboro Village.

"Your old stomping grounds," Johnny said as he maneuvered his truck through the bustling neighborhood.

Astoria craned to see where an apartment tower had replaced an old red brick building. "When did they tear down Boscoe's?" she asked.

"Boscoe's been gone a long time. That sports bar we used to hit up is gone, too, and they've fancied up the Belcourt Theatre."

"The *historic* Belcourt Theatre?" Astoria asked, face still pressed to the window, processing the unrecognizable new features of the old neighborhood.

"Exactly."

They found the young woman's apartment. It was on the second floor of a 70s-era complex. Johnny had to stop and catch his breath twice as he and Astoria wrestled the couch up the concrete stairs. The young woman thanked them profusely, offering Johnny twenty dollars for his delivery services.

"I ain't gonna take your lunch money for the week," Johnny said.

The girl blushed.

"I'm glad you didn't take her money," Astoria said when they were back in the truck, idling out of Hillsboro Village and onto the Interstate.

They bounced along in silence as Johnny drove towards East Nashville, orbiting downtown on I-40, then merging onto I-24. The once-distinct skyline peeked out from the center of the city, now crowded with iridescent high-rises that sparkled in the afternoon sun as if bidding her adieu.

"City's changing," she said. "But I guess that's what we do in America. Change or die, right?"

Johnny fished a pack of cigarettes from the dashboard and popped one out, taking it between his lips. She wanted him to say something, but he just lit his cigarette and rolled down the window.

"I'm gonna get out as soon as I can," he said after they rode on in silence and he sucked down half the cigarette. "Save up some money, buy a little hideaway on a mountain somewhere."

"Whatever makes you happy, Johnny, I want that for you."

He blew a funnel of smoke out the window, easing the truck off the freeway onto Shelby Avenue. They cruised past dotted lines of red brick public housing.

"I've been thinking about the ferry rides my parents took me on as a kid," Astoria said, staring straight ahead. "You can ferry anywhere in northwest Washington. You drive your car right onto the boat. It's disorienting to see all these cars floating on water, with the mountains and ocean pressing in. It doesn't matter what kind of car you drive; all that nature is so close, reminding you it can swallow you up in an instant, rich and poor alike. And yet, riding those ferries always made me feel like I could go anywhere."

Both hands gripping the wheel, cigarette hanging from his lips, Johnny squinted out the windshield.

"I'm excited to get back on the road," Astoria said, talking entirely to herself now. "Study the mileposts. Probably take a ferry ride when I get home."

From Shelby Avenue, they turned left on Sixteenth Street. Shadows and sunlight dappled the rooftops of the colorful Craftsman homes. Soon, the trees would bloom red, yellow, and gold. More people would come and go. Whether anyone noticed or not, Nashville would tuck itself into another autumn, shiver through a frigid winter, and bloom into spring.

Johnny whipped the truck around the corner onto Russell Street, rolling to an abrupt stop in front of Astoria's empty apartment.

She shifted to face him, wanting him to look at her, offer something meaningful, show her that he cared.

The truck idled anxiously like a little boy wanting to play.

"Safe travels," he said, saluting two fingers atop the steering wheel.

She smiled, waves of love and anger and sadness coursing through her. She climbed out but turned to look back up at him, squinting against the afternoon sun. "Make it a good one, Johnny."

She shut the door and walked away.

***

With Lightning 100 coming through clear on the dial of her AM/FM radio, she wriggled her hands into a pair of yellow rubber gloves, filled a bucket with hot water and Pine Sol, grabbed a sponge, and set to work.

Later, she walked down to the community gathering spot for one last cocktail and to say goodbye.

"We'll tell the others you're leaving," said the bartender. "You and your lame-ass two-drink minimum will be missed."

She took one last stroll through Lockeland Springs, its quiet streets and quaint homes filled with couples, children, and families, all carrying on with the joys and quarrels of life. The rocking chairs waited empty on the firehouse porch. Streetlights buzzed. The air hung heavy and thick with the last days of summer.

Her apartment smelled like a car freshener, having been scrubbed from the cupboards to the baseboards.

Astoria crammed books, shoes, clothes, and stacks of notebooks into her car like a game of Tetris. The only things left to pack were a pillow, a pile of blankets, and her air mattress, inflated on the living room floor.

With a DVD of The Office: Season 3 playing on her laptop, she sat cross-legged on the mattress, drinking bottled water and laughing at the everyday quirks of the American workplace, her face bright in the screen's glow, the soft night wrapping itself around her.

***

She called Ace from a truck stop somewhere west of Minneapolis.

"You already go see your friend in Mississippi?" he asked.

"I went and interviewed some people for her in a town called Marigold. They make beautiful pottery—it'll make a good story."

"And you're already in Minnesota? Better watch your speed. You might drive like your mother."

"I know a trick if the cops catch me speeding," she said. "Hey, I gotta go to Seattle to see about a gig up there. I might go explore the Sound like we used to do when I was a kid. Remember?"

"Think you'll have to live in Seattle for work?"

"No, but I will have to fly back to Mississippi in a month or two, but the world has the internet now, Ace. I can work from anywhere."

"Maybe we can get some of that high-speed stuff here at the house. Wireless, they call it."

"Get to work on it. I'll come see ya in a few weeks."

***

At a Motel Six near the interstate in Sioux Falls, she woke in the night, electricity in her bones. The red numbers on the alarm clock said three-thirty-three, but her head was clear; she was ready to get back on the road.

Long-haul trucks rumbled in the parking lot. To the east, a scratch of orange light was burning into the day. The air was dry but cold.

Astoria yanked a sweatshirt from a stack of clothes in her back-seat, pulled it over her head, then lingered, drinking coffee from a Styrofoam cup and watching the men and their trucks. The smell of coffee making her feel nostalgic for things like the Elks Lodge and cool fall mornings back home, she wondered about the cargo on the trucks, the senders and receivers of all that commercial transport, and the manufactured complexity of it all.

Three eighteen-wheelers lumbered out of the lot.

It was her turn; she was ready to go.

***

The morning broke in layers of silver and blue. Light danced in and out of the badlands as she drove west with the windows down, clean air billowing around her. Goosebumps bubbled on her skin; newness and hope flooding her senses. The radio picked up an FM station out of Rapid City, and the DJ played Waylon, Willie, Kristofferson, and Cash singing "Highwayman."

Astoria pulled off the road, cut the engine, and climbed out of the car. Loose gravel crunched beneath her Chuck Taylors as she walked down the bank.

Low-slung hills and plateaued rock formations spread out to the horizon. Dry grass danced in the wind. The sweet smell of sage floated on the charged air. The land shifted with the light, shades of lavender and gray pooling in the shadows. Joy stirred within her—an aperture opening between a life endured and one unfurled. Hers would be a banner staked in the quiet purpose of her creation, its beauty in soft breezes and the strongest winds.

Acknowledgements

Across the rooftops and through the trees, I will forever praise the radical souls I've encountered in my adventures who have granted me grace, love, and opportunities and have helped me down the path: Jennifer Macha-Hebert, Mary Margaret Andrews, Sheila Thomas, Rebecca Gervais, Heather Collins, Jen Patterson, and Robin and Dave Kempf (Dave, as usual, you're in the company of a bunch of wise, wonderful, good-looking women).

Endless thanks to Jennifer Lauck and the talented members of the Blackbird Studio for Writers in Portland, Oregon, and eternal gratitude to Mary Adkins and all the brilliant minds associated with The Book Incubator.

Each of you is proof that life is beautiful and people are good.

I love you all.

About the Author

Amanda Sapp works as a brand marketing consultant during the day and writes in her spare time. She lives in the forest in Oregon with her dog. She publishes cultural observations and short stories on Substack: amandasapp.substack.com. *Something of Yourself* is her first novel.